Hungarian Sketches in Peace and War

Constable's Miscellany of Foreign Literature

Vol. I

by

Mór Jókai

Hungarian Sketches in Peace and War
Constable's Miscellany of Foreign Literature
Vol. I
by Mór Jókai

ISBN: 978-93-62764-89-8

Published by

DOUBLE 9 BOOKS
2/13-B, Ansari Road
Daryaganj, New Delhi – 110002
info@double9books.com
www.double9books.com
Tel. 011-40042856

This book is under public domain

ABOUT THE AUTHOR

Moricz Jokay of Asva, also known as Mor Jokai, was a Hungarian novelist, dramatist, and revolutionary. Outside of Hungary, he was known as Maurice, Maurus, or Mauritius Jokai. He was a key figure in the Hungarian Revolution of 1848, which began in Pest. His romantic works quickly became famous among Victorian England's elite, and the press frequently compared him to Charles Dickens. One of his most famous admirers was Queen Victoria. He was born in Komarom, Kingdom of Hungary, to Jozsef Jokai of Asva (1781-1837), a member of the Asva branch of the historic Jokay aristocratic family, and noblewoman Maria Pulay (1790-1856). Jokai was inspired to pursue his craft after receiving appreciation from the Hungarian Academy of Sciences for his debut play, Zsido fiu ('Jewish Boy'). In 1845, he relocated to Pest, where Petofi introduced him to literary groups. Pesti Divatlap released his first notable work as a serial that same year, followed by a hardback version in 1846. It was met with widespread critical acclaim. The following year, Jokai was appointed editor of Eletkepek, Hungary's main literary journal, and formed a network of young authors around himself.

CONTENTS

PREFACE

Jokai is one of the most popular of the Hungarian prose writers of fiction that sprang up a few years before the late war. His wit, flowing style, and vivid descriptions of Hungarian life as it is, joined to a rich fancy and great intensity of feeling, soon made him a favourite with Hungarian readers.

Among the earlier of his productions, those best known are a novel entitled, "The Common Days," and a collection of minor tales, published under the title of "Wild Flowers."

The present volume has been written for the most part since the late memorable national movement, and embodies descriptions of several of the direst scenes in the civil war which devastated Hungary from the year 1848 to 1850.

Most of the Hungarian literati were, at the close of the war, either roaming in foreign countries, or wandering in disguise through their native land; and the field of literature for a long time threatened to remain neglected and barren—a monument of national grief and desolation! Those patriotic writers who had for years wielded the pen with the noblest impulses thought to do their duty best by letting their highest faculties lie dormant; and laid aside the lyre rather than bring unacceptable offerings to a fatherland laid low, and at the mercy of foreign swords. And who will deny that there is sometimes great virtue in silence, and that the tongue that speaks not is often more eloquent and heroic than that which dares to utter sublime truths even at the foot of the gibbet? Many of the noble-hearted of Hungary resigned themselves to such a martyr-like silence, and persevere in it to the present day; while the great bulk of the people, unwilling to enhance the triumph of their victorious enemies by a show of unavailing lamentation, followed their example. Pesth, which had been the scene of literary activity, was at once deserted; the bards of Hungary, abandoning their homes to the wantonness of a foreign soldiery, went back to the districts whence they had come, there to mingle with those peasants whose chivalry and patriotism afforded constant themes to their lyres. Their renewed intercourse with their rustic countrymen served again to revive their hopes, quenched as in the grave.

In the sketches of Jokai, the reader will find many original delineations of Hungarian life among the middle-class nobility—a race of men whose manner of life and thought cannot fail to be interesting, however cursorily described. But the Hungarian peasant is in his way no less attractive. Nothing can be wilder than his dress, consisting of a sheepskin cloak (bunda), or a similar habit of the coarsest cloth, a shirt, scarcely reaching below the waist, and wide linen drawers, to which boots do not often form the necessary complement; yet his easy demeanour, delicate feelings, and especially his language, are such as to put him on a level with the educated classes. In conversation he will often use a more dignified style than a noble, who, by his exclusive privileges, has had ample scope for oratory in the county assemblies—select with astonishing tact the best lyrical productions of the day, and immortalize the lay by a tune of his own composition. These qualities of the Hungarian rustic—an insight into whose character will be given to the reader by a few camp scenes contained in this volume—must appear the more striking if we remember that the class to which he belongs was for centuries in a state of serfdom, from which it was only liberated by the late Revolution.

Independently of the various other calamities which prevented the development of the physical and mental resources of Hungary during the last three hundred years, the feudal system alone was an insurmountable barrier in the way of progress. The privileged classes were for the most part devising how to kill the time, while the labour of the peasant provided them with the means of gratifying their propensities, rarely disquieted by the backward state of the country, which in their eyes seemed all perfection. Properly speaking, it was only since the year 1825 that matters had begun to exhibit a material change in this respect. Many of the most conceited and thoughtless among the nobles had gradually allowed themselves to be convinced that arts and sciences might add to the charms of an easy life; and that national greatness demanded something more than hospitable roofs, fertile plains, and vast herds of cattle. The political and literary activity displayed by Counts Szecheny and Kolcsey found noble followers, and produced unexpected and astonishing results during the last twenty-five years. Still, compared with other countries, the progress of literature was slow; and the works of the most popular authors, though thrown off in comparatively small impressions, were long of reaching second editions. The cause of this result must be sought in the fact that reading is by no means universal among the Hungarians. Among the nobles, who had the means of buying books, only a few cared to do so, while the condition of the peasants prevented them from becoming in any way the patrons of literature. This apathy was undoubtedly owing in great part to the absence of a central national government; the effect of Hapsburg rule had always been to crush the political institutions of the country, and repress its noblest efforts, regarded as the sure forerunners of revolution. The Court of Vienna, besides excluding from public office and emolument such as were known for their independent principles and national feelings, now began gradually to arrogate to itself the right of censorship—an institution which alone would have sufficed to cripple the intellectual progress of the country.

Such, however, was the mental activity of the present generation, that Hungarian literature, despite the numerous obstacles it had to encounter, made rapid progress, and created in the minds of the people a spirit of inquiry and a desire after intellectual pursuits hitherto unknown. Never before had the cultivated tongues of the West been so much studied, or so many valuable translations made from the German, French, and English literatures. That the influence of the first was originally the strongest, and that several of the leading writers in philosophy and history took for their model the German school, will appear no matter of surprise. The rising writers of a more recent date, however, insensibly turned their attention to the more lively literature of France, and afterwards to that of Britain; and while some read with rapture the fictions of Scott, Bulwer, and Dickens, politicians learned to admire the doctrines of Adam Smith and Jeremy Bentham. Of poets, none were more extensively read and more generally admired than Byron and Moore. Thus did the merely literary progress march on boldly and combine with the new political movement to further a change which had already made itself felt in every grade of society, and which was the more remarkable and satisfactory from having followed a too long period of stagnation.

A few words will suffice, and perhaps not be superfluous, to bring to the English reader's mind the deplorable causes of this long neglect.

The fifteenth century, which illumined the sky of Italy, and thence reacted on the rest of Europe, brought for Hungary nothing but an endless series of wars, distinguished by dazzling military achievements, against the hosts of the Sultans, and turning out in the end but useless victories, productive of most ruinous effects and general exhaustion. The next age proved still more disastrous. The race of the Hunyadis, who in the preceding century had struck terror into the hearts of the Ottomans, had disappeared; the weak princes that ruled after them perished among the carnage of battle, to leave the crown of St. Stephen vacant, and to open a way for the Hapsburgs to the Hungarian throne. At this juncture, coinciding with the great religious movement in Germany, which was rapidly spreading to the banks of the Theiss, the position of Hungary became more desperate than ever, although the events that followed far surpassed the gloomiest anticipations. While the majority of the people chose a native for their king, a part of the aristocracy declared for Ferdinand of Austria. The rival kings, unable to vanquish each other, called in to their aid the two most powerful monarchs of Europe. The former invoked the assistance of Solyman the Great; Ferdinand found a willing ally in his brother, Charles V. Thus it happened that, till the beginning of the eighteenth century, Hungary presented the aspect of a vast camp, exposed to the insolence of foreign mercenaries and the tyranny of the Hapsburg emperors, and at once protected and laid waste by its allies the Turks. Unfortunately, the Mussulman military colonies, which subsisted in Hungary from the time of Solyman to Achmet III., while adding to the distress of the people continually menaced by famine even during the years of temporary peace, were more ignorant than those whom they affected to protect, and therefore failed to produce on the Hungarians those effects which the Moors, in circumstances somewhat similar, had wrought upon the Spaniards. Nor is anything now left to call to mind the presence of the Turks in Hungary, except a few words that slipped into the Hungarian language.

The state of the country in the eighteenth century, somewhat relieved by the reign of Maria Theresa, was, after such a long series of calamities, not much calculated to foster the cultivation of science and poetry; nor did any fresh symptoms of the national life spring clearly into view before the beginning of the present century. True, that even amid the storms of the past generations, there appeared from time to time writers, whose names survive to the present day. But, with a few exceptions, chiefly in the department of poetry, all the works of that time were but insipid imitations which aspired to be thought original, but were little fitted either to please or to instruct.

After such a gloomy past as has been here shortly described, it will seem very natural, that with the awakening of the national mind the career of literature, suddenly interrupted by the late war, should be bold, steadily progressive, and triumphant, despite the narrow and contemptible canons of censors. As to prose fiction, it must be observed that it is of quite recent growth. The beginning of this species of composition was made about fifteen years ago by Baron Nicholaus Josika, who soon found successful rivals in Kuthy and Baron Eötvös. Jokai, who is now the favourite of the public, belongs, as has been already observed, to the younger staff of writers.

It would be a mistake to imagine, from the Eastern origin of the Magyars, that the tales and romances to be found in the Hungarian language bear any resemblance to the *Arabian Nights*, or the familiar poetry of the East in general. None of the writers above mentioned carries the reader to fairy realms, and superhuman characters. In plot, tendency, and execution, Hungarian prose fiction is identified with the modern novel of the rest of Europe—deriving, withal, its most pleasing characteristics from the peculiar features of Hungarian life and history, as well as from the native idiom, which differs entirely in its figures, and many of its expressions, from the other cultivated languages. It must, however, here be added, that the more the time approached to the great catastrophe, the more the general literature partook of a political character—a circumstance attributable to the censorship, which did not allow political questions to be discussed in their proper place. The novel or romance writer, not being so suspicious to the censor as the politician, often intermingled his love scenes and adventures with single touches, unfinished periods, and marks of exclamation, which escaped the vigilance and attention of the scissors-holder, but were only too well understood by those to whom they were addressed. Even the literary journals, sternly interdicted from meddling with politics, swarmed with allusions to the questions of the day; and while tending to cultivate the taste of the public, their usefulness was greater than might have been expected in rearing new labourers for the field of literature. In the presence of a public eminently conservative as regards book buying, not a tenth part of the more highly gifted youth would have gone farther than the composing of some slight specimens while at college, had it not been for the encouragement given by three weekly journals. The first of these periodicals, entitled the *Honderu*, was started by Lazarus Horvath, a gentleman who had travelled much in Europe, and was familiar with high life, and who is known as the unsuccessful translator of *Childe Harold*. The two other journals, started afterwards, were conducted by Frankenburg and Vachot. It was through the medium of these latter papers that the young bard Petöfi sent forth his wild, touching strains, and that Jokai, his intimate friend, became gradually known, when the unexpected events of 1848 changed the face of the whole country. Disastrous civil feuds, commenced on the one hand by the Slavonic population in the south of Hungary, and on the other by the Wallachians or Roumins in Transylvania, were followed by a desolating general war; and for nearly two years nothing was heard but the din of arms. Two or three daily papers alone testified that literary life was not yet extinct in the nation. As almost every one did who felt in any way capable of serving his country, Jokai followed the Government (obliged to abandon the capital to the Austrians in the beginning of 1849) to the town of Debreczin, on the other side of the Theiss, where he conducted for a short time a small political Journal. The rapid progress of the Hungarian arms in the same year, followed by the Russian invasion, was, as the reader may be aware, suddenly converted into a most disastrous defeat. The subjugated country was handed over to General Haynau; the nationality of its people was destroyed, and its noblest defenders fled into other lands, or awaited certain death in their own. The country people, struck with fear and amazement, confined themselves in sombre silence to their homes, which were filled with disguised literati, and other classes of delinquents; the different races of the population, their hands yet wet with blood, gazed confusedly on the ruins of their own working; the streets of Pesth, the gay capital, were deserted, and the single voice that broke the deep silence was that which pronounced in its official organ sentences of death, imprisonment, and confiscation. In such a state the country continued for several months, when even Haynau, a few days before being removed from his post, began to loathe his work, and to sign pardons as carelessly as he had hitherto subscribed sentences of death. It was at that juncture that a few straggling literati, gradually assembling at Pesth, commenced to issue a literary periodical, to which Jokai largely contributed. The press, it must be observed, was placed under the control of the police, established on an Austrian model. The head and chief members of the police belonging to the other parts of the Austrian empire, and totally ignorant of the Hungarian language, were naturally obliged to employ some natives to peruse the literary productions and translate their contents; after due consideration of these, the verdict was passed. The consequence of such a state of things was, that very frequently a single seemingly portentous phrase, or even the mere title, doomed to oblivion the most innocent work of the brain, while more substantial writing was allowed to make its way into the country, and frequently to be again prohibited, after having become familiar to thousands.

Most of the sketches contained in this volume, and which Jokai wrote under the name of Sajo, underwent this fate. The latest production of Jokai's pen is a novel entitled *The Magyar Nabob*, which is highly praised. His strictly historical pieces, depicting scenes of the civil war, though recalling the more vividly to mind the dreary and not yet forgotten past, were most eagerly read in Hungary; nor will the English reader peruse without deep emotion the fate of the Bardy family, contained in this volume.

Within the last two years, the state of literature in Hungary, if judged by the number of new books published, appears astonishingly progressive. The chief reason of this phenomenon may be found in the denationalizing measures of the Government, attempting to suppress the national idiom by excluding it from the public schools, and substituting in its place the German—a policy attempted without success by Joseph II. about the end of the last century.

That the people—though now perhaps more willing than ever to give their full support to literature—are inclined to look with some suspicion at the productions of a press in the hands of foreign authorities, and that many branches of a more serious nature than novel-writing must remain excluded from the sphere of literary activity in a country subjected to martial law, need hardly be remarked.

Besides, some of the more prominent and elder authors still persevere in their sad mournful silence, while others have sunk from a state of patriotic gloom into mental imbecility. But whatever shape Hungarian literature may henceforth assume, it is undoubtedly true that much that has issued within the last few years from the Hungarian press is worth translating; and I believe that the present volume, presented in a faithful and easy translation, and likely to be soon followed by several others of a similar class, will be found to introduce the English reader to scenes hitherto undescribed, and to characters as interesting as unusual.

Emeric Szabad.

DEAR RELATIONS

One evening, towards the end of summer, my uncle, Lorincz Kassay, the sub-sheriff of the county, was seated on a bench before his *porte-cochère*, which stood wide open, without bar or gate, as beseemed the entrance to the house of an hospitable Hungarian gentleman.

True, half a dozen dogs, nearly as large as bears, were lying lazily about the court, and might have rendered the entrance embarrassing to persons of hostile intention; but as for strangers in general, these honest guards were too well accustomed to see them treated as the angels were by Abraham, to take any further notice than by a friendly bark, and a slow shake of the tail.

Uncle Lorincz Kassay sat enjoying his pipe, and calling across the road to his assistant, who was likewise seated at the door of his house, enveloped in the same comfortable fumes. The conversation might have been carried on with more facility had one of these worthy gentlemen crossed to the other side—the road being wide, and a stentorian voice necessary to make one's-self understood—but the mud lay so deep between the two houses, that it was severe work for carts and carriages to get through; and when it was absolutely necessary to cross the road, the passenger was obliged to make a considerable circuit, by the garden and meadow, holding on by the rail, besides returning the same way: consequently Uncle Lorincz and his ally found it less troublesome, and more convenient on the whole, to exert their lungs in the manner above mentioned.

Meanwhile my readers may be curious to learn how I am related to this worthy gentleman; but this indeed I cannot tell. I only know that he is called by all who know him Lorincz Kassay, bacsi;1 and I would advise my friends likewise to adopt him as such, for he is a thoroughly honest and honourable country gentleman, and will never give them cause to blush at his name. Let us keep up the good old Magyar custom of calling our elders by the familiar titles of uncle and aunt, while we are privileged to those of nephews and nieces.

[1] *Bacsi*, contraction for *batya*—"elder brother," or "uncle."

Uncle Lorincz belonged to that medium class whose duty is to manage the laws and rights of the people, keep up their national prerogatives, look after their interests, in short, to labour without noise or fame,—a man of whom neither history nor poets speak, for the upright and honourable man is not so rare a character among us as to render it necessary to emblazon his name in history; and what could a poet make of an honest man who has neither romance enough to carry off his neighbour's wife, nor to shoot his best friend through the head for looking askance at him? Such a man as Uncle Lorincz, for instance, who comes into the world without the aid of star or horoscope, grows up without becoming a virtuoso on the piano, goes through his classes satisfactorily, and without occasioning any mutiny, and, finally, returns like a dutiful son to his parents, who assist him to look out for a good wife, whom he marries without any poetical occurrences; and who, when his parents are gathered to their fathers, inherits their blessing and their property unencumbered by debt—for this class of our countrymen consider debt as a species of crime; their principle being that an honest man should not spend more than his income. This principle had taken such root in Uncle Kassay's mind, that, rather than run up an account at the shoemaker's, he has been known, in his scholar days, to feign illness and keep his room, when his boots needed mending, until the necessary money arrived from home; and the same sense of honour, combined with the most lavish hospitality, characterized him through life.

Having been directly called upon by the county, he had accepted the situation of szolgabiro or sheriff—which the Hungarian takes upon himself *ex nobili officio*—from a generous sense of duty, rather than for the lucrative advantages attached to it, which by no means compensate for the dinners he is obliged to give; but he readily makes a sacrifice for the honour of the employment, and the confidence of the people in that incorruptible conscience which is chosen as the earthly providence of an entire district, to keep order and administer justice among twenty or thirty thousand people.

At the time our story commences, Lorincz and his worthy assistant were actually discussing some affair of great moment across the road, when their attention was attracted by shrill voices, and, looking in the direction of the sounds, they perceived a conveyance which it will be worth while to describe at length, as such things are not to be met with every day, particularly now that railroads are making so great innovations in our old habits and fashions.

It was a gentleman's calèche; the leather was somewhat spotted and gray, which may be easily accounted for, however, by the continual roosting of poultry on its roof. When or where the machinery had been contrived, it would be impossible to decide, for, according to historical date, suspended calèches existed in the days of Lajos I. The form of the body might be compared to a water-melon cut in half, which body was so convulsed by its four high springs at each irregularity of the road, that the tongues within ran the risk of being severed in twain when they attempted to speak, while their owners would certainly have been pitched out, had they not held well on by the sides. It was as impossible to open the doors as it was to shut them, for which reason they were permanently secured by well-knotted ropes. Above the two hinder wheels a large bundle of straw was attached, which threatened at every jerk to light on the heads of the inmates. Before this worthy ancestral memorial three very quiet horses were attached, a pie-bald, a bay, and a white, all three up to their ears in mud, and assisting one another with their shaggy tails to whip the reins out of the coachman's hand, while their hides exhibited various graphic traces of the whip.

In truth, the noble animals did not lack good-will, but only the necessary capabilities for the station they now filled, being honest cart-horses, neither born nor bred to draw an iron-springed calèche; and, sensible no doubt of their inability, they paused every ten minutes to draw breath instead, and to regard each other with doleful expressions.

On one of these occasions—namely, when the horses paused, and did not seem disposed to proceed further—one of the four individuals inside thrust forth a head, and called in a shrill voice to the coachman to stop.

The voice proceeded from one of the fair sex, whom we cannot at present describe, as the shawls and mufflers in which she was enveloped only permitted a glimpse of her respectable nose to be seen; three other individuals filled the vehicle. Beside the lady sat a figure in a fur mantle, whose only visible points were a vast beard and a meerschaum pipe, the bowl of which must have been guarded by some singular providence, from having its neck broken at every jolt of the carriage.

Opposite to mamma sat a hopeful sprig, whose head was so well thrust into his lambskin cap, that only two scarlet ears protruded to view, turning and perking with unwearied scrutiny to suit their owner's curiosity. The last place was occupied by a smaller boy, whose large wondering eyes were fixed on the muddy world around, and whose legs and feet coming constantly in contact with those of the gentleman opposite, obliged the latter to draw up in the most inconvenient manner possible.

The horses having again paused, the lady, working her way with great exertions through various cloaks and mufflers, called to the coachman as before to stop, and, addressing one of the bystanders, who stood gaping at the carriage, asked various questions relative to the position of Mr. Lorincz Kassay's house; and having received satisfactory answers, she once more muffled herself in her wrappings, and desired Marczi to proceed; on which he gave a lash to one horse, and the half-turned pole giving a blow to the second, the third took the hint, and they all three began to move, and proceeded in order for a few minutes, until they arrived in the village, where they once more paused and hung their heads, while the lady, for the third time, called to Marczi to stop, fixing as usual on some person whom she wished to address.

This time, the gentleman of the fur cloak and meerschaum pipe, losing all patience, cried out, "Zsuzsi, my dear, why the tartar are you calling to Marczi again, when the plague is our having to stop so often?"

"Cannot you see, you thick-skull?" rejoined the fair lady sharply, "that is just the reason I call to him to stop, that folks may not see we cannot get on!"

Fortunately the last person addressed happened to be the sheriff's footman, who offered to conduct them to the house, desiring the coachman to follow, which was easy to say, but not so easy to put in execution, until the good steeds had recovered breath in due time.

Meanwhile, Uncle Lorincz, observing that the carriage was coming to his house, blew the embers out of his pipe, and arranging his beard in two points, advanced to meet his guests. After a good deal of labour, the vehicle at length struggled into the court, and, unfortunately, in the confusion occasioned by the general efforts to rise from the heaps of wrappings, the good man managed to tread on some sensitive member of his wife's foot. She returned the compliment with a thrust from her elbow, which caused him to stumble, thereby bringing the hot bowl of his pipe in contact with the face of his youngest boy, who, uttering a cry of pain, raised both hands to protect his face, at the same time striking up the pipe, which broke between the old gentleman's teeth.

"Which of you did that?" cried he furiously, pulling the piece out of his mouth, and raising his hand threateningly over the heads of the youngsters. But before the stroke of chastisement could be administered, Marczi, throwing back his muddy coat, directed it so skilfully as to fall right over the boys' heads, filling the eyes of the whole party with dust and mud; and in the confusion of this unexpected attack, the delinquent thought fit to make his escape as best he could out of the carriage, smearing his clean white trousers with the wheels. All these accidents took place in a much shorter period than I have taken to describe them.

The sub-sheriff, his footman, and other retainers, had now come up to the assistance of the travellers, and after many ineffectual efforts to open the carriage doors, they were obliged to give up that point, and lift out the inmates like so many bundles.

The noise had brought down the lady of the mansion, who waited at the foot of the stairs to welcome her guests. She was a comely little round-faced woman, attired in a simple but well-made costume, to which the small flounced apron and blue-ribbon cap gave an air of coquettish smartness. She held by the hand a little, dark-eyed, strawberry-lipped maiden of about six years old, who, half hiding behind her mother's dress, looked like an amourette preparing to take aim.

The travellers being at last safely landed, the lady advanced to Uncle Lorincz with an air of amiable confidence, and began a formal introduction.

"Dear and worthy cousin, I have the pleasure of presenting to you in my own person Susanna Sajtari, a cousin on the maternal side; being *en route*, we could not think of passing our dear cousin's house."

"Welcome, welcome; God bless you!" cried Uncle Lorincz, saluting the lady with several hearty kisses on each cheek. "I am overjoyed at this unexpected happiness; pray come in, the servants will carry up everything directly."

"Allow me to present my husband," began the lady.

"Whist! don't tell my name," interrupted the gentleman in the fur cloak; "let me see if my dear cousin remembers me," and laughing heartily, he seized both of Uncle Lorincz's hands, and waited for him to remember.

It was rather an embarrassing situation for Uncle Lorincz, who had not the slightest recollection of ever having seen his dear cousin before.

"Pooh! how can he recognise you in that cap?" cried his faithful partner, snatching from her husband's head the prodigious two-eared fur cap, and exposing a good-natured countenance, with a large, bald forehead, and features which we meet in a thousand faces, without ever distinguishing one from the other.

"Ay, do you know me now?" asked the worthy gentleman in a tone of confidence.

Uncle Lorincz blushed to the ears, and would have given his best meerschaum to have been helped out of the unpleasant dilemma.

"Oh! certainly, I remember—quite well," he replied, rubbing his forehead with the tip of his forefinger; "perfectly remember; only the name will not come into my head."

"Well, do you remember when we sat together at the Gyor elections in 1830?"

"Exactly, the name is on the tip of my tongue."

Among the four thousand people who had assembled for the Raab elections ten years before, it would have been difficult to recall the features of one in particular.

"Well, I am that Menyhert Gulyas" —

"Gulyasi!—exactly, so you are! Welcome with all my heart!" cried Uncle Lorincz, much relieved at being at length freed from such a tax on his memory, although not a bit the wiser even after hearing the name.

"And these are my two sons, Sandor and Peter," continued the worthy lady. "Go and kiss your aunt's hand, boys."

Sandor and Peter rushed forward in obedience to their mother's command; the younger succeeded in taking possession of his aunt's hand, which he fervently pressed against lips and nose, while she slily put the other behind her back.

"You are too old to kiss hands, my dear nephew," she said, at the same time proffering her cheek to Sandor, who was so embarrassed at the idea of kissing his aunt, that he scarcely knew what he was about; and, after the ceremony, was thrown into such a tremor, that he trode successively on his father's, mother's, and brother's toes.

The great house-dogs now approached to take their part in the patriarchal reception, thrusting in their cold noses, and licking the hands of the guests. And here we must observe, the house-dog is an infallible index of his master's character. Where the great fellow comes forward with marks of affection, you are always sure of a hearty welcome; but where, on the contrary, he lies still and growls, you may expect the question: "When will you be pleased to continue your route?"

Having entered the hall, the compliments were renewed, according to the Hungarian fashion: "Hozta Isten (God has brought you); receive us into your good graces," &c. &c. Bundas and pelisses, shawls and kerchiefs, began to unwind from the persons of the travellers, and by degrees each assumed his natural form.

The worthy father of the family was a simple, good-natured looking man of about fifty, though the blackness of his teeth, caused by incessant smoking, made him look considerably older. An amiable grin played on his large, good-humoured countenance, while the colour which bloomed on his cheeks might have still passed for that of the spring-time of life, had not the deeper tint in his nose told more of autumn, and the good red grape.

He wore a green dolmany, descending to the knees, with broad braid, and oval buttons; and, standing with his hands behind his back, and his two spurred feet apart, he looked round on the company with a good-natured smile.

His worthy partner was a short, spare figure, with a tolerably good-looking face, the most remarkable feature of which was the nose. This nose could be turned up or down, and twisted right and left, at its owner's inclination, to suit the pleasure or displeasure she desired to express; and the family had learned to interpret its various evolutions so well, that in strange company their eyes were constantly fixed upon it, as the steersman's on the prow; and good Mr. Menyhert Gulyasi has been observed, on more than one occasion, to stop short in the midst of his speech at some sudden contortion of the leading feature of his better half.

Nephew Sandor was a long strip of a youth, with smooth, puffy cheeks, and a snub nose. Nature had amply provided him with hands and feet, of which he seemed painfully aware; for he kept the former in perpetual motion, as if endeavouring to get rid of them, while the latter had a peculiar call for stumbling over and treading on everything they came in contact with.

The smaller boy never left his mother's side, holding fast by her dress—finding it at the same time a convenient place of refuge for his nose.

When the guests were made tolerably comfortable, and their hosts had sufficiently insisted on their considering themselves at home, the lady of the house disappeared for a few minutes to give some hasty orders in the kitchen, to the execution of which, sudden cacklings of various feathered tribes in the court-yard bore conclusive testimony.

When she returned, Uncle Lorincz invited Menyhert and nephew Sandor to his own sitting-room, to smoke a pipe with him. Before reaching the apartment, however, it was necessary to pass through several doors, at each of which a scuffle ensued with nephew Sandor, who could not be prevailed on to enter before Uncle Lorincz. There was a cheerful fire in the open stove, with a large wood-basket beside it; comfortable arm-chairs were ranged around, and the pipe-stand stood forth invitingly with its many silver-covered meerschaums.

"Pray sit down," said Uncle Kassay, rolling out the arm-chairs, and showing his guests a good example.

Gulyasi seated himself opposite; but Sandor could by no means think of such a thing.

"He is not accustomed to much sitting," observed his father.

"Well, well, let him do as he likes," said Uncle Lorincz, leaving him to stand like a propping-post against the wall; for he was not aware that our nephew required to have the chair pulled under him, and to be forcibly pushed into it, before his modesty would allow him to accept such an offer.

"Take a pipe," said Uncle Lorincz, handing to him the tobacco-bag. The youth declined.

"Much obliged," said his father for him; "Sandor does not smoke." He did smoke, however; but was too well brought up to let strangers see that he knew anything of the comforts of life.

Uncle Lorincz and his guest were soon engaged in an interesting conversation, by which it appeared that Menyhert had his own ideas, and ventured to express them too, in the absence of his better half, and uninfluenced by the motions of her nose.

He declared, in the first place, that it would be much more prudent to make steam-horses to draw boats instead of steam-boats, and there would be no risk of the boats being blown up if the boiler burst. Then he remarked that it would be advisable to propose at the next Diet a prohibition of the cultivation of potatoes, as the increase of this article in the market would be highly prejudicial to the growth and sale of wheat.

Then he uttered imprecations against the new system of pasturage, by which Government proposed introducing sheep instead of the great studs which had hitherto been kept on the heaths; "so that in case of war," continued the worthy gentleman, "the noblemen would be obliged to ride on sheep-back."

Finally, he expressed his opinion that the rising generation should be interdicted the use of mantles, as the students were in the habit of concealing their violins beneath them, and amusing themselves at the public houses, dancing and fiddling, to the neglect of their studies, thereby making this garment a cloak to all bad morals.

A loud "Ha, ha, ha! he, he, he!" suddenly broke forth from the corner in which Sandor was standing. Both gentlemen turned to see what was the matter.

"Father's shadow on the wall is so funny when he speaks!" exclaimed the youth, holding both hands over his mouth to restrain his laughter.

"Perhaps you are cold, nephew, as you are standing with your back against the stove?" said Uncle Lorincz, fearing that Menyhert was about to reprove his hopeful son. "Come, my boy, you will never get a wife if the girls catch you standing behind the stove."

"That would be a sad story," said the father, making grimaces to his son; "for we are now *en route* to get a wife for him."

"The tartar!" exclaimed Uncle Lorincz, turning to the stripling with interest; "so we have a bridegroom here! come, man, let us look at you a little nearer."

But it would have required a large pair of tongs to draw our nephew from behind the stove.

"And what does the young man say to the prospect of a fireside of his own? and who is the chosen fair one?" asked Uncle Lorincz.

Menyhert crossed his legs and looked up to the ceiling, as he was wont to do when discussing matters of weight. "Well, the girl is no other than Carolina Berkessy, the only child of my worthy friend, Gabor Berkessy, pronotarius of the county of Csongrad; her father promised her to my eldest son, when she was still in the cradle."

"Well, all I can say is, she is a very fine girl," replied Uncle Lorincz; "a very fine family altogether, and not a thing to be rejected, if he gives his consent."

"Gives his consent!" cried Menyhert, not without some offence; "and why should he withhold his consent?"

"Why, only because my nephew is rather young—that's all," replied Uncle Lorincz.

"What of that?" said his father proudly; "he has sense enough: I will venture to say that in any company. He attained eminence in every department at school—But what the tartar smells so strong? You are singeing your coat, boy! I desired you not to lean against the stove."

Sandor lifted up one of the flaps of his coat, in which a large hole was already burned.

"Sit down, you ass!" said Menyhert to his accomplished son, who eyed the damage, as if considering how to get it washed out.

Uncle Lorincz, seeing that the conversation was taking rather an unparliamentary turn, endeavoured to revive the former subject. "And probably my nephew has passed his examination too?" he asked.

"And with great credit," replied his father, forgetting the burnt coat; "that severe G——, who puzzled all the young men, was an examiner. Tell us what he asked you, Sandor; come, say it off."

Sandor was quite ready to say it all off, but he required to be pressed.

"Well: *Quomodo*" —

But at that instant the wood-basket swallowed up our nephew, who had sat down upon it, and, unfortunately, not having been intended for such service, the lid had broken under him, and he disappeared inside, with the exception of his hands and feet, which still remained without.

At this sight Uncle Lorincz could no longer contain himself, but burst into such a hearty laugh that he almost rolled off his chair. Happily, by dint of struggling, the basket overturned, and Sandor succeeded with some difficulty in creeping forth.

His father, having first looked to see that no bones were broken, prepared to make a terrible explosion; and it is impossible to say how the affair might have ended, had not the footman entered to announce that supper was ready.

Meanwhile Aunt Zsuzsi had also initiated her hostess in the mysteries of their journey, with all its circumstances, and various innocent additions, such as, that her son Sandor had attained the highest honours, and that all the girls in their neighbourhood were desperately in love with him, although he never looked at one of them, considering it his duty only to fall in love with whoever his parents should choose for him, and so forth. This interesting conversation was suddenly interrupted by loud cries issuing from the nursery; and little Klarika appeared, sobbing out that Peterke had first twisted her doll's neck, and then threatened to strike her.

"You naughty boy!" said mamma, as the little urchin came sliding in behind, "where shall I find a rod to punish you with? Is this the way you behave in your aunt's house? Come here, directly."

Peterke not only would not come out, but retreated under the bed, looking out from below at dear mamma, and neither threats nor entreaties could prevail on him to quit his position. Supper was now announced.

"Just stay where you are," said mamma, "and I shall lock the door till we return from supper."

The head of the family having entered with his guests, the whole party proceeded to supper, with the exception of little Peterke, and took their places round the table, which latter ceremony, however, did not take place without a good deal of trouble, each person paying compliments to his neighbour, during which the lady of the house was obliged to use force to make her guest sit at the head of the table; while a complete struggle took place at the opposite side between Uncle Lorincz and Sandor; the former, however, being the stronger of the two, at last succeeding in placing our nephew beside him.

"You must learn, my dear boy," said Uncle Lorincz, "what the high sheriff of Bihar taught me while I was his clerk; when I was invited to my principal's table, and I too pleaded for the lowest place—'Just sit down where you like,' said the excellent man, 'and rest assured, wherever that is, it will always be the lowest place.'"

When a blessing had been asked, the savoury gulyas hus2 was brought round, the very name of which, even on paper, seems to emit that delicious flavour which every Hungarian housewife knows so well to give it.

[2] A favourite national dish. It is a stew or hash of beef, with onions and red pepper, and other spices.

After the gulyas came the fogas;3 fortunately the footman carried it round, otherwise the company would have been obliged to draw lots who should be helped first. When it came to Sandor's turn, he declined, to the surprise of every body.

[3] A fish said to be peculiar to the Balaton or Platten Lake in Hungary, and to the Black Sea and the Wolga. It is the *Perca Lucioperca*.

"You don't eat fogas?" said Uncle Lorincz, opening his eyes wide.

"Thank you," replied his father for him; "he eats very little in general."

"Hm! perhaps the boy is particular," thought Uncle Lorincz.—"Well, there may be something else which he will be able to eat."

Then came a dish of good turos galuska,4 the crisp pastry smiling from out of the rich curds and cream, and still hissing on the dish.

[4] Balls of pastry in curds.

"You will eat some of this?" said Uncle Lorincz, turning to his neighbour, as the dish came round.

"I thank you, I am not hungry; and I have a little headache."

But our nephew was as hungry as anybody else, and had not the slightest headache. The fact was, he was not accustomed to eat till after he had been pressed a dozen times, and his plate filled perforce.

For once, however, there was short work with our nephew's customs; for Uncle Lorincz, believing what he said, sent on the good turos galuska with a sigh, admitting it was certainly no cure for a headache; and consequently Sandor was obliged to keep up the farce during the whole time of dinner, while his eyes were actually starting from his head with hunger.

"Drink something, at least, if you do not eat—it will do your headache good," said Uncle Lorincz, taking up the good Eger5 wine. But Sandor would never have forgiven himself had he not snatched aside his glass as Uncle Lorincz was in the act of pouring out the wine.

[5] From Eger or Erlau, a town between Pesth and Tokay.

"Much obliged," said his father, "but he does not drink wine."

"The tartar! he does not!" exclaimed Uncle Lorincz; "well, he is a rare child—neither eats, drinks, nor smokes! why, he will be a millionnaire! I am heartily sorry that you have got a wife for him already; otherwise I should have asked you to wait until my girl is marriageable."

Meanwhile there was another individual who followed quite a different course from that of nephew Sandor, and that was little Peterke.

Finding himself locked in, he first only pettishly came out from his stronghold, waiting for some one to coax him to come to dinner; but, finding that the door was locked, and that knives and forks were actually clattering without him, he took it quite to heart, and began calling to mamma to let him out.

"Never mind him, let him cry," said mamma, who found this little episode highly interesting. But the kindly Klarika, when she thought nobody was observing, hastily concealed a turkey's pinion and a large piece of apple-tart, and ran off with them to the nursery—contenting herself with this generous revenge for the havoc done to her playthings. On this the little urchin became quiet.

When supper was over, the mutual compliments were repeated, during which Sandor took an opportunity of thrusting into his pocket a roll of bread, which he had not ventured to touch at dinner.

Aunt Zsuzsi now opened the door with great solemnity, to release the little delinquent, whom they found dancing about with greasy cheeks, and holding up in triumph the remains of the turkey's leg.

"Oh, you rascal!" exclaimed mamma, catching hold of him, and wiping his cheeks; "go directly and kiss your aunt's hand, and beg her pardon for being so rude."

Peterke slid over, drawing his mouth and nose to one side, as if he expected that the hand he was ordered to kiss was preparing to give him a box in the ear; and it was only on being convinced of the contrary that he resumed his former confidence, and ventured to ask for another piece of apple-tart, on receiving which he had the complaisance to show the company, by way of a return, how a large piece of pastry might be crammed into two cheeks.

Who was enduring greater torment than our nephew Sandor all this time? Hungry as a wolf, with only a small white roll in his pocket—and how to eat it! Wherever he went, he was sure to be seen; his only resource was to wait till everybody went to bed, and then eat it in the dark; but the two gentlemen, meanwhile, got so deeply engaged in conversation, that there was no saying when it might end.

At last he summoned up courage to say he would go out a little, and walk in the garden.

"In the garden!" repeated Uncle Lorincz; "why, it is quite dark, and the mud is very deep."

"I will sit upon a bench."

"That will be a fine walk—ha, ha, ha!"

"Perhaps the air would do my head good."

"Well, do as you like, my boy; you are at home here."

Sandor, finding himself at liberty, descended to the garden in great delight. Just below the back window of Uncle Lorincz's apartment, which looked out upon the garden, stood a winter pear. Uncle Lorincz thought he heard this tree shaking, and going to the window, he could distinguish our nephew pulling the unripe pears, and cramming them into his mouth.

"Well, he is a strange youth!" thought Uncle Lorincz, as he returned to his seat.

Before retiring for the night, the guests took leave of their kind hosts—declaring that they must set out at break of day, and would not disturb them—after which they were conducted to their apartments, and soon lay buried in the great down feather-beds and snow-white pillows, with their neat laced and ribboned covers. The coachman had been desired to harness the horses at four o'clock, and not to awake anybody; but when our provident guests rose in the morning, they found the whole household on foot, and a comfortable breakfast prepared, of coffee, rolls, cold meat, and plum brandy. This time, Uncle Lorincz gave his bashful nephew no peace until he had actually forced down his throat all that was eatable and drinkable—seeing that he was in the habit of being thus treated. When breakfast was over, there was a mutual interchange of affectionate speeches, and Uncle Lorincz once more packed up his guests in their cloaks and furs, thrusting a long cylindrical bottle of plum-brandy into Uncle Menyhert's pocket, while his wife put a large, fresh-baked cake into Aunt Zsuzsi's hand, and little Klarika provided the young Sphinx with an ample supply of cold pastry; and after exacting from their guests a promise to visit them again on their return, they all took leave—Uncle Lorincz accompanying them a few miles on horseback, to point out the best road across the plains.

And now we must beg our readers to draw on their three-leagued boots, and step into the neighbouring county. Here, too, the roads lie deep in mud; for the rain continues during seven weeks in these districts, as it does in the East Indies. Here, too, are villages on the highroad, and houses with open doors, and travellers hastening towards them. But now it is question of a house whose doors are shut, and of travellers who do not stick in the mud.

A handsome carriage, drawn by four spirited grays, was driven by a young gentleman, while the smart-liveried coachman sat beside him.

The youth was slightly flushed with the exercise: he wore a low-crowned hat, and light summer dolmany, while his embroidered fur cloak lay across the seat. Guiding the horses dexterously over the difficult roads and rickety bridges, he finally turned aside about half way through the village, and drove rapidly towards a dilapidated house, before which he was obliged to rein up his horses, as the *porte-cochère* was closed.

"Hej! ho!" cried the coachman, leaping from the box, and knocking at the door.

"Go in at the side-door, and open the *porte-cochère* yourself, Matyi; but take the whip with you, or else the dogs will tear you to pieces."

The coachman did as he was desired. No sooner had he reached the court, than a terrible encounter took place between the dogs and Matyi, who swore and lashed away with his whip until he had succeeded in opening the gate.

The tumult brought out a buxom dame, whose appearance betokened somewhat more than a cook, and somewhat less than the lady of the house. Standing at the entrance, with her arms a-kimbo, she exclaimed in a sharp, shrill voice: "What diabolical noise is this, I should like to know? are the Turks or the French coming, eh?"

Meanwhile, Matyi having opened the *porte-cochère*, the carriage drove into the gateway; and the young man, leaping from the box, and throwing the reins to the coachman, stepped up to the dame, who eyed him askance, with an expression of dried plums, as if doing her best to make herself as disagreeable as possible to the new-comers.

"Ah! my sweet Boriska," said the young man gaily, "how handsome you have grown since we last met! I thought you were to be married that carnival; but I suppose it was premature, eh?"

"Well, you have grown ugly enough yourself, Master Karely, since I saw you last: you were a pretty child, but I should not have known you again."

"Thank you, Boriska, dear. Is my uncle at home?"

"Where else should he be?"

"Because I have come to see him, with my mother and sister."

"What! are they here too?" said the dame, fixing her sharp eyes on the carriage, like a two-pronged fork. "Well, I can't understand how folks can leave home, and wander abroad for weeks."

"Call my uncle, there's a dear girl, and you can help one another to scold."

The beauty cast another sour glance at the vehicle, and disappeared into the kitchen. Karely, meanwhile, opened the carriage door, and the mud being deep in the gateway, he lifted out the two ladies in his arms. One was his mother—a calm, ladylike person about forty, with a sweet, melancholy expression: the other was his sister—a merry, mischievous looking little fay of about twelve, with bright sparkling eyes and rosy cheeks, and a constant smile on the never-closed lips.

"Welcome kindly! We will not wait for them," said Karely, laughing, as he lifted them out and opened the door, which Boriska had shut behind her.

Our readers having had a slight glance at the travellers, I must inform them that the lady who has just arrived is Mrs. Erzsebet Hamvasi, sister of Abraham Hamvasi, to whose house they have come, and which had been left equally to the lady and her brother by their parents—although Erzsebet Hamvasi, subsequently Tallyai, had left her brother in undisturbed possession, only desiring an occasional reception when *en route*.

As Karely opened the door, Boriska appeared at the farther end of the room, calling into the stove: "Come out; you have guests here." To which a voice from within responded: "Let them wait." After a few minutes, a door opened behind the stove, and a man of spare bent figure advanced towards the travellers. His face was disfigured by small-pox, and rendered grotesque by a pair of stiff gray moustaches, which grew straight forward from under the nose, leaving only the extremities of the lips visible, and giving him very much the appearance of an otter. He wore an old stuff coat—too cool for winter and too warm for summer—the sleeves of which were turned up to the elbow; for he had just come out of the stove, which he had been plastering, and both hands were covered with mortar.

To judge by his countenance, he certainly did not seem endeavouring to look pleased to see his dear relations; and though the lady greeted him amiably, he did not seem much inclined to open the other side of the door at which she was standing, waiting for her brother's welcome.

"What! so many of you!" he exclaimed, pushing open the door with his elbow; "where the tartar are you all going?"

The lady shook her head placidly, and pointing to her brother's dirty hands—"How now, dear brother!" she said, in a half reproachful and half jesting tone; "must you really do such work yourself?"

"It is no shame to work," replied her brother; "never trust to others what you can do yourself."

"I would kiss your hand, dear Uncle Abris, if you would put on gloves," said Karely, laughing.

"Easy enough for fine gentlemen like you to speak, but a poor man must do what he can.—Boris! bring me a bowl of water to wash my hands, for these gentle folks are ashamed to stand in the room with me."

"Dirty the dishes, indeed!" cried Boris sharply; "there is the tub."

Master Abris went and washed in the tub; then, lifting up the bed-quilt, he wiped his hands and face in the sheet, with so many grimaces, that it was evident he was undergoing an unusual penance.

The guests meanwhile entered the sitting-room. Every room has its own peculiar perfume. On entering some apartments an agreeable friendly odour, which we cannot account for, greets the sense, while others are so close and so unpleasant that we involuntarily retreat. The apartment of Uncle Abris was among the latter. The walls were soiled and daubed with pencil scrawls of several years' standing; there was a thick carpet of straw and feathers beneath the beds; the furniture was an inch deep in dust, and it was impossible to see out of the windows, which had cobwebs in every corner.

The lady sighed deeply as she entered this apartment; one could almost read on her countenance, that she was recalling brighter days, when everything in the house looked very different from what it did now.

Uncle Abris, having very coldly kissed each of the party, endeavoured to smile a little; but not succeeding, he gave it up, and his features resumed their usual hard, anxious expression.

His guests would gladly have taken off their cloaks, but where should they put them down? It would have been ruin to clean clothes to come in contact with anything in the room.

"I should like to sit down somewhere, Uncle Abris," said Sizika, looking round her with innocent scrutiny.

"Well, my dear, here are plenty of chairs, and a sofa," said Uncle Abris.

"What! *may* I brush off all this pretty dust?" asked Sizika roguishly. "I thought it was put here to dry."

Karely laughed; while his mother put her finger to her lips, and shook her head; and Uncle Abris answered quietly, "Dust we are, and unto dust we must return, and therefore we need not despise dust;" and, in order to strengthen the golden precept, he lifted the flaps of his coat, and, wiping three chairs for his guests, seated himself on a fourth.

The lady placed herself down opposite to her brother. One was silent, the other did not speak; and so they remained nearly an hour. Occasionally one or other would sigh deeply, "Heighho!" on which the other would reply, a quarter of an hour after, "Ay, ay!"

Karely having gone out to look at the horses, Erzsike went to the window, and, wiping one of the panes with her pocket handkerchief, tried to look through it. You must not be perplexed, dear readers, at our having first called this merry little fairy Sizika, then Erzsike; both denominations come from the same source, and there is perhaps no name in the Hungarian language which admits of so many variations to represent the various gradations from the utmost refinement to the greatest coarseness; hence the tender, caressing Siza, the gay, roguish Erzsike, the robust, noisy Erzsu, and the dirty, untidy Boske.

It never entered Uncle Abraham's head to ask his guests if they wanted anything; he only sat and sighed. Matyi, the coachman, a smart lad from Lower Hungary, now entered; he had been a csikos,[6] and was an inveterate specimen of cleverness and roguish insolence.

> [6] *Csikos*, who take care of the horses and studs of the vast meadows or heaths, called *puszta*.

"Is there any hay to be sold here, sir?" he asked, saluting the master of the house.

"Hay! hay! for whom do you want hay?"

"Not for myself, sir, but for my horses—that is, not for my horses, but for my master's."

"Well, let's see; I believe I can give you a little," said Hamvasi, weighing each word, as he took the key of the barn from his pocket, and went out. The guests could hear the murmurs of Boris outside the door:—"The tartar take them all! to come to an honest man's house with four horses, just that they might devour more hay, as if two were not enough!"

Master Abraham gave the key to Matyi, making him promise not to drop any of the hay about, because it was dear; and, after watching till he had returned, he re-entered, and resumed his seat without speaking.

In a few minutes, Matyi came in again: "Where shall I find a tavern sir?"

"A tavern! what do you want a tavern for?"

"Not for the horses, sir, but for myself. I want to get a glass of wine."

"Well, I will give you one just now," said Uncle Abris, and taking the key of the cellar, he went out, desiring Matyi to wait at the entrance.

Boriska stormed and dashed about, scolding and holding forth to herself.

Scarcely had the old gentleman re-entered and silence resumed her reign, than Matyi appeared a third time: "Boriska wants to know, sir, what she shall cook for supper?"

"Supper! are you used to sup?" asked Uncle Abris, turning to his guests.

"That we are," replied Karely quickly, before his gentle mother had time to say the contrary.

Master Abris sighed deeply, rose and went into the kitchen, whence he was heard talking in a low voice to Boriska, who, on the contrary, spoke as loud as possible, so as to be heard in the next room.

"What! that beautiful fowl!—have you lost your senses? I make a fire now! there is no wood cut. Let them eat cheese, there is plenty of bread. Indeed I shall not open the pot of preserves—I can't knead puddings, I've a sore hand. I am not a cook; and why don't you keep one, if you want to turn innkeeper?"

All this was heard distinctly by the guests within. And now, for once, Uncle Abris really got into a passion, and, going out to the court, he struck down a renowned cock with the rolling-pin, and, lighting a fire himself, he set to work to pluck it, till Boriska, seeing it was in vain to oppose, snatched the cock from his hands and turned him out of the kitchen.

In about two hours the banquet was ready. The unhappy cock had been burnt to a cinder, and his bones were not harder than his flesh. The half-baked bread stuck to the knife when it was cut, and to the palate when it was chewed; and the dishes were so full of salt and cayenne that tears came into the eyes of the eaters.

The lady sat at the head of the table, and scarcely tasted anything; she sighed deeply on seeing the worm-eaten holes in her dear mother's table-linen, the well-known knives and forks loosened from their deer's-horn handles, and the old family plate all bruised and broken. What may not a man come to who has no wife to keep his house in order!

During supper Uncle Abris, having taken some wine, ventured to break the silence, and asked his sister whither she was *en route*.

She replied, smiling, that they were going to visit Gabor Berkessy.

"What! to that detestable man!" exclaimed Uncle Abris, somewhat under the influence of the wine.

"Why is he a detestable man?" asked Karely, half amused, half annoyed.

"Because when I was a student in Debreczen he informed upon me once for visiting a tavern. I was punished by twenty-four hours' confinement, and I have never forgotten it since."

And yet it was good thirty years ago!

"And what are you going there for, if I may ask?" continued Uncle Abris.

The lady did not answer; on which Siza took up the conversation: "We are going to look out for a wife. Mr. Berkessy has a daughter who would just suit my brother."

"Hm!" replied the old man, ungraciously looking over his shoulder at Karely; "you are still a child."

"That is just the reason we want to get him married," replied Sizike demurely. "He is a good lad, but somewhat unsteady; when he has a wife, his understanding will come. And then," she continued, "it is much better to marry young, than to grow old, and fall into the hands of some virago."

The child spoke these words with such peculiar gravity, that Karely could scarce restrain his laughter; her mother shook her head, and Uncle Abris looked as if he were sharpening his teeth to devour her.

"Hm! you know how to talk at least; can you bake bread too?"

"Oh! that I can, uncle, though I do not know that I could dress the szalonna7 for it."

[7] Szalonna is a kind of fat which they are fond of eating with bread in this district; but the same name is applied to the wet dough which is found in badly-baked bread.

Uncle Abris saw that he was losing ground, and moved back his chair, which was a signal to the rest of the party to rise; and, after the usual ceremonies on leaving table, the guests asked to be shown to their apartments, whither Uncle Abris conducted them, giving each a candle, which he begged them to put out as soon as they went to bed.

There were rooms enough in the house, but it was melancholy to see them. Pease, maize, and onions lay in every corner; and the beds were just in the condition in which they had been left by the last occupants.

Karely went to the smaller of the two rooms which had been allotted them, and in a few minutes he was in bed.

"Dear mamma, we shall freeze here," said little Sizike, feeling the ice-cold pillows; "what shall we do?" and knocking at Karely's door, she asked if he were asleep.

"What do you want, Sizike?"

"We cannot undress here, Karely, there are no curtains on the windows."

"Well, blow out the candle."

"O dear! I am afraid in the dark!"

"Then lock the door."

"The door will not shut properly."

"Well, wait, Boske, I will get up and sleep there, and you can come here with mother," and, jumping up and out of bed, he dressed and came into the next room, putting the ladies into his.

"And now confess, Erzsu," he said, trembling with cold; "why did you cheat me out of my warm bed into this cold one?"

"Because you had warmed it already," replied Erzsike, merrily.

There is nothing gayer than the childish mirth between brother and sister. Even the mild lady laughed heartily. But it was no easy matter to get warm, even under feather beds. Such rooms attract the cold all the winter; and even in summer, if the weather is damp, one is apt to get chilled and cold. Scarcely had our travellers fallen into an uneasy sleep, than an inconsiderate cock crew loudly just under their windows.

"Karely, do you hear the ghost of the cock we ate last night?" cried Sizike, waking up.

It was out of the question trying to sleep again; and in a short time they all rose and dressed, feeling in every limb as if they had been beaten.

There is a great art in making beds. In some beds you fall asleep immediately on lying down: the pillows, which have been placed out in the sun, have still the freshness and natural heat which they have attracted; the mattresses and feather-beds are so skilfully arranged, that every limb feels at home, and on whichever side you lie, you awake on it next morning; while in others, turn which way you will, you can never find a place—now shivering, now perspiring, you try to sleep, but start up in a fright,—the woodworm gnaws and bores, the bed creaks and cracks. If at last you do fall asleep, it is to dream of robbers, and when you awake you cannot turn your head. Strange that no book has yet been written on this very necessary science!

Our travellers had still a grievous ordeal to go through, and this was breakfast. They would gladly have avoided it; but Uncle Abris gravely declared, that having fulfilled his part of the obligation—having roasted the coffee, and boiled the milk—they must not be wasted. So they all sat down; and although the coffee was a little burned, and the milk a little run, and the rolls somewhat stale, no one grumbled; but, finishing as quickly as possible, prepared to depart. The carriage then drove up, and Uncle Abraham assisted his guests into it. He now smiled in good earnest. "They are off at last, and will want nothing more"—it was easy interpreting his smile. Having kissed them all, and wished them a prosperous journey, he thought he had passed all dangers, when Matyi exclaimed: "I quite forgot to drink that glass of brandy which your honour wanted to give me."

Uncle Abris once more grew pale, and retreating into the parlour, came out with a glass about as large as a thimble.

"Is this all for me, sir?" asked Matyi, holding up the little glass in surprise; and having emptied it, he looked round, as if to say, Was there anything in it?

"Will you have half a glass more?" asked Uncle Abris, with extraordinary generosity.

"Thank you, sir," replied Matyi; "I am afraid of overturning the carriage. Bless your honour! bless you, Boriska! we shall be back again in a week."

It was lucky that the horses now set off, for the party could no longer contain their laughter. Uncle Abris and Boriska thrust their heads out of the door, and it was not until the carriage had totally disappeared from view that they ventured to return into the house.

Boris never ceased scolding all that day. "Is it for this, indeed, one has relations—that they may come and lay waste the house, while we are stinting all the year round just to stuff these locusts! The cows don't eat so much in a week as they used for their horses; and that little, saucy girl could only make bullets of the good bread, and throw it about. She will eat it some day though, I'll answer for that, the delicate dear! And then the work they gave folks!" In fine, good Mrs. Boriska summed up her complaints by declaring, that if they ever set foot in the house again she should leave it, and let Master Abris shift for himself; and then, slamming the door in his face, she left him to his solitary reflections.

Our readers are by this time aware that there is a certain Gabor Berkessy who has a marriageable daughter, to obtain whose hand two marriageable young men are hastening from different parts of the country, accompanied by their respective families, as beseemed.

We entreat our readers' patience to accompany us once more to a third county, and then we shall all hasten to Uncle Berkessy's together.

In the capital town of the county of S——, a young widow resided, called Julia Csalvari. It was the general opinion among the ill-natured gossips of this town that the fair widow was a great coquette. The fact is, that Julia, during the few years of her wedded life, had been kept very strictly by her husband—an old gentleman, who was miserly, stupid, and jealous in an equal degree; and consequently, after his death, the restrained feelings of a vivacious nature burst out the more vehemently. Her husband had left her the mistress of a considerable fortune, and thus the handsome young widow found herself surrounded by admirers, who flattered her vanity without touching her heart. She rode, gave soirées, and frequented balls, and dressed in great style; all this was enough to make her be spoken of in the capital town of S——. Besides, an old gentleman who had formerly been an assessor, who was a sort of uncle of Julia, and lived with her as protector and secretary, supplied the good neighbours with constant theme. Everything that occurred in Julia's house was repeated by him in the noble and bourgeois casinos of S——; even that she never wore the same pair of silk stockings more than once, and that she was vaccinated every year! In short, the smallest circumstances, from love-quarrels downwards, might be procured fresh-hatched every morning from Uncle Nanasy, who was thus continually getting into scrapes—at one time running the risk of being called out by one of his niece's reported admirers, while at another some discarded cavalier threatened to thrash him; and more than once he was obliged to remain at home for fear of being shot through the head. And then he had even more to endure from the fair Julia's caprice than from the dangers without. But all this did not cure the old gentleman: he still gossiped as much as he could, denied as much as he could, and bore the results with wonderful patience.

Julia's relations constantly pressed her to marry, and give up this sort of life; but Julia was little disposed to exchange her present freedom. And indeed she was so wilful and capricious, that had she preferred any one person in particular, she was quite capable of rejecting his suit, and never seeing him again, if her relations urged her to marry him. Her marriage was thus put off from year to year; as soon as anything serious began to be reported, some quarrel was sure to take place on one side or other, and not unfrequently the whole affair would pass over, while those most nearly concerned knew nothing of it.

About the time when our story commences, Uncle Nanasy entered the kitchen one afternoon to discover what was being cooked, after which he announced himself to the *dame de compagnie*, to ascertain in what humour his fair niece was to be found that day; and having satisfied himself on that point, he entered Julia's room, to tell her all that had been spoken of in the *cafés* that morning. He found her at her toilet; her maid was curling her long golden hair, while she reclined carelessly in her arm-chair and played with the silken tresses, which descended to the floor.

"Good morning, my sweet pretty little niece!" lisped Uncle Nanasy, tripping over to Julia with galopade steps, and seizing her small hand, which he covered with kisses from the wrist to the tips of the nails, exclaiming between each one: "Ah, what a dear little hand! how charming to get a box on the ear from such a soft hand! And how is my sweet little niece to-day? whose head is she going to turn with these long ringlets *à l'Anglaise*? Ah, you merciless Penelope! do you know that a duel took place on your account this very morning? The handsome Lajos, that dark-eyed youth, got a cut across his forehead, he, he, he!—he is a lucky man. Let me arrange this ribbon—there's a love, just through these tresses. See, is it not tastefully placed? would not Uncle Nanasy make a capital tirewoman?—he, he, he!"

Julia did not wish to laugh at all this nonsense; and turning to her maid, desired her to bring her shoes.

"No, I shall not allow anybody to bring them but myself!" cried Uncle Nanasy, holding back the maid, and running to fetch them; then, kissing them a dozen times, he placed them before her, while Julia took off her small embroidered slippers, and let Uncle Nanasy put on her satin shoes, as little embarrassed by his presence as if he had been her maid. Then rising, she continued her toilette before the Psyche; while Uncle Nanasy stood by, exclaiming, "How angelic! how lovely!" until he almost poked his chin out of joint with admiration and wonder.

"Nanasy bacsi," said Julia gravely, and still looking at herself in the mirror, "I am going to intrust you with a very serious affair, and one about which you must not gossip until it has been duly brought into execution."

"Well, my love; am I not the most trustworthy keeper of secrets?"

Julia frowned. "I am not joking, bacsi; but I tell you seriously, that if you speak of this affair to anybody before it takes place, I will tear your hair."

"Nanasy bacsi will be grateful for the favour," said the old gentleman, pulling off his peruke and holding down his head, which was as smooth as a water-melon. At this sight, the waiting-damsel burst into an immoderate fit of laughter; on which her mistress, frowning, ordered her to leave the room.

Uncle Nanasy tried every means to amuse his niece—put on his wig awry, opened his snuff-box with a variety of grimaces, performing pirouettes and courtesies of the *renaissance* era; but all in vain—Julia would not laugh.

When they were alone, she shut the doors, seated the old gentleman on the balzac, and standing before him—"Listen to me now, Nanasy bacsi," she began; "I am going to be married."

Nanasy bacsi became all surprise and curiosity.

"You must go to-day," she continued, "to V——, find out the high sheriff, and get me a dispensation.8 You need not come back from there, but go straight on to Pesth, and order all that is requisite for a wedding—what that is, you know better than I do; arrange everything for this day week at the latest. I want to have it all over by that time."

[8] A dispensation is required when the marriage is not proclaimed three times in the church.

"Depend upon me, my angel—in three days all shall be ready, or you will hear that Nanasy bacsi is no more."

"You must have my bridal dress made in Pesth, within the shortest time possible."

"Depend on me, my darling; I shall employ the most celebrated milliners, Varga or Sovari—and if I do not bring the most magnificent bridal dress within a week, advertise me in the papers as a stray dog, for which the lucky finder will receive five florins!"

"Write to my relations at the same time," continued Julia, "and invite them to the ceremony on this day week; but for this you will have time enough in Pesth. I have ordered the carriage, and now you have nothing to do but to get into it and drive off."

"Yes, my dear, I understand; but what am I to say to our relations?"

"Why, what have we been talking about?—that I am going to be married!"

"Yes, but to whom?"

"Why, is it necessary to know that too?"

"Ha, ha, ha, ha! why, that is the *facit* of the matter."

"How odd!—well, say Kalman Sos."

"Kalman Sos—Kalman Sos; I have heard the name once before. How do you spell it—with two o's or two s's?"

"With as many as you like!"

"Who, or what is this fine young man?"

"A poet!" replied Julia, with a grave sigh.

"But what else?"

Julia stared at her uncle, partly in surprise, partly in anger, as if to say, How simple you old people are! and then, with a disdainful shrug, she replied, "Fate was generous enough, I think, in bestowing on him a rich mind, without adding a rich position too."

Nanasy bacsi did not understand this logic, but contented himself by thus filling up the rubric: Whoever he may be, actor, dancing-master, or what else, she will certainly be able to manage him.

Julia left the old man to think what he pleased, while she prepared with her own hands all that was necessary for his journey—not forgetting his shaving materials—wrote her commissions in a pocket-book, in which she placed a heap of uncounted notes, and, thrusting it into Uncle Nanasy's pocket, she assisted him to put on his great-coat and fur cloak, drew his travelling-cap over his head, and would not let him breathe until she saw him seated in the carriage, that he might have no time to betray her secret.

Nanasy bacsi, however, bursting with the importance of his mission, happened to meet one or two friends as he was passing through the town, and, thrusting his head out of the carriage, without stopping, he told the first that his niece was going to be married in a week, the second, that he was on his way for a dispensation, and the third, that he was going to Pesth for dresses and confectionary; and, in about an hour afterwards, the whole town was talking of the secret marriage, and guessing who the happy bridegroom might be—for Nanasi bacsi had not told his name, husbanding his news, like all true gossips, that he might have something new to relate when he came back.

Meanwhile, Julia returned to her room, with the placid conviction of having arranged all her affairs to satisfaction, and gave orders to her servants not to admit any person except Kalman.

In a short time the sound of steps echoed along the corridor, and Julia assumed her sweetest smiles; for our readers are no doubt aware that, under such circumstances, namely, when one is in love, even the sound of a boot-heel may be recognised. In this respect, only the editors of newspapers have a finer instinct—who, it is said, tell, even from the sound of a step in the street, whether it is the postman with subscribers or a poet with his verses. In this case the magnetism was reversed; Julia expected the poet, not the postman, and she was not deceived—

Kalman Sos opened the door.

He was a pale, interesting youth—not that his paleness alone made him interesting, but he entered the room as Hamlet is expected to enter with the skull, and, walking with pathetic steps towards Julia, he raised the fair lady's hand to his lips, where he held it for a long time, and would probably have been holding it still, had not Julia withdrawn it, exclaiming, "Something is the matter, Kalman, that you are so sad to-day?"

"Sad I am, indeed!" replied the poet.

"For mercy's sake!" exclaimed Julia, in alarm, "what has taken place?"

"Nothing, nothing," replied Kalman, but in a tone which left his fair bride to surmise the worst; and then, sinking into an arm-chair, he gazed vacantly before him.

"Yes, yes, there is something the matter with you," cried the lady, really frightened; "I entreat, I desire you will tell me instantly!"

The poet rose *à tempo*, and once more taking Julia's hand, he gazed long and earnestly into her eyes. "Do you believe in presentiments?" he asked at last, in a faltering voice.

"How! Why?"

"Have you never known that feeling, something like a waking dream, which overtakes us in our gayest hours, as if some cold hand passed across the brow, and the smile which had risen on the lip dies away; as if suddenly a magic mirror rose before us, reflecting our own countenance, but pale and dark, as if warning us not to rejoice?"

"O stop!" cried Julia, on whom these words made an uncomfortable impression; "it is not right to speak of such things; let us talk rather of our wedding. Have you heard from your relations yet?"

Kalman assumed a Byronic look, and, turning up his eyes, "You are happy, Julia," he replied; "ah! you are still a child, and can rejoice at everything."

"Now, what nonsense, Kalman! you know I am at least five years older than you are, if not more."

"Ah, Julia! years alone do not constitute time. You are still a child at eight-and-twenty, while I am an old man at twenty-four. Not he who is furthest from the cradle is the oldest, but he who is nearest the grave. It is the weight of days, not their number, that brings wrinkles. I have suffered as much as would suffice for a life of fifty years!"

"Poor Kalman!" sighed Julia, laying her fair hand on the poet's shoulder. Her delicacy prevented her asking what the deuce had caused him so much suffering; besides, Kalman might have been shocked at hearing her give utterance to such an expression.

"See!" continued Kalman, "at the very moment when I first beheld your angel face, and my heart began to burn with the thought that I might possess you—call you mine for ever—an ice-cold whisper seemed to say, 'Rejoice not, all is uncertain till the day has come.'"

"But it is certain now," replied Julia, "for I have sent for the dispensation, and invited my relations; we shall celebrate the wedding this day week."

"Ha! this day week! do you not know that will be the thirteenth of the month!"

"Indeed, I did not consult the calendar."

"Ah, Julia! that number has a fearful influence over my fate!"

"Well, let it be the previous day."

"Julia, you speak as securely as if you held the hand of fate within your own."

"Well, if you wish it, and I have no objection, should I speak otherwise than of a certainty?"

Kalman raised his finger, and with it his eyes, so that Julia began to think he had discovered a spider's web hanging from the ceiling, and was pointing it out to her. "Fate hangs over us," he exclaimed, "and fate is capricious, Julia; broken hearts and withered hopes are offerings in which she takes delight. Ah, Julia! you are happy if this feeling has never breathed across your soul; if within your bosom's world there are no magic chords on which the hand of prophecy strikes wildly; it would have banished the roses from your face, as it has done from mine."

Julia was getting tired of all these unpleasant visions and magnetic influences; and to give the conversation another turn, she seated herself at the piano, and began to play a gay fantasia.

Kalman leant his elbow on the back of her chair; his dark countenance seemed to pierce the future, while his eyes glared, and his hair stood erect— Julia could observe all this in the opposite mirror. Then, again, he folded his arms and drooped his head on his bosom, till, no longer able to bear the excess of his feelings, he started up, struck his forehead, and exclaimed, in a state of exultation, "Ah! one such moment were sufficient for life; to hear those sweet accents, and, hand in hand, heart to heart, expire together, breathing forth our souls in one long embrace. Julia, do you not desire to die with me?"

"Indeed it will be very nice, when we have both of us reached a good old age; meanwhile let us live a little while together."

Kalman gazed at Julia with an expression of pity: he felt with pain how far beneath his own must that mind be, which could not comprehend the fearful ecstasy of two persons dying together, who have nothing at all the matter with them. He rose and paced the room several times, like a wandering spirit who had no other calling than to terrify the living; then seizing his hat with suicidal determination, he stepped up to Julia, and exclaimed, in heart-rending accents: "Farewell, farewell! Heaven grant that my forebodings be not realized!" And then, tearing himself from her, he rushed out of the room as if in desperation.

Poor Julia was truly in despair, and fearing she knew not what, despatched her servant after Kalman, to see that he did not harm himself; and it was not until the man returned, and assured his mistress that he had seen the young gentleman in the casino eating roast-meat and green garlic, that she could at all compose herself.

Julia was occupied all that afternoon by visitors; and, much to her surprise, she received calls from various persons who had not crossed her threshold for several years before, who all endeavoured, by hints and delicate advice, to allude to the secret which she thought was already twenty miles off—in fact, the whole town seemed perfectly aware of her intended marriage.

She had now no other resource but to shut herself up in her own apartment, and to see nobody. Reflecting upon Kalman's late visit, she reproached herself for her prosaical remarks, which must have ill accorded with the poet's sublime rhapsodies, and endeavoured to force on her imagination some of those strange feelings, which she supposed might resemble the unpleasant sensations caused by a cold in the head, derangement of the stomach—and having worked herself up to a state of nervous excitement, she sat down to her escritoire, and began a long letter to her bridegroom.

As she was in the act of revising a composition which she herself scarcely understood, her maid entered the room with a letter.

Annoyed at being interrupted, Julia snatched it from her hand, and glancing hurriedly at the address, recognised Kalman's handwriting.

Seriously alarmed, she held the letter in her hand without daring to break the seal, in case she should read: "When these lines meet your eye, the writer will be"—the thought was too horrible! Motioning to her maid to quit the room, she opened the epistle with a trembling hand: there were four pages closely written.

"Adorable Julia!—Angel never to be forgotten!—Have you ever seen two stars so close to one another in the blue vault of heaven, that with the naked eye you might take them to be but one, and which, ever since their creation, have been revolving round one another—when suddenly an unexpected phenomenon takes place: one of these two stars, impelled by an irresistible power, quits his companion, and rushing forward through the universe, becomes a comet, whose fate is to wander beyond the worlds, threatening the trembling stars with destruction." . . . .

Julia's patience was not sufficient to go through four pages of astronomy, and turning impatiently to the end of the letter, she read as follows:—

"As my father's wishes in regard to me are iron fetters, which enchain me like Prometheus to the rock; and since he absolutely insists upon my marrying the daughter of Gabor Berkessy, pronotarius of the county of Csongrad, there remains no alternative but to die or—to obey. Were I to consider myself alone, it were bliss to choose the former. But I can think of you alone—the despair, the derangement, probably, my selfishness might cause you; and therefore I live and obey for your sake, my adorable Julia! for your peace alone; and with tears in my eyes, and anguish in my heart, trace these few lines, each word of which is a dagger in the soul of him who can never forget, and lives alone in your remembrance.

Kalman Sos."

And these were the fatal forebodings, the mysterious visions! Julia fell from the stars.

After a moment's brief reflection, however, the fair lady coolly folded the letter, without deigning it a second perusal, and throwing it into the fire with the one she had just written, she rang the bell; then writing a few hurried lines, she sealed the note and handed it to her maid, saying: "Desire the groom to get a fleet horse instantly, and ride after Nanasy bacsi to the sheriff's: should he find him there, he may leave the letter and return; if not, he must go on to Pesth. My uncle generally lodges at the Golden Eagle; but let him find him out, and spare no expense."

Uncle Gabor Berkessy was a man of about sixty years of age, with hair and beard snow-white; but though old in years, he was as young in spirit and as active in limb as a youth of twenty.

He was the life and soul of every company, without ever offending by his jests. His anecdotes were celebrated in the country; and when he began to tell a story after dinner, it was impossible for the company to keep their seats; and finally, when he himself joined in the laugh, it might have been heard at the end of the town; for the thundering peal could only be compared to what a lion's might be, if the risibility of that mighty king of beasts could be excited. On more than one occasion, when he had happened to be present at a comedy, the actors were obliged to stop in the midst of their performance. First it began slowly—ha! ha, ha! ha, ha, ha! holding his handkerchief to his mouth, and pretending to cough; until at last, as if a bomb had burst within him, the fearful sounds would break forth—ha, ha, ha, ha, ha! tears would roll down his cheeks, he would strike the board before him with his fist, stamp on the ground, and engage the attention of all the spectators; so that at last, whenever an actor heard the first ha! he hurried over whatever was to be said, knowing that he had no chance afterwards of being listened to at all.

I have descanted rather at length on Uncle Gabor's laughing faculty, because, according to my theory, if a man can laugh heartily, he must not only be a good-hearted, but a well-informed man; and as such Berkessy was acknowledged in all the district. His countenance was a faithful interpreter of his mind: the jolly round face and laughing eyes, with their silver lashes; the knolly, flexible brows; the healthy teeth and red lips; and the expression of goodness, impossible to mistake, impressed on every feature, gave such a charm to his countenance, that it was impossible not to feel comfortable in his vicinity; and even the Christmas Legatus would have taken courage in his presence.

Uncle Berkessy was thirty years old when he married; and his wife was an excellent soul, with whom he lived sixteen years of peaceful life, without however being blessed by children. At last, when least expected, the blessing arrived in the form of a little girl.

The happy pair were now twice as happy as they had been before; the little Linka was the joy and light of their eyes, and the hope and glory of both. They lavished upon her all the affection and tenderness of their nature, hastening to gratify her slightest fancies—for every thought seemed concentrated in their only child; and, strange providence! this indulgence not only did not spoil her, but rendered her from day to day more amiable and more loving. The slightest hint from her mother's eyes was sufficient to direct her, and she knew no greater happiness than that of pleasing her parents; all their care and tenderness found a kindly grateful soil within her gentle heart, and was richly repaid. How unlike to most indulged natures, which are generally like vinegar—the more sugar you put in, the stronger will the acid be.

Lina was scarcely ten years old when she lost her mother—the greatest loss a little girl can experience. All a father's attention can never make up for the want of a mother's care; much will remain unobserved by him which could not escape the ever-watchful spirit of a tender mother.

Although this misfortune did not change Lina, she was more thoughtful afterwards; but the cares of a household devolving upon her, left her no time to indulge in melancholy. A great safeguard for a young girl are her household cares: they teach her to respect herself, they banish sadness, keep down the passions and false feeling, and give true life to the young mind.

The little girl was the greatest comfort in her father's bereavement: and as she grew up, her sweetness and amiability, and excellent management, were the surprise and admiration of all the families around; and no less than three suitors, as we have already seen, were on their way to Uncle Berkessy on matrimonial speculation. Our sweet little heroine's exterior, though pleasing in the extreme, was not such as is called in the language of poets, beautiful. And here I cannot help observing, that the manner in which these poetical gentlemen dictate to the world in general is certainly most unfair. According to their ideas, it is only a perfect beauty who dare lay any claim to happiness; while all the others, whose faces cannot be compared to lilies and roses, are born only to be deceived, and but for their wealth would never appear in a romance at all. Real life, however, gives them the lie; for we see family happiness bloom even in households where the ladies are not painted for annuals. And how many a mild and unpretending being do we find gifted with that delicacy and true poetry of mind, which give to features not created for a painter's model an attraction and loveliness that it would be impossible to describe, for we can scarcely say what it is we find so agreeable; and although we might turn with cold indifference from a mere sketch of the features, no sooner do we see them lighted up by a smile, or hear an accent of sympathy cross the lips, than a sweet fascination rises within us—the eyes, the lips, the whole countenance, wins new attractions; the soul assumes its power over the clay, and charms into beauty what in itself is not so. Fortunately, nature seldom bestows on any one the consciousness of being less handsome than her neighbour; for that woman could scarcely be good-humoured, who, when she looked in the glass, could not discover something which rendered her countenance agreeable, and which others also will no doubt remark after some observation. These ideas may, I fear, hurt the classic understanding, and the lovers of art will be shocked to hear that the not beautiful can also be subjects of poetry; but if mankind has so increased upon earth as to mottle the Olympic regularity with many variations, who can help it? The negro and the Laplander have their beauties; and some are even bold enough to affirm that the mind of itself may render beautiful.

All these deviations must not weary you, gentle reader, for you know it is now a question of matrimony, and therefore you must read patiently and not in vain.

Day was just dawning; the sound of bells broke the silence of the village, and, one by one, the green blinds opened as the sun shed his first rays on the windows of Uncle Berkessy's house. Two windows alone remained closed—those of the room in which the old gentleman slept; the others were all open, and the rooms filled with the fresh morning air. The valuable old furniture was already dusted, and the polished floors were shining like mirrors. In the first room, a great glass chiffonnière stood opposite the windows, ornamented by pillars supported by gilded angels. Among the china and cut crystal arranged within, was that which Uncle Gabor's grandmother had received as a bridal gift, and which she used until she was eighty-two years old, and left in the same admirable order to her children. At the other side of the room, stood two large beds, on whose heavy curtains a stag-hunt was portrayed. Although nobody slept in those two beds, they were turned down every sunny day, and the great feather pillows placed within the double windows to air. Opposite the beds stood an antique cabinet, ornamented by various carvings and pillars, of which it would be difficult to discover all the quaint recesses and the secret drawers. Between the windows stood an ancestral mirror, with its frame of ornamental cut glass, the centre of which was decorated by a garland of everlasting flowers, which might have hung there at least half a century. In one corner stood a large cabinet clock, and in the other a high spinning-wheel, used by grandmamma in ancient times; and which was always kept in the same corner from a feeling of respect, although nobody ever used it. And, as we are come on matrimonial speculations, I may inform you, gracious reader, that the lower part of the chiffonnière contains real old silver-plate for forty-eight persons; and that the large cabinet is filled with the finest table-linen, among which is still preserved that which grandmamma had spun with her own hands. And now we shall proceed into the next room. This had been fitted up with the newest furniture by Uncle Gabor as a surprise on one of his daughter's birthdays, and was filled with comfortable arm-chairs, spring sofas, and elegant work-tables. There was a grand pianoforte too, and a glass chiffonnière, in which all her little birthday and holiday gifts were arranged. The rich worsted-work carpet was an example of the young lady's personal industry, for, besides keeping the house in perfect order, she found time for various other female employments. A pretty bookcase was filled with choice books, selected by her father, while on her little embroidery table lay the Athenæum and the Regelo,9 with extracts from the latest Hungarian works.

[9] *Regelo*—title of a literary magazine.

Lina's sleeping apartment opened from this room; surprising neatness and order reigned in every part of the little sanctuary; and the snow-white curtains of the bed and windows pleasantly contrasted with the dark, polished floor. The airy windows opened on the garden, from whence the large harvest roses peeped in. A pretty brass cage, with a canary bird, hung on the wall; and whenever its mistress appeared, the little tenant would sing as if its small heart were going to burst. Beyond this room was an ante-chamber which opened into the old gentleman's apartment, which we will not disturb, as he is still asleep.

In the opposite wing of the building were the guests' chambers, the kitchen, servants' rooms, and store-rooms; and beyond these was a pavilion, provided with comfortable seats, in the centre of which a fountain played; and here the host was wont to sit and smoke with his guests, sheltered equally from sun or rain.

The court-yard was already full of business and activity; the reapers preparing to set out, the old gray-headed labourer leading his oxen with their decorated horns to the well; the footman was standing at the door of the out-house polishing his master's silver-spurred boots, so that he might have shaved in them. A comfortable odour of soup proceeded from the open kitchen-door, and in a few minutes, our little lady herself stepped across the corridor, and appeared in the court to distribute bread and brandy to the reapers. Her cheeks were flushed, for she had just come from the fire, and a neat white handkerchief was arranged round her head. For the young girls, who were as yet innocent of the virtues of brandy, she had prepared a good warm soup, that they might not go hungry to their work. It was not with any idea of parsimony, but rather to see that each person had sufficient, that she came out herself; and she was never contented till every person had partaken of her gifts. Having wished their young mistress a hearty *Aldja Isten* (God bless you), the reapers then set out in the greatest good humour, the young lads and lasses singing and jesting, and the elders walking soberly together.

Lina still lingered a few minutes to enjoy the fresh air, and listen to the tinkling bells of the oxen as they disappeared, and then she called her flock of poultry, which had collected round the millstone where the labourers had breakfasted, and distributed their portions also; after which, she returned to the kitchen to superintend the roasting of the coffee for her father's breakfast; for when she left it to the servants, they were sure either to roast it unmercifully, or burn it, or do something else which gave it an unpleasant taste. Covered fireplaces were not yet known in those days— everything was cooked on the flames or hot embers, and consequently the proper management of the fire was then a source of much greater trouble to cooks, who had to guard against smoking, burning, or singeing their dishes; and cooking was at that period a far more difficult business than in these more enlightened times.

Meanwhile, the footman had covered the table, and the old gentleman, being awakened by the rattling of cups and spoons, soon made his appearance in complete attire, with his polished silver-spurred boots, and his fur dolmany thrown across his shoulders; his thick gray hair was uncovered, and a pipe, quite full, in his mouth. The footman wished him "a happy good morning," while three huge greyhounds sprang from under the table to meet him. Having patted and caressed them all, Uncle Gabor walked into the kitchen to light his pipe, well knowing that he should find his daughter there. Linka's hands were full, and, as her father entered, she exclaimed, in the sweetest voice imaginable, "Good morning, dearest father; just hold out your hand here one instant, dear papa."

"For what?" exclaimed the old gentleman, holding out his hand at the same time.

It was just that Lina might stoop down and kiss it, for both her hands were occupied.

The old gentleman patted his daughter's face, and then, taking a bride's eye (a bright-burning ember) between his fingers from the fire, he lit his pipe and stood watching Lina's operations. When breakfast was ready, Lina prepared her father's coffee; she knew exactly how black and how sweet to make it, and the old gentleman was so spoilt in this respect, that he could never drink coffee except at home.

We have now seen the little lady at her various occupations, but we have still to see her when she scolds, for this is infallibly requisite in good housekeeping, and to overlook faults is in itself the greatest fault; but the question is, how to scold that your servants may neither fear nor laugh at you; and Lina could scold both gracefully and agreeably—indeed the manner in which it was done was generally the means of establishing good humour.

While she was sipping her coffee, out of a cup not much larger than a nut-shell, all at once she heard a noise of barking and running in the kitchen, as if some person was hunting her little greyhound.

She immediately jumped up, and ran into the kitchen. "Who is teasing my little dog?" she asked, in a voice of dove-like anger.

The servants all laughed, and the footman, trying to compose his features, replied, "It was Feeske, who was leaping up on the fireplace."

"Well, and must you strike the poor dog for that!—he feels it just as much as you would."

"Nobody beat him, Miss; only he put his head into the milk-ewer, and could not get it out again."

"Yes, because you are all so disorderly.—Come here, little Feeske! You should not have left the milk-ewer on the fireplace—come here, my poor little dog; did these bad people hurt you?"

She was obliged to break the ewer to free the little dog's head.

"Sure it's the pretty ewer that's to be pitied," said one of the servants, laughing.

"Well, I would not let the dog suffer for the sake of a ewer;" and then she returned to her father with a beaming countenance. "Have I not scolded them all well!"

Towards the end of breakfast, the footman entered with the letters and newspapers, which the messenger brought weekly from town.

Uncle Gabor opened the Jelenkor newspaper, and followed Espartero and Zummalacarreguy with great attention, while Linka glanced over the peaceful columns of the Regelo—for it was only in the evening that she had time to read it through. As she opened the last page, her eyes fell on a sonnet, entitled, "To Lina B——ssy." She started as if she had looked into a book of incantations, and closed the paper so suddenly, that the old gentleman, who was just standing before the cannons of a naval engagement, cried out, "What's the matter, my child?"

"Nothing at all, papa," replied Linka, changing colour, "only the paper nearly fell out of my hand."

So far was true. Uncle Gabor hastened back to the engagement, lest anything should have taken place in the mean time.

Lina folded the paper quite small, and thrust it into the pocket of her apron; then, taking up her watering-pot, she glided noiselessly out of the room, and ran into the garden. She was determined not to read the paper. She would either burn it, or put it away where nobody should find it. With this firm intention, she began to water her carnations and violets, all the time turning in her mind where she could most conveniently hide the sonnet—for, after all, it would be very hard-hearted to burn it.

At last she remembered the glass-house, and hastened thither with the intention of putting the paper under one of the great cactus pots. She looked round on entering, to see that she was quite alone. Loneliness is the godmother of every weakness, and when she took the paper out of her pocket she could not withstand the temptation of looking once more into it—nobody would see if she blushed—and, with trembling hands, as if she were committing something very scandalous, she unfolded the paper, and read with a beating heart the lines addressed to her.

The verses were of that kind which our young literature produced about twenty years ago—for we have always had a *young* literature, which never attained maturity—whose constrained inspirations, insipid taste, and high-sounding problems, had at least this one advantage, that, possessing no feeling at all, they were incapable of exciting any. Lina, blushing deeply, was forced to recognise herself in "the rosebud whose perfume is intoxicating bliss;" as "Heaven's loveliest angel, the night of whose glossy ringlets might form a pall beneath which it were ecstasy to expire, while the sunny radiance of her dark eyes would wake to life again." The sonnet was signed, "Kalman S—s."

Lina knew the youth. She had frequently met him in Sz——, at the county meetings, and having read the lines, she did not think them so very dreadful after all, except of course in a poetical point of view.

As she was still holding the open paper in her hand, a voice called from the garden door, "Miss Lina!"

Starting up, she once more thrust the paper into the pocket of her apron, and, turning very pale, ran to the door.

"Guests have arrived, Miss Lina! make haste home," said the servant, who had been sent for her.

An ancestral conveyance, with three unhappy horses, was standing at the door!

Our readers will guess to whom it belonged.

Lina took the handkerchief from her head, smoothed her hair with her hands, and hastened into the room, where numerous voices were to be heard all talking together with exclamations of joy.

It was just themselves, dear reader; the good-natured country gentleman, the dictatorial lady, our nephew Sandor, and his amiable little brother, Peterke.

They had passed the night in the neighbouring village, for a variety of excellent reasons; of which the principal were, first, that the horses might rest, so as to be able to gallop into Uncle Gabor's court next morning; and, secondly, that the family might equip *en gala* for the occasion.

The worthy dame wore a large cap decorated with rainbow-coloured ribbons, the border of which encompassed her face, like the portrait of the sun in an almanac. Her dress, of bright-green silk, was short enough to show the embroidered petticoat beneath; a large bronze buckle secured her waist-band almost under her arms, and the *tout ensemble* was relieved by a silver-coloured shawl with crimson flowers, thrown negligently over her shoulders.

Uncle Menyhert was shaved, and his hair brushed up smartly; his shirt-collar would fain have stood upright, but not having quite enough of starch for that, was obliged to be satisfied with the good intention; his waistcoat had been white piquet, but was now somewhat yellow. A huge watch betrayed itself in his side-pocket, partly by its size, partly by its ticking, which seemed to take part in every conversation, and was worn round his neck by a thick silk cord resembling a sword-belt. Instead of the green attila, he now wore a chocolate-coloured coat, whose long narrow tails nearly reached the ground, and his light Hungarian hose were exchanged for pantaloons of yellow angine, very wide above and narrow below. All this was crowned by a long cylinder hat, which was now placed on the table for universal admiration.

Our nephew Sandor wore his Juratus attila, with a vest of cherry-coloured velvet. It was clear he felt himself a different man in the attila to what he had been in his bonjour. The latter completely cast him down, humiliated, and put him to shame; the attila inspired him with confidence and courage.

He now neither stood behind the stove nor kissed the footman's hand; in short, he had become quite superior to himself, and jested with everybody. This is characteristic of his age: when a youth of that time of life has an inferior coat, he will be sure to get out of your way, to avoid saluting you; whereas if he happens to be satisfied with his appearance, he will cross you on every occasion, and expect you to salute him.

Even the cadet had undergone a change. He had been washed and combed, and boxed into submission. Indeed, at the last station he had undergone a severe chastisement, to prevent any misbehaviour at Uncle Berkessy's; and having cried the whole way thither, he was now tolerably quiet and subdued.

As Lina entered, Aunt Zsuzsi rose, and, running across the room, threw her arms round her neck, to the utter derangement of cap and frill, and, with a face beaming with triumph, she led forward the blushing girl, and introduced her to the other members of her family. "Well, you rascal!" she exclaimed, turning to Sandor with motherly pride, "have we not chosen a fine girl for you, eh? You do not deserve her, I can tell you!"

Our nephew looked at Lina with a rueful smile, as if he had expected something far prettier; but it may have been the extreme tightness of his boots which made it an unpleasant gymnastic exercise to rise from his seat.

This cordial introduction at first surprised Linka, and, with a modest blush, she took refuge beside her father, as if soliciting his protection against such an unexpected attack. The old gentleman, observing her embarrassment, put his arm playfully round her. "No! you shall not carry off my little Linka so easily, my dear niece!" he exclaimed.

"Ah, but we shall indeed," replied Aunt Zsuzsi, "or else we shall leave Sandor with you."

"That's right! with all my heart, I shall be delighted if you will leave both the boys with me. They shall be my sons."

At these words, little Peterke, in great alarm, stationed himself between his father's knees, and began crying out, "I will not be that bacsi's son—take me home, I will stay with tate (daddy)."

Uncle Gabor burst into one of his fearful laughs, while papa lifted up the little urchin, and placed him beside his mother. "Hang on there, my brave boy."

"Never mind," said Aunt Zsuzsi, "when we take him to be married, I daresay he will not cry at being left with a pretty girl. If my uncle had but one little girl more for him!"

"Hush, wife!" interrupted Menyhert, feeling himself called upon to say something wise; "don't you see who you are speaking before? Here is a young innocent girl, who blushes at the very name of marriage; we must not mention these things before the girls, till it comes to their turn. I must say, I think it is a most excellent custom of the Turks not allowing the bride to see her bridegroom"—

But at that instant Menyhert, happening to glance towards his wife's nose, perceived in its evolutions such marked symptoms of displeasure, that he began to stammer, forgot what he had been saying, and finally broke down entirely.

"Shall we go and look at the stud?" said Uncle Gabor.

"With all my heart," replied Menyhert, glad to change the subject, and speculating on the handsome curricle and four which Uncle Gabor would give his daughter on her marriage.

"Meanwhile, I shall go and take a look at the garden," said Aunt Zsuzsi.

"And gather pretty flowers," exclaimed Peterke, springing up.

"No, no, you little fool," said dear mamma, "you must not touch the flowers; but you may catch as many butterflies and beetles as you like."

Sandor seemed undecided whether he should go and look at the horses, or undertake to gather butterflies and beetles too; and Lina waited to see what her father would say, when the prudential Aunt Zsuzsi interposed: "We will leave the young people together; let them amuse themselves speaking, and get acquainted: such innocent intercourse should never be hindered. Come away, fathers."

It was useless to oppose Aunt Zsuzsi's plans, and so the parental society went out together, leaving the young people to get acquainted; and the latter, seeing there was nothing else to be done, resigned themselves to the innocent intercourse.

Linka, having recovered her presence of mind, sat quietly down to her embroidery-table in the window; while Sandor drew himself up, and began admiring a large oil-painting of a pretty shepherdess on the wall opposite, the frame of which seemed to attract his particular notice.

"You are thinking," said Lina, to begin the conversation, "that that portrait is very like me, are you not?"

"Like you?" said Sandor; "ohoho! what an idea!"

"It has much more colour than I have."

"Oh! much more."

"And is much taller than I am."

"Oh! much taller."

Linka began to think that she had at last met some person who was perfectly sincere. "I do not know," she continued, "why that painter should have made me prettier than I am."

Sandor perceived that he had been giving very stupid answers, and hastened to repair his fault. "That is to say, Miss Lina, the portrait is not prettier than you are; on the contrary, it is uglier, for one side of the face is larger than the other."

Lina, perceiving that the young gentleman did not understand painting or perspective, tried another theme.

"You have lived in Pesth, and are no doubt acquainted with some of the poets there?"

"O yes; indeed, there were several students among us who were terrible spendthrifts,10 but I never spent much myself; six florins a month were sufficient for me."

[10] "Spendthrift," In Hungarian *kolto*, means also "a poet," as the verb *kolteni* signifies "to poetise," or "to expend."

Linka laughed heartily at what she supposed to be a pun of Sandor's. "Oh! I did not mean that kind of *kolto*," she exclaimed, "but verse writers."

"Ah, indeed!" replied Sandor, looking vacantly out of the window; "I did not see any such in Pesth."

"But you have read their works? for instance, Vorosmarty."

"O yes, certainly; that was what Kisfaludy wrote, was it not?"

"Ah no! Vorosmarty himself was the author."

"Aha! I know now: it was he who wrote Kisfaludy."

"How you are quizzing me! You cannot make me believe that you do not know the Magyar poets."

"Umph! singular! Well, if I do not know one, I know another; I am very fond of poetry, and I can repeat some verses by heart."

"Pretty ones? Perhaps you will write a few in my album; who are they by?"

"Well, the prettiest are by Vad Janos."

"Vad Janos! and who is Vad Janos?"

"Ah, now! you see you do not know him, although he was poetical præceptora."

"And has he published many works?"

"Why, I believe so. That beautiful poem called 'Spring;' then his 'Ode to a Sausage' — that's a capital thing; and then the 'Maize King's complaint against the Trailing Bean' — ah, that is superb!"

"And where are they all published?" asked Linka humbly.

"Why, in the *Hippocrene*," replied Sandor confidently.

"And what is that?" asked Lina again, with pious awe.

"It is the name of a newspaper."

"I have never heard of it," sighed the poor girl. "And where does it appear?"

"Why, in Koros."

"And who is the editor?"

"The students write it themselves,11 whoever has the best hand; and then we take it about to all the pretty girls to read—that is, I never brought it to anybody," said Sandor, hastening to justify himself, lest he might be suspected of visiting pretty girls.

[11] This is really done in the smaller towns.

How many are there who never learn anything after they leave school, and grow old with the same ideas they brought from their classes! I had a schoolfellow about fourteen years ago, who could tell a pleasant anecdote pretty well. I met him again this year; we had only exchanged a few words, when he began the old anecdote.

While the two old gentlemen were looking at the stud, Aunt Zsuzsi had stepped into the garden—not exactly to look at the flowers, but to find out what sort of things Lina kept for the kitchen use; while Peterke ran up and down the beds, looking for butterflies and beetles. In the midst of his career, he happened to upset one of the bee-hives; and the bees consequently stung him so furiously, that his whole face was swelled like a bladder, and the eyes almost entirely disappeared. On hearing his cries, mamma ran up, and taking him by the hand, led him into the house. On any other occasion, he would have been severely punished, besides having been stung; but here everybody endeavoured to be sweet-tempered, as if the whole family were made of milk and butter.

This misfortune put an end to the innocent intercourse, and Linka ran away to get something for the dear boy's face. Each person proposed a different remedy—cold and hot applications, oil, brandy, &c. &c. In vain; the swelling still continued, and there was nothing for it but to go to bed.

Linka then went to superintend her kitchen duties, glad to have a few minutes to herself. She had not been long away, however, when sounds of wheels were heard again driving up to the door; but Linka paid no attention to the noise—she was too much occupied with the arrangement of her dishes. This did not prevent the inquisitive servants from running to the window to see who had arrived.

"Oh, Miss Lina," cried one, "what a beautiful calèche! and such a smart coachman!—not like that Matyi. See what beautiful linen sleeves!"12

[12] In summer, the coachman's dress is a coloured vest over a white linen garment with wide sleeves embroidered round the neck and shoulders; also wide linen drawers with fringes, and a broad hat decorated with feathers.

"Oh, Miss Linka!" cried another, "see what a handsome young cavalier has just got down off the box! and now he is helping out a fine lady and a little rosy girl. That is a youth for a bridegroom, Miss Lina."

But Miss Lina was very angry. "What are you all chattering about?" she exclaimed; "you had far better attend to your dishes."

They had scarcely turned from the window, when another sound excited their curiosity. The galloping of a horse was heard in the court; and presently afterwards, a voice, talking in an affected tone through the nose, addressed the old gentleman, who had come to the door to receive his guests.

"Permit me to introduce myself as Kalman Sos," said the horseman, "come to pay my respects"—

As Linka heard these words, she threw the egg-shells into the dish instead of the yolk, and snatching the Regelo from her pocket, without further reflection, she threw it into the fire.

"What have you done, Miss Linka?" exclaimed the portly cook; "all your burnt paper has got into my dishes."

And to put the *comble* to her distress, the old gentleman entered, his face beaming with pleasure, and, going maliciously up to his daughter, he looked in her face, and smiled knowingly without saying a word, while the poor girl only wished that the floor might open by some miracle and permit her to sink into the cellar.

"Do you want anything, dearest papa?" she ventured at last to ask.

"I do not want you to stay in the kitchen!"

"And why not, dear father?"

"Because you will be sure to salt everything to-day."13

[13] Sos, salt salted.

Poor Linka! if she could have blushed still more deeply she would have done so, for she understood her father's meaning too well; and, moreover, the cook increased her embarrassment, by adding, "Indeed, sir, you will do well to carry off the young lady, for she is not at all like herself, poor thing!

and giving us much unnecessary trouble; only a few minutes ago, she put the egg-shells into the pudding instead of the yolk; and then she burnt" —

Lina tried to silence the cook, who, however, only talked the louder—so she was compelled at last to yield; and, taking her father's arm, she made up her mind with a sigh to the great sacrifice of leaving the kitchen and going to her guests. And what a place of refuge the poor girl had often found there on such occasions!

Meanwhile the guests were assembled in the sitting-room. On one side of the sofa sat Aunt Zsuzsi, endeavouring with great vehemence, and frequent application of her finger to the side of her nose, to explain something in an under tone to a mild lady, in whom we recognise Mrs. Tallyai, who was sitting beside her listening patiently to her tales.

Our nephew Sandor sat at the table, evidently a good deal put out by seeing so many strangers; although it never crossed his imagination that he had two rivals among them.

His father sat beside him, administering wise counsel about various matters, such as how to behave when he was addressed, how to sit at table and use his knife and fork, not to put his nail into the salt-cellar instead of the point of his knife, or to wipe his mouth with the table-cloth, or drink the water out of the finger-glass. With these and such-like salutary precepts did good Mr. Menyhert Gulyasi endeavour to enlighten his son, till the poor youth lost all the little courage with which his attila had inspired him.

Opposite Sandor sat Karely Tallyai—a handsome, manly youth, in whose gay countenance and easy manners no holiday restraint was to be seen. He was carrying on a jesting conversation with his sister, the little mischievous Siza, whose roguish eyes were ever and anon glancing at the opposite side of the table, while she constantly discovered something to arrange in her brother's neckerchief or ruffles, or an atom of down to pick off his coat, all of which she did with an air of mysterious prudery, as if "nobody but ourselves" was to remark it.

Last, though not least in his own opinion, stood Kalman the poet, apart from the rest, with his arms folded and his back against an arm-chair, his countenance vainly endeavouring to express unutterable sadness. Such expressions have great effect on young girls—the pale, moonlight face; the secret sigh; the sad smile when others laugh heartily; the retirement to a corner where he can be seen by everybody, when others are amusing and enjoying themselves; the gentle cough now and then—and if asked why, the laying of the hand with pensive calmness on the breast, the speaking of approaching autumn, of falling leaves, and of sweet sleep among those leaves; remarking that the sound of coughing is like knocking at the gate of another world, and such-like poetic similes. All this is certain of success if directed skilfully against a young and inexperienced heart.

Thus the three rival parties were arranged to begin the attack. The family of Gulyasi were no doubt the strongest; they claimed the old gentleman's earlier friendship and former promise, besides which, his own speculations too allotted them the first place.

Kalman considered himself quite dangerous enough to enter the lists in single combat, and without a second, having already opened the attack by pouring forth his secret vows in verse; while the least favourable place fell certainly to Karely. With an honourable heart, and lips that despised flattery, he had also the misfortune to possess a simple-hearted mother, who, instead of clothing her son in every virtue, even exposed his faults, declaring that he was a sad, wild youth, who spent a great deal of money, besides various other misdemeanours which she spoke of in the sincerity of her heart, so that poor Karely might have hung the basket on his arm14 beforehand, as there was every chance of his receiving it.

[14] It was an old custom to present a basket as a mark of refusal to the rejected suitor.

Uncle Gabor entered the room with Lina on his arm, and led her up to Mrs. Tallyai. The young girl kissed her hand, and gracefully saluted the rest of the party. Then the two ladies placed her between them on the sofa, and it was really amusing to see how Aunt Zsuzsi contrived to occupy her whole attention, overwhelming her with praises, flattery, and ill-timed questions, while Mrs. Tallyai had not an opportunity of putting in a single word.

"What a pretty, dear girl! quite a child still, and yet such a good housewife. I saw your garden, quite an example—such cauliflowers! you must know they are my favourite vegetable. I have looked at your preserves, and they do the greatest credit to these pretty little white hands; but I must teach you by and bye to make medlar and grape jelly—when we are at Makkifalva, you know. You never tasted anything better—Sandor is so fond of it! indeed he is fond of all sweets, quite his father's son; but he had not hitherto seen the sweetest of all sweets!—Come, you must not blush so, you naughty girl, though I must confess it is most becoming."

The poor girl was actually sitting on thorns during the whole of this conversation, till, fortunately, Sizike interrupted it by running over and throwing her arms round her neck, which gave Lina an opportunity of withdrawing with her young companion into an adjoining room.

The two girls did not return till they were summoned to dinner, and then they were already *per tu*. Friendship is very quickly formed between girls, and, notwithstanding the difference of age—for Siza was yet a child—a "holy alliance" had been concluded in a few minutes, and it was evident that Lina looked more favourably on Karely than on Sandor, although Kalman still remained the most dangerous in her regard, and she never ventured to look except by stealth at the hero of the lines, conscious that his eyes were always fixed upon her.

At dinner, the two matrons sat at the head of the table, and Uncle Gabor at the foot, with the two girls at each side of him; Karely sat beside Linka, and Sandor opposite him, beside Siza. The poet sat beside Aunt Zsuzsi, and Menyhert beside Mrs. Tallyai. Soup was served, and the spoon being an innocent weapon, nothing particular took place during its requisition, except that Sandor, observing Kalman hold his spoon between his first finger and thumb, tried to imitate him, and at the first experiment emptied the soup over his coat. Afterwards, when the knives and forks came into requisition, and the first glass of wine began to inspire courage, Menyhert related his own heroic deeds of 1809—a period which Berkessy, on the other hand, did not exactly wish to recall. Kalman began eating with his left hand, and Sandor, desirous of following his example, pitched the meat off his fork into his neighbour's lap. Aunt Zsuzsi then talked of the want of principle in the young men of the capital, on which Kalman asked her if she had seen *Janesi Parlagi*;15 and then again incurred her wrath by pouring out a glass of water backwards, on which the good lady declared that the next time he did so, she would not drink it.

[15] *Janesi Parlagi*, a popular play. The question was asked in derision of the "country bumpkin."

Sandor having been desired by his mother not to refuse anything, lest it might offend the young lady of the house, ate and drank of everything that came in his way. The good Eger wine seemed only to renew his vigour in attacking the dishes, inspiring him at the same time with as much confidence as if he were sitting among his Juratus colleagues, opposite the golden flask. He laughed and jested, stumbled into everybody's conversation, played on the bottles and glasses, and threw about balls of bread. At last, in the height of his merriment, he stretched his limbs under the table, and, having reached a little foot opposite, which he took for Lina's, began to press it gently with his own. The foot happened, however, to be Karely's, who, being deeply engaged in conversation with his neighbour, allowed this tender *quiproquo* to go on unnoticed.

Towards the end of dinner, when hearts and mouths were ever opening wider, that amiable confusion began in which everybody speaks at once, and nobody can hear himself, though he understands his neighbour. As one anecdote gave rise to another, the company laughed till the tears ran down their cheeks; and the ladies entreated the gentlemen not to make them laugh more, as they were already quite fatigued; while the young people laughed too, pretending to join in the joke, although it was something quite different they were laughing about. Reader, would you understand their mirth? You must be young, and in love.

Kalman the poet alone maintained a Parnassus repose of feature. His countenance was never discomposed by a smile, while his eyes were constantly fixed on the young lady of the house, or straight before him—not on Uncle Menyhert, but beyond him on the opposite wall, on which a large mirror was suspended. This mirror seemed to divide his attention with Lina; and to judge by his countenance, he was perfectly satisfied with the appearance reflected within—watching every motion of his hands as he ate his dinner, or picked his teeth.

Nobody seemed to observe him excepting little Sizike, whose mischievous eyes nothing escaped. Her *naïve* ideas kept the old gentleman in constant mirth; and once or twice he was very nearly breaking out into one of his terrible explosions, when, pointing to Sandor, who was stretching his foot under the table, she whispered: "See, bacsi, the student is disappearing!" in allusion to one of his own stories of a student who disappeared under the table.

The general gaiety had reached its climax, when Kalman rose from his seat, and, drawing his fingers through his hair, filled his glass, and coughed slightly, to signify to the company that he was about to speak.

The noise ceased; each person hushed his neighbour, and endeavoured to assume a befitting length of countenance. The poet gazed around him for a few moments, and then, raising his glass, began:—

"There is a sea, beneath which a lovely pearl lies concealed." . . .

"See, bacsi," whispered Sizike in Uncle Gabor's ear, "how Kalman looks at himself in the glass!"

Uncle Gabor glanced at the poet, whose eyes were fixed intently on the mirror with the most extraordinary self-complacency, totally unconscious of the mirth he excited.

"This pearl," he continued, with great pathos, "is dearer than Cleopatra's far-famed pearl, purer than those in the Brazilian emperor's diadem! To win this gem, it were small sacrifice to descend into the depths of the ocean: to die for it were bliss!" . . . .

"See, bacsi, how he offers himself the glass in the mirror," whispered Sizike again.

Uncle Gabor seemed ready to burst, like an over-heated steam-boiler. His vast chest rose and fell, his face grew purple, he clenched his fists.

Karely, meanwhile, observing that Sandor was pressing his foot very affectionately, and not wishing to leave the kindly intention unresponded to, felt for Sandor's corn, and trod upon it with all his strength.

"Yai!" roared Sandor in the midst of the pearly simile, giving the bottle before him such a push, that the red wine flowed to the opposite end of the table.

This was all that was wanting for Uncle Gabor. The restrained laughter now broke out in all its fury; he threw himself back in his chair, and struck the table till all the bottles danced. The young people laughed too; and the ladies were so startled at the wine which was running towards them, that they retreated from the table. Kalman alone maintained a profound gravity, waiting with dignified mien till the noise had subsided, to continue his speech; but in vain. Three times he made an attempt to recommence; but no sooner did Uncle Gabor look at him, or hear his voice, than the explosion was renewed, which he was utterly incapable of restraining.

Kalman was obliged to sit down at last without finishing his speech. The old gentleman was evidently annoyed, but it could not be helped; if Kalman had spoken from the pulpit, he could not have kept his gravity. To relieve the general embarrassment, Karely took up a glass and added gaily:

"May the pretty pearl of which our friend Kalman speaks long be an ornament amongst us, more especially as it does not grow on a cold shell, but adorns the bosom of a true-hearted son of Hungary, who, instead of salt sea-water, offers all explorers plenty of good Turkish blood!"[16]

[16] The Eger wine is so called, from the many battles fought there.

"Eljen! eljen!" cried the whole party: even Uncle Gabor heartily clapped his hands in approval. Kalman alone could not forgive Karely, for having followed up the effusion of his brilliant genius with such commonplace wit. But it is vain attempting to say wise things after dinner, and still more vain to expect people to listen to them.

As soon as the company rose from table, Uncle Berkessy invited his guests to drive out in his grounds with him; and all having readily accepted, orders were given to the coachmen from each party.

Menyhert went into the stables, to consult with Matyi as to the possibility of his horses undertaking the drive; and the result being unfavourable, it was agreed, on the promise of a pint of wine Matyi should receive on their return, that the latter was to pretend to be unfit to drive.

Meanwhile the other carriages had driven out, and the ladies were preparing to step in. Kalman brought forward his steed, with its tail cropped à l'Anglaise, and all were ready, when Menyhert appeared coming out of the stables in great wrath.

"What the tartar are we to do? my coachman is so drunk that it is impossible he can drive us. I am shocked to think that this should have taken place here, but I shall turn him off as soon as ever we go home."

"Don't annoy yourself, my good friend," exclaimed Berkessy, "there's plenty of room, and we can arrange so as to take you all in. Your lady will sit beside Mrs. Tallyai; Karely likes driving at all events, and the girls will not object to having a cavalier with them."

Kalman had just got one foot in the stirrup, when hearing that there was a place in the carriage beside Lina, he turned suddenly to Sandor, who was standing beside him admiring the horse, and asked, with amiable condescension, if he liked riding.

"That I do," replied Sandor grinning; "but I have no horse."

"Would you like to ride mine?"

"Really! may I indeed?"

"Most welcome; my back is already tired with riding all the morning, and I can get a place beside one of the coachmen."

It was not necessary to repeat the offer; Sandor put one foot into the stirrup, and, after dancing about a considerable time on the point of the other, succeeded in placing himself in the saddle. The rest of the party had arranged themselves according to Uncle Gabor's directions, and Kalman was fortunate enough to obtain a place in Berkessy's carriage opposite the two girls.

It was only now the company perceived that Sandor had mounted Kalman's horse, on which he made rather a remarkable appearance—his legs being very long, and the stirrups drawn up very short, consequently obliging his knees almost to meet round the horse's neck.

Unfortunately, this horse had the bad habit of rearing whenever he felt a stranger on his back; and he now began by throwing up his head with a strange, drawn-out neigh, backing by degrees, and finally rearing.

Aunt Zsuzsi now started from her seat. "Sandor!" she cried, "you fool! get off that horse directly; you will break your neck."

It would appear unnecessary telling a man to get off a horse whose intention it is to give his rider all possible assistance in dismounting. But Sandor neither heard nor saw; and if we apply the term of "all ear" to an attentive listener, we may perhaps affirm of Sandor that he was "all horse."

The steed, finding that Sandor did not fall off as he intended, neighed once more, and pricking up his ears, made a start for the gate, and then set off full gallop across the garden and over the meadow, bearing his unhappy rider with him, who in despair let go the bridle, and with both hands held fast by the saddle before and behind.

"My son, my son! he will be killed!" shrieked Aunt Zsuzsi, wringing her hands; "will nobody save him?"

"Oh, never fear," said her worthy husband; "he is safe enough, depend upon it, and a throw or two won't break his neck. Did you not see that he spurred the horse purposely? Let us go on, he will soon overtake us."

Whereupon the whips cracked, and the carriages proceeded at a quick pace along the road; Aunt Zsuzsi calling to every person she met, to ask if they had seen her son—nobody hearing her, of course, owing to the noise of the carriages.

Having arrived at Uncle Berkessy's farm, where the harvest was going on, they turned into a beautiful avenue planted on each side with trees; here and there the wheat and barley were in stacks, the maize was still ripening luxuriously, and the golden melon and citronil peeping out among the stubble. But neither corn nor melons had any charms for Aunt Zsuzsi— she could only think of her lost son; till Mrs. Tallyai having suggested the probability of Sandor's having returned home, the good lady became tolerably calm, and was able to estimate the value of each plot of melons, and bushel of corn.

Having amused themselves some time watching the reapers, the party drove home again. Aunt Zsuzsi's first word was to inquire for Sandor; but nobody knew anything about him.

The good lady then gave vent to her lamentations. "I am undone!" she exclaimed, "my son Sandor is lost for ever! One has been nearly stung to death by bees, and now the other is killed by a mad horse. Oh! why did we ever come here at all?—But it is all your fault, you old fool," she continued, turning to her husband; "why did you want to marry your son so young? Now he is gone for ever, and you may go after him yourself, with your ass of a coachman. And you, sir," she added, turning her wrath on Kalman, "how dared you let him mount your confounded horse? where is he now, I ask you?—where is my son Sandor?"

"And where is my horse?" exclaimed the poet, not less alarmed at the idea of Sandor's having carried off his horse, than the good lady at the horse's having carried off her son Sandor.

"Oh, heavens! how am I to go home without my son?" said Aunt Zsuzsi, bursting into tears.

"And how the tartar am I to get home without my horse?" said the sentimental poet, forgetting himself.

Not content with blaming her husband and Kalman, Aunt Zsuzsi included the whole family in her wrath: the girls because they had not taken Sandor with them, and Uncle Berkessy for having allowed him to drink so much wine, as otherwise he never would have dared to mount the horse; and finally, she broke out in invectives against the whole party for standing with their mouths open, instead of running to look for her lost son.

At last Menyhert's patience was exhausted: "What are you yammering about?" he exclaimed; "nobody made this fuss about me when I went to the elections at Raab, when several gentleman were shot there! Never fear! bad money is not so easily lost; depend upon it, he will come back again. They don't steal people in this country, and they won't begin with Sandor; and if the rascal does not return soon, we shall have him advertised."

These cruel words fell with indescribable bitterness on Aunt Zsuzsi's sensitive heart. That a father should speak thus of his lost son! She had no words to reply; but, rushing into the room where Peterke was lying eating cake, she threw herself on her only remaining son, and began sobbing bitterly, on which Peterke turned the cake out of his mouth and began roaring too.

Uncle Berkessy, much annoyed at the good lady's distress, sent messengers in every direction, on foot and on horseback, to search for the lost youth.

Meantime our readers may have no objection to follow too, and see what has become of him.

Having crossed the garden, the steed went full speed across the fields, and out into the highroad, where he continued in full gallop, Sandor having surrendered himself to his fate, wondering whether he should be carried off to Ukrania, as Mazeppa had been before him.

Now and then he ventured to look hastily round, and saw the place they had left always at a greater distance, till at last it disappeared entirely, and only the tower of the village church was to be seen; finally, that too disappeared, and he began to see the towers of some unknown town rising out of the horizon before him.

Now and then he called to the people he met on the road to catch the horse, but they all understood that they were to keep out of the way, taking it for granted that he was riding for a bet, or else that he was a messenger sent for a doctor or fire-engines.

It was six days since the pretty widow had sent Uncle Nanasy abroad to make preparations for her wedding and to assemble her relations. All her orders had been scrupulously attended to. And the *estafette* whom Julia had sent to recall him having arrived half an hour too late at each place, Uncle Nanasy returned to S—— without having seen him, and entered his niece's apartment with a huge bandbox under his arm.

"Here I am, darling!—I have executed all your orders," he exclaimed; "and here are your bridal dresses—this Varga made, and is it not splendid? And this is from Keresztessy, worthy of an empress! And here is the dispensation in my pocket—and the confections are in that great case outside—and all our relations will be here: went about myself, darling, and invited them all—But what's the matter? You are not pleased with the dresses?"

Julia, trembling with vexation and rage, had pushed away the box violently, and it rolled on the floor, crushing all the finery.

"Take these dresses out of my sight!" she exclaimed, in a voice choked with passion. "I don't want to see them—nor the dispensation, nor confections, nor relations, nor yourself either, you facetious, meddling, old fool!"

Uncle Nanasi's eyes and mouth opened wide at this unexpected reception; his jaws moved, as if endeavouring to articulate, though he was utterly incapable of pronouncing a syllable.

When a man discharges all the business confided to him in the most punctual way possible, just as he expects to receive at least a kiss in return, and instead of it, has a box thrown at his head amid a storm of abuse, what is he to suppose?

Nanasy bacsi was beyond supposition; and, to add to his amazement, his fair niece had thrown herself down on the sofa, and was sobbing bitterly.

At that instant the sound of horses' hoofs was heard in the court, and Julia's maid burst into the room with a look of astonishment, "Miss!—Madam!—gracious lady! Master Kalman's horse!"

"Don't dare to admit him," cried the lady, starting passionately from her seat.

"But it is not Master Kalman, only his horse, with a strange young gentleman."

"Who?"

Who, indeed, but the unfortunate Sandor, who had been carried across the district to the principal town of the neighbouring county, and set down before a strange house half dead with terror and fatigue!

Kalman had been accustomed to visit Julia every day on horseback, and on these occasions the fair lady used to feed the horse with sugar from her own delicate hands, so that when he passed up that street the animal would frequently carry his master perforce into the court of Julia's house, and now, having been six days absent, he had consequently been six days without sugar, and, naturally enough, finding himself unchecked, set off, and never stopped till he arrived in the court of Julia's house, where he stood still, and began neighing for the sugar.

This is the most natural way of explaining the psychology of the circumstance, at least as far as we are capable of comprehending the ideas of a horse.

Sandor tumbled off the horse's back as soon as it stopped, and tottered towards the wall with aching and distorted limbs: presently, he crept up to the door with great difficulty, just as Julia with her maid had appeared on the staircase to see who was there.

"Who are you?—what do you want?—how did you come here?" were the first questions put to the unhappy stranger.

"Don't ask me anything," groaned the horseman. "I am lost—I am dying—my back is broken—put me to bed and call a surgeon. I am just going to die!"

Julia saw with real sympathy that the youth was in great suffering, and, sending her servant immediately in search of medical and surgical aid, she put the tortured adventurer to bed, and bestowed every possible attention which female tenderness could suggest. At last the arrival of the doctors relieved her as to the state of the invalid—assuring her that the young man was only saddle-sick, and that a few hours of rest would put all to rights.

At Gabor Berkessy's, matters became more serious every hour. Mrs. Gulyasi would let nobody draw breath till she had turned out the whole household in search of her son, while she herself wandered about distracted, asking every new comer what they had done with her son! At last she was seized with violent cramps, and was obliged to go to bed to tea and warming-pans.

Poor Lina and Mrs. Tallyai kept watch by her bedside, and never closed their eyes all night; while Menyhert slumbered with a calm conscience in the next room, snoring so loudly that they were obliged to rouse him once in each five minutes for fear of disturbing the invalid.

At last, towards morning, she fell asleep, overcome by fatigue and groaning, and Mrs. Tallyai also sank down on the sofa to get a few minutes' rest, when all at once the footman was heard beating the gentlemen's coats in the corridor.

The two girls ran out eagerly and desired him not to make such a noise, as the ladies had only just fallen asleep.

As the footman retreated with the coats, Sizike observed something lying on the floor, and running over, picked up an open pocket-book, on the outside of which was printed in large golden letters, "Journal," and the initials "K. S."

Who could blame severely two young girls, when the journal of a young man—not entirely without interest in their eyes—had fallen into their hands, that they should be unable to withstand the temptation of peeping just a very little into it? At all events it was very natural. The two girls ran whispering and tittering behind a pillar, and hurriedly turned over the leaves of the mysterious book. It was full of verses; here and there dried flowers, or a forget-me-not of plaited hair peeped out between the leaves, which they carefully replaced, and amused themselves with reading the verses, stifling their laughter as they gaily snatched the book out of each other's hands. Suddenly Lina's eyes fell on some well-known lines. She looked again; they were indeed the very same which she had read the day before in the Regelo, with this slight difference, that they were not addressed to herself, but to Julia Cs——, and instead of dark hair and eyes, these spoke of forget-me-not eyes and golden hair; otherwise it was quite the same—every angel and charmer in its place, the same heartaches, the same readiness to die, and promises to meet in a better world!

Lina felt herself precisely in the situation of a person who accepts a compliment, and then perceives it was intended for another. She hastily closed the Journal and retreated to her room, to hide the blush of shame which covered her face, as if a hundred eyes were turned upon her. For once in her life, a feeling of vanity had crossed her heart; but now she was severely punished for it: all those beautiful similes and sweet words had not been written for her at all, but only translated from fair to dark! She was completely disenchanted.

The sun had already risen, when one of the messengers who had been despatched on Sandor's traces returned, with the consolatory news that he had discovered the young gentleman, and that nothing was the matter with him; on the contrary, he was in excellent hands, under the care of a beautiful lady, who would not let him go until he had entirely recovered from the fatigue occasioned by his ride—meanwhile, she hoped that his worthy parents would come and be her guests until the young gentleman was thoroughly restored.

At this news, Aunt Zsuzsi suddenly came to herself, rose from bed, and ordered her carriage; and without even waiting for breakfast, thanked her host for all his kindness, hurried her husband and little Peterke, with tied-up jaws, into the conveyance, and desired the coachman to drive for life and death to S——. The lad who had brought the message was seated beside the coachman as a guide, having forgotten the lady's name on his way back, but hoped to be able to find the house again.

Uncle Gabor shook hands cordially with Menyhert, who was already in the coach, exclaiming gaily: "But for all this our process must not fall to the ground—*liquidum est debitum*; and if it cannot be arranged otherwise, we must enforce the execution."

Menyhert laughed heartily, understanding an allusion to the long-promised marriage.

The whole household accompanied the carriage to the road, where they once more parted, and the horses set off as fast as they were able.

Uncle Gabor then returned to the house with his guests; Linka was evidently out of spirits that morning, while Siza could scarcely contain her joy on seeing the Gulyasis set off.

"Miss Lina's sunny countenance is clouded to-day," said the poet in a theatrical tone.

Lina, without condescending a reply, turned to Karely, with whom she began to converse, and they entered the house together.

Kalman was thunderstruck. "Why is Miss Linka so ungracious to-day?" he asked Sizike, who still remained out.

"Oh! did you not hear Mr. Menyhert Gulyasi threaten her father with an execution?"

"Who? the old gentleman?" asked Kalman, much shocked.

Siza had spoken carelessly, without an idea of being believed; but Kalman's look did not escape her quick eye—for at twelve years old she had more sharpness than most people have at forty. Without rectifying the mistake, she answered gravely: "Yes, certainly, old Berkessy; but you must not speak of it to anybody."

"Impossible!" cried Kalman, in great agitation; "he is considered a very rich man."

"Ah! there are many considered rich who are not really so," said Sizike; and, carelessly humming a tune, she tripped into the house.

Kalman paced up and down with folded arms: he was quite confounded. How could he imagine that a child of twelve years old should think of making a fool of him? He might indeed have doubted had he heard it from a grown-up person; but why should a child say such a thing, unless she had heard it from those around her? In that case, it would be better to return to Julia,—people said ill-natured things of her, to be sure, and she was rather volatile and capricious; but at all events she was rich, and very pretty. It might not be so difficult, after all, to begin again: a few well got up scenes— an attempt at suicide if necessary, and all would be right.

A horse was the only thing wanting—perhaps Berkessy would lend him one; and with this hope the poet entered Uncle Gabor's apartment. Berkessy was sitting on a large arm-chair, and Karely was standing before him.

Kalman paused as he approached, to consider how he should arrange his speech so that the old gentleman might suppose, and yet not suppose that it was no longer his intention to propose for his daughter. And here his evil genius again placed a looking-glass before him; and again forgetting himself, he drew up his collar, brushed up his hair, and the "Sir" with which he began his speech was apparently addressed to himself.

Uncle Gabor, who had been observing his strange attitude in the mirror, suddenly burst into one of his uncontrollable fits of laughter, which Kalman was obliged this time to take to himself. He grew red, then pale again, while his lips trembled with rage.

The old gentleman suddenly checked himself, and asked in the gravest tone—"In what can I oblige you, nephew?"

"Sir," replied Kalman, scarcely able to articulate with fury, "I thought—I expected to find in you a cultivated man, who despised the superstition of the last century, which considered a poet as something ridiculous."

"I do not consider poets ridiculous, sir," replied Berkessy gravely, "as the walls of my room and my library will prove, where you may see the portraits and the works of our best authors; but I despise that bastard poetry which sucks the parent stem, and grows green without ever producing fruit. I honour and revere those great minds, uniting brilliant genius with vast study, who fulfil their glorious career to the glory and honour of their country; but to mistake every reed whistle for an Æolian harp, is what I cannot do. The real poet elevates our mind by his ideas, while those who only call themselves so because they invent rhymes can but excite a smile; and if nature has given to my smile a somewhat louder tone than usual, it is not my fault. Really, my dear nephew, the properties I first mentioned are rather rare, while the latter certainly abound—and this you must not take amiss from an old man."

No dictionary hitherto published contains words sufficiently expressive of all that Kalman felt at this moment. To accuse a man of stealing a silver fork, is nothing in comparison of telling him he is a bad poet. At last, after a few moments' silence, he began in a dignified tone: "Sir, if I did not consider that I am in your house"—

"That need not incommode you in the least: in my house the guests are the masters."

"The insult you have offered me should be washed out with my blood," continued Kalman (he did not yet presume to say with anybody's else).

"I am not a surgeon," replied the old man, with quiet sarcasm.

Karely now stepped in between them, and taking Kalman's arm—"Comrade," he whispered, "you are playing a very ridiculous part, in disputing thus with an old gentleman."

"Why has he not a son, that I might demand satisfaction?"

"Take comfort, if that is all you want: I am his son, for I am going to marry his daughter, and I am ready to give you all the satisfaction you desire, but don't let us make a noise about it. I believe you are going home at all events; so, if you will drive with me to S——, we can settle this affair with our friends."

Uncle Gabor did not hear what the young men were saying; and as Karely declared that he was obliged to go to S——, and would take Kalman with him, he was quite satisfied, and ere long the two young men drove away in the Tallyai carriage.

Meanwhile the Gulyasis arrived happily at S——, and were received by the fair widow with the greatest amiability, and conducted to the chamber of the sick youth, in whom Aunt Zsuzsi recognised her lost son. He was reposing on a divan, arrayed in a rich silk dressing-gown, embroidered slippers, and gold-tasselled cap, formerly the property of the fair lady's husband.

Of course, Aunt Zsuzsi remarked nothing of all this at first, she could only see her long-lost son; and falling on his neck, she sobbed passionately for several minutes, after which she poured forth her thanks and compliments to the pretty widow for her son's extraordinary preservation, and the careful attendance bestowed upon him, repeating at least ten times over—"Oh! if my son Sandor had such a wife, I should be at rest as to his fate—I should then be sure of having placed him in good hands!"

Julia smiled charmingly, and brought the worthy family through all her fine apartments—showed them her porcelain, her silver services, and finally her jewellery. Aunt Zsuzsi was beside herself; praised everything to the skies, and scarcely knew what to look at first.

Meanwhile Uncle Nanasy took Menyhert up stairs into his smoking-room, and spoke a great deal of Julia's fortune, of her various merits, and of the brilliant alliance she would make for the first family in the country, and of her late husband's admirable arrangement, allowing his widow a handsome income in case of her marrying again—to all of which Menyhert listened attentively, and the hours passed rapidly away until dinner was announced.

During dinner, the surprise and admiration of the family reached its highest climax. They did not know which to admire most—the meats, or the dishes in which they were served. Little Peterke alone seemed perfectly decided in his opinion as to the tarts, and had his own way of proving it—what he could not eat he thrust into his pockets, and Julia helped him to fill his cap with sweetmeats.

"Well, Peterke," said Aunt Zsuzsi after dinner, taking the dear boy in her arms, "tell me which you like best, Aunt Julia or Aunt Lina?"

"I don't love Aunt Lina, because she would not give me chocolate when I asked her."

"Well then, you love Aunt Julia best, don't you?"

"Uhum!"

Mamma smiled, and gently patted the dear boy's cheek.

It was now the seventh day, and the report had already spread through the whole town, that the pretty widow was to be married on that day. Her relations began to arrive, and one calèche followed another till the house was quite full of gaily dressed people, among which the indefatigable Uncle Nanasy was seen receiving everybody, and looking more mysterious than ever.

"Where is the bride?" and "Where is the bridegroom?" was in every mouth; but, for once in his life, Nanasy bacsi answered discreetly—that Julia was at her toilet.

Meanwhile Julia had arrayed herself in her bridal attire, in which she really looked like a fairy queen, and was in the act of placing the wreath on her head when the door opened, and who should enter but—Kalman Sos!

Julia, who was standing before the mirror and saw him enter, had just time to check the start of astonishment which his appearance caused, and, turning calmly round, "O you bad man!" she exclaimed in a voice of gentle reproach, "to have put me to such an unmerciful trial. If I had not known you so well, I might have been quite desperate on your account."

"Then you never doubted me?"

"Doubted you! how could I imagine that you would forsake me, when everybody knew we were going to be married! I must have had a very low opinion of you indeed, had I thought for an instant that you could have so basely betrayed a woman who loved you. Oh, no! I knew it was only a poetical caprice on your part to prove the strength of my confidence. I knew you would return, and so I did not even put off my guests, but made all the preparations for the day appointed, so well did I read your character."

"Yes, Julia! you read truly," murmured Kalman, enchanted; "it was only a trial, which you have overcome, and my love will now be a thousand times stronger than ever."

Julia turned from her mirror, and, courtesying low, with a smile of bewitching coquetry, asked, "Am I pretty?"

"Oh, lovely!—Oh, angelic!" murmured the poet, throwing himself at Julia's feet.

At that instant Uncle Nanasy entered to announce that the reverend gentleman had arrived for the ceremony.

Julia poured some *Ess bouquet* on her handkerchief, and, taking Nanasy's arm, who stepped forward *à pas de menuet*, she descended to the apartment where the guests were assembled.

The company hastened to greet the lovely bride, each according to his own mode, and one and all seemed lost in admiration of her beauty.

At last the reverend gentleman stepped forward, and, rubbing his hands with a business-like countenance, asked the name of the "happy bridegroom."

Julia looked round with one of her sweetest smiles, while Kalman hastened across all the corns in the company in his haste to join the beautiful bride; but Julia's hand had already been placed in that of nephew Sandor, whom she presented to the clergyman as her future husband!

Kalman tottered towards the wall, and so completely lost his presence of mind, that he tripped successively over three chairs into the lap of a fat dowager lady; and then, starting up, rushed to the nearest door, but finding it was a cupboard had to return across the room; and when at last he found the door and got down stairs, the first person he happened to meet being a little kitchen-maid, he addressed her as "My lady aunt!" and begged her to get him a glass of water, for he was *very cold*!

There was only one other person in a greater perplexity than himself, and this was the bridegroom. When Julia led him towards the clergyman, he stared as if he had heard sentence of death passed upon him. The affair had been already made up between the elders, who considered it superfluous to mention the subject to Sandor beforehand, and Julia was too secure in the power of her charms to doubt of their success in this undertaking.

Sandor allowed himself to be led before the table arranged for the ceremony, and when the clergyman asked him, "Do you love this honourable lady whose hand you hold?" he only stared at the worthy man, till his father cried out, "Well, do you love her? Of course you love her—how should you not love her?" on which Sandor recovering his senses, went through the rest of the marriage formula pretty well, though it cannot be denied that his teeth chattered not a little.

After this all went on well. The *fêtes* which succeeded the ceremony removed every constraint; and I must not omit, for the satisfaction of our readers, that the happy bridegroom even danced after supper, and thereby managed to trip up and tumble over several of the guests.

Early next morning three young men were walking in the gardens outside the town. One was Karely, and the other two his comrades, who were to act as seconds in his encounter with Kalman.

The latter had quitted Julia's house with a greater desire of fighting than ever, and declared in several coffeehouses that he was determined to shed either his own blood or that of another, and that he would not be content with sending a ball through Karely's brain alone. In vain his friends hinted that it was imprudent to publish his sanguinary intentions beforehand, as he might be taken up. He cared not; they might imprison him or take his life, but they should not touch his honour!

Karely and his friends had waited full half an hour after the time appointed. At last Kalman's seconds arrived — alone! and, with countenances expressive of anger and disgust, handed a letter to their opponents. Karely opened it impatiently, and read as follows: —

"Gentlemen, — Reflecting more coolly on this affair, I have come to the conclusion that greater obligations than those at present incurred forbid my risking a life not my own. The genius which fate has intrusted to me is not mine alone. It belongs to my country — to humanity in general.

"There is another thing we must not lose sight of; a duel should only take place between individuals of equal rank, and I need not explain to you that the mind has its aristocracy as well as society. When you have selected one of my own grade, I will gladly measure arms with him; meanwhile I quit this ungrateful town, probably for ever, to seek elsewhere a circle more suited to my tastes," &c. &c.

The seconds stared at one another; some laughed, others cursed, and Karely seeing there was nothing more to be done, took leave of his comrades, and, stepping into the carriage which was waiting for him, drove back to Berkessy's.

About half way he met their calèche, with his mother and sister, and old Berkessy and his daughter, who all uttered exclamations of joy on seeing him.

Some friend who had heard Kalman's threats in the *café* hastened that very evening to inform them of it, and they were now driving for life and death to S— —, and were infinitely relieved and rejoiced to meet Karely returning, especially when he assured them that the affair had gone off without any bad consequence.

Berkessy proposed going home with Karely, to give the ladies more room, and they all drove back together.

Uncle Gabor then questioned Karely as to the cause of the duel, and having heard it was on *his* account, he opened his eyes in astonishment.

"And what right had you to demand satisfaction in my name?"

"That right which a son has in his father's name."

The old gentleman smiled. "But you are not my son."

"But might I not be?"

"Hm! nephew, you are certainly a fine, good-hearted lad, but they say you are very extravagant."

"Well, perhaps they are right; but had I not been so hitherto, I might have been hereafter."

"But how can I be sure that you will not be hereafter what you have been hitherto?"

"Please, dear uncle, give me a year's trial. If within that time you should hear anything against me, never admit me into your house again; if, however, I can prove that I have resolution to keep my word" —

"Then I will never let you leave my house again," said Uncle Gabor, shaking his hand.

Karely kept his word. A year had passed by, and daring all that time no temptation could prevail on him to diverge in the slightest degree from the resolution he had formed; and though he attended the county meetings as usual, he had not once been seen to gamble; and after a great dinner, he was sure to be the only sober one of the party. Meanwhile, he put his estate in order, and employed his leisure hours in studying languages. In the course of a year, he was looked upon as the most regular, as well as the most accomplished man in the district. He continues to be so still. He married Lina, whom he loves sincerely and faithfully; and seven years have not disturbed their family peace. Happiness is easily read in a woman's countenance, and the lapse of years has only beautified Lina's.

Sandor is also happy. He has a handsome wife with plenty of money; and Aunt Zsuzsi visits them every year, and wears her daughter-in-law's old-fashioned silk dresses.

Uncle Abris is happy in his own way. He has married Boriska; and is no longer obliged to pay her wages.

Uncle Lorincz Kassay is happy too. The visits from his relations never diminish—his house is always full; and among the many suitors for his pretty daughter's hand, "little Peterke," now a handsome youth, is not the *least* in favour.

Kalman alone is unhappy. Dissatisfied with the world, misunderstood by everybody, his hopeful genius has turned to misanthropy. Gentle reader, if you ever read bad verses, think of him with pity!

THE BARDY FAMILY

We are far amidst the snow-clad mountains of Transylvania.

The scenery is magnificent. In clear weather, the plains of Hungary as far as the Rez promontory may be seen from the summits of the mountains. Groups of hills rise one above the other, covered with thick forest, which, at the period when our tale commences, had just begun to assume the first light green of spring.

Toward sunset, a slight purple mist overspread the farther pinnacles, leaving their ridges still tinged with gold. On the side of one of these hills, the white turrets of an ancient family mansion gleamed from amid the trees.

Its situation was peculiarly romantic. A steep rock descended on one side, on whose pinnacle there rose a simple cross. In the depth of the valley beneath lay a scattered village, whose evening bells melodiously broke the stillness of Nature.

Farther off, some broken roofs arose among the trees, from whence the sound of the mill, and the yellow-tinted stream, betrayed the miners' dwellings.

Through the meadows in the valley beneath, a serpentine rivulet wound its silvery way, interrupted by numerous falls and huge blocks of stone, which had been carried down in bygone ages from the mountains during the melting of the snows.

A little path, cut in the side of the rock, ascended to the castle; while, higher up, a broad road, somewhat broken by the mountain streams, conducted across the hills to more distant regions.

The castle itself was an old family mansion, which had received many additions at different periods, as the wealth or necessities of the family suggested.

It was surrounded by groups of ancient chestnut trees; and the terrace before the court was laid out in gardens, which were now filled with anemones, hyacinths, and other early flowers. Now and then the head of a joyous child appeared at the windows, which were opened to admit the evening breeze; while various members of the household retinue were seen hastening through the corridors, or standing at the doors in their embroidered liveries.

The castle was completely surrounded by a strong railwork of iron, the stone pillars of which were overgrown by the evergreen leaves of the gobea and epomoea.

It was the early spring of 1848.

A party, consisting of thirteen persons, had assembled in the dining-room. They were all members of one family, and all bore the name of Bardy.

At the head of the board sat the grandmother, an old lady of eighty years of age, whose snow-white hair was dressed according to the fashion of her times beneath her high white cap. Her face was pale and much wrinkled, and the eyes turned constantly upwards, as is the case with persons who have lost their sight. Her hand and voice trembled with age, and there was something peculiarly striking in the thick snow-white eyebrows.

On her right hand sat her eldest son, Thomas Bardy, a man of between fifty and sixty. With a haughty and commanding countenance, penetrating glance, lofty figure, and noble mien, he was a true type of that ancient aristocracy which is now beginning to die out.

Opposite to him, at the old lady's left hand, sat the darling of the family—a lovely girl of about fifteen. Her golden hair fell in luxuriant tresses round a countenance of singular beauty and sweetness. The large and lustrous deep-blue eyes were shaded by long dark lashes, and her complexion was pale as the lily, excepting when she smiled or spoke, and a slight flush like the dawn of morning overspread her cheeks.

Jolanka was the orphan child of a distant relative, whom the Bardys had adopted. They could not allow one who bore their name to suffer want; and it seemed as if each member of the family had united to heap affection and endearment on the orphan girl, and thus prevent her from feeling herself a stranger among them.

There were still two other female members of the family: Katalin, the old lady's daughter, who had been for many years a widow; and the wife of one of her sons, a pretty young woman, who was trying to teach the little prattler at her side to use the golden spoon which she had placed in his small fat hand, while he laughed and crowed, and the family did their best to guess what he said, or what he most preferred.

Opposite to them there sat two gentlemen. One of them was the husband of the young mother, Jozsef Bárdy—a handsome man of about five-and-thirty, with regular features, and black hair and beard; a constant smile beamed on his gay countenance, while he playfully addressed his little son and gentle wife across the table. The other was his brother, Barnabas—a man of herculean form and strength. His face was marked by small-pox; he wore neither beard nor moustache, and his hair was combed smoothly back, like a peasant's. His disposition was melancholy and taciturn; but he seemed constantly striving to atone, by the amiability of his manners, for an unprepossessing exterior.

Next to him sat a little cripple, whose pale countenance bore that expression of suffering sweetness so peculiar to the deformed; while his lank hair, bony hands, and misshapen shoulders awakened the beholder's pity. He, too, was an orphan—a grandchild of the old lady; his parents had died some years before.

Two little boys of about five years old sat opposite to him. They were dressed alike, and the resemblance between them was so striking, that they were constantly mistaken. They were twin-children of the young couple.

At the lower end of the table sat Imre Bardy, a young man of twenty, whose handsome countenance was full of life and intelligence, his figure manly and graceful, and his manners courteous and agreeable: a slight moustache was beginning to shade his upper lip, and his dark hair fell in natural ringlets round his head. He was the only son of the majoresco, Tamas Bardy, and resembled him much in form and feature.

Beside him sat an old gentleman, with white hair and ruddy complexion. This was Simon Bardy, an ancient relative, who had grown old with the grandmother of the family.

The same peculiarity characterized every countenance in the Bardy family—namely, the lofty forehead and marked brows, and the large deep-blue eyes, shaded by their heavy dark lashes.17

> [17] There is a race of Hungarians in the Karpath, who, unlike the Hungarians of the plain, have blue eyes, and often fair hair.

"How singular!" exclaimed one of the party; "we are thirteen at table to-day."

"One of us will surely die," said the old lady; and there was a mournful conviction in the faint trembling tones.

"O no, grandmother! we are only twelve and a half," exclaimed the young mother, taking the little one on her knee. "This little fellow only counts half on the railroad."

All the party laughed at this remark; even the little cripple's pale countenance relaxed into a sickly smile.

"Ay, ay," continued the old lady, "the trees are now putting forth their verdure; but at the fall of the leaf, who knows if all, or any of us, may still be sitting here?"

Several months had passed since this slight incident.

In one of the apartments of the castle, the eldest Bardy and his son were engaged in earnest conversation.

The father paced hastily up and down the apartment, now and then stopping short to address his son, who stood in the embrasure of one of the windows. The latter wore the dress of the Matyas Hussars18—a gray dolmany, with crimson cord; he held a crimson csako, with a tricoloured cockade in his hand.

[18] Part of the free corps raised in 1848.

"Go," said his father, speaking in broken accents, "the sooner the better; let me not see you!—do not think I speak in anger; but I cannot bear to look at you, and think where you are going. You are my only son, and you know how I have loved you—how all my hopes have been concentrated in you. But do not think that these tears, which you see me shed for the first time, are on your account; for if I knew I should lose you—if your blood were to flow at the next battle, I should only bow my head in the dust and say, The Lord gave, and the Lord has taken away, blessed be His holy name! Yes, if I heard that you and your infatuated companions were cut to pieces, I could stifle the burning tears; but to know that your blood, when it flows, will be a curse upon the earth, and your death will be the death of two kingdoms"—

"They may die now; but they will regenerate"—

"That is not true; you only deceive yourselves with the idea that you can build up a new edifice when you have overthrown the old one. Great God, what sacrilege! Who has intrusted you with the fate of your country, to tempt the Almighty? Who authorized you to lose all there is for the hope of what may be? For centuries past, have so many honourable men fought in vain to uphold the old tottering constitution, as you call it? or were *they* not true patriots and heroes? Your companions have hissed their persecuted countrymen in the Diet; but do they love their country better than we do, who have shed our blood and sacrificed our interests for her from generation to generation, and even suffered disgrace, if necessary, to keep her in life?—for though that life has been gradually weakened, still it is life. You promise her glory; but the name of that glory is *Death!*"

"It may be so, father; we may lose our country as regards ourselves, but we give one instead to ten millions, who were hitherto our own people, and yet strangers in their native land!"

"Chimera! The people will not understand you. They never even dreamt of what you wish to give them. The true way to seek the people's welfare is to give them what they need.

"Ask my dependants! Is there one among them whom I have allowed to suffer want or ruin, whom I have not assisted in times of need?—or have I ever treated them unjustly? You will not hear a murmur. Tell them that I am unjust notwithstanding, because I do not call the peasant from his plough to give his opinion on forming the laws and constitution,—and what will be the consequence? They will stare at you in astonishment; and yet, in mistaken wrath they will come down some night and burn this house over my head."

"That is the unnatural state of the times. It is all the fault of past bad management, if the people have no better ideas. But let the peasant once be free—let him be *a man*, and he will understand all that is now strange to him."

"But that freedom will cost the lives of thousands!"

"I do not deny it. Indeed I believe that neither I nor any of the present generation will reap the fruits of this movement. I think it probable that in a few years not one of those whose names we now hear spoken of may still be living; and, what is more, disgrace and curses may be heaped upon their dust. But a time *will* come when the great institutions of which they have laid the foundation will arise and render justice to the memory of those who sacrificed themselves for the happiness of future generations. To die for our country is a glorious death; but to carry to the grave with us the curses of thousands, to die despised and hated for the salvation of future millions, oh! that is sublime—it is Messiah-like!"

"My son—my only son!" cried his father, throwing himself passionately on the young man's neck, and sobbing bitterly, "do you see these tears?"

"For the first time in my life I see them, father—I see you weep; my heart can scarcely bear the weight of these tears—and yet I go! You have reason to weep, for I bring neither joy nor glory on your head—and yet I go! A feeling stronger than the desire of glory, stronger than the love of my country, inspires my soul; and it is a proof of the strength of my faith that I see your tears, my father—and yet go!"

"Go!" murmured his father in a voice of despair. "You may never return again, or, when you do, you may find neither your father's house nor the grave in which he is laid! But know, even then, in the hour of your death, or in the hour of mine, I do not curse you—and now, leave me." With these words he turned away, and motioned to his son to depart.

Imre silently left the apartment, and as soon as he had closed the door the tears streamed from his eyes; but before his sword had struck the last step his countenance had regained its former determination, and the fire of enthusiasm had kindled in his eye.

He then went to take leave of his Uncle Jozsef, whom he found surrounded by his family. The twins were sitting at his feet, while his wife was playing bo-peep with the little one, who laughed and shouted, while his mother hid herself behind his father's arm-chair.

Imre's entrance interrupted the general mirth. The little boys ran over to examine the sword and golden tassels, while the little one began to cry in alarm at the sight of the strange dress.

"Csitt baba!" said his mother, taking him from his father's arms; "your cousin is going to the wars, and will bring you a golden horse."

Jozsef wrung his nephew's hand. "God be with you!" he exclaimed; and added in a lower voice, "You are the noblest of us all—you have done well!"

They then all embraced him by turns, and Imre left them, amidst the clamours of the little ones, and proceeded to his grandmother's apartments.

On the way, he met his Uncle Barnabas, who embraced him again and again in silence, and then tore himself away without saying a word.

The old lady sat in her great arm-chair, which she seldom quitted, and as she heard the clash of Imre's sword, she looked up and asked who was coming.

"It is Imre!" said the fair-haired maiden, blushing, and her heart beat quickly as she pronounced his name.

Jolanka felt that Imre was more than a brother to her, and the feeling with which she had learnt to return his affection was warmer than even a sister's love.

The widow lady and the little cripple were also in the grandmother's apartment: the child sat on a stool at the old lady's feet, and smiled sadly as the young man entered.

"Why that sword at your side, Imre?" asked the old lady in a feeble voice. "Ah, this is no good world—no good world! But if God is against us, who can resist His hand? I have spoken with the dead again in dreams: I thought they all came round me and beckoned me to follow them; but I am ready to go, and place my life with gratitude and confidence in the hand of the Lord. Last night I saw the year 1848 written in the skies in letters of fire. Who knows what may come over us yet! This is no good world—no good world!"

Imre bent silently over the old lady's hand and kissed it.

"And so you are going?—well, God bless and speed you, if you go beneath the cross, and never forget in life or in death to raise your heart to the Lord;" and the old lady placed her withered hand upon her grandson's head, and murmured, "God Almighty bless you!"

"My husband was just such a handsome youth when I lost him," sighed the widow lady as she embraced her nephew; "God bless you!"

The little cripple threw his arms round his cousin's knees, and, sobbing, entreated him not to stay long away.

The last who bade farewell was Jolanka. She approached with downcast eyes, holding in her small white hands an embroidered cockade, which she placed on his breast. It was composed of five colours—blue and gold, red, white, and green.19

[19] Blue and gold are the colours of Transylvania.

"I understand," said the young man, in a tone of joyful surprise, as he pressed the sweet girl to his heart; "Erdely20 and Hungary united! I shall win glory for your colours!"

[20] Transylvania.

The maiden yielded to his warm embrace, murmuring, as he released her, "Remember me!"

"When I cease to remember you, I shall be no more," replied the youth fervently.

And then he kissed the young girl's brow, and once more bidding them all farewell, he hurried from the apartment.

Old Simon Bardy lived on the first floor: Imre did not forget him.

"Well, nephew," said the old man cheerfully, "God speed you, and give you strength to cut down many Turks!"

"It is not with the Turks that we shall have to do," replied the young man, smiling.

"Well, with the French," said the old soldier of the past century, correcting himself.

A page waited at the gate, with two horses saddled and bridled.

"I shall not require you—you may remain at home," said Imre, as, taking the bridle of one of the horses and vaulting lightly into the saddle, he pressed his csako over his brow and galloped from the castle.

As he rode under the cross, he checked his horse and looked back. Was it of his grandmother's words, or of the golden-haired Jolanka that he thought?

A white handkerchief waved from the window.

"Farewell, light of my soul!" murmured the youth; and kissing his hand, he once more dashed his spurs into his horse's flanks, and turned down the steep hill.

Those were strange times. All at once the villages began to be depopulated; the inhabitants disappeared, none knew whither. The doors of the houses were closed.

The bells were no longer heard in the evening, nor the maiden's song as she returned from her work. The barking of dogs which had lost their masters alone interrupted the silence of the streets, where the grass began to grow.

Imre Bardy rode through the street of the village without meeting a soul; few of the chimneys had smoke, and no fires gleamed through the kitchen windows.

Evening was drawing on, and a slight transparent mist had overspread the valley. Imre was desirous of reaching Kolozsvar21 early on the next morning, and continued his route all night. About midnight the moon rose behind the trees, shedding her silvery light over the forest. All was still, excepting the echo of the miner's hammer, and the monotonous sound of his horse's step along the rocky path. He rode on, lost in thought; when suddenly the horse stopped short, and pricked his ears.

[21] Klausenburg.

"Come, come," said Imre, stroking his neck, "you have not heard the cannon yet."

The animal at last proceeded, turning his head impatiently from side to side, and snorting and neighing with fear.

The road now led through a narrow pass between two rocks, whose summits almost met; and a slight bridge, formed of one or two rotten planks, was thrown across the dry channel of a mountain stream which cut up the path.

As Imre reached the bridge, the horse backed, and no spurring could induce him to cross. Imre at last pressed his knees angrily against the trembling animal, striking him at the same time across the neck with the bridle, on which the horse suddenly cleared the chasm at one bound, and then again turned and began to back.

At that instant a fearful cry rose from beneath, which was echoed from the rocks around, and ten or fifteen savage-looking beings climbed from under the bridge, with lances formed of upright scythes.

Even then there would have been time for the horseman to turn back, and dash through the handful of men behind him; but either he was ashamed of turning from the first conflict, or he was desirous, at any risk, to reach Kolozsvar at the appointed time; and instead of retreating by the bridge, he galloped towards the other end of the pass, where the enemy rushed upon him from every side, yelling hideously.

"Back, Wallachian dogs!" cried Imre, cutting two of them down, while several others sprang forward with their scythes.

Two shots whistled by, and Imre, letting go the bridle, cut right and left, his sword gleaming rapidly among the awkward weapons; and, taking advantage of a moment in which the enemy's charge began to slacken, he suddenly dashed through the crowd towards the outlet of the rock, without perceiving that another party awaited him above the rocks with great stones, with which they prepared to crush him as he passed.

He was only a few paces from the spot, when a gigantic figure, armed with a short broad axe, and with a Roman helmet on his head, descended from the rock in front of him, and seizing the reins of the horse, forced him to halt.

The young man aimed a blow at his enemy's head, and the helmet fell back, cut through the middle, but the force of the blow had broken his sword in two; and the horse, lifted by his giant foe, reared, so that the rider, losing his balance, was thrown against the side of the rock, and fell senseless to the ground. At the same instant a shot was fired towards them from the top of the rock.

"Who fired there?" cried the giant, in a voice of thunder.

The bloodthirsty Wallachians would have rushed madly on their defenceless prey, had not the giant stood between him and them.

"Who fired on me?" he sternly exclaimed.

The Wallachians stood back in terror.

"It was not on you, Decurio, that I fired, but on the hussar," stammered out one of the men, on whom the giant had fixed his eye.

"You lie, traitor! Your ball struck my armour; and had I not worn a shirt of mail, it would have pierced my heart."

The man turned deadly pale, trembling from head to foot.

"My enemies have paid you to murder me?"

The savage tried to speak, but the words died upon his lips.

"Hang him instantly—he is a traitor!"

The rest of the gang immediately seized the culprit and carried him to the nearest tree, from whence his shrieks soon testified that the sentence was being put in execution.

The Decurio remained alone with the young man; and hastily lifting him, still senseless, from the ground, he mounted his horse, and placing him before him, ere the savage horde had returned, he had galloped to some distance along the road from whence the youth had come, covering him with his mantle as he passed the bridge, to conceal him from several of the gang who stood there, and exclaiming: "Follow me to Topanfalva."

As soon as they were out of sight, he suddenly turned to the left, down a steep hilly path, and struck into the depth of the forest.

The morning sun had just shot its first beams across the hills, tinting with golden hues the reddening autumn leaves, when the young hussar began to move in his fevered dreams, and murmured the name "Jolanka."

In a few moments he opened his eyes. He was lying in a small chamber, through the only window of which the sunbeams shone upon his face.

The bed on which he lay was made of lime-boughs, simply woven together, and covered with wolves' skins. A gigantic form was leaning against the foot of the bed with his arms folded, and as the young man awoke, he turned round. It was the Decurio.

"Where am I?" asked the young man, vaguely endeavouring to recall the events of the past night.

"In my house," replied the Decurio.

"And who are you?"

"I am Numa, Decurio of the Roumin22 Legion, your foe in battle, but now your host and protector."

[22] The Wallachians were, in the days of Trajan, subdued by the Romans, with whom they became intermixed, and are also called *Roumi*.

"And why did you save me from your men?" asked the young man, after a short silence.

"Because the strife was unequal—a hundred against one."

"But had it not been for you, I could have freed myself from them."

"Without me you had been lost. Ten paces from where I stopped your horse, you would inevitably have been dashed to pieces by huge stones which they were preparing to throw down upon you from the rock."

"And you did not desire my death?"

"No, because it would have reflected dishonour on the Roumin name."

"You are a chivalrous man, Decurio!"

"I am what you are: I know your character, and the same feeling inspires us both. You love your nation, as I do mine. Your nation is great and cultivated; mine is despised and neglected, and my love is the more bitterly devoted. Your love for your country makes you happy; mine deprives me of peace. You have taken up arms to defend your country without knowing your own strength, or the numbers of the foe; I have done the same. Either of us may lose, or we may both be blotted out; but though the arms may lie buried in the earth, rust will not eat them."

"I do not understand your grievances."

"You do not understand? Know, then, that although fourteen centuries have passed since the Roman eagle overthrew Diurbanus, there are still those among us—the now barbarous people—who can trace their descent from generation to generation, up to the times of its past glory. We have still our traditions, if we have nothing more; and can point out what forest stands in the place of the ancient Sarmisaegethusa, and what town is built where once Decebalus overthrew the far-famed troops of the Consulate. And alas for that town! if the graves over which its houses are built should once more open, and turn the populous streets into a field of battle! What is become of the nation, the heir of so much glory?—the proud Dacians, the descendants of the far-famed legions? I do not reproach any nation for having brought us to what we now are; but let none reproach me if I desire to restore my people to what they once were."

"And do you believe that this is the time?"

"We have no prophets to point out the hour; but it seems yours do not see more clearly. We shall attempt it now; and if we fail, our grandchildren will attempt it again. We have nothing to lose but a few lives; you risk much that is worth losing, and yet you assemble beneath the banner of war. Then what would you do if you were like us?—a people who possess nothing in the world, among whom there is not one able or one instructed head; for although every third man bears the name of Popa, it is not every hundredth who can read: a people excluded from every employment; who live a miserable life in the severest manual labour; who have not one noble city in their country, the home of three-fourths of their people! Why should we seek to know the signs of the times in which we are to die, or be regenerated? We have nothing but our wretchedness, and if we are conquered we lose nothing. Oh! you did wrong for your own peace to leave a nation to such utter neglect!"

"We do not take up arms for our nation alone, but for freedom in general."

"You do wrong. It is all the same to us who our sovereign may be, only let him be just towards us, and raise up our fallen people; but you will destroy your nation—its power, its influence, and privileges—merely that you may live in a country without a head."

A loud uproar interrupted the conversation. A disorderly troop of Wallachians approached the Decurio's house, triumphantly bearing the hussar's csako on a pole before them.

"Had I left you there last night, they would now have exhibited your head instead of your csako."

The crowd halted before the Decurio's window, greeting him with loud vociferations.

The Decurio spoke a few words in the Wallachian language, on which they replied more vehemently than before, at the same time thrusting forward the kalpag on the pole.

The Decurio turned hastily round. "Was your name written on your kalpag?" he asked the young man, in evident embarrassment.

"It was."

"Unhappy youth! The people, furious at not having found you, are determined to attack your father's house."

"And you will permit them?" asked the youth, starting from bed.

"I dare not contradict them, unless I would lose their confidence. I can prevent nothing."

"Give me up—let them wreak their bloody vengeance on my head!"

"I should only betray myself for having concealed you; and it would not save your father's house."

"And if they murder the innocent and unprotected, on whom will the ignominy of their blood fall?"

"On me; but I will give you the means of preventing this disgrace. Do you accept it?"

"Speak!"

"I will give you a disguise; hasten to Kolozsvar and assemble your comrades—then return and protect your house. I will await you there, and man to man, in open honourable combat, the strife will no longer be ignominious."

"Thanks! thanks!" murmured the youth, pressing the Decurio's hand.

"There is not a moment to lose; here is a peasant's mantle—if you should be interrogated, you have only to show this paszura,23 and mention my name. Your not knowing the language is of no consequence; my men are accustomed to see Hungarian gentlemen visit me in disguise, and having only seen you by night, they will not recognise you."

[23] Everything on which the double-headed eagle— the emblem of the Austrian Government—was painted, engraved, or sculptured, the Wallachians call *paszura*.

Imre hastily took the dress, while the Decurio spoke to the people, made arrangements for the execution of their plans, and pointed out the way to the castle, promising to follow them immediately.

"Accept my horse as a remembrance," said the young man, turning to the Decurio.

"I accept it, as it would only raise suspicion were you to mount it; but you may recover it again in the field. Haste, and lose no time! If you delay, you will bring mourning on your own head, and disgrace on mine!"

In a few minutes the young man, disguised as a Wallachian peasant, was hastening on foot across the hills to Kolozsvar.

It was past midnight.

The inhabitants of the Bardy castle had all retired to rest. The iron gate was locked and the windows barred, when suddenly the sound of demoniac cries roused the slumberers from their dreams.

"What is that noise?" cried Jozsef Bardy, springing from his bed, and rushing to the window.

"The Olahok!"24 cried a hussar, who had rushed to his master's apartments on hearing the sounds.

[24] *Olah*, Wallachian—*ok*, plural.

"The Olah! the Olah!" was echoed through the corridors by the terrified servants.

By the light of a few torches, a hideous crowd was seen before the windows, armed with scythes and axes, which they were brandishing with fearful menaces.

"Lock all the doors!" cried Jozsef Bardy, with calm presence of mind; "barricade the great entrance, and take the ladies and children to the back rooms. You must not lose your heads, but all assemble together in the turret-chamber, from whence the whole building may be protected." And, taking down two good rifles from over his bed, he hastened to his elder brother Tamas's apartments.

He found him already dressed in his richest costume, with his jewelled sabre by his side, and walking calmly up and down the room. The turret-chamber opened from his apartments, and overlooked the court.

"Have you heard the noise?" asked his brother as he entered.

"I knew it would come," he replied, and coolly continued to pace the room.

"And are you not preparing for defence?"

"To what purpose?—they will kill us all. I am quite prepared for what must inevitably happen."

"But it will not happen if we defend ourselves courageously. We are eight men—the walls of the castle are strong—the besiegers have no guns, and no place to protect them; we may hold out for days, until assistance comes from Kolozsvar."

"We shall lose," replied Tamas coldly, and without the slightest change of countenance.

"Then I shall defend the castle myself. I have a wife and children—our old grandmother and our sister are here, and I shall protect them, if I remain alone."

At that instant Barnabas and old Simon entered with the widowed sister.

Barnabas had a huge twenty-pound iron club in his hand; grinding his teeth, and with eyes darting fire, he seemed capable of meeting single-handed the whole troop.

He was followed by the widow, with two loaded pistols in her hand, and old Simon, who entreated them not to use violence, or exasperate the enemy.

"Conduct yourselves bravely!" replied the widow, drily; "let us not die in vain."

"Come with me—we shall send them all to hell!" cried Barnabas, swinging the club in his herculean arm as if it had been a reed.

"Let us not be too hasty," interrupted Jozsef; "we will stand here in the tower, from whence we can shoot every one that approaches, and if they break in, we can meet them on the stairs."

"For Heaven's sake!" cried Simon, "what are you going to do? If you kill one of them, they will massacre us all. Speak to them peaceably—promise them wine—take them to the cellar—give them money—try to pacify them! Nephew Tamas, *you* will speak to them?" continued the old man, turning to Tamas, who still paced up and down, without the slightest visible emotion.

"Pacification or resistance are equally vain," he replied coldly; "we are inevitably lost!"

"We have no time for delay," said Jozsef impatiently, "take the arms from the wall, Barnabas, give one to each servant—let them stand at the back windows of the house, we two are enough here. Sister, stand between the windows, that the stones may not hit you; and when you load, do not strike the balls too far in, that our aim may be the more secure!"

"No! no!—I cannot let you fire," exclaimed the old man, endeavouring to drag Jozsef from the window. "You must not fire yet—only remain quiet."

"Go to the hurricane, old man! would you have us use holy water against a shower of stones?"

At that instant several large stones were dashed through the windows, breaking the furniture against which they fell.

"Only wait," said Simon, "until I speak with them. I am sure I shall pacify them. I can speak their language, and I know them all—just let me go to them."

"A vain idea! If you sue for mercy they will certainly kill you, but if you show courage, you may bring them to their senses. You had better stay and take a gun."

But the old man was already out of hearing, and, hurrying down stairs, he went out of a back door into the court, which the Wallachians had not yet taken possession of.

They were endeavouring to break down one of the stone pillars of the iron gate with their axes and hammers, and had already succeeded in making an aperture, through which one of the gang now climbed.

Old Simon recognised him. "Lupuj, my son, what do you want here?" said the old man. "Have we ever offended you? Do you forget all that I have done for you?—how I cured your wife when she was so ill, and got you off from the military; and how, when your ox died, I gave you two fine bullocks to replace it? Do you not know me, my son Lupuj?"

"I am not your son Lupuj now; I am a 'malcontent!'" cried the Wallachian, aiming a blow with his heavy hammer at the old man's head.

Uttering a deep groan, Simon fell lifeless to the ground.

The rest of the party saw the scene from the tower.

Barnabas rushed from the room like a maddened tiger, while Jozsef, retiring cautiously behind the embrasure of the window, aimed his gun as they were placing his uncle's head upon a spike, and shot the first who raised it. Another seized it, and the next instant he too fell to the earth; another, and another, as many as attempted to raise the head, till, finally, none dared approach.

The widow loaded the guns, while Tamas sat quietly in an arm-chair.

Meanwhile Barnabas had hurried to the attics, where several large fragments of iron had been stowed away, and, dragging them to a window which overlooked the entrance, he waited until the gang had assembled round the door, and were trying to break in; when, lifting an enormous piece with gigantic strength, he dropped it on the heads of the besiegers.

Fearful cries arose, and the gang, who were at the door, fled right and left, leaving four or five of their number crushed beneath the ponderous mass.

The next moment they returned with redoubled fury, dashing stones against the windows and the roof, while the door resounded with the blows of their clubs.

Notwithstanding the stones which were flying round him, Barnabas stood at the window dashing down the heavy iron masses, and killing two or three men every time.

His brother, meanwhile, continued firing from the tower, and not a ball was aimed in vain. The besiegers had lost a great number, and began to fall back, after fruitless efforts to break in the door, when a footman entered breathless, to inform Barnabas that the Wallachians were beginning to scale the opposite side of the castle with ladders, and that the servants were unable to resist them.

Barnabas rushed to the spot.

Two servants lay mortally wounded in one of the back rooms, through the windows of which the Wallachians were already beginning to enter, while another ladder had been placed against the opposite window, which they were beginning to scale as Barnabas entered.

"Here, wretches!" he roared furiously, and, seizing the ladder with both hands, shook it so violently that the men were precipitated from it, and then, lifting it with supernatural strength, he dashed it against the opposite one, which broke with the force of the weight thrown against it, the upper part falling backwards with the men upon it, while one of the party remained hanging from the window-sill, and, after immense exertions to gain a footing, he too fell to the earth.

Barnabas rushed into the next room grinding his teeth, his lips foaming, and his face of a livid hue: so appalling was his whole appearance, that one of the gang, who had been the first to enter by the window, turned pale with terror, and dropped his axe.

Taking advantage of this, Barnabas darted on his enemy, and, dragging him with irresistible force to the window, he dashed him from it.

"On here! as many as you are," he shouted furiously, the blood gushing from his mouth from the blow of a stone. "On! all who wish a fearful death!"

At that instant, a shriek of terror rose within the house. The Wallachians had discovered the little back door which Simon had left open, and, stealing through it, were already inside the house, when the shrieks of a servant girl gave the besieged notice of their danger.

Barnabas, seizing his club, hurried in the direction of the sounds; he met his brother on the stairs, who had likewise heard the cry, and hastened thither with his gun in his hand, accompanied by the widow.

"Go, sister!" said Jozsef, "take my wife and children to the attics; we will try to guard the staircase step by step. Kiss them all for me. If we die, the villains will put us all in one grave—we shall meet again!"

The widow retired.

The two brothers silently pressed hands, and then, standing on the steps, awaited their enemies. They did not wait long.

The bloodhounds, with shouts of vengeance, rushed on the narrow stone stairs.

"Hah! thus near I love to have you, dogs of hell!" cried Barnabas, raising his iron club with both hands, and dealing such blows right and left, that none whom it reached rose again. The stairs were covered with the dead and wounded, while their death-cries, and the sound of the heavy club, echoed fearfully through the vaulted building.

The foremost of the gang retreated as precipitately as they had advanced, but were continually pressed forward again by the numbers from behind, while Barnabas drove them back unweariedly, cutting an opening through them with the blows of his club.

He had already beaten them back nearly to the bottom of the stairs, when one of the gang, who had concealed himself in a niche, pierced him through the back with a spike.

Dashing his club amongst the retreating crowd, he turned with a cry of rage, and, seizing his murderer by the shoulders, dragged him down with him to the ground.

The first four who rushed to help the murderer were shot dead by Jozsef Bardy, who, when he had fired off both his muskets, still defended his prostrate brother with the butt-end of one, until he was overpowered and disarmed; after which a party of them carried him out to the iron cross, and crucified him on it amidst the most shocking tortures.

On trying to separate the other brother from his murderer, they found them both dead. With his last strength Barnabas had choked his enemy, whom he still held firmly in his deadly grip, and they were obliged to cut off his hand in order to disengage the Wallachian's body.

Tamas, the eldest brother, now alone survived. Seated in his arm-chair, he calmly awaited his enemies, with a large silver chandelier burning on the table before him.

As the noise approached his chamber, he drew from its jewelled sheath his broad curved sword, and, placing it on the table before him, proceeded coolly to examine the ancient blade, which was inscribed with unknown characters.

At last the steps were at the door; the handle was turned—it had not even been locked.

The magnate rose, and, taking his sword from the table, he stood silently and calmly before his enemies, who rushed upon him with fearful oaths, brandishing their weapons still reeking with the blood of his brothers.

The nobleman stood motionless as a statue until they came within two paces of him; when suddenly the bright black steel gleamed above his head, and the foremost man fell at his feet with his skull split to the chin. The next received a deep gash in the shoulder of his outstretched arm; but not a word escaped the magnate's lips, his countenance retained its cold, and stern expression, as he looked at his enemies in calm disdain, as if to say,—"Even in combat a nobleman is worth ten boors."

Warding off with the skill of a professed swordsman, every blow aimed at him, he coolly measured his own thrusts, inflicting severe wounds on his enemies' faces and heads; but the more he evaded them, the more furious they became. At last he received a severe wound in the leg from a scythe, and fell on one knee; but, without evincing the slightest pain, he still continued fighting with the savage mob, until, after a long and obstinate struggle, he fell, without a murmur, or even a death-groan.

The enraged gang cut his body to pieces, and in a few minutes they had hoisted the head on his own sword. Even then the features retained their haughty and contemptuous expression.

He was the last man of the family with whom they had to combat, but more than a hundred of their own band lay stretched in the court and before the windows, covering the stairs and rooms with heaps of bodies; and when the shouts of triumph ceased for an instant, the groans of the wounded and the dying were heard from every side.

None now remained but women and children.

When the Wallachians broke into the castle, the widow had taken them all to the attics, leaving the door open, that her brothers might find a refuge in case they were forced to retreat; and here the weaker members of the family awaited the issue of the combat which was to bring them life or death, listening breathlessly to the uproar, and endeavouring, from its confused sounds, to determine good or evil.

At last the voices died away, and the hideous cries of the besiegers ceased. The trembling women believed that the Wallachians had been driven out, and, breathing more freely, each awaited with impatience the approach of brother—husband—sons.

At last a heavy step was heard on the stairs leading to the garret.

"That is Barnabas's step!" cried the widow joyfully, and, still holding the pistols in her hand, she ran to the door of the garret.

Instead of her expected brother, a savage form, drunken with blood, strode towards her, his countenance burning with rage and triumph.

The widow started back, uttering a shriek of terror, and then, with that unaccountable courage of desperation, she aimed one of the pistols at the Wallachian's breast, who instantly fell backwards on one of his comrades, who followed close behind. The other pistol she discharged into her own bosom.

And now we must draw a veil over the scene that followed.

What happened there may not be witnessed by human eyes. Suffice it to say, they murdered every one, women and children, with the most refined and brutal cruelty, and then threw their dead bodies out of the window from which Barnabas had dashed down the iron fragments on the besiegers' heads.

They left the old grandmother to the last, that she might witness the extermination of her whole family. Happily for her, her eyes had ceased to distinguish the light of the sun, and ere long the light of an eternal glory had risen upon them.

The Wallachians then dug a common grave for the bodies, and threw them all in together. The little one, whom his parents loved so well, they cast in alive, his nurse having escaped from the attics and carried him down stairs, where they had been overtaken by the savages.

"There are only eleven here!" cried one of the gang, who had counted the bodies; "one of them must be still alive somewhere—there ought to be twelve!" and then they once more rushed through the empty rooms, overturning all the furniture, and cutting up and breaking everything they met with. They searched the garrets and every corner of the cellars, but without success.

At last a yell of triumph was heard. One of them had discovered a door which, being painted of the same colour as the walls, had hitherto escaped their observation. It concealed a small apartment in the turret. With a few blows of their axes it was broken open, and they rushed in.

"Ah! a rare booty!" cried the foremost of the ruffians, while, with bloodthirsty curiosity, the others pressed round to see the new victim.

There lay the little orphan with the golden hair; her eyes were closed, and a death-like hue had overspread her beautiful features.

Her aunt, with an instinctive foreboding, had concealed her here when she took the others to the attics.

The orphan grasped a sharp knife in her hand, with which she had attempted to kill herself; and when her fainting hands refused the fearful service, she had swooned in despair.

"Ah!" cried the Wallachians, in savage admiration, their bloodthirsty countenances assuming a still more hellish expression.

"This is common booty!" cried several voices together.

"A beautiful girl! A noble lady! ha, ha, ha! She will just suit the tattered Wallachians!" and with their foul and bloody hands, they seized the young girl by her fair slight arms.

"Ha! what is going on here?" thundered a voice from behind.

The Wallachians looked round.

A figure stood among them fully a head taller than all the rest. He wore a brass helmet, in which a deep cleft was visible, and held in his left hand a short Roumin sword. His features bore the ancient Roman character.

"The Decurio!" they murmured, making way for him.

"What is going on here?" he repeated; and seeing the fainting girl in the arms of a Wallachian, he ordered him to lay her down.

"She is one of our enemies," replied the savage insolently.

"Silence, knave! Does one of the Roumin nation seek enemies in women? lay her down instantly."

"Not so, leader," interrupted Lupuj; "our laws entitle us to a division of the spoil. This girl is our booty; she belongs to us after the victory."

"I know our laws better than you do, churl! Due division of spoil is just and fair; but we cast lots for what cannot be divided."

"True, leader: a horse or an ox cannot be divided, and for them we cast lots; but in this case" —

"I have said it *cannot*, and I should like to know who dares to say it *can*!"

Lupuj knew the Decurio too well to proffer another syllable, and the rest turned silently away from the girl; one voice alone was heard to exclaim, "It can!"

"Who dares to say that?" cried the Decurio; "let him come forward!"

A young Wallachian, with long plaited hair, confronted the Decurio. He was evidently intoxicated, and replied, striking his breast with his fist: "*I* said so."

Scarcely had the words escaped his lips, than the Decurio, raising his left hand, severed the contradictor's head at one stroke from his body; and as it fell back, the lifeless trunk dropped on its knees before the Decurio, with its arms round him, as if in supplication.

"Dare any one still say it can?" asked Numa, with merciless rigour.

The Wallachians turned silently away.

"Put the horses immediately to the carriage; the girl must be placed in it, and brought to Topanfalva. Whoever has the good fortune of winning her, has a right to receive her as I confide her to you; but if any one of you should dare to offend her in the slightest degree, even by a look or a smile, remember *this*, and take example from it," continued the Decurio, pointing with his sword to the headless body of the young man. "And now you may go—destroy and pillage."

At these words the band scattered right and left, leaving the Decurio with the fainting girl, whom he lifted into the carriage and confided to some faithful retainers of the family, pointing out the road across the hills.

In half an hour the castle was in flames; and the Wallachians, descending into the cellars, had knocked out the bottoms of the casks, and bathed in the sea of flowing wine and brandy, singing wild songs, while the fire burst from every window, enveloping the blackened walls; after which the revellers departed, leaving their dead, and those who were too helplessly intoxicated to follow them.

Meanwhile, they brought the young girl to the Decurio's house; and as each man considered that he had an equal right to the prize, they kept a vigilant eye upon her, and none dared offend her so much as by a look.

When the Decurio arrived, they all crowded into the house with him, filling the rooms, as well as the entrance and porch.

Having laid out the spoil before them on the ground, the leader proceeded to divide it into equal shares, retaining for himself the portion of ten men, after which most of the band dispersed to their homes; but a good many remained, greedily eyeing their still unappropriated victim, who lay pale and motionless as the dead on the couch of lime-boughs, where they had laid her.

"You are waiting, I suppose, to cast lots for the girl?" said Numa drily.

"Certainly," replied Lupuj, with an insolent leer; "and his she will be who casts highest. If two, or ten, or twenty of us should cast the same, we have an equal right to her."

"I tell you only one can have her," interrupted Numa sternly.

"Then those who win must cast again among each other."

"Casting the die will not do: we may throw all day long, and two may remain at the end."

"Well, let us play cards for her."

"I cannot allow that: the more cunning will deceive the simpler."

"Well, write our names upon bricks, and throw them all into a barrel; and whichever name you draw will take away the girl."

"I can say what name I please, for none of you can read."

The Wallachian shook his head impatiently.

"Well, propose something yourself, Decurio."

"I will. Let us try which of us can give the best proof of courage and daring; and whoever can do that, shall have the girl, for he best deserves her."

"Well said!" cried the men unanimously. "Let us each relate what we have done, and then you can judge which among us is the boldest."

"I killed the first Bardy in the court, in sight of his family."

"I broke in the door, when that terrible man was dashing down the iron on our heads."

"But it was I who pierced his heart."

"I mounted the stairs first."

"I fought nearly half an hour with the noble in the cloth of gold."

And thus they continued. Each man, according to his own account, was the first and the bravest—each had performed miracles of valour.

"You have all behaved with great daring; but it is impossible now to prove what has happened. The proof must be given here, by all of you together, before my eyes, indisputably."

"Well, tell us how," said Lupuj impatiently, always fearing that the Decurio was going to deceive them.

"Look here," said Numa, drawing a small cask from beneath the bed— and in doing so he observed that the young girl half opened her eyes, as she glanced at him, and then closed them. She was awake, and had heard all.

As he stooped down, Numa whispered gently in her ear: "Fear nothing," and then drew the cask into the middle of the room.

The Wallachians stared with impatient curiosity as he knocked out the bottom of the cask with a hatchet.

"This cask contains gunpowder," continued the Decurio. "We will light a match and place it in the middle of the cask, and whoever remains longest in the room is undoubtedly the most courageous; for there is enough here to blow up not only this house, but the whole of the neighbouring village."

At this proposition several of the men began to murmur.

"If any are afraid, they are not obliged to remain," said the Decurio drily.

"I agree," said Lupuj doggedly, "I will remain here; and perhaps, after all, it is poppy-seeds you have got there—it looks very like them."

The Decurio stooped down, and taking a small quantity between his fingers, threw it into the Wallachian's pipe, which immediately exploded, causing him to stagger backwards, and the next instant he stood with a blackened visage, sans beard and moustache, amidst the jeers and laughter of his comrades.

This only exasperated him the more.

"I will stay for all that," he exclaimed; and lifting up the pipe which he had dropped, he walked over and lit it at the burning match which the Decurio was placing in the cask.

Upon this, two-thirds of the men left the room.

The rest assembled round the cask with much noise and bravado, swearing by heaven and earth that they would stay until the match was burned out; but the more they swore, the more they looked at the burning match, the flame of which was slowly approaching the gunpowder.

For some minutes their courage remained unshaken; but after that they ceased to boast, and began to look at each other in silent consternation, while their faces grew paler every instant. At last one or two rose and stood aloof; the others followed their example, and some grinding their teeth with rage, others chattering with terror, they all began to leave the room.

Only two remained beside the cask: Numa, who stood with his arms folded, leaning against the foot of the bed; and Lupuj, who was sitting on the rim of the cask with his back turned to the danger, and smoking furiously.

As soon as they were alone, the latter glanced behind him, and saw that the flame was within an inch of the powder.

"I'll tell you what, Decurio," he said, springing up: "we are only two left, don't let us make fools of each other; let us come to an understanding on this matter."

"If you are tired of waiting, I can press the match lower."

"This is no jest, Numa; you are risking your own life. How can you wish to send us both to hell for the sake of a pale girl? But I'll tell you what—I'll give her up to you if you will only promise that she shall be mine when you are tired of her."

"Remain here and win her—if you dare."

"To what purpose?" said the Wallachian, in a whining voice; and in his impatience he began to tear his clothes and stamp with his feet, like a petted child.

"What I have said stands good," said the Decurio; "whoever remains longest has the sole right to the lady."

"Well, I will stay, of course; but what do I gain by it? I know you will stay too, and then the devil will have us both; and I speak not only for myself when I say I do not wish that."

"If you do not wish it, you had better be gone."

"Well, I don't care—if you will give me a golden mark."

"Not the half: stay if you like it."

"Decurio, this is madness! The flame will reach the powder immediately."

"I see it."

"Well, say a dollar."

"Not a whit."

"May the seventy-seven limbed thunderbolt strike you on St. Michael's day!" roared the Wallachian fiercely, as he rushed to the door; but after he had gone out, he once more thrust his head in and cried:—

"Will you give even a florin? I am not gone yet."

"Nor have I removed the match; you may come back."

The Wallachian slammed the door, and ran for his life, till exhausted and breathless he sank under a tree, where he lay with his tunic over his head, and his ears covered with his hands, only now and then raising his head nervously, to listen for the awful explosion which was to blow up the world.

Meanwhile Numa coolly removed the match, which was entirely burnt down; and throwing it into the grate, he stepped over to the bed, and whispered in the young girl's ear: "You are free!"

Tremblingly she raised herself in the bed, and taking the Decurio's large and sinewy hands within her own, she murmured: "Be merciful! O hear my prayer, and kill me!"

The Decurio stroked the fair head of the lovely supplicant.

"Poor child!" he replied gently, "you have nothing to fear; nobody will hurt you now."

"You have saved me from these fearful people—now save me from yourself!"

"You have nothing to fear from me," replied the Dacian proudly; "I fight for liberty alone, and you may rest as securely within my threshold as on the steps of the altar. When I am absent you need have no anxiety, for these walls are impregnable; and if any one should dare offend you by the slightest look, that moment shall be the last of his mortal career. And when I am at home you have nothing to fear, for woman's image never dwelt within my heart. Accept my poor couch, and may your rest be sweet!—Imre Bardy slept on it last night."

"Imre!" exclaimed the girl, starting. "You have seen him, then?—oh! where is he?"

The Decurio hesitated. "He should not have delayed so long," he murmured, pressing his hand against his brow; "all would have been otherwise."

"Oh! let me go to him, if you know where he is."

"I do not know; but I am certain that he will come here if he is alive—indeed, he must come."

"Why do you think that?"

"Because he will seek you."

"Did he then speak—before you?"

"As he lay wounded on that couch, he pronounced your name in his dreams. Are you not that Jolanka Bardy whom they call 'The angel'? I knew you by your golden locks."

The young girl cast down her eyes. "Then you think he will come?" she said in a low voice. "And my relations?"

"He will come as soon as possible; and now you must take some food and rest. Do not think about your relations now; they are all in a safe place—nobody can hurt them more."

The Decurio brought some refreshment, laid a small prayer-book on the pillow, and left the orphan by herself.

The poor girl opened the prayer-book, and her tears fell like raindrops on the blessed page; but, overcome by the fatigue and terror she had undergone, her head ere long sank gently back, and she slept calmly and sweetly the sleep of exhausted innocence.

As evening closed, the Decurio returned; and, softly approaching the bed, looked long and earnestly at the fair sleeper's face, until two large tears stood unconsciously in his eyes.

The Roumin hastily brushed away the unwonted moisture; and as if afraid of the feeling which had stolen into his breast, he hastened from the room, and laid himself upon his woollen rug before the open door.

The deserted castle still burned on, shedding a ghastly light on the surrounding landscape, while the deepest silence reigned around, only broken now and then by an expiring groan, or the hoarse song of a drunken reveller.

Day was beginning to dawn, as a troop of horsemen galloped furiously towards the castle from the direction of Kolozsvar.

They were Imre and his comrades.

Silently and anxiously they pursued their course, their eyes fixed upon one point, as they seemed to fly rather than gallop along the road.

"We are too late!" exclaimed one of the party at last, pointing to a dim red smoke against the horizon; "your castle is burning!"

Without returning an answer, Imre spurred his panting horse to a swifter pace. A turn in the road suddenly brought the castle to their view, its blackened walls still burning, while the red smoke rose high against the side of the hill.

The young man uttered a fierce cry of despair, and galloped madly down the declivity. In less than a quarter of an hour he stood before the ruined walls.

"Where is my father? where are my family? where is my bride?" he shrieked in frantic despair, brandishing his sword over the head of a half-drunken Wallachian, who was leaning against the ruined portico.

The latter fell on his knees, imploring mercy, and declaring that it was not he who had killed them.

"Then they are dead!" exclaimed the unhappy youth, as, half-choked by his sobs, he fell forward on his horse's neck.

Meanwhile his companions had ridden up, and immediately surrounded the Wallachian, whom, but for Imre's interference, they would have cut down.

"Lead us to where you have buried them. Are they *all* dead?" he continued; "have you not left one alive? Accursed be the sun that rises after such a night!"

The Wallachian pointed to a large heap of freshly-raised mould. "They are all there!" he said.

Imre fell from his horse without another word, as if struck down.

His companions removed him to a little distance, where the grass was least red.

They then began to dig twelve graves with their swords.

Imre watched them in silence. He seemed unconscious what they were about.

When they had finished the graves they proceeded to open the large pit, but the sight was too horrible, and they carried Imre away by force. He could not have looked on what was there and still retained his senses.

In a short time, one of his comrades approached and told him that there were only eleven bodies in the grave.

"Then one of them must be alive!" cried Imre, a slight gleam of hope passing over his pale features; "which is it?—speak! Is there not a young girl with golden locks among them?"

"I know not," stammered his comrade, in great embarrassment.

"You do not know?—go and look again."

His friend hesitated.

"Let me go—I must know," said Imre impatiently, as the young man endeavoured to detain him.

"O stay, Imre, you cannot look on them; they are all—headless!"

"My God!" exclaimed the young man, covering his face with both his hands, and, bursting into tears, he threw himself down with his face upon the earth.

His comrades questioned the Wallachian closely as to what he knew about the young girl. First he returned no answer, pretending to be drunk and not to understand; but on their promising to spare his life, on the sole condition that he would speak the truth, he confessed that she had been carried away to the mountains, where the band were to cast lots for her.

"I must go!" said Imre, starting as if from a trance.

"Whither?" inquired his comrades.

"To seek her! Take off your dress," he continued, turning to the Wallachian, "you may have mine in exchange;" and, hastily putting on the tunic, he concealed his pistols in the girdle beneath it.

"We will follow you," said his comrades, taking up their arms; "we will seek her from village to village."

"No, no, I must go alone! I shall find her more easily alone. If I do not return, avenge this for me," he said, pointing to the moat; then, turning to the Wallachian, he added sternly, "I have found beneath your girdle a gold medallion which my grandmother always wore suspended from her neck, and by which I know you to be one of her murderers, and, had I not promised to spare your life, you should now receive the punishment that you deserve. Keep him here," he said to his comrades, "until I have crossed the hills, and then let him go."

And taking leave of his friends, he cast one glance at the eleven heaps, and at the burning castle of his ancestors, and hastened towards the mountains.

The hoary autumn nights had dyed the leaves of the forest. The whole country looked as if it had been washed in blood.

Deep amidst the wildest forest the path suddenly descends into a narrow valley surrounded by steep rocks, at the foot of which lies a little village half concealed among the trees.

It seemed as if the settlers there had only cleared sufficient ground to build their dwellings, leaving all the rest a dense mass of forest. Apart from the rest, on the top of a rock, stood a cottage, which, unlike the others, was constructed entirely of large blocks of stone, and only approachable by a small path cut in the rock.

A young man ascended this path. He was attired in a peasant's garb, and although he evidently had travelled far, his step was light and fleet. When he had ascended about half way, he was suddenly stopped by an armed Wallachian, who had been kneeling before a shrine in the rock, and, on seeing the stranger, rose and stood in his path.

The latter pronounced the Decurio's name, and produced his pazsura.

The Wallachian examined it on every side, and then stepped back to let the stranger pass, after which, he once more laid down his scythe and cap, and knelt before the shrine.

The stranger knocked at the Decurio's door, which was locked; and an armed Wallachian appeared from behind the rock, and informed him that the Decurio was not at home, only his wife.

"His wife?" exclaimed the stranger in surprise.

"Yes, that pale girl who fell to him by lot."

"And she is his wife?"

"He told us so himself, and swore that if any of us dared so much as lift his eye upon her, he would send him to St. Nicholas in paradise."

"Can I not see her?"

"I would not advise you; for if the Decurio hears of it, he will make two halves of you; but you may go round to the window if you like—only let me get out of the way first, that the Decurio may not find me here."

The stranger hastened to the window, and, looking in, he saw the young girl seated on an arm-chair made of rough birch boughs, with a little prayer-book on her knee; her fair arm supporting her head, while a mass of golden ringlets half veiled her face, which was pale as an alabaster statue; the extreme sadness of its expression rendering her beauty still more touching.

"Jolanka!" exclaimed the stranger passionately.

She started at the well-known voice, and, uttering a cry of joy, rushed to the window.

"Oh, Imre!" she murmured, "are you come at last!"

"Can I not enter? can I not speak with you?"

The young girl hastened to unbar the door, which was locked from the inside, and as Imre entered she threw herself into his arms, while he pressed her fondly to his heart.

The Wallachian, who had stolen to the window, stood aghast with terror, and, as soon as the Decurio arrived, he ran to meet him, and related, with vehement gesticulations, how the girl had thrown herself into the peasant's arms.

"And how did you know that?" asked Numa, coldly.

"I saw them through the window."

"And how dared you look through my window? Did I not forbid you? Down on your knees instantly, and pray!"

The Wallachian fell on his knees, and clasped his hands.

"Rebel! you deserve the punishment of death for having disobeyed my commands; and if you ever dare to open your lips on the subject, depend upon it, you shall not escape!" And with these words, he strode away, leaving the astonished informer on his knees, in which posture he remained for some time afterwards, not daring to raise his head until the Decurio's steps had died away.

As Numa entered the house, the lovers hastened to meet him. For an instant or two he stood at the threshold, regarding the young man with a look of silent reproach. "Why did you come so late?" he asked.

Imre held out his hand, but the Decurio did not accept it.

"The blood of your family is on my hand," he whispered. "You have let dishonour come on me, and mourning on yourself."

The young man's head sank on his breast in silent anguish.

"Take his hand," said Jolanka, in her low, sweet accents; and then, turning to Imre, "He saved your life—he saved us both, and he will rescue our family too."

Imre looked at her in astonishment.

The Decurio seized his arm, and drew him aside. "She does not know that they are dead," he whispered; "she was not with them, and knows nothing of their fate; and I have consoled her with the idea that they are all prisoners. She must never know the horrors of that fearful night."

"But sooner or later she will hear it."

"Never! you must leave the place and the kingdom. You must go to Turkey."

"My way lies towards Hungary."

"You must not think of it. Evil days await that country; your prophets do not see them, but I know, and see them clearly. Go to Turkey; I will give you letters by which you may pass in security through Wallachia and Moldavia; and here is a purse of gold—do not scruple to accept it, for it is your own, it belonged to *them*. Promise me, for her sake," he continued earnestly, pointing to Jolanka, "that you will not go to Hungary."

Imre hesitated. "I cannot promise what I am not sure I shall fulfil; but I shall remember your advice."

Numa took the hands of the two lovers, and, gazing long and earnestly on their faces, he said, in a voice of deep feeling, "You love one another?"

They pressed his hand in silence.

"You will be happy—you will forget your misfortunes: God bless and guide you on your way! Take these letters, and keep the direct road to Brasso,25 by the Saxon-land.26 You will find free passage everywhere, and never look behind until the last pinnacles of the snowy mountains are beyond your sight. Go! we will not take leave, not a word—let us forget each other!"

> [25] Brasso, or Kronstadt, a town in the south-east of Transylvania, on the frontiers of Wallachia.
>
> [26] A district inhabited by a colony of Saxons.

The Decurio watched the lovers till they were out of sight; and called to them, even when they could hear him no longer, "Do not go towards Hungary!"

He then entered his house. The prayer-book lay open as the young girl had left it; the page was still damp with her tears. Numa's hand trembled, as he kissed the volume fervently and placed it in his bosom.

When night came on, the Roumin lay down on his wolfskin couch, where the golden-haired maiden, and her lover before her, had slept; but it seemed as if they had stolen his rest—he could not close his eyes there, so he rose and went out to the porch, where he spread his rug before the open door; but it was long ere he could sleep—there was an unwonted feeling at his heart, something like happiness, yet inexpressibly sad; and, buried in deep reverie, he lay with his eyes fixed on the dark blue starry vault above him till past midnight. Suddenly he thought he heard the report of some fire-arms at a great distance, and at the same moment two stars sank below the horizon. Numa thought of the travellers, and a voice seemed to whisper, "They are now happy!"

The moon had risen high in the heavens, when the Decurio was roused from his sleep by heavy footsteps, and five or six Wallachians, among whom was Lupuj, stood before him.

"We have brought two enemies' heads," said the latter, with a dark look at the Decurio; "pay us their worth!" and, taking two heads from his pouch, he laid them on Numa's mat.

The Wallachians watched their leader's countenance with sharp, suspicious glances.

Numa recognised the two heads by the light of the moon. They were those of Imre and Jolanka, but his features did not betray the slightest emotion.

"You will know them, probably," continued Lupuj. "The young magnate, who escaped us at the pass, came for the girl in your absence, and at the same time stole your money, and, what is more, we found your pazsura upon him also."

"Who killed them?" asked the Decurio, in his usual calm voice.

"None of us," replied the Wallachian; "as we rushed upon them, the young magnate drew two pistols from his girdle, and shot the girl through the head first, and himself afterwards."

"Were you all there?"

"And more of us besides."

"Go back and bring the rest. I will divide the money you have found on them among you. Make haste; and should one of you remain behind, his share will be divided among the rest."

The Wallachians hastened to seek their comrades with cries of joy.

The Decurio then locked the door, and, throwing himself upon the ground beside the two heads, he kissed them an hundred times, and sobbed like a child.

"I warned you not to go towards Hungary!" he said bitterly. "Why did you not hear me, unhappy children? why did you not take my word?" and he wept over his enemies' heads as if he had been their father.

He then rose, his eyes darting fire, and, shaking his terrible fist, he cried, in a voice hoarse with rage, "Czine mintye!"27

[27] *Czine mintye!* —a Wallachian term signifying revenge.

In a few hours, the Wallachians had assembled before the Decurio's house. They were about fifty or sixty, all wild, fearful-looking men.

Numa covered the two heads with a cloth, and laid them on the bed, after which he opened the door.

Lupuj entered last.

"Lock the door," said Numa, when they were all in; "we must not be interrupted;" and, making them stand in a circle, he looked round at them all, one by one.

"Are you all here?" he asked at last.

"Not one is absent."

"Do you consider yourselves all equally deserving of sharing *the booty*?"

"All of us."

"It was you," he continued, turning to Lupuj, "who struck down the old man?"

"It was."

"And you who pierced the magnate with a spike?"

"You are right, leader."

"And you really killed all the women in the castle?" turning to a third.

"With my own hand."

"And one and all of you can boast of having massacred, and plundered, and set on fire?"

"All! all!" they cried, striking their breasts.

"Do not lie before Heaven. See! your wives are listening at the window to what you say, and will betray you if you do not speak the truth."

"We speak truth!"

"It is well!" said the leader, as he calmly approached the bed; and, seating himself on it, uncovered the two heads and placed them on his knees. "Where did you put their bodies?" he asked.

"We cut them in pieces,.and strewed them on the highroad."

There was a short silence. Numa's breathing became more and more oppressed, and his large chest heaved convulsively. "Have you prayed yet?" he asked, in an altered voice.

"Not yet, leader. What should we pray for?" said Lupuj.

"Fall down on your knees and pray, for this is the last morning which will dawn on any of you again."

"Are you in your senses, leader? What are you going to do?"

"I am going to purge the Roumin nation of a set of ruthless murderers and brigands. Miserable wretches! instead of glory, you have brought dishonour and disgrace upon our arms wherever you have appeared. While the brave fought on the field of battle, you slaughtered their wives and children; while they risked their lives before the cannon's mouth, you attacked the houses of the sleepers, and robbed and massacred the helpless and the innocent. Fall down on your knees and pray for your souls, for the angel of death stands over you, to blot out your memory from among the Roumin people!"

The last words were pronounced in a fearful tone. Numa was no longer the cold, unmoved statue he had hitherto appeared; he was like a fiery genius of wrath, whose very breath was destruction.

The Wallachians fell upon their knees in silent awe, while the women, who had been standing outside, rushed shrieking down the rocks.

The Decurio drew a pistol from his breast, and approached the cask of gunpowder.

With a fearful howl, they rushed upon him—the shriek of despair was heard for an instant, then a terrible explosion, which caused the rocks to tremble, while the flame rose with a momentary flash amidst clouds of smoke and dust, scaring the beasts of the forest, and scattering stones and beams, and hundreds of dismembered limbs, far through the valley, and over the houses of the terrified inhabitants!

When the smoke had dissipated, a heap of ruins stood in the place of Numa's dwelling!

The sun arose and smiled upon the earth, which was strewed with the last leaves of autumn, but where were those who had assembled at the spring-time of the year?

The evening breeze whispered mournfully through the ruined walls, and strewed the faded leaves upon eleven grassy mounds!

The pen trembles in my hand—my heart sickens at the recital of such misery.

Would that I could believe it an imagination—the ghastly horror of a fevered brain!

Would that I could bid my gentle readers check the falling tear, or tell them: "Start not with horror, it is but romance—the creation of some fearful dream—let us awake, and see it no more!"

CRAZY MARCSA

There are as yet no institutions in our country for those unhappy beings in whose minds the "image and likeness" to their Divine original has been destroyed. Hence every town and village in Hungary has its lunatic or idiot, familiar to everybody, from the child to the old man, who often remembers him from *his* childhood—for such unhappy persons generally live a long time.

They are looked upon as public orphans by the people, and are allowed to wander about as their innocent inclinations may suggest; seeking wild-flowers in the lonely woods, singing through the streets, lying abroad in the sun, or roaming by moonlight; and none wish to deprive them of the blessed free air, to check their strange gibberish, or their love for the pathless woods and the mysterious moon. They are sure to find good souls, who feed them when they are hungry, and clothe them when they are in want, or give them shelter at the close of day, to continue their ceaseless pilgrimage next morning. And when the power of darkness comes, and they run through the streets, or shout up at the windows, they are merely greeted with "jo bolond" (good fool), or some such familiar expression; but none try to silence or confine them, for it is known that silence and confinement are torment to a fatuous person.

Some are born thus—perhaps *they* are happy; but for those whose countenances were once as bright and intelligent as any other, what chords have been rent asunder in the heart, what sudden revolution has overturned the mind, that the soul should no longer know itself! Some retain a few words from the memory of the past, and those who hear the strange sentence only shake their heads, and exclaim, "Poor fool!" little knowing what a world of grief, what a tale of ruined hope and withered life, lies concealed in these few unintelligible words!

A few years ago, I spent some time in the county of Csongrad,28 a very beautiful and populous district, where I had many opportunities of mixing with the peasants and farmers of the country. In this district the farmers, however wealthy, bear the name of peasant, and still retain their simple costume, the linen *kontos*,29 and the *brenda*.30

[28] In the east of Hungary.

[29] *Kontos*, short Hungarian coat.

[30] *Brenda*, the cloak bordered with fur.

At the house of one of these worthy peasants in particular, I was a frequent visitor; his simple but vigorous mind, and the wit and pertinence of his remarks, often entertained me. I partook of his hospitality at all their family *fêtes*—the vintage, kukoricza gathering,31 and birthdays; and indeed the good people would have taken it amiss had I remained behind.

[31] "Kukoricza gathering," the cutting of the maize or Indian corn—a great *fête* in Hungary, like the vintage.

On one occasion I happened to enter as they were baking, and was received in the kitchen, where the wife, a rosy-faced, buxom young woman, was standing beside the stove superintending the motions of five or six servants, though she herself was more busy than any, with her own hands kneading the loaves, and tossing them on the baking-shovel. The husband stood there too, under pretence of lighting his pipe, but in reality for no other purpose than to tease his wife, who, during the important affair, scolded everybody who did not move as quickly as she did, which became her very well.

Already ten large bannocks, fried with goose fat, and enriched with preserved plums, lay smoking on the hearth; these the good woman, immediately on my entrance, began arranging in her best dishes, and offered to me with a welcome smile, her husband assuring me that she had baked them herself, and adding something about a certain wine which was particularly good to drink after them.

In the midst of all this work, during which Mistress Kata several times applied the long handle of the baking tongs to the shoulders of such as did not bestir themselves quickly enough to please her, the door was softly pushed open, and the figure of a very old and shrivelled woman appeared on the threshold; at first she only put in her head, and looked around with a ghastly and vacant smile, caressing the dogs, which ran up to her, and speaking to them as if they were the dearest friends she had in the house; she then slowly advanced into the room, pausing every now and then, as if waiting to be invited, and again taking courage to proceed.

Nobody seemed to notice her except myself; they were either too much engaged, or the fearful-looking creature who advanced towards them was too familiar a sight to strike them as she did me, who saw her for the first time.

Her figure was so bent and shrivelled that she did not appear to be more than four feet high; her head was uncovered, and a mass of perfectly white hair hung in a long plait down her back, as young girls used to wear it. The face was furrowed by a thousand wrinkles, and the vacant and half-closed eyes seemed ever gazing on the same spot, while her lips were distended in a continual unearthly smile, while every now and then she made an idiotic motion with her head; her petticoat and apron were composed of bright-coloured rags sewed together; in one hand she carried a large bunch of wild-flowers and weeds, and in the other two billets of wood.

On seeing a stranger, she endeavoured, with an odd and embarrassed *naïveté*, to conceal her face behind her large nosegay; and, shuffling up to Mistress Kata, who had just placed her last loaf on the baking-shovel, she tapped her on the shoulder with the flowers, exclaiming, with a weird laugh, "Hühü! Mistress Aunt, here I am, you see!"

"That's right, Marcsa," said Mistress Kata; "I was just expecting you,—don't you see?"

"Hühü!—I have brought you some beautiful flowers to plant; then I heard you were baking, and I have brought wood," and she placed the billets in Mistress Kate's arms.

"Now, you see, if you had not brought me this, we could not have kept up the fire. Well, will you have a bannock?"

"Hühü! that I will," said the old woman, stretching out her shrivelled arms.

"There, now—eat it," said Mistress Kata, handing her a large cake. "But you must eat it before me."

"Hühü! I will take it to Joska bacsi!"

"Joska bacsi doesn't want it. Joska bacsi has sent to say that you are to eat it yourself."

"Really! did he say that?" asked the old woman; and then, with a deep sigh, she began to swallow the bannock. She did not bite it, not having wherewithal, but pushed the pieces into her mouth and swallowed them, heaving a deep sigh at every mouthful; and, when she thought nobody was observing her, she hastily concealed the remainder in her apron, and looked round in great glee at having succeeded so cleverly.

"What will she do with the piece she has hidden?" I asked Mistress Kata.

"She keeps it, poor fool, for Joska bacsi!"

On hearing Joska bacsi mentioned, the old woman looked eagerly up, and asked, "What does Joska bacsi say?"

"He says you must count how many poppy-seeds32 there are in that plate," said one of the maids, laughing.

[32] Poppy-seeds are much used in Hungary, in bread, puddings, cakes, &c.,—a favourite ingredient worked up into crust for different pastries.

The old woman rose without a word, and, approaching the plate, began eagerly counting the seeds grain by grain.

"Why do you trifle with her?" said I, pitying the poor, witless creature; while Mistress Kata came forward and took hold of her arm.

"Leave it alone, good Marcsa; Erzsi is telling a story—that was not what Joska bacsi said."

But the poor idiot would not leave off counting till Kata said, pointing to me, and making a sign that I should acquiesce, "Look here, Marcsa; this gentleman has just come from Joska bacsi, and he has brought a message from him that you should go home and remain quiet, and not wander so much about the Theiss—did he not, sir?"

I of course assented, on which the idiot shuffled joyfully up to me, and, taking my hand, looked long into my face with her fearful, vacant eyes, and then said coaxingly, "Hühü! I do think he is almost as beautiful a lad as my own Joska bacsi!"

This was very flattering, though I would have been better pleased had this hapless creature not gazed upon me thus, with her fixed and witless eyes, and hastily taking a piece of silver out of my pocket, I offered it to her.

Idiots are always fond of money, and as soon as I had put the coin into her hand, she immediately wished everybody good-night, and set off in great haste.

"Well, there's something more for Joska bacsi," said Mistress Kata, laughing.

"How—how?" I eagerly asked, my curiosity being much excited.

"She will throw it into the Theiss where the water is deepest. Whatever she gets that she can give to Joska bacsi, all goes into the Theiss!"

"And who is this Joska bacsi?"

"Nobody at all: dear heart! such a creature never existed on earth. It is only a fancy, such as all idiots have."

"And was she always mad?"

At these words an old peasant, who had been sitting in the chimney-corner, and silently observing us, exclaimed, "No, sir, that she was not."

"Well, I have never seen her otherwise, since I remember anything," said Mistress Kata.

"You are not yet thirty years old, Mistress, and this happened long before your birth."

"Do you know something about her, then?" I asked, turning with interest to the old man.

"He know, indeed!" said Mistress Kata scornfully; "he just likes to tell stories, when he can find a fool who will listen to him. But don't be taken in, young gentleman, take my word for it."

I paid no attention, however, to Mistress Kata's warning, and questioned the old man further: "Perhaps it was love that drove this poor woman mad?"

"Love, indeed!—what nonsense!" cried Mistress Kata; "as if a peasant would go mad for love! Bless your soul! only great folks can do that—peasants have something else to do."

"And were you not yourself madly in love with me, eh?" interrupted her husband, putting his arm round her waist.

"Get along!" cried his wife, striking his hand and blushing to the eyes; "I'd like to know for what?"

The old peasant meanwhile pulled my cloak, and whispered, "I don't like speaking here, sir, for they only laugh at me; but if you would like to hear, come this evening. I will be standing in the porch, and there I can tell you. It is a sad story enough, and may interest you to hear it."

Mistress Kata reverted frequently to the subject, exclaiming ever and anon, as the bread baked, and she took each loaf out of the oven and turned up its shining crust, "Well, that is an idea!—go mad for love of you, forsooth, as if you were worth going mad for!"

I did not forget my evening tryst, and found the old man in the porch. I greeted him with "Adjon Isten,"33 and placed myself beside him on the bench.

[33] *Adjon Isten*, God give—an abbreviation for, God give
good day, &c.

The old man returned my salutation, and, emptying his pipe, began striking fire with a flint. "Permit me, sir, to light my pipe again; for I cannot now think much unless I see the smoke before me;" then, drawing his cap far over his brow, he began his tale:—

"Nobody remembers anything about it now, for full sixty years have passed since it happened; I was myself a barefooted boy, and it is only a wonder that I have not forgotten it too. That poor idiot whom you saw there, that wrinkled old creature, was then a beautiful young girl, and that Joska bacsi of whom she always speaks was—my own brother! There was not a handsomer pair among all the peasants than those two; I have seen many a rising generation since, but never any like them! Our parents were mutually sponsors. Marcsa's mother held my brother and me at our baptism, and my mother held Marcsa. We played together, we went to school together, and to the Lord's Table on Easter Sunday. Hej! that was a good priest who christened and catechized us; he has been long since preaching in heaven; and the worthy chanter who instructed us too, is up striking time among the angels!

"The lad and the young girl had been so attached from their childhood, that they never dreamed they could live otherwise than together. Our mother always called Marcsa her little daughter-in-law; and when she and my brother were each nineteen years old, their parents decided that if God pleased to preserve us all till the next Carnival, they should be married. My brother often entreated them not to wait till the Carnival, 'for who knows,' he said, 'what may happen before then?' and with reason did his heart misgive him, poor fellow! for at the vintage Marcsa's father and ours went to the cellars to make the wine, and the deadly air34 struck them—we found them both dead!

> [34] The wine-cellars, which every peasant possesses, are not in their cottages, but out in their vineyards; it frequently happens that there is a malaria in the vaults, which is certain death to any who remain in them above a certain time.

"The mourning was very great in both houses—the two fathers cut off at one stroke; but in Marcsa's house the distress was still greater than in ours, for the old man, having been sacristan, had been intrusted with certain sums, of which two hundred florins were missing after his death. Where he had put them, or what had become of them, was never known, for death had struck him too suddenly. The reverend gentlemen who examined the accounts had so much consideration for the poor widow, that they did not bring the affair to light, and even promised to wait a whole year, during which time the family must endeavour to make up the sum, as after that period it could no longer be kept secret.

"Our mother was much distressed when she heard of this affair, and there was no more said of the carnival wedding: she was a poor but an honest woman, and how could she allow her son to marry the daughter of a man in whose hands the public money had been lost, and whose goods would probably be sold at the end of a year to repay the scandalous debt? The young lovers cried and lamented loudly, but it was all in vain; my mother said if the sum should be restored within a year she would receive the girl, but never otherwise. She prohibited my brother from holding personal intercourse with Marcsa during that entire period; and in order that he might keep his word the more easily, she bound him apprentice to a Theiss miller, and then—the water parted them.

"Meanwhile, Marcsa's mother very soon died of grief and care, and the girl was left alone. But love wrought wonders in her; and when the poor girl had not a creature in the world to help her, she came over to our mother and said: 'You will not allow your son to marry me unless my father's debt be replaced—good, I have still a whole year, and I will work day and night; I will endure hunger, fatigue—everything, but I will earn the money.'

"And then she began to put her promise into execution.

"Oh, sir! you do not know what a great sum two hundred florins is for a poor peasant, who has to earn it all by hard and honest labour, the work of his hands and the sweat of his brow, and to collect it penny by penny.

"From this day forward, the good girl was scarcely ever seen away from her work. All through the winter, she sat for ever at her wheel, spinning a yarn like silk, which she wove herself; there was no linen like hers in the village, as I have heard the old folks say. She looked after the poultry in the morning, and carried the fowls and eggs herself to market. There was a little bit of a garden behind the house, where she kept flowers and vegetables; and earned more by it than many who had four times as much ground. In summer she joined the reapers, and all that she got for her work she turned into money—fruit, or poultry, or little sucking pigs. Throughout that blessed year, sir, nobody ever saw smoke arise from her chimney: a bit of dry bread was all her daily sustenance; and yet the Lord took such good care of her, that not only her beauty did not diminish, but she looked as healthy and as rosy as if she were living on milk and butter. Love kept the spirit in her, poor girl!

"My brother was not allowed to go to her, but I was the messenger between them. Often, in the fine summer evenings, when I was down at the mill with my brother, he would take his flute and play those beautiful melodies, which none could do better than he; and the girls on the other side, who were filling their pitchers in the stream, or standing with their white feet in the water, washing linen, would hear the air, and join in the chorus. But my brother only heard one voice, and that was the sweetest and the saddest I ever listened to, and brought tears into the eyes of every one who heard it: you could have recognised her voice among a thousand.

"Sometimes his master gave my brother leave of absence for an hour or two, and those were happy days for Joska: he would send me to bid Marcsa come down in the evening toward the Willow Island. This was a little sandbank covered with willow-trees, about three or four fathoms from the shore. Hither would my brother also come in his little boat, while his true-love sat opposite to him upon the shore, and there would they converse till morning across the stream—thus satisfying their own hearts, and obeying my mother's orders. They met, and yet were separated.

"On this footing things remained until the vintage. Marcsa was considered not only the prettiest, but the best girl in the village. The new wine was not yet clear, when one morning the good girl came into my mother's, and counted out two hundred florins on the large oak table—all in good huszasok,35 not one small piece was wanting—and begged my mother to take them with her to the reverend gentlemen, who gave a sealed receipt for the amount. None but ourselves ever knew that it was all our pretty Marcsa's hard earnings.

[35] *Huszas*—a silver piece containing twenty kreutzers, worth eightpence.

"On returning, my mother took Marcsa home with her, and plaited her long hair with pretty rainbow-coloured ribbons, put a string of garnets round her neck, and a pair of fine shoes on her little feet; and all gaily dressed, she took her—none of us knew whither.

"I followed them, however, to the Theiss, when my mother bade me go and ask the ferryman to take us across to the mill, where my brother was serving; and we all three sat down in the boat.

"Even now I think I see the beautiful girl: it seems as it were but yesterday that she sat in the boat before me by my mother's side, blushing modestly, her sparkling eyes cast down. Her heart told her whither we were going.

"My brother recognised us from a distance, and seeing that we were rowing towards him, and his beloved sitting by his mother's side and on her right hand, he rushed joyfully down to his boat, and pushing it off, leaped in and rowed to meet us.

"When he came up to us, and he and his bride raised their eyes towards each other, the poor things scarcely knew what they were about for joy—they looked as if they could have flown, to rush the sooner into one another's arms. Joska guided his boat alongside of ours that we might step in, and coming to the bow, he stretched out his arms to Marcsa, who trembled like the delibab36 with joy and emotion.

> [36] The mirage, or *Fata Morgana*, frequently seen on the puszta, and which sometimes appears to tremble like a reflection in a troubled stream. The traveller is sometimes deceived by seeing a village or castle before him, which trembles and vanishes by degrees as he approaches.

"At that moment the boat overbalanced, and my brother suddenly fell between the two boats, and disappeared from our sight.

"The unhappy bride, who had stretched out her arms to the bridegroom for whom she had endured so much and worked so hard, uttered a fearful cry, and threw herself after him into the Theiss.

"My poor mother and I wrung our hands, and called for help, which brought out the millers from the other side, who hastened down to their boats, and put off towards us: in a short time they took up Marcsa, whose wide dress floated on the surface; but they could not find my brother, and we never saw anything more of him from that hour, except his wreathed bonnet37 floating on the water.

> [37] The Hungarian peasants in some districts wear small pointed hats, in form like the Tyrolian, always adorned with a wreath of flowers.

"Three days afterwards, my mother was struck with apoplexy, and the poor bride lay insensible in a violent fever. For six weeks she continued more dead than alive; and when at last she was able to rise, her beauty was all gone—you could scarcely have recognised her as the same person.

"For some time we only remarked that she was very sad and thoughtful, and would sit all day without speaking a word; but by and bye, to our astonishment, she would go down to the river, and when the miller's boys came over in their boats, would ask, 'What news from Joska bacsi?'

"At first we thought this was still only the effect of fever,—for during her illness she had raved incessantly of Joska; but as time wore on, and she was always doing stranger things, our eyes began to open to the melancholy truth. One day she went home, and telling us she was going to arrange her house, that it might be in order when Joska bacsi came, she began turning up all the chairs and tables, whitewashed the house, killed her little poultry one after the other, and then began cooking and baking to prepare for the wedding. All at once, however, she became quite distracted: knew no person by name, would speak aloud in the church, and pray and sing along the roads; she would do no work, and was indeed quite incapable—entangled all her yarn, saying she would get more money for it if in that condition, and set out empty egg-shells for market. At last, the wandering mania came upon her. One evening she disappeared from her house; and after searching everywhere for five days, we found her among high reeds by the river's side—her face disfigured, and her clothes all torn. Since that time, the poor creature has remained insane. Her beauty had passed away like the wind, and in four years she was the broken-down old woman you now see her, and that was full sixty years ago.

"Every one has now forgotten the event, for few are living who witnessed it; and the oldest man remembers her since his childhood as Crazy Marcsa, who minds neither cold nor hunger, fasts for days together and eats whatever is placed before her, collects every gaudy rag and sews it on her dress, calls old and young *nene* (elder sister), and asks but one question—'What news from Joska bacsi?'

"The folks laugh at her, but none know that her bridegroom lies below the Tisza water; and the merry girls in the spinning-rooms have little thought, when they make fun of Marcsa, that the wrinkled and fearful old creature was once as gay and smiling—ay, and prettier far than any of themselves. Such is life, good sir!"

The old man emptied his pipe: it was getting late. I thanked him for the tale, and pressing his hand, returned slowly and thoughtfully home.

"Strange, that a peasant should go mad for love! Only great folks can do that!"

I heard another case, in Bekes, of an idiot who was to all appearance a very quiet and industrious man. One could scarcely perceive any symptoms of insanity about him; but if the name Gyuri (George) were uttered in his hearing, he would start up—whether he was eating or working, or from whatever his employment might be—dash down his spoon or his saw, and run without stopping till he fell down from utter exhaustion.

Mischievous boys would sometimes make him run thus for their senseless amusement; at other times, the name, unguardedly dropped, would send him rushing to and fro: but otherwise, he was the quietest, gentlest creature in the world, and one might converse with him as with any other person.

His story was as follows:—

It happened once, that on a bright December day he and another shepherd boy had gone out to the plains with their flocks. It was a remarkable fine winter; there had been no frost as yet, and the whole plain was as green, and the sun as warm, as on a day in spring.

The two boys had driven their sheep to a great distance, when all at once, towards evening, a sharp and biting wind arose from the north. In an hour the weather had changed, and the horizon was overcast with heavy dark-blue clouds, which seemed angrily contending with the north wind. The ravens, those avant-couriers of the snowstorm, assembled in vast flocks, mingling their cries with the howling of the wind.

The shepherd boys hastily assembled their sheep, and began to drive them home. Scarcely had they proceeded a few hundred yards, however, when the horizon had completely darkened, the snow fell thickly, driven about by the wind, and in a few moments the path which guided them was covered. Meanwhile, the cold had sensibly increased, the ground was soon frozen quite hard, and the boys had lost all traces of their homeward way—they ran hither and thither, listening, and looking around them. No glimmering light was to be seen, nor the barking of a dog to be heard. Night had come on, and they had strayed into the puszta!

What was to be done? It was impossible to drive the sheep farther, for they crowded all in a heap, with their heads together.

"We will do like the sheep," said the herd-boys; and spreading their Izurok38 upon the ground, they lay down close to one another, endeavouring by the heat of their bodies to keep out the frost: and thus, with their arms clasped tightly round each other, they awaited the long stormy night, during which the snow never ceased an instant, and soon covered them both.

[38] The peasant's mantle of coarse white flannel.

Pista—so one of them was called—could not close his eyes all night: he heard the cries of the ravens incessantly above his head, and the roaring of the storm, which seemed hushed at intervals only to burst out more furiously, like the wrath of some huge monster, while the chill blast seemed to pierce him through, and turn his blood to ice. But his comrade Gyuri slept soundly, although he continually called in his ear in order to awake him; for he feared to listen to his heavy snoring, and to be alone awake. At length the sleeper ceased to snore, and breathed quietly for a time, till by degrees the breathing too became fainter and fainter.

When at last the fearful night had passed, and the clouds of snow had cleared away, and day began to break upon the hoary world, Pista tried to rise and wake his companion, who was still sound asleep, and kept his arms clasped tightly round his neck; but all his exertions could not wake him.

"Gyuri, awake!" he cried, shaking the sleeper; but Gyuri did not wake.

"Gyuri, awake!" he repeated in terror; but Gyuri's sleep was an eternal one—the boy was frozen.

When Pista saw that his comrade was dead, he tried in vain to release himself from his grasp; but the stiff dead arms were clasped so tightly round his neck, it was impossible to extricate them.

The terrified boy, finding himself face to face with the dead, who held him with such irresistible power in his fearful embrace, while the glazed and motionless eyes looked straight into his own, struggled fearfully through the snow, and dashed into the rushes, where the villagers who had come out to search for them most providentially found him, still crying out—"Gyuri, awake! Gyuri, let me go!"

They freed him with great difficulty from his companion's arms, but terror had deprived him of reason from that hour.

He never does any harm, or quarrels with anybody; and he speaks sensibly and quietly, unless his comrade's name is mentioned, when he will take to his heels and run as long as he has breath in his body.

Mental derangement does not always assume a melancholy form: here and there we meet with most grotesque examples, whose peculiar slyness and original ideas are most amusing. Outwardly they are always gay: who may know what passes within?

We had an instance of the latter species of madness in Transylvania. *Boho Boris* (silly Barbara) was known through the whole district.

She was never seen for one week in the same place, but wandered continually about; her whole travelling apparatus consisting of a guitar, which she slung around her neck, and went singing away to the next neighbour or the nearest town.

She found her table always covered; for she was quite at home in every gentleman's house, never waiting to be invited, and ordered all the servants about whether they would or not. Her apparel seemed to grow like the flowers of the meadow, without the assistance of tailors or *marchandes de modes,*—not that petticoats and ruffles actually sprang out of the earth on her account, but whenever she was tired of any article of apparel, or did not fancy wearing it longer, she would doff it at the first gentleman's house she came to, and put on a dress belonging to the lady of the mansion, declaring with the utmost gravity that it suited her very well; and the Transylvanian ladies were too generous not to leave her in her confidence, and in undisturbed possession of the new dress.

Once a great lady, Countess N— —, pitying poor Boris's uncertain mode of life, invited her to her castle, promising to keep her as long as she lived.

Now this good lady had one or two little peculiarities. In the first place, she was very sentimental, and always dreaming of some hero of romance; secondly, she was extremely sensitive, and if any person unmercifully wounded her tender heart, she was always sure to swoon away; and thirdly, having swooned away, she always waited till the whole household had assembled round her, and could not be brought to herself as long as one member of it failed.

Boho Biri being constantly with the Countess, had the full benefit of her eccentricities. This, however, did not seem to annoy her in the least: when the lady spoke of her love affairs, Boris spoke of her own; when the Countess sighed deeply, Boho Biri sighed still deeper; if the Countess described her injuries or her bitter fate in prose, Biri illustrated hers in verse; and when the Countess, overcome by her emotions, fainted away on a sofa, Boho Biri fainted on another, and always remained full half an hour longer in her swoon than the lady herself. If it were necessary to take cramp, when the Countess had only commenced, Boho Biri was already roaring so as to bring the whole household to the rescue.

Finally, however, it became too much for Boris. One day, taking up her guitar, and putting a roll in her pocket, she announced her intention to depart.

The good lady in astonishment asked why.

Boho Biri struck an accord on her guitar, and raising herself on the tips of her toes, she answered, with dignified composure: "Two fools are one too many in one house!"

COMORN

Monument of war! unhappy and deserted town! where are thy churches and thy towers—thy hospitable mansions and thy lively inhabitants? Where are the cheerful bells, calling the people to prayer, and the sound of music to mirth?

Alas! what a contrast from the proud fortress of former times, when the pinnacles of many a tower or steeple were seen glistening from afar, with their single and double crosses, their eagles and golden balls!

There were churches in Comorn unrivalled in Hungary for their beautiful frescoes. There was the great Universal Academy, opposite the Reformed Church; the old County-house, crowning three streets; the gigantic Town-hall; the great Military Hospital; the fine row of buildings on the Danube, which gave the town the air of a great city; the High Street, with its quaint edifices; the Calvary,39 and the romantic promenade in the centre of the town.

[39] In most Roman Catholic towns abroad, there is what is called a Calvary hill, with its fourteen *"stations of our Lord,"* and the crucifixion and chapel crowning the hill, whither the devout make little pilgrimages, and where they perform their devotions.

In the midst of the Danube there is a little island—whoever has seen it in former days, may have an idea of paradise! On crossing the bridge which united it to the town, an alley of gigantic palm-pines extended from one end of the island to the other, through which the rays of the sun gleamed like a golden network. The island was beautifully laid out in gardens, which furnished the town with fruit. In summer, the gay population held many a *fête* here.

Then in winter, when the cold confined the inhabitants to the town, what merriment and cheerfulness were to be seen everywhere! The young men of the district assembled for the Christmas tree and the Carnival festivities. Every mansion was open, and its hospitable landlord ready to receive alike rich and poor.

On Sundays and holidays, as soon as the early bells began to toll, a serious and well-conditioned population were seen crowding to the churches—the women in silken dresses, the men in rich pelisses fastened with heavy golden clasps; and when an offering was wanting, none were found remiss. At one oration by a popular preacher, the magnates deposited their jewelled clasps, buttons, and gold chains, in heaps at the threshold of the church; and with this gift the vast school was built which stood opposite the Reformed Church.

All this *was*—and is no more! Two-thirds of the edifices have been reduced to ashes; three churches—among them the double-towered one with the fine frescoes, the Town-hall, the County-house, the Hospital, the High Street, the Danube row, and the entire square, with more than a thousand houses, have been burnt to the ground! What remained was battered to pieces by the balls, and destroyed by the inundation and the ice in the following spring.

The beautiful island was laid waste, the trees cut down, and the bridge destroyed! Where are the joyous scenes of the past, the pleasant intercourse, and the gay society? The carnival music and the holiday bells are mute; the streets are empty, the houses roofless, and the people wretched!

It was a fearful night—raining, freezing, and blowing hard, while the shells were bursting over the town, and whistling like wingless demons through the midnight air. The congreve rocket ascended in its serpentine flight, shaking its fiery tail; while the heavy bomb rose higher and higher, trembling with the fire within, till, suddenly turning, it fell to the earth with a fearful crash, or, bursting in the air, scattered its various fragments far and wide upon the roofs below.

The szurok koszorus[40] descended like falling meteors, while here and there a fiery red ball darted up between them, like a star of destruction rising from hell. It seemed indeed as if the infernal regions had risen against heaven, and were venting their fury against the angels,—bringing down hosts of stars with the voice of thunder.

[40] Globes covered with tar, and filled with combustible matter.

Several houses on which the bombs descended had taken fire, and the wind carrying the sparks from roof to roof, a church, which had hitherto escaped destruction, was soon enveloped in flames. It was the Reformed Church. Some zealous partisans of this faith endeavoured to rescue their church; but they were few, and, after great exertions, amidst showers of balls, which whistled incessantly around, they succeeded at last in preventing the fire extending further, but there were not enough of hands to save the church—the flames had already reached the tower.

The light of the burning church gleamed far through the darkness on a troop of horsemen, who were hastening towards the fortress. They were hussars; their leader was a short, strong-built man, with light-brown hair and a ruddy complexion, which was heightened by the glare of the fire. His lips were compressed, and his eye flashed as he pointed towards the burning tower, and redoubled his speed. On reaching the Danube they were promptly challenged by the sentinel; and the leader, snatching a paper from his bosom, presented it to the officer on guard, who, after a hasty glance, saluted the stranger respectfully, and suffered the troop to pass across into the town.

At the extremity of the street which leads to the Vag,41 and where there was least danger to be apprehended from the enemy's battery, their progress was arrested by a crowd of men, principally officers of the national guard, who were standing gazing on the fire.

[41] Comorn is built at the junction of the Danube and the Vag.

The leader of the troop rode up to them, and inquired, in a voice of stern command, what their business was in that quarter.

"Who are you, sir?" replied a stout gentleman, with a large beard and a gold-braided pelisse, in a tone of offended dignity.

It was easy to judge by his appearance that he was one of those representative dignitaries, ever jealous of their authority before the military.

"My name is Richard Guyon!" replied the stranger; "henceforward commander of this fort. I ask again, gentlemen, what do you want here?"

At the mention of this name, some voices among the crowd cried, "Eljen!" (vivat!)

"I don't want Eljens," cried Guyon, "but deeds! Why are none of you assisting to extinguish the fire?"

"I beg your pardon, General," replied the municipal major sheepishly, assuming a parliamentary attitude before the commander, "but really the balls are flying so thickly in that direction, it would be only tempting Providence and throwing away lives in vain."

"The soldier's place is where the balls are flying—move on, gentlemen!"

"Excuse me, General, probably you have not witnessed it; but really the enemy are firing in such an unloyal manner, not only bombs of a hundred and sixty pounds' weight, and shells which burst in every direction, but also grenades, and fiery balls of every description, which are all directed against those burning houses." The worthy major endeavoured to introduce as much rhetoric as possible into his excuses.

"Will you go, sir, or will you not?" cried the General, cutting short his oration, and drawing a pistol from his saddle bow, he deliberately pointed it at the forehead of the argumentative major, indicating that his present position was as dangerous as the one he dreaded in the midst of bombs and fiery balls.

"Mercy!" he stammered; "I only wished to express my humble opinion."

"I am not used to many words. In the hour of danger, I command my men to *follow*, not to *precede* me; whoever has any feeling of honour has heard my words;" and, dashing his spurs into his horse, he galloped forward.

In a few seconds the place was empty—not a man remained behind. An hour afterwards, thousands were eagerly working to extinguish the fire. The commander himself, foremost in the danger, seemed to be everywhere at once; wherever the balls flew thickest and the fire raged most furiously, his voice was heard exciting and encouraging his men. "Never mind the balls, my lads, they never strike those who do not fear them."

At that instant the aide-de-camp at his side was struck down by a twenty-four pounder. The General, without being discouraged by this *mal-à-propos* sequel to his words, only added—"Or when they do, it is a glorious death!"

A universal "Eljen!" rose above the thunder of the cannon and the howling of the elements.

"On, lads! save the spire!" continued the General.

The bells of the tower had already fallen, one by one, into the church, but the fire was visibly decreasing, and the people redoubled their exertions, working hard until the morning. Their efforts were crowned with success; and the tower, with its great metal spire, stands to this day; thanks to the energy and courage of the hero of Branyisko.42

[42] In Upper Hungary, where Guyon obtained a victory.

The day following, the principal officers of the fort hastened to present themselves to their commander. He reproached them for their negligence in allowing the fortress to be bombarded by troops which were scarcely more than the garrison of the place, and quietly suffering them to place their batteries on the hill opposite, from whence they fired incessantly into the town. The officers retired in great confusion, promising their commander that the evil should soon be repaired.

The town dignitaries next made their appearance, to pay their respects to the new governor—a most honourable set of periwigged worthies dating from 1790. The General received them graciously, and invited all those who had called on him to dinner, assuring them, in broken Hungarian, that they should have capital entertainment.

Everybody was charmed with the condescension and affability of the future commander; although, "It must be allowed," they added, "he treats the Magyar language with as little mercy as he does our enemies."

"If our *vis-à-vis* would only give us peace for a time," remarked the above-mentioned municipal major, who, in consideration of his official dignity, was desirous of keeping on good terms with the commander. The rest of the worthy gentlemen present signified, by their gestures, that they considered the remark not altogether unreasonable.

The major, judging by Guyon's thoughtful expression that he was duly considering the matter, ventured to add his humble opinion, that it might be advisable to propose a cessation of hostilities on the day of the entertainment, in order to celebrate in peace, and with all due honours, the arrival of their most excellent commander.

"It would be useless," replied the General, calmly, "for they would not give it."

"In that case," replied the major, "there is a spacious hall in the subterranean apartments of the bastions, where two hundred might dine commodiously."

"Indeed!" replied the General.

"Certainly; and plenty of room for a band of music besides."

"And cannot the bombs get in there?"

"O dear! no—not even the hundred and sixty pounders; the vaulted roof is strong an a rock, besides twelve feet of rock above. We can eat, drink, and give toasts," continued the major, "to our heart's content; the band may play, and the young folk dance, without endangering a hair of our heads!"

"Ah! a capital idea, truly! Perhaps you have already given *fêtes* there?"

"Oh, almost every day in winter; while the enemy were raising entrenchments over our heads, and trying their best to throw shells into the town, we were dancing quite snugly under the ramparts, and only laughing at them through the loopholes—ha, ha, ha!"

The major seemed to consider this an excellent joke, while the other dignitaries were cutting wry faces, recollecting that on such occasions but few, and those not the *élite*, remained without to protect the fort.

The General neither laughed nor looked displeased; he appeared satisfied with the major's plan, and dismissed the deputation, promising them that the next day's entertainment should be the most agreeable they had ever yet partaken of.

At the hour appointed, a large party, in gala costumes and with holiday demeanour, assembled in the pavilion of the fort.

The General received his guests with his usual cordiality, and, as soon as the attendants announced that the banquet was prepared, he invited them to accompany him thither.

It was a glorious spring evening. The soldiers greeted the brilliant *cortège* with loud "Eljens!" as they passed the gates of the castle.

Among the guests was our bearded major, who took the utmost pains to insinuate himself into the good graces of the General, constantly addressing him in the most facetious manner, so that those who heard the conversation might have supposed they were on the most intimate footing possible.

"Your excellency is pleased to survey the ramparts?" he remarked in the softest tone imaginable, which he had learnt as a lord-lieutenant.

"I surveyed them all early this morning," replied the General; "they are in good condition."

"Especially that one which your excellency was pleased to hear me mention yesterday."

"And where we are going to dine to-day," pursued the General.

"He, he! indeed!" The major was ready to burst with pride. "I am truly flattered, rejoiced, that my humble opinion has met with your excellency's approbation."

They had now entered the court of the old fortress. The bastion in question, with its gigantic, massive walls, is built over the Danube. Its roof is protected by the high walls of the fortress, which, covered with beautiful green turf, formed the most agreeable promenade possible. To the east of the bastion there was a small rondella, where the former governor, Bakonyi, was in the habit of spending his leisure hours with his friends in those good old times when people lived on more friendly terms than they do now.

There were placed before this rondella about half a dozen tables, sumptuously covered with superb confections and flowers, relieved by bottles of every description.43

[43] In Hungary, as on the Continent in general, the dessert is put down at first, to decorate the table.

The rondella itself was tastefully decorated with evergreens and banners of the national colours.

The approaching guests perceived these tables laid out on the top of the bastion, with a curious sensation, unlike that which we are wont to experience at the sight of a dinner-table under ordinary circumstances. The major alone did not seem to take the matter into consideration, and, turning to the entrance of the bastion tunnel, he officiously offered his services to lead the way to the subterranean hall.

"Not there!" cried the General, "but upon the top of the bastion! Do you not perceive, gentlemen, our tables are prepared there?"

The major attempted to smile, but his teeth chattered.

"Your excellency is pleased to jest, he! he!—surely the hall is far pleasanter, and more convenient."

"Are you dreaming, major? lock one's-self up this beautiful evening in a dank hole, where scarce a ray of light enters two spans of loophole! It would be sinning against nature; here in the open air we shall enjoy ourselves famously!"

The major would willingly have been excused such enjoyment.

"And are we all to dine up there?" he asked, while his chin trembled visibly.

"Certainly, of course," replied the General; and perceiving it was one of those occasions in which the word *follow* must be substituted for *on*, he deliberately ascended the steps to the bastion, his guests reluctantly following, more like a troop of victims brought to unwilling martyrdom, than a festal procession approaching a banquet.

The municipal major not only relinquished his position close to the General's ear, but actually managed to fall behind—evidently evincing an inclination to make himself scarce when the opportunity should offer. The General's condescension, however, was so great as to seek him out, take his arm, and lead on to the ramparts, where he engaged him in close conversation.

"What a glorious view! See how the Danube washes the walls of the bastion! Mark the enemy's ramparts, where the great guns are pointed towards us—why, we can actually see into them! There stand the howitzers, and a bomb-mortar—remarkably clear atmosphere, major! See now, an artilleryman has just come out on the ramparts; one can distinguish his facings perfectly, even at that distance! Superb weather, major, is it not?"

It is quite certain that if the General had not forcibly retained his man, keeping him in conversation until they sat down to dinner, the worthy major would have slipped through his fingers like an eel; as it was, there was no other course for him but to resign himself to his fate, while he heartily wished that this transparent atmosphere would give place to so dense a fog, that they should not be able to distinguish each other across the table.

The guests had taken their places with no small uneasiness, each eyeing his neighbour's countenance, in the vain hope of discovering some degree of that confidence which he lacked himself—but resignation was the utmost that could be traced in any expression.

The General placed the major on his right hand: he was desirous of distinguishing him in his military dress.

Meanwhile, as the dishes were served and the wine circled, the spirits of the guests began to rise, and the clouds of uneasiness which had darkened each brow dissipated by degrees before the inward light which the good wine diffused. The conversation flowed more freely; some even ventured to jest, afterwards to laugh heartily.

The unhappy major alone did not seem to partake of the universal dissipation. He elbowed his loquacious neighbour with tears in his eyes, trod on the feet of his *vis-à-vis* under the table, accompanying these actions with an imploring gesture that they should speak and laugh less loudly; while he himself used his knife and fork with the utmost caution, looking every now and then over his shoulder at the cannon, howitzers, and artillerymen opposite—now spilling the soup down his neck, and now conveying to his ear the morsel intended for his mouth, or biting the empty fork from which the meat had fallen, while he sprinkled large quantities of cayenne and salt over the confections, and finally drank the vinegar intended for the salad, to the infinite amusement of the spectators. Even the General regarded his victim with inward satisfaction, though it was not his custom to express any visible emotion. He frequently recommended him one or other excellent wine; but the major would not be persuaded to drink anything but water, which he swallowed in large quantities, declaring that he was exceedingly warm—which was not improbable.

At the height of the entertainment, when the roses of good humour bloomed on every countenance, the major summoned all his resolution, and sidling close up to the commander, whispered in his ear: "It is very well that the besiegers are dining also at present, and therefore have not observed us, otherwise it might be no joke if they caught a glimpse of us."

"True; the poor devils would then have to leave their dinners, and amuse themselves firing at us."

The major would gladly have been excused such amusement.

"Meanwhile," pursued the commander, "we shall give them a toast;" and pouring out a glass of genuine tokay, he rose from his seat.

There was a universal silence.

"Gentlemen!" cried the governor, in a loud clear voice, "let us drink to the land of the Magyar!"

A tremendous cheer burst from every mouth, and the guests rising, struck their glasses together. Every idea of fear seemed banished at the word. Three times three the cheer was repeated, with such thundering applause that the very bastion trembled.

The poor major extended his arms in utter despair: he looked like a man vainly endeavouring to stifle the explosion of a revolution; and to add to his distress, scarcely had the third cheer died away, than the military music which was concealed in the rondella struck up the Rakoczy March.

"We are betrayed! we are undone!" he exclaimed, throwing himself violently back in his chair. "Sir Governor, Sir Commander, now is the moment for us to leave the place! The enemy's guns are directed towards us—we shall have the bombs pouring upon us!"

"That would be only giving ourselves trouble," replied the General coolly; "and besides, I should like to see how they aim."

"But I don't want to see; my life is not my own, it belongs to my country. It is not permitted to risk it thus; the Diet would not allow it."

"Set your mind at ease, my dear major; I will take the whole responsibility of your precious life before the Diet. Meanwhile, orders have been given that none shall quit the bastion until I go myself."

The major's anguish was not altogether without foundation; for the music having attracted the attention of the besiegers, their cannon began firing one by one, and several balls whistled past the revellers.

"Aha! in this case we must protect ourselves," cried the General; and without moving from his seat, he desired his attendants to prepare the battery.

This battery consisted of champagne bottles well preserved in ice, the popping of which most ludicrously parodied the cannons of the enemy, while the generous wine increased the good humour of the reckless company.

The music continued to play one national air after another; as soon as the first band ceased another struck up, the company joining their voices in full chorus to the most familiar airs.

Meanwhile the bombs were falling right and left: some, splashing into the Danube, burst at the bottom, or without extinguishing, struck the water again and again. Others whistled past the pavilion, and burst above it; but none as yet came near the tables.

The merry party made light of it all, crying "good speed" to those which flew over their heads, offering a glass to renew their strength, promising to let down ropes to such as fell into the moat. In short, what they had looked upon with awe from a distance, they now considered capital diversion.

The poor major suffered the most exquisite pangs of terror: bobbing his head each time a shell flew over the ramparts at the distance of a hundred fathoms, or starting aside from the passing balls; and as often as a bomb burst, he almost fell on his back in the most violent contortions.

Meanwhile, as the day closed, the sounds of music, as well as the beauty of the evening, had attracted various groups of well-dressed people to the ramparts; and notwithstanding the thundering of the cannon, the fair sex formed no small portion of the curious, whose desire of amusement overcame their timidity.

The moon rose brilliantly upon the landscape; and by its bewitching light the youth abandoned themselves to the dance, with as little thought as if the thundering around were a salute in honour of a bridal festival.

The national dance seemed especially to please the General; and once, when he expressed his admiration by a hearty 'bravo' at some dexterous turn, a merry little dark-eyed sylph tripped up to him, and succeeded in leading him forth to the "Wedding of Tolna"—a favourite dance, where he allowed himself to be wheeled about through all the mazes, performing each manœuvre required of him with that almost English coolness which characterized him.

A little episode now occurred, which caused a short interruption. A grenade fell burning, almost at the feet of the General. Several of the dancers fled, while the boldest of the party wished to pour water over it, and others in jest proposed to cover it with a hat.

"Let all remain in their places!" cried the General.

At this command everybody remained stationary. Even the women endeavoured to conceal their fear, and one or two of the girls peeped inquisitively forward, scarcely comprehending the danger with which they were threatened.

The bearded major, however, seemed fully alive to all the horror of his situation; for no sooner did the grenade fall hissing among them, than he broke at once through all constraint, and with a roar like a bull, as if in compensation for all he had hitherto endured in silence, rushed from the spot as if he were possessed by legion, and without looking right or left, precipitated himself into the moat, regardless of its height. Providentially he reached the bottom, at a depth of four-and-twenty feet, with bones unbroken, and there lay upon his stomach, with closed eyes, awaiting the issue of the hideous catastrophe.

The grenade meanwhile turned quickly round like a spinning-top on the spot where it had fallen, the rocket flame from within describing a bright circle round it. The bystanders breathlessly awaited the moment of its explosion.

Suddenly it ceased turning, and the fiery circle disappeared. Whoever is acquainted with the nature of these balls, will know, that between the spinning round of the grenade-rocket in its flame and that instant in which— the spark having reached the powder—it explodes, there is an interval of a few seconds, in which the grenade stands still.

In this interval it was that the commander suddenly rose, and approaching the grenade, lifted it in his hands and dashed it into the moat.

The sudden explosion which instantly followed proved that the ball had just been thrown in time, while the yell which immediately succeeded seemed to indicate that the direction had not been equally well chosen; and in truth the grenade had burst scarcely two spans from the unlucky major, although, strange to say, with no more serious consequence than that from that day forward he has heard with difficulty with the right ear.

After this little bravado—whose authenticity more than one eye-witness can guarantee—the General allowed the company to disperse; and from that day fear seemed banished from all hearts; and grenades, and other fiery implements, were looked upon with even greater coolness than before.

On taking leave of his guests, the General promised them a tranquil night, to compensate for the agitation of the day; and he was as good as his word, for that very night he made a sally with some troops above the Nadorvonal,44 and compelled the enemy to withdraw their battery.

[44] Palatine's line.

Time flies; the past is gradually forgotten, and with it the past glory. Where are the glorious hopes—the bright dreams? All are gone. Comorn! monument of war! deserted and unhappy town! what remains of all thy power and glory? The blackened ruins, and the Comorn Honved officers!45

[45] When the fortress capitulated, the officers of the national guard were suffered to quit the country free—one of the conditions for which they had stipulated.

MOR PERCZEL

In the January of 1848 it had not yet entered the most speculative imagination that war might break out before the year had ended. Our humane patriots thought of anything in the world rather than of the manufacture of gunpowder; and when, during some unusually riotous municipal elections, one or two of our noble countrymen were shot through the head, the papers, for several weeks afterwards, were full of comments on the horrors of such unheard-of bloodshed.

It was about this time that the journals were much occupied with the wonders of a certain magnetic somnambulist, who foretold various strange things, which, to the astonishment of all who heard them, actually came to pass.

She foretold, among other things, the ruin of Comorn! Unhappy town! it might have been well for her if all her misfortunes had been included in this prophecy, but alas! her fate was doomed to exceed even this, in the direful results of the siege. Another of the prophecies of the somnambulist was, that the country should be visited by cholera, and that those whom it carried off would be the happiest.

When Mor (Morice) Perczel was sent as deputy to Presburg, he was obliged to pass a night at Vacz, where he heard so much of this marvellous somnambulist that he determined not to leave the place without seeing her, and accordingly he got an acquaintance to escort him in the evening to her lodging.

On entering the apartment, he beheld, by the dim light of a lamp, a very young girl, whose extreme paleness gave her an almost supernatural appearance; her face was thin, and her skin transparent; her eyes, which were very large, and of a pure blue, were half closed, and her lips and hands trembled exceedingly.

She was lying motionless in a large arm-chair; and her physician had just entered. He had recommended the use of magnetism for the cure of spasms at the heart, and it was now the sixth week that she had been under the magnetic influence. She was seldom awake, but still seldomer asleep; her usual state being something between the two—a constant unconscious reverie, accompanied by acute sensibility to the pleasure or pain of others, and a total absence of personal feeling. As her physician approached, and she came within the magnetic influence, she slowly opened her eyes, and fixed them steadfastly on his face without moving her eyelids. When he took her hand, a cold, faint smile passed over her countenance, and the trembling ceased; her physician then began to stroke her face, arms, and breast, with the tips of his fingers, at first slowly, but quickening the motion by degrees, while he kept his eyes steadily fixed upon his patient.

The girl continued motionless; her eyelids alone seemed to contend with the irresistible power which always gained upon her, closing by degrees and then opening wide again, while the pupils were unusually dilated.

Her whole countenance gradually underwent a wonderful change: her features assumed a character inexpressibly sweet and sad; she sighed and wept, her lips parted, while a calm smile settled on them. At last, her head sank on the cushion of her chair, and she fell asleep.

The physician now motioned to Mor Perczel to approach within the magnetic circle. Suddenly the girl's countenance assumed an expression of surprise and uneasiness.

"Who is this?" asked the physician, in a low, familiar tone.

The girl answered slowly, and with hesitation, "One of—our future—greatest leaders!"

Perczel smiled. "Perhaps in the camp of the Diet," he thought to himself.

"No, not in the Diet," replied the girl, to whom he had not communicated his thoughts; "on the field of battle!"

"And what fate awaits him there?" asked the physician.

"Let him beware of his own name!"

Before the termination of that year, Mor Perczel was a General in the Hungarian rebel army, had raised troops, and fought several battles, without ever recalling the prophecy of the Vaczi girl.

It was on the 30th December that the memorable action near Mor46 took place, in which the Hungarians were defeated with considerable loss.

[46] South-west of Pesth, in the county of Stuhlweissenberg.

The real cause of the loss of this battle has never been clearly proved up to the present day. It was enough, and more than enough to Perczel, that the battle was lost, his troops scattered, his positions occupied, his colours taken, and the gallant Zrinyi battalion, the flower of his army, cut to pieces or taken prisoners.

When he returned to Pesth after this battle, one of the town magistrates, ever ready with a jest, maliciously observed, "Ocsem47 Mor, your namesake did not receive you well."

[47] Nephew—younger brother.

"Indeed!" replied the General, without taking offence, "now I remember, that the somnambulist foretold me this just a year ago. If I did not believe that Görgei was the cause of our losing the battle, I should be inclined to think there had been witchcraft in it. Well, the Germans shall keep their name's-day by and bye!"

After this loss, the Hungarians were obliged to retreat from Pesth. The Government and treasury were removed to Debrecsen, and Perczel was intrusted with their escort thither.

Having accomplished this, he advanced with a small army towards Szolnok, where the enemy had encamped, and were fortifying themselves during the cold season.

One fine misty morning, Perczel crossed the Tisza48 on the ice to the enemy's nearest position, and, opening fire upon them, obliged them to retreat to Czegled, whither he pursued them.

[48] Szolnok is built on the river Tisza, or Theiss.

The imperial troops had just crossed a village vineyard. Perczel saw the last dragoon disappear behind the acacia trees which skirted it, and, striking his spurs into his horse, he ordered his troops to advance, that the enemy might not escape them.

At that moment he was arrested by a stranger, who unceremoniously rode up to him, and, seizing his mantle, accosted him in French.

"N'allez pas là!" said the unknown, pointing to the vineyards.

The General looked at him in astonishment. The stranger was an old man, simply attired en civile, but there was something peculiarly striking in his martial air and keen glance.

"And why should I not go there?" asked Perczel.

"The enemy will bring you into a snare!"

"I should like to see that."

"You will see it. Behind those vineyards there is undoubtedly a concealed battery, from which you will receive a cross fire."

"Why do you imagine this?"

"Because it follows naturally from the position."

"Ah! we must not let our apprehensions retain us on such grounds; we have no time to speculate," cried the General, and, shaking off the importunate stranger, he once more galloped forward.

They were now scarcely a thousand paces from the vineyards. A Suabian peasant, whose cart had been overturned in endeavouring to pass the artillery, was standing by the roadside, uttering lamentations over his damaged goods.

"What village is that, good fellow?" asked Perczel out of mere curiosity, pointing to the village at the foot of the vineyards.

"Perczel!" replied the boor.

"That is I," said the General; "but I asked you the name of that village."

"May be your excellency is called after it, for its name has been Perczel since the beginning of the world."

The General stopped short. The words of the somnambulist recurred to him; he looked round for the old man—he was riding among the troops.

Perczel motioned to him to approach, and said, "Do you really believe that there is a battery concealed behind those vineyards?"

"I am certain of it. The slightest experience in tactics might determine that."

"And accordingly you consider the position unattainable."

"On the contrary—but on such occasions it is usual to make a *détour*."

"For which a very rapid movement were requisite, and our infantry is too much fatigued."

"We can manage that; intrust me with a battalion of infantry and two squadrons of cavalry, and wait here in reserve until I start the game from its cover."

"Do so," said the General, and, giving some directions to his aide-de-camp, he watched the stranger's movements with interest.

The old man put the infantry in the hussars' stirrups, and conducted them with the utmost expedition across the wood.

The idea was as natural as that of Columbus in regard to the egg, and yet it had occurred to no one before.

In a few minutes the rapid discharge of musketry announced that the stranger had not been mistaken; and the batteries, which were actually lying in ambush behind the hill, appeared retreating from either side.

Perczel then advanced with the reserve to meet his troops. They returned in triumph with the little, grayhaired stranger, who rode calmly on as if nothing had happened, his brow still blackened with the smoke from the gunpowder. The troops could not sufficiently extol his coolness and intrepidity.

"I owe you much," said Perczel, not ashamed to acknowledge the stranger's superiority. "May I know whom I have the honour of addressing?"

"My name is Henry Dembinszki," replied the stranger coldly.

Perczel respectfully saluted him, and placed the marshal's baton in his hand. "It is your due; henceforward let *me* serve in your ranks."

GERGELY SONKOLYI

After all, it cannot be denied that my uncle, Gergely Sonkolyi, was an excellent man; and how well I remember him, as he hunted me in the forest through bush and brake, while I never expected to rest until we had made the circuit of the world.

I think I see him still, his cornelian-wood brass-headed cane in his hand, and his cherry-wood pipe with its acorn-shaped bowl, which he never took out of his mouth, even when he scolded—and with what eloquence he could anathematize the sons of men! the raging of the elements is like the notes of a clarionet in comparison! I was not one who considered courage, under all circumstances, as a peculiar virtue; and as soon as I perceived the storm gathering, I no longer took the matter in jest, but looking about for the first loophole, valiantly took to my heels, trusting to their speed to place me beyond its reach.

But in order to explain why my uncle, Gergely Sonkolyi, hunted me through the forest, I must turn up an early letter in the alphabet of memory, and begin my story at the usual point—namely, the beginning.

When? I cannot precisely state the date; though so far I may confidently affirm,—it was after the French war, and before the cholera, that I was turned out of school in disgrace.

Ah yes, I behaved very ill indeed! I sinned against civilisation by refusing to wear square-toed boots, and for this enormity I was banished from the classes; and yet, nothing could induce me to wear anything but sharp-nosed csizmas.

I went home; and my father, after inflicting severe corporal punishment, threatened to bind me apprentice to a butcher. But, unfortunately for this speculation, the resident executioner of oxen declared that the trade required wit; otherwise I might now have possessed a two-story house in Pesth.

"You hit where you have your eye, master, don't you?" I asked the worthy slayer of cattle as he raised his axe, observing (for he squinted hideously) that he fixed his right eye on the bullock, and the left one on me.

"Eh! to be sure I do," replied the big man.

"Then I will just place myself beside you," I said, fearing he might look out of the wrong eye.

"Never fear," said the big man; and with one blow the work was done.

"Well now, Master Janos, tell me what peculiar talents are requisite here?"

"Heigh! you would not do for this trade. You see we have a different way of reckoning from what you students have."

"I believe you are right, Master Janos; for my mother is always complaining of your system of twice two."

And now this man is a landed proprietor, and I—a landless one!

Having been rejected by the schoolmaster and the butcher, I was considered a hopeless subject, and left to my own devices. What should I do at home? From morning till evening there was not wherewithal to stain my teeth; so for want of better employment, I began to look about the village. This certainly did not require much genius, for our house was on an eminence, from whence we had a view of the whole place; and when I mounted the great corn-stack in our yard, I could see directly into some of our neighbours' courts.

Here it was that I became initiated in certain hidden mysteries,—for example, how some of our village dames, who would launch forth on holidays all smartness and finery, were up to their elbows in dirt at home, and to their knees in mud—their heads vying with those unowned hay-stacks which are kicked at by every passing colt; while their lips, which were so daintily prim on holiday occasions that one could scarcely believe them capable of pronouncing the letter R, now raised the very dust on the roads with their abuse.

Then there was a house which had two doors to it; and whenever the goodman made his exit at the one door, somebody else entered by the other.

At another house, whenever the master came home late, his wife laid his dinner outside, upon the millstone table, with the servants; and the best of the matter was, that with this too familiar exception, he was held in vast respect by the whole household.

All this was very well to contemplate from a distance; but I happened at last to stumble upon something, a nearer view of which would have been by no means disagreeable to me.

Our next neighbour was my excellent uncle, Gergely Sonkolyi. His house was pretty ancient; and I remember, in my childish days, pulling the reeds49 out of the roof to look for sugar. In those days the walls were painted partly blue and partly yellow; but afterwards the old man had them all rough-cast, and then it was not necessary to paint them again.

[49] Reeds—*nad*. Cane sugar is called *nad czukor*.

The house lay below the garden, and there were little plots before the windows, which were always filled with bouquets of musk and carrot flowers; and from a square hole in the roof sundry bunches of pepper blushed forth, in the warlike vicinity of an outstretched scythe.

Several large mulberry trees in the court-yard formed a roosting-place for the poultry; and opposite the kitchen door was the entrance to the wine-cellar, over which hung a variety of pumpkins. Beyond this was a large pigeon-house, farther on a pig-sty, then a two-yard measure, then a draw-well; while various implements of industry appeared in the perspective—such as ploughs, harrows, waggons, &c. And if to all these I add nine dogs, two speckled bullocks, and a flock of geese, I have before me a very perfect view of my Uncle Sonkolyi's court-yard.

The nine dogs kept watch at the entrance when my uncle was not hunting, feasting in imagination upon the savoury odour of gulyas-hus50 which issued from the grated door of the kitchen, where a large fire burned incessantly in the broad grate, with various huge pots hissing among the flames, while a squadron of linen servants,51 each one redder than the other, hurried to and fro under the direction of old Mrs. Debora.

[50] The herd's meat; a hash composed of beef, with various spices, and a quantity of onions and pepper.

[51] The kitchen-maids and boys wear linen dresses, and wide linen drawers.

Beyond the kitchen were several other apartments, for a description of which I must refer my readers to the county chronicles, where all such goods and chattels are particularly delineated. For my part, I only remember the little back room, with its large white stove, the old eight-day clock, two great tent-beds standing side by side, a double-leaved oak table in the middle of the room, and the history of Joseph and his brethren on the walls. A casement door, opening inside, disclosed another chamber, whose walls were hung with hunting-bags, whips, bugles, swords, and saddle accoutrements, each one more rusty than another. But among all these reminiscences, the most interesting in my regard is an old black leather sofa: ah! it was on that very old sofa—but I must not anticipate.

Well, it was here that my dear uncle lived—the honourable and nobly-born Gergely Sonkolyi.

But he might have lived here or anywhere else for aught I might have known or cared, had it not been for the prettiest—the very prettiest little girl that mortal eyes e'er rested on.

She was the old man's daughter. Little Esztike was a most lovely creature: often, very often did sleep forsake me thinking of her, although I still oftener dreamt of her—of those small soft hands, and those large dark eyes, one half glance of which I would not have exchanged for the Chinese emperor's finest cap. I was never tired of standing guard all day long on the top of the corn-stack, from whence I could see my little darling when she came out to the court to water her flowers, or feed her doves. Each motion, each turn—in short, everything about her, was so engaging and so attractive, that I often forgot while watching her whether it was morning or evening.

But all this was not sufficient for happiness: it was like sucking the honey through the glass, to dream of so much sweetness.

I would have given kingdoms, had I possessed them, to any one who would have helped me with good counsel; but good counsels are not mushrooms, growing where they are not sown.

Everybody knew that my uncle, Gergely Sonkolyi, was a peculiar man,—who did not understand a joke in certain matters, and had a strange fancy of never allowing any of the male sex to approach within nine paces of his daughter. "Whoever wanted to marry her" (this was his argument) "will ask for her; and if not, he shall not make a fool of her." And his usual reply to suitors for his daughter's hand was: "Will you have her to-day, nephew, or wait till to-morrow?" indicating that she was still very young, and not fit for the charge of a *ménage*. But all this I considered a very matter-of-fact view of life; and I must confess that it annoyed me extremely at the time, though afterwards I acknowledged he was right.

Notwithstanding my uncle's caution, however, there were times when I contrived to make little Esztike sensible of my feelings towards her. But there was one terrible fatality—that old Mrs. Debora, who never moved from home, but kept watch for ever, like a dragon over treasure; and wo to the unhappy youth who dared to visit Esztike—there were few who had courage to make a second trial.

Some said that this Mistress Debora was a sister of the old man; others, that she was his wife. Indeed she might have been his grandmother, for she looked older than the Visegradi tower.[52]

[52] An ancient fortress on the Danube.

It was six whole years since I had shaken the school dust from my boots, and still the gates of paradise were barred against me.

One evening, when the old gentleman had gone out, I could no longer control my impatience; and leaping over the garden wall, I slipped to the back of the house, where I could at least see the windows of the room in which Esztike sat; and there I stood, with a beating heart, and eyes fixed on the shadow of a hand which I distinctly saw through the muslin curtains, moving up and down at some needle-work, while I actually devoured it with my eyes.

Suddenly the hand advanced and knocked violently at the window; it was impossible not to see that it was intended for me, and, while I was hesitating whether to fly towards it or from it, the window burst open, and I thought the Egyptian seven years of leanness had thrust its head out—it was Mistress Debora!

"What do you want there, you good-for-nothing, long-legged horihorgas,53 staring like a calf at a new gate, eh? Get along about your business, or I will set the dogs after you; if you have nothing better to do, go and seek for grass to make your wisdom-teeth grow;" and with this compliment she closed the window violently.

[53] "Horihorgas," *hobbledehoy.*

It was several minutes ere I could collect my scattered senses. At last, I drew my cap over my eyes, and went home with a heavy heart. I lay gazing all night at the starry heavens; the very thought of sleep was banished from my senses. How could it be otherwise? as often as I tried to think of my little Esztike's beautiful face, the hideous vision of old Mistress Debora rose before me; and to increase my ill humour, all the cats in the neighbourhood seemed to have collected to squall and trill under my window. I contented myself for some time with patiently anathematizing them; but perceiving at last that they were rehearsing operas from end to end, I jumped up, and, seizing a rolling-pin—the first implement which came to my hand, I dashed it amongst the choristers. It was certainly a theatrical stroke, and from that night forward I never had cause to repeat it.

Next morning, however, the black soup54 awaited me. My father entered the room, with his fox-headed mantle over one shoulder and his lambskin cap drawn over his brow.

[54] "Black soup" or black dose, *désagrément.*

"Well, my lad, you have done for yourself now," he exclaimed; "you knocked out the brains of Mrs. Debora's pet cat last night."

"Phu! this is a bad job indeed! Is there actually no life in him?"

"All gone, *ab intestato,*" said my father, holding up the great fat animal, with its four legs hanging down, and its white teeth grinning at me.

I shook my head in despair. If Mistress Debora ever finds this out, there is an end to all hope, and I shall never be able to marry. Alas! why did I allow the cats to put me out of temper? A thought suddenly struck me, and, dressing hastily, I laid the deceased neatly, out in my handkerchief, and, tying up the four corners, started for Mistress Debora's.

At the gate, I found the nine dogs disputing with a Jew, in whose cloak they had made sundry air-holes, while the unfortunate man roared and struggled, to the infinite amusement of the servants.

This was so far propitious for me, as otherwise they might have required my passport also, and it would have been no jesting matter to have struck my uncle's dogs; but happily I got through the kitchen without observation, and looking once more at the four corners, to see that all was right, I knocked humbly at Mistress Debora's door.

"Who is there?" said a voice like the sound of broken crockery.

I opened the door. At the memorable window sat Mistress Debora, who turned round and squinted at me from beneath her spectacles. Her hair—or more probably some other person's—was twisted up behind with a giraffe comb, and the face, which was the colour of brown leather, had more wrinkles than could well find room.

At the other window sat my little ruby at her work. There was not much to be seen from her window, poor child! for a large vetch-stack was piled up before it. As I entered, she blushed to the very shoulders, or at least I fancied so; but her eyes were cast down, and she never ventured to raise them.

"Well, what have you got there?" said Mistress Debora,—instead of wishing me good morning.

I advanced, and, taking up her bony fingers, pressed them against my teeth—bah! I have never been able to pick a bone since. "Ah! my dear, worthy aunt, have you forgotten me? I am that little, fair-haired Peter Csallokozi, who used to bring young pigeons so often to his dear aunt."

"And who used to break my windows so often with pebbles. Well, you have grown big enough, at any rate."

"But my dear aunt has preserved her looks quite wonderfully, or rather I should say, grows younger."

"Ay, I was handsome enough in my day; folks can tell you that I used to wash my face every evening with warm milk, which made my skin so white, one can see that still—(it required imagination); there is not so handsome a girl in the country as I was in my young days—your father may remember that—('when you were young the priest was not born that christened my father,' thought I, but did not say it). For some years past I have lost much of my looks, certainly. Ay, ay, there is nothing lasting under the sun!"

Meanwhile I had been drawing nearer to Esztike, which the dragon observing, desired her to go out and see if the labourers were come. Esztike rose and went out.

"Well, let me hear what you have to say, nephew; and tell it quickly, for we are always busy here."

"To come to the point then, I must observe, dear aunt, that in these days we cannot be too cautious; misfortune meets us at every step, and" —

"Therefore we should stay at home and mind our business. Nothing can happen to us at home."

"Not to ourselves perhaps, but there are other creatures about us, aunt; for instance, you have cats and so have we" —

"Only that ours are handsomer."

"Perfectly true. Well, these cats frequently pay visits—yours to ours, and ours to yours" —

"I know that well enough, for your cats gnaw all the sausages in our attics; but ours don't need to go to you, for they have enough to eat at home. Go, Estike," continued the hag, as the little girl re-entered, "and see if the young peacocks have been fed."

("A time will come, you old witch, when I shall crack nuts with your bones," thought I, but did not say it.) "Well, dear aunt, last night, as I was saying, these innocent creatures had assembled, and were singing away together—it was quite delightful to hear them—when some cruel and treacherous hand knocked out the brains of the handsomest among them."

"Served you right! what business had the cat to be out?"

"It was not our cat that was killed, but yours, dear aunt," I replied, untying the handkerchief, and producing the remains of her favourite.

I shall never forget the look of rage, despair, and horror, which I was doomed to encounter at that moment, and which has often haunted me since, even in my dreams. I pinched myself at last, to assure myself that I had not been turned to stone.

"*My* cat!" she shrieked, while her eyes glared, and her lips foamed, and, tearing it out of my hands, she began kissing and fondling it like an infant. "Cziczuskam! cziczuskam! look at me—look at me!" she cried, pulling its eyes open. At last she laid it on the table, and, throwing herself upon it, began to weep bitterly.

At that moment Esztike re-entered, and sat down before her little table. Taking advantage of Mistress Debora's emotion, I slipped up to her—to Esztike, not to Mrs. Debora—and, pressing her small white hand in mine, asked, in a tremulous voice, "You are not angry with me, dearest Esztike, are you?"

"Why should I be angry?" said the artless little girl, casting down her eyes, and drawing her hand out of mine.

It was a foolish question, I allow; but when one is in love, wise questions do not always present themselves.

I had scarcely time to look at my little violet, before Mistress Debora again grumbled out, "Esztike, go and see if your father is coming!"

Tartar take the old vampire! I thought she was bewailing her cat. Once more alone with her, however, I endeavoured to console her, spoke of the weather, of the maize crop, of the vines—all in vain. At last she started up—

"Wait, you worthless scamp!" she cried; "whoever you are, who murdered this little innocent creature—I'll find you out, and revenge it on your children's children—(Merciful Heaven! she means to live three generations longer!) I will place the affair before the county, and begin a suit immediately, a *violentialis, infamisationalis* suit. You shall be avenged, my cruelly murdered, innocent, speckled cat, and I will make you a fearful example to generations still unborn!"

"You are quite right, my dear aunt, your determination is excellent; he deserves the utmost rigour of the law, and I promise you I shall be the first to look out for him."

"Will you really promise that?" exclaimed Mistress Debora; and then followed what I had dreaded might be the consequence of my generous speech. She actually seized and embraced me!

"My dear nephew, you were always a good lad; your father was a worthy man—I love all your family. Find out the murderer of my cat, and I will bless you for it, even after your death!"

"I would rather bless *you* under those circumstances," I thought, but did not say it; and, promising to do all in my power to hasten the *criminalis* inquisition, she proceeded to enumerate her favourite's merits—how he could purr, how he would leap on the table, and drink coffee out of a saucer, how sagacious, and how knowing he was; and then followed anecdotes illustrative of the virtues of her poor lost cat, to all of which I listened with unheard-of patience.

I at length suggested the prudence of removing the object of her emotion, and, after a most affecting scene, she consigned the precious relics to my arms, to be buried under her window, and I took leave, promising to return as soon as possible with some information relative to the murderer.

I then buried the cat, and raised a monument of sods above its grave, by which means I thoroughly ingratiated myself in Mistress Debora's favour.

Meanwhile, she seemed to have forgotten that she had sent Esztike out to watch for her father; and when, with a beating heart, I hurried to the gate, I found my little charmer still there.

"For whom are you waiting so long?" I asked, by way of conversation.

"For my dear father," she replied, twisting the little tassel of her apron.

"Poor little Esztike! how much you have to suffer from that old Mrs. Debora!"

She did not speak, but the large tears filled her eyes.

It was then I first remarked how beautiful black eyes look when they weep: tears do not become blue eyes, I like *them* best when they smile.

"Ah, Esztike! it should not be thus if—but I won't let you be annoyed if I can help it, that I won't."

She did not answer. I confess I should not have liked if she had been able to answer every word I said.

"Nobody loves me," I continued, "in the wide world: my life is very lonely and sad; but surely Heaven will smile upon us yet."

My little dove looked as if she wished to go, yet fain would stay; but as I behaved discreetly, she remained. A cold wind began to blow, and she had only a slight silk handkerchief round her neck.

"Why don't you put on a warmer handkerchief?" I asked. "You might catch cold and die."

"It would be no great pity," said the poor child, sadly; "I would go to a good place, I hope, and nobody would miss me."

"Oh! do not say that, unless you wish to break my heart (here my voice was somewhat choked)! You must live a long time yet, dearest Esztike; for if you die, I shall soon know how deep the Danube runs!"

And then I hastened away; and when I reached home, I found that my cheeks were wet, and that I was sobbing like a child. Ay, the heart of man makes him a strange animal!

For some time I had no occasion to fear my uncle's dogs, knowing that Mistress Debora would not set them at me; but I generally watched till the good man went out to wage war on the hares, and then I hastened to our neighbour's with all the information I had collected as to the murderer of the cat—describing, from his cap to his slippers, a being very unlike myself, and whose supposed existence nearly turned Mistress Debora's head.

But this could not continue very long; and my aunt at last began to forget her pet's untimely end, and no longer received her dear nephew so graciously as before.

After a lapse of some days, I called on pretext of speaking to my uncle (I had watched till I had seen him go out, with gun and dogs); and after poignant regrets at not finding him at home, I asked Mistress Debora if she had heard what had happened in the village. As nothing had happened, she naturally had not heard, and therefore was the more curious to know; and I accordingly proceeded to repeat all the gossip I had collected from some old gazettes with as much eloquence as I could—and (Heaven forgive me!) I fear, as much invention—till the old lady was ready to drop off her seat at my histories. She would listen for hours; and though I dared not speak to Esztike, we had frequent opportunities of exchanging sighs, and our eyes carried on most interesting dialogues together.

On one pretext or other I was honourably received for some time, and even allowed to bring Esztike books, which I had borrowed from a cousin in the village. True, they were only German books; but what could I do? Had I brought such unholy things into the house in the Hungarian language, I should have been banished from it for ever; for, if I remember rightly, they were romances and love tales, by Wieland and Kotzebue. But they passed for good books; and Mistress Debora (the worthy soul knew no other language than Magyar) would frequently insist on my translating the salutary effusions, which of course I did in as touching a style as possible, while the tears ran down the furrows in her cheeks.

One day, after taking leave (I generally had an instinctive feeling as to the time when my uncle would return), I was in the act of opening the house door, when it was pushed towards me, and the next instant my noble and honourable uncle, Gergely Sonkolyi, with pipe and brass-headed cane, stood before me.

How to escape was my first impulse; but seeing this was impossible, my next was to put a brave face on the matter.

"Well, nephew," said my uncle, twisting his moustache; "red, stammering, out of breath—eh? So you visit here, do you?"

What could I answer? I was not fool enough to say I had come to visit Esztike; and should I say I was visiting Mistress Debora—she may be his wife, I thought, and then he will shoot me through the head!

"I know your errand," continued my uncle, pertinaciously holding the handle of the door. "Storms and thunder! don't think to put your fingers in my eyes! Ten thousand fiery devils! if ever you dare to come within my door again, I swear by the woods of Karpath that I will make leather belts of your skin!"

"Thank you, uncle," I replied, delighted to get off so easily, as, once more commending me to the devil, he entered, and shut the door behind him; while I heard his allegorical phrases—or, as an impartial world would call them, his oaths—echoing wrathfully through the house.

What was to be done? I found myself just where I had been before the death of the cat.

I now considered it prudent to avoid the dogs.

From this day forward, I had very seldom an opportunity of seeing Esztike, except across our gardens; and even then, I exposed myself to the danger of being shot through the head, if my uncle should see me.

On one occasion Esztike gave me to understand by signs, that she dared not approach nearer. I pointed to the attic windows, which my little sweetheart understood at once; and from that day we frequently carried on a pantomimic conversation from our attics. I often laugh when I think how much we contrived to say, and how quickly we comprehended each other's gestures.

One day I heard that my uncle had set out on a long journey, and that the dogs had been tied up, which none would have dared to do till the old man had fairly erased the frontiers of the county.

I immediately went out into the woods, and spent several hours in filling my hat with mushrooms, which I brought to our neighbour's.

The old man had probably turned the house upside down on the occasion of my last expedition; for every one, from the first cook to the last dog, looked askance at me.

As I opened the door of the sitting-room (I had only one leg and one arm inside), my progress was arrested by Mistress Debora, who hastened over, and shutting the door on my other arm and leg, which consequently remained outside, exclaimed, with hospitable consideration: "Just stay where you are, nephew, and say what you want."

"I only want to beg my dear aunt's acceptance of some mushrooms, which I have gathered for her."

"Eh, well!" she exclaimed, releasing me from my ignominious position. "You have brought mushrooms? that is another thing. Come in."

I entered, and produced the mushrooms.

"That is a good lad! Well, what have you been about? do you still go to school?"

"Oh, dear, no! I have finished my studies."

"So soon! And what business are you going to take up?"

"I am an oculist, aunt."

"Indeed! already?"

"At your service, aunt."

Little Esztike tripped up to me: "Now you are joking, bacsi," she whispered, with a mischievous smile.

"Well, you must carry on the joke," I whispered in reply.

"And why?"

"Merely because I wish my dearest Esztike to hand me Aunt Debora's spectacles over the wall this evening; I am going to make a little improvement in them."

"Well," interrupted Aunt Debora, who had been examining the mushrooms; "and so you are an oculist? Ay, ay!"

"At your command. But I will not inconvenience you further," I said, taking up my hat.

"Oh, stay a little longer," said the good dame—at the same time pushing me towards the door, which she opened to let me out.

I got the spectacles that evening; and removing the magnifying glasses with great care, I substituted a pair which I had cut out of the smoothest pane of glass with a diamond.

Next morning I rose early and replaced the spectacles on Aunt Debora's table, after which I obtained admittance with a basket of cherries.

"We are really much obliged to you," said Mistress Debora, speaking in the plural number, though she gave none to anybody but herself.

"Oh, it is not worth mentioning."

"But I must just look if they have any inhabitants," she added; "this fruit generally has." And searching for her spectacles, she placed them on her nose and began examining the cherries, holding them first close, then at a distance, and then taking off her glasses and wiping them to look again.

"I don't know what is the matter," she exclaimed at last; "I can't see in the least to-day." ·

"Eh, how? what is the matter?"

"Just try these glasses, nephew, and tell me if they magnify."

I looked through them. "Why, aunt, the hairs on my skin look like porcupines' quills."

"O dear! then I must be becoming blind, for I can see nothing through them."

"My dear aunt," I exclaimed, with a look of alarm, turning her round to the light, "what can be the matter with your eyes? St. Gregory! you are going to get a white cataract! Why don't you take more care of yourself?"

"A white cataract!" she shrieked, covering her eyes with both her hands. "Oh! I am lost! I am undone! Nephew, dear nephew! can you not help me?"

"Hm!" I replied, with a look of anxious importance, making a few doctor's grimaces; "have you no sensations of paralysis in the tunica choroidaia?"

She knew what the tunica choroidaia was! and replied that she certainly had some sensations of the kind.

"Do you awake often at night?"

"I do indeed, every night."

"Hm! a bad symptom. Show me your tongue."

She produced it. "A very bad tongue indeed (here, at least, I spoke truth). If these symptoms should be accompanied by pains in the elbows (I knew the good lady was subject to this), I fear, my dear aunt, it may end in—marmaurosis!"

"O dear! O dear!—my elbows ache constantly; but what is the marmaurosis?"

"That is when the retina gets apoplexia, and the patient remains in total ablepsia."

She did not comprehend much of this, but what she did was quite enough for her.

"For Heaven's sake, don't let me get blind, dear nephew!—what shall I do, or what can I take?"

"There is not a moment to lose: you must go to bed instantly, while I prepare some medicine."

I went home and mixed a little liquorice and rose-water, and found my patient in bed on my return.

Having rubbed her eyes with the rose-water, and tied up her face so that only her chin protruded from beneath the bandage, I ordered her to keep quite quiet, and by no means to remove it until I gave her leave, as otherwise total ablepsia might be the consequence.

And now I could speak to my little Esztike without disturbance; and (Heaven forgive me!)—I gave her a hearty kiss!

"Esztike!" cried Aunt Debora, suddenly starting up.

Esztike had slipped out of the room.

"Csitt!" I replied softly, "Esztike is not here."

"What was that smack I heard just now?"

"I was drawing the cork from the medicine-bottle."

"O dear! the medicine!"

"Yes, dear aunt; but you must not talk or make the least exertion, for you will certainly get the *black* cataract if you do."

"This will not do," thought I; "for if she has not eyes, she has ears, and good ones too."

After a few minutes, I sat down beside her and felt her pulse.

"You must know, dear aunt, that we oculists have ascertained by anatomy that the ears and nose serve, like garret windows, to communicate fresh air to the nerves of the eyes. When, however, the nerves are in a state of inflammation, the danger is, that the air, passing through all these windows at once, may occasion a draught, which would irritate the inflammation; and therefore, according to Doctor Smilax, on such occasions one of the passages must be stopped with cotton. So now, dear aunt, you may have your choice; which do you consider the most convenient to have closed up—the nose or the ears?"

She naturally preferred dispensing with her ears. And now, at last, this living house Statuarium was not only blind, but deaf and dumb too, and for the first time in her life she left her fellow-creatures in peace.

And thus days glided by—centuries of bliss they might have been, for aught I knew or cared. Mistress Debora was still under strict medical discipline, and my little Esztike was as good as she was lovely; and I—I don't wish to praise myself. Sufficient to say, we were happy, and forgot all but our own happiness, as if it were to last for ever; but alas! when does a man in love ever think of the future?

One evening, later than usual, as I was still sitting beside Esztike (I could not tear myself away, and besides, it was raining hard), I thought I heard some person knocking at the outer door, but took no notice of it; for, with my little dove by my side, what cared I if the world were falling to pieces around us? The old clock ticked cheerfully; and Esztike and I had so many pretty things to say about nothing, as we sat together on the same seat (the old black leather sofa), and consequently not very far apart.

All at once we heard a noise in the kitchen.

"Holy Saint Stephen! it may be thieves!" cried Esztike trembling, and drawing still closer to me.

Who would not feel courageous under such circumstances? For my part, I felt capable of unheard-of heroism; and assuring her that she had nothing to fear from a dozen robbers as long as I was there, I seized a pistol (without a trigger) from the wall, while Esztike, encouraged by my boldness, took the candle, and we advanced, to the door. I opened it. Esztike uttered a loud scream, and extinguished the light. The outer door was open, and a dark form advanced towards us.

"St. Barbara, help!" I sincerely ejaculated. "Who is there?" I exclaimed, in as loud a voice as I was master of, at the same time presenting the triggerless pistol at the black form.

"Thunder and storms! and who are you, I should like to know? Lightning and fury!" —

"Uyüyü! my worthy uncle!" I cried, each word sounding like a squib let off at my ear; and making a dash for the door, the next instant I was outside. But here I was stopped; the flaps of my coat having been caught in the heavy gate, I could neither turn nor extricate myself, but remained hanging by my wings like a cockchafer.

In vain I pulled and kicked, praying that the flaps of my only holiday coat might be torn off, while I heard my uncle deliberately opening the door behind me.

"He will make mince-meat of me," thought I; and exerting all my remaining strength, I tore myself from the flaps and fell to the ground.

"Now for it—fly!" I exclaimed; and starting up, my legs bore me with supernatural agility towards the forest.

"Stop, rascal!" roared my pursuer behind me, "or I will shoot you through the head."

I only ran the faster.

"Stop!" he roared again, "or I will shoot you through the legs."

As I had not stopped for the sake of my head, I naturally had no superior partiality for my legs; and so we continued to run—Heaven knows how long!—until we were a good way through the forest. Neither of us had the slightest idea of capitulating; but I began to perceive that the distance between us was gradually decreasing (the old man had learned to run in 1809),55 and I began to smell the brass-headed cane very near me.

[55] Alluding to the flight of the Hungarian volunteers at Raab, before Napoleon.

My worthy uncle had been endeavouring to reach my back with this cane for some minutes, when, just as he was about to aim a cruel blow, I disappeared from his sight.

The good man had not much time for astonishment; for the next instant the earth opened beneath him, and he too fell head foremost, from depth to depth, as I had done, wondering in which part of the lower world we should alight.

On reaching the bottom, we found ourselves in total darkness.

"O me! O me!" groaned the worthy man; "I am d——d—dead and d——d! there is no doubt of it. Wo to my sinful soul! The good priest always warned me not to swear, or the devil would carry me away; and now he has me—with the guilt of meditated murder on my soul, too! Oh! Heaven be merciful to my sinful soul, and I will never swear again, nor poach! I will pay the priest's tithes, as much as is due, and give my daughter to her lover—only let me be saved from perdition!"

The good man trembled like a jelly, firmly believing he was at least in the vestibule of purgatory. Meantime, I had a good opportunity of hearing his resolutions of amendment; and plainly enough, too, for we had both fallen into the same wolf's trap, full twelve feet under ground, and were thus in tolerably good arrest for the present.

I began to reflect that although I had escaped one danger, I had probably fallen into another not less alarming; for, if a troop of wolves came tumbling in upon us, our resurrection would certainly be divested of all fleshly encumbrances.

However, it was no use to be afraid. One thing was certain: if the wolves came they would devour us, and if they did not come they would not devour us; but in either case, fear was useless. And, consoling myself with this argument, I took my pipe and tobacco-pouch from my pocket—for the pit was filled with innumerable gnats.

"Mercy on my sinful soul!" roared my uncle, starting up as he saw the light of my pipe in the darkness.

Of course I sat as still as a hare, determined to let him tremble a little longer; but, in the excess of his despair, he hit me such a kick with his spurred foot, that I was under the necessity of addressing him.

"Don't be uneasy, uncle," I exclaimed; "it is certainly an unfortunate occurrence, but you need not break your neighbour's bones."

"Nephew!" cried my uncle, in a voice of joy, "Nephew Peti! are you here too? are we alive? or where are we both, and how came we here?"

"Just as the rain comes from heaven, uncle, without a ladder; but let us rejoice that we have reached the bottom with sound limbs."

"Well, but where are we?"

"Why, in a wolf's pit."

"A wolf's pit! ten thousand fiery"—

"Softly, softly, uncle; remember the promises you have just made."

"Just made! did I know I was in a wolf's pit? I thought I was in a far more honourable place. How the tartar are we to get out of this? Three-and-thirty centuries of devils' livers! how the scorpion can I annihilate the accursed philosophy which dug a pit here? The leprosy take the idiot who invented it!—nine bucketfuls of dragons' nails! how the Alp can we be heard from this infernal hole?" and in this strain he continued, till the pit resounded with his elocution. At last, turning to me, "Nephew," he said, "just let me get up on your shoulders and see if there is any way of getting out of this, and if I succeed, I will help you up afterwards."

I submitted, and he mounted me, shouting to the full extent of his voice, while his enormous weight, and the exertions he made at each shout, made my position somewhat painful.

"You had better not make so much noise, dear uncle," I said, hoping he would dismount, "for if the wolves come in upon us we shall need no help out again."

At last my worthy uncle dismounted, and sat down, muttering and swearing to himself.

"Chains and dungeons! what is this?" he exclaimed, drawing a white heap from under his feet.

It was the dead goose which was placed on the top of the pit to allure the wolves, and had made its descent into the pit with us.

"But what are we to do here till the morning?" said my uncle; "the gnats will devour us. I thought the devils were pinching me with fiery tweezers!"

"Just do as I do, uncle; light your pipe and fumigate them."

"Well, you are a man, nephew; I swear there's something in you;" and, seeing there was nothing better to do, he lighted his pipe, and we smoked together as if for a wager.

"But now, nephew," began my uncle, after some silence, speaking with his pipe in his mouth, while he stirred the bowl with his little finger, "what the tartar have you to do in my house, eh?"

"Well, uncle, here or there, why should I deny it, I am in love with Esztike."

"But the proper way would have been to speak to me first."

"I am not in love with you, uncle."

"Nor I with you; but to come to the point, what business have you with the girl? love her, if you will, and as much as you like, but don't come near her; you can love her just as well nine miles off!"

"But that won't do, uncle. I don't want to love Esztike from such a distance. It was far enough between our two roofs; but if she has no objection, and no peculiar animosity to me—here, in the wolf's pit, with all solemnity, I demand her dear little hand, and if Mrs. Debora is to go with her, I will take her too."

"Take the tartar! why, she is my stepmother! You don't want to be my son and my father at once, do you? But I'll tell you what, nephew, you are still a child, and, what's more, you have nothing to break into your milk."

"Very true, uncle, nor the milk to break anything into; but the Almighty is rich, and He will assist us."

"Heaven does not make banknotes for anybody," said the old man, holding his pipe in the palm of his hand; "and you need not expect roasted sparrows to fly into your mouth, though you hold it open till doomsday!"

"Well, but what is not may yet be; in the beginning there was nothing, as the Bible tells us. I will go to Pesth, finish my studies, and be a *tekintetes ur* 56 and advocate."

[56] *Tekintetes ur*, respectable sir—a title.

"A starving candidate!" interrupted my uncle; "it would have been better if you had been a priest; your father always wished it, honest man! but you were an obstinate rascal all your life. You might have been a chaplain now, and the deuce would not have brought us here; but I've said my word, and I'll make two out of it. Hark ye! the elections are approaching, and you may profit by them if you like; we will join the national meeting, and see what can be made of you."

"And then Esztike will be mine?"

"Storms of Karpath! can you think of nothing but Esztike?"

"Uncle, they may make a lord-lieutenant of me if they like, only let me have Esztike."

"When you get as far as that I should not care, hang you! but one syllable does not cross your lips, nor do you approach my house before the elections, or, by the wars of Attila! nothing shall come of it."

I was too happy not to promise anything, and we ended with a hearty embrace, and my uncle saying, "Give me a light, my son,"—a peculiar mark of favour on his part, for he always lighted his own pipe.

After this, I laid the old man's head on my breast, and he slept soundly, and snored as loud as if he were blowing a bassoon with each nostril. It was impossible for me to sleep—the very pit trembled with the sounds; so I lay awake, thinking of my good fortune, and smoking the gnats off us. At last the morning dawned, and, as our appetites began to sharpen, we renewed our efforts to obtain delivery, shouting by turns till we had no voices left, and then we sat down again and smoked in despair.

Chance at last brought two foresters in our direction, who, observing the smoke of our pipes from some distance, came to the rescue.

Luckily they happened to be two of my uncle's own men, and as they drew us out of the jaws of death, he promised to turn their skins inside out if ever they dared disclose where they had found us.

It was fortunate that we returned when we did, for the good folks were just about to advertise us both.

For two long months I never spoke to Esztike, though I often saw her, poor child! with swelled eyes and pale cheeks, and felt as if my heart would burst; but I had promised, and I wished to keep my word.

At the end of the two months, the elections closed. It was all very fine indeed, though, at this present moment I have no particular recollection of anything, except that there was one fat lad advanced, two others degraded, several more kicked out, and that, when it came to my turn, I was taken by the throat, my hair cut, my attila slit up the sides, one of my masticators drawn, and the oath administered.

Some days after the election, my uncle gave a great supper, to which all the aunts and uncles of the village were invited, and myself among the rest, though I was neither aunt nor uncle to anybody.

What this grand supper consisted of I know not; indeed I had important reasons for remaining in ignorance till the present day.

The large table in the arbour was laid out for forty-eight persons, and when I arrived the company was already assembled.

My little Esztike was busy with her guests, serving everybody, with her sweet rosy face—for she had just come from the fire—and now and then turning bashfully away, as one or other uncle tried to embrace her; but with all her sweetness, and all her blushes, she still looked very sad, poor child!

I bowed low as I entered, striking my spurs together, but the little girl was so startled by my appearance that she overturned the Polish soup she had in her hand over the head and ears of a certain uncle, who complained of dulness of hearing ever afterwards.

"You are welcome, nephew!" cried Uncle Gergely, "though you come late; you presume on your character of bridegroom."

My little Esztike grew very pale, and looked very sad too. Something had fallen into her eyes, she said, turning away; but it was tears that were in them.

"Really to see how these young people grow up!" said an important assessor, who always sat on two chairs at once; "my niece Esztike will very soon be marriageable."

"Not at all very soon," said Uncle Gergely, severing at one cut the fork stuck in the goose's back, as if it had been a fibre; "she is now a bride."

It needed no more for poor Esztike. She turned to go out, but the landscape must have looked very confused, for she could scarcely find the arbour door.

It never once entered her head, bless her! that she was my bride and I her bridegroom, and that we were to be a pair.

"Esztike, bring the sugar-box," cried Mistress Debora, who enjoyed what she believed to be our mortification. She had never ceased exciting

Uncle Gergely against Esztike and me since that memorable day, and indeed she had reason enough, poor soul! for I had kept her a week and a half in bed, with eyes blindfolded and ears stuffed,—and, moreover, she now believed that I had killed her cat.

"Nephew!" cried Uncle Gergely, beckoning me; "run after her," he whispered, "and console her a little, poor child! or she will cry her soul out."

This needed no repetition. I darted after Esztike, and, seizing her hand, pressed it to my lips. "Esztike, dear Esztike, one word!"

"Excuse me," she said faintly; "I feel very ill."

"My Esztike, do you know your future bridegroom?"

"May I die sooner than know him!"

"Then do not die, for he is now so near you that none can be nearer."

For the first time, the whole business began to dawn on her; and in an instant all the blood rushed to her cheeks, and dyed them a deep crimson.

Had I not caught her in my arms, she would have fallen. How quickly her heart beat!—and oh! that sigh, which released it! I felt its deep throb. Once more I strained her to my heart, and whispering—"But it is all still a secret," I tore myself away, and hurried back to the arbour.

Meanwhile, Uncle Gergely had announced the news, to the joy of all the assembled guests, but the rage of Mistress Debora; and when I returned I was received with such a burst of congratulations, that I was quite overpowered.

"I will bet you anything," said Uncle Gergely, "that this girl will bring anything back with her except the sugar-box, which she was sent for."

He might have betted what he liked; when little Esztike returned, her artless countenance beamed with some joyful mystery, but there was no sugar-box in her hand.

Every eye was turned upon her; it was no wonder, therefore, that she blushed like the morning sky.

"Well, where is the sugar-box?" cried Mistress Debora impatiently.

Esztike blushed still deeper, looked still more confused; but at last, when she saw that everybody began to smile on her, she ran over to her father and hid her burning face in his bosom. The old man laughed, and kissed the little bride again and again, making her face still redder with his rough beard.

"I will go for the sugar myself," said I; for I felt as if thorns were under my feet.

"Certainly, go for it, both of you," said Uncle Gergely, putting Esztike's hand in mine.

"And now I will answer for it, we shall not see the sugar box to-night," remarked the assessor on the two chairs.

We went into the house together.

Who can presume to compare his happiness with mine? Who would be so audacious as to seek words to express such happiness? I am silent; for that small white hand, that smiling but fitful glance, those artless lips, whose silence spoke so much—all were mine; and their possession made me wealthier than if an empire had been conferred on me. O God! what a beautiful thought of thine was love!

When we returned to the arbour with the sugar-box, the company had long forgotten that they had drunk coffee; and we excused ourselves by saying that there was no sugar in the box when we went into the house. Fortunately they did not investigate the matter farther. So far was true—the box was empty when we went for it; but when we returned with it—there was still nothing more in it!

"This day two months I will be glad to see you all at the wedding." And with these words, my uncle closed the *fiançailles*.

But the will of poor mortals is in the keeping of God.

Before the two months were over, my uncle was obliged to take a long journey—so long, that he could not even take his pipe with him! He blessed us both, and died like a good Christian, scarcely cursing the doctor and the medicines; and we buried my good uncle, Gergely Sonkolyi.

Esztike and I mourned for him a whole year—outwardly; for in our hearts we remember him as tenderly to this day as if he had died but yesterday. And this was the reason that I could never call him 'father,' for there is no advancement in death: in whatever relation we die, there we remain.

When the year was out, that happy moment arrived when my earthly paradise was at last attained, and I pressed to my heart my own dear Esztike.

Never, indeed, did such sweetness meet my lips, as when for the first time she kissed me of her own good-will. I remember it all well to this day.

And yet it was a long while ago.

That beautiful little sylph-like form, which in those days I could have spanned, has now so increased in size that I have enough to do to embrace it with both arms; but for all that, I love her as my very soul's core.

Mistress Debora still lives and rules, though unable to move a member of her body—her tongue always excepted. This member is still sound and healthy; and she has engaged herself to teach our grandchildren to speak. Heaven may grant it to her; but it is not my prayer.

THE UNLUCKY WEATHERCOCK

It seems as if fortune delighted in extending her hand favourably towards some individuals, while to others she only puts it forth to deceive and buffet them through life. Her caprices have furnished us with a lively example in both manners of dealing. We relate the simple facts as we heard them, without adding a word.

Towards the close of 1848, war was the only theme in vogue. In Pesth especially, the word *peace* was quite out of fashion. The hotels were filled with guests who met for the purpose of discussing the favourite topic; martial music was heard from morning till night: the European war was preparing.

Two personages were sitting together before a small table at the hotel "Nagy Pipa,"[57] to whom the German saying might have been applied—"*Der eine schweigt, der andere hört zu,*"[58] for one of these two personages seemed attentively considering the probable or possible cause of his companion's silence, casting, from time to time, a scrutinizing glance on his countenance, intended to penetrate whatever dark project might be passing within.

[57] Great Pipe.

[58] "One keeps silence, the other listens to him."

This observant individual was no other than the humane Master Janos, Police-corporal, and vice-jailer of the noble city of Pesth; and when we inform our readers that he occupied this post during Metternich's time, and that, notwithstanding that minister's overthrow, he still retained his position, unlike the usual fate of the adherents of a fallen ministry, they will surely admit that the favourite of fortune could not be better personified than by the same Master Janos; nor can it be denied that the individual opposite was no less persecuted by the fickle goddess, not only because he was the object of honest Master Janos's suspicious glances; but more especially because a nailsmith's apprentice from Vienna could think of coming to Hungary of all places on earth—a country where the craft is carried on wholesale at the corner of every village, by the Wallachian gipsies.

Master Janos had not studied Lavater, but long experience had led him to conclude, after minute examination of the man's countenance, that some counter-revolutionary scheme was turning in his head.

Consequently he drew his chair nearer, and determined to break the silence.

"Where do you come from, sir? if I may presume to ask," he inquired, with a wily glance at his companion.

"Hyay! from Vienna," sighed the stranger, looking into the bottom of his glass.

"And what news from that city?"

"Hyaee! nothing good."

"Eh, what? nothing good!—what bad, then?"

"Hyay! war is much feared."

"Feared! what audacity!—how dare they fear?"

"Hyay! sir, I do not fear either at thirty leagues' distance; but once I heard from the cellar how they were bombarding the streets, and I found nothing agreeable in it."

Master Janos found still greater reason for suspicion. He resolved to make him drink, and he would probably come on the traces of some dangerous plot.

How much does a nailsmith's stomach require? At the second pitcher his head sank slowly back, and his tongue moved with difficulty.

"Now for it!" thought Master Janos, filling his glass. "Eljen! liberty!" he exclaimed, waiting for the nailsmith to strike glasses.

The latter was not long in responding to the invitation, and echoed the "Eljen!" as far as his thickening tongue permitted.

"Now it is your turn to give a toast," said the vice-jailer, slily eyeing his victim.

"Indeed, I am not used to give toasts, sir; I only drink them."

"Come, don't play the egotist, but drink to whoever you consider the greatest man in the world!"

"In the whole world?" replied the nailsmith, reflecting that the world was very large, and that he knew very little about it.

"Yes, in the whole world!—the whole round earth!" pursued Master Janos, confidently.

The nailsmith hesitated, scratched his nose, scratched his ear, scratched his whole head, and, finally, cried out, "Success to Master Slimak!"

The vice-jailer shuddered at this public demonstration. It was quite clear that this Master Slimak was some gunpowder-sworn commander-in-chief—there was no doubt of it, and, without any further ado, he seized the nailsmith by the collar, and, *brevi manu*, escorted him to the town-hall, where he dragged him into a narrow, ominous-looking chamber, before a stout, red-faced gentleman.

"This man is a suspicious character," he exclaimed. "In the first place, he has the audacity to fear war; in the next place, he sat from seven o'clock until half-past nine, two whole hours and a half, without opening his lips; and, finally, he was impious enough to give a public toast to a certain Master Slimak, who is probably quite as suspicious a character as himself."

"Who is this Master Slimak?" asked the stout, red-faced gentleman, sternly.

"Nobody, indeed," replied the trembling Viennese, "but my former master, an honest nailsmith, whom I served four years, and would be serving still, had his wife not beaten me."

"Impossible!" ejaculated the fat, red-faced gentleman. "It is not customary to give public toasts to such personages."

"But I don't know what the custom is here."

"If you wished to give a toast, why did you not drink to constitutional liberty, to the upper and lower Danube armies, or to freedom of the press, and such toasts?"

"Hyay, sir! I could not learn all that in a month!"

"But in three months I daresay you will be able to learn it well enough. Master Janos, take that man into custody."

The humane Master Janos again seized the delinquent by the collar, *ut supra*, and escorted him to the place appropriated to such malefactors, where he had time to consider why he was put there.

The three months passed slowly enough to the nailsmith. It was now the middle of March.

Master Janos punctually released his prisoner, and the honest man, in order to prove the reform in his sentiments, and thereby rise in Master Janos's opinion, greeted him with, "Success to liberty, and the Hungarian arms!"

Master Janos stumbled against the wall in speechless horror, and as soon as he had regained his equilibrium, he seized the astonished nailsmith, who, when he had recovered his terrified senses, found himself again in the narrow, ominous chamber; but now, instead of the stout, red-faced gentleman, he stood before a lean, black gentleman, who, when he understood the charge against the prisoner, without permitting any explanation, condemned him to three months' imprisonment, informing him that henceforth, unless he wished to fare worse, he would exclaim, "Success to the imperial armies, the great constitution, and the one and powerful Austria!"

And the nailsmith, having made three steps beyond his prison door, was brought back to renew his captivity, and ponder over his strange fate.

The three months had again passed over. It was some time in June.

The humane Master Janos did not fail to release his captive. The poor man began at his prison door to declaim the redeeming words of "Long live Prince Windischgrätz! success to glorious Austria!"

Master Janos laid his hand upon his sword, as if to protect himself from this incorrigible man.

"What! was it not enough to imprison you twice? Have you not yet learned what you should say? Have the kindness to step in here."

And for the third time they entered the narrow chamber.

Instead of the meagre, black gentleman, it was again the fat, red-faced gentleman before whom our victim was called in question for his repeated crime.

"Obstinate traitor!" he exclaimed; "are you aware of the extent of your offence, and that if I did not condemn you to an imprisonment of three months on my own responsibility, instead of giving you up to justice, you would be cut into four quarters, as you deserve?"

The unhappy nailsmith must needs rejoice, in his extreme terror, at the mildness of the punishment.

"But what should I have said?" he asked his lenient judge, in a voice of despair.

"What should you have said? why, Success to the republic! Success to democracy! Success to revolution!"

The poor man repeated the three injunctions, and promising faithfully to attend to them, he resigned himself patiently to a new lease of his dark abode.

During the ensuing three months, everything had changed except the good fortune of Master Janos. Neither time nor chance could succeed in displacing him, as they had so many others. He was still vice-jailer of the noble city of Pesth, as he had formerly been.

It was now September. The nailsmith's penalty was out, and Master Janos called him forth.

The prisoner's countenance expressed something unusually important, and no sooner did the vice-jailer approach, than, seizing his hand, he exclaimed, between his sobs, "Oh, Master Janos, tell the black gentleman that I humbly kiss his hand, and wish him from the bottom of my heart, 'Success to the Republic!'"

As the hungry wolf pounces on the lamb, Master Janos once more seized the nailsmith by his ill-used collar; and indeed, so shocked was the worthy jailer, that, having brought his prisoner into the narrow chamber, it was some time before he could recover himself sufficiently to explain the circumstance to the lean, black gentleman, who once more occupied the place of the fat, red-faced one; and great was his vexation when this individual, instead of sentencing the delinquent to be broken on the wheel, merely awarded him three months more imprisonment!

On the third of November 1849, all who had been imprisoned for slight political offences were released from their confinement, and among others the nailsmith.

As Master Janos opened the door, the unfortunate man stopped his mouth with his pocket-handkerchief, giving the humane jailer by this pantomime to understand, that he would henceforth keep his demonstrations to himself.

It might have been some consolation to him to know that he was not the only one who cried out at the wrong time!

THE TWO BRIDES

Some years ago, there lived in Szolnok a widow with her two daughters. It was a long time since the lady had been made a widow, and yet she still wore her weeds; and every year she grew paler and weaker, as she drew nearer to her husband's grave. But two sweet buds still blossomed beside the withered stem; and Ilka and Aniko grew more and more lovely as their bridal-day approached,—for they each wore betrothal rings, and their young bridegrooms were noble, handsome, and generous youths. They were both in the army; and though far from their native land, every month brought a letter from each, full of affection and of hope. It was now two months, however, since news had come. "They are surely coming home themselves," said Ilka and Aniko, and there was comfort in the thought.

It was the last day of the year—that day of thanksgiving for the past, and hope for the future, which we love to pass in the midst of friends and family, while many a national song and warm greeting are exchanged, as the bowl passes round the hospitable board.

But the last day of 1848 saw no wassail bowl in Szolnok, no hospitable meetings to hail the new-born year.

All day and through the night the whistle of the train was heard, as it came and went incessantly; and the arrivals and departures being at uncertain hours, the terminus was crowded with people wearing gloomy and anxious countenances, while the new-comers gazed perplexed around them, ignorant whither to turn in the confused and unknown town.

Beyond the terminus, heavy baggage-carts had overturned numerous unclaimed wares; while, farther off, uncovered waggons stood about, and great guns, chests bearing the Government seal, arms, vessels, and articles of clothing, lay strewn unheeded all around.

Again the train came in with cold and anxious passengers, while outers pressed into the vacant seats; and many who had waited all day in vain, finding no places, were obliged once more to return weary and disconsolate.

Armed and official men alighted from the nearest coaches, and again the terminus was crowded. Women closely veiled and muffled, pale trembling girls, and little children were there also, taking a hurried farewell, or waiting anxiously for expected friends and relatives; and many were the unheeded inquiries—an hundred questions put for every answer.

And now the train was filled with military, whose wild songs chimed strangely with the noise of the machinery.

Meanwhile, all was hurry and confusion within the town: each individual seeming occupied by his especial grievances—each felt alone among the thousands who surrounded them. The new-comers went from house to house, asking lodgings and warmth from inmates more wretched than themselves. Powerful magnates, whose palaces had been scarcely large enough for their numerous guests and retinues, were glad to find shelter on the earthen floor of a reed cottage; while ancient enemies, whose feuds had made a kingdom too small to contain them, now shared their broken fortunes in one room; and high-born maidens, accustomed to every refinement, received with thankfulness the benches proffered by strangers, who found a scarcely harder bed upon the earthen floor.

On the other side of Szolnok, numerous vehicles pursued their course in long unbroken lines, moving with difficulty on the frozen uneven roads, and filled with men, women, and children—cold and anxiety depicted in every countenance. Whole caravans passed on foot, in miserable clothing, carrying empty sacks, and followed by carts loaded with iron machines and broken weapons, on the tops of which women and children lay huddled together in blankets and rugs. One or two noblemen's calèches, with the windows drawn up, were obliged to follow slowly in the rear of these creaking machines, which the badness of the roads, or the steep banks, made it impossible to pass.

Thus closed the last day of the old year, and the first day of the new was a weary repetition of similar scenes.

The trains moved again all day and all night, bringing more anxious and gloomy countenances, baggage, coaches, and cannon. Those who had arrived yesterday hastened on to-day, while the fresh comers again sought shelter from house to house, and the lingerers still awaited the next coaches—searching in vain for relatives, or friends, or trunks.

On the opposite side of the Theiss, the carriages of the fugitives seemed to have no end. Here and there a few mat-covered vehicles might be seen, where a mother, hastening to join her husband's flight, had brought her infant in its cradle; but the rest being mostly uncovered, were exposed to the chill blast and the drifting snow, which seemed to turn every face to stone.

Travellers were seen crossing the inhospitable waste from morning till night, and all night again till morning; while the little inns, at the distance of a day's journey on the puszta, were empty and deserted.

Troops of riders, and heavy cannon, pursued their doubtful path among the hills, or, stopped up by the snow, were obliged to remain stationary till chance should bring them assistance, or they should perish in the cold.

And so it continued on the second, third, fourth, fifth day; on the sixth the movement ceased, and all was silent. The train brought only one or two passengers—taciturn and moody, like the rest. Clerks and officials left their places and retired; the lingerers took their lonely and sad way home; and the cannon, chests, and baggage, which had not hitherto been removed, were left on the roads to the care of fate.

The last fugitives had left the town with break of day: all was calm, silently awaiting the mysterious future.

Towards noon, the beating of drums and the sound of the trumpet announced the entrance of the Hungarian army. The troops had an hour's rest, and received a hearty welcome from citizens who willingly shared their last morsel with the national guards, after their many vicissitudes, and days and nights of hardship and privation.

A hussar officer rode up to the widow's house. He was a handsome, slender youth, whose raven hair and moustache formed a striking contrast to the olive paleness of his complexion. He wore a double gold cord on his crimson csako, and his breast was already decorated. As he entered the house his dark eye flashed with pleasure, and all his efforts to be serious could ill restrain a smile.

That smile betrayed him!

"Gejza!" exclaimed the widow and her daughters together; and then there was a rush, and a mutual embrace—the first affectionate, the next playful, and the last long and warm.

"I knew you would come," whispered Ilka, as he pressed her again and again to his heart. "How long will you stay with us?"

"As long as we remain in Szolnok."

"And how long will that be?"

"Perhaps an hour."

"Only one hour! And when will you return?"

"Perhaps soon, perhaps—never."

Ilka clung weeping to her lover's neck, who drew her still closer to his heart.

The other sister now approached, and gently chiding Ilka's tears, she asked in a low, tremulous voice: "Where is Laszlo?"

"He will be here this evening, I believe."

"Why did he not come with you?"

The hussar hesitated. "I am retreating, but he is pursuing."

The colour left the young girl's cheek.

"He joined the cuirassiers," continued Gejza, "about two months ago, and now—we are in opposite ranks."

The sisters looked at each other in consternation.

"*You* fight against each other!" exclaimed Ilka; "my bridegroom against my sister's!—O merciful Heaven!"

"And did you not think of us, then?" said Aniko.

"It is the soldier's fate, my friends: he may love, and be happy; but when the trumpet sounds he must forget love and happiness, and think only of stern duty."

"Ah, Gejza! you must not fight against each other; we must gain one of you over to join the other."

"It cannot be, my friends; I know Laszlo well, and he is what I am. A soldier's place is beside his standard: whereever that leads he must follow— be it to death, or against his own brother."

"And if you should meet upon the field?"

"It nearly happened a short time ago. In the skirmish of Teteny we were scarcely fifty paces apart, when we recognised each other. He suddenly turned his horse's head, I did the same—we both sought another enemy; and when the battle was over, both our swords were red. It is the soldier's fate!"

"And could you have killed him?"

"Far rather die myself; and therefore I do not love the sword—I like the cannon much better. Those soldiers are far happier; they never see the faces of those they kill, or hear their dying groans. More than once, when the madness of glory has made my brain giddy, I have heard my name repeated by the enemy I had cut down—calling to me, 'Thanks, comrade!' as he fell from his horse; and I have recognised some old school-fellow, or some officer who had left our own regiment. And then, when I am alone, that 'Thanks, comrade' always"—

The trumpet sounded before the window. It was the call to march.

The hussar took leave: a short word, a long kiss, a tear hastily brushed aside, and the next moment he was on his impatient charger, and neither the tear nor the kiss were to be traced on his calm countenance.

Again the trumpet sounded—the troop marched forward, white handkerchiefs waved from the widow's window—an hour afterwards, Szolnok was once more deserted and silent.

Towards evening, the sound of martial music was again heard; helmets and cuirasses gleamed in the setting sun. It was the imperial army, well clothed and mounted, and in perfect order. Their troops formed a striking contrast to those which had passed in the morning, who were dejected by want and suffering.

A young cuirassier had quartered himself in the widow's house; he was the gayest officer in his regiment, and more particularly now, as the bridegroom of one of the two fair sisters.

Unlike the young hussar, there was no sadness in his tone; and when he could think of aught but Aniko's bright eyes, victory shone in his glance—for he loved his profession, and was ready to shed his blood or win laurels of glory for it.

"Do not fear, sweet friend!" he exclaimed, seeing Ilka turn away with tearful eyes to weep alone; "I will bring back your bridegroom from the first battle to pass his captivity with you."

But the jest pained Ilka.

She replied with pride: "Gejza will sooner die than be taken prisoner."

Weeks and months passed away, and Laszlo's bride was soon to be his wife.

"The first victory," he said, "shall celebrate our marriage!"

"The first victory," sighed Ilka, "will be *his* defeat!" and then she wept bitterly. But when the sisters were together, each restrained her smiles and her tears so as not to grieve the other.

One day Laszlo whispered gravely to Aniko, "This day week there will be a battle!" and the warm pressure of his hand seemed to say, "and our victory;" while the deep blush on the bride's cheek seemed to reply, "And our wedding!"

Both girls prepared a dress in secret for that day. Aniko's was white embroidery, as for a bridal; Ilka's was simple black!

The imperial troops remained several months in Szolnok, during which time they had raised strong fortifications.

An extensive redoubt guarded the *tête de pont* on the opposite side of the Theiss. Palisades were constructed to screen the *tirailleurs* between the entrenchments, before which a little willow thicket concealed a battery of field-pieces.

Within the fortifications was the pontoon bridge, which the imperial army had formed after having burnt the great bridge in January.

Before the bridge could be taken, the enemy had first to drive the troops from their strong entrenchments, and should they even effect this, they would still be exposed to the cross fire of the redoubt and the battery concealed in the thicket, and it was impossible to make a circuit, for the Theiss surrounds two-thirds of the place.

Szolnok is built on the opposite side, and was protected on one side by the river Zagyva and the impassable morasses of the Theiss, and on the other by strong ramparts and entrenchments. Within the *tête de pont* there were three half-moon bastions, well fortified, and protecting each other.

The terminus, which lay within gun-shot of a bastion running along the Theiss, was also strongly fortified by moats and artillery, whose guns commanded all the defiles leading to it; to the west stood a chapel, built on a knoll—the only elevated position near the place.

An assault from this side was almost impracticable, according to the rules of tactics, for these bastions could only be taken by a large force, with guns of great calibre; and, in case of a repulse, the besiegers would be cut off from all retreat, and exposed to the whole concentrated main body of the imperial forces in Pesth.

The Zagyva morasses alone remained partly unprotected, an attack from that side being considered impracticable.

Patrols were stationed along the right bank of the Theiss, as far as Czibakhaza, which served as a point of passage to the Hungarians, though, according to the information of spies, there were no forces there at present, excepting a few reserve corps, the two Hungarian *corps d'armée* having united at Torokszentmiklos, under Vecsey and Damjanics.

The attack was consequently expected from that quarter; and, according to the spies' reports, the day was fixed, and the station appointed on the opposite side of the Theiss.

There is a ferry between Szolnok and Czibakhaza, and the boat is guided by the simple means of a rope drawn across the river.

The boat was now on the opposite side, some persons having just crossed with the permission of the imperial party, who kept a patrol to guard the passage.

On the evening of the expected day, two hussars rode up to the ferry from the opposite side.

"Do you see that boat?" cried the elder of the two, as they reached the bank.

"I see it, corporal," replied the other, who appeared to be a recruit.

"Whether you see it or not, we must cross there."

"Very well, corporal."

"Don't argue with me when the order is to cross; we *must* cross, were a thousand fiery devils on the other side!—Hej! come out, thou slug!" he continued, knocking at the door of the boatman's hut.

"*Thou*, indeed!" grumbled a voice from within; "I'll hear something more civil first!"

"No arguing, nephew, but turn out, unless you wish your house turned upside down, and yourself left under the clear sky!"

An old grayheaded man appeared. "It is a long time since I was called 'nephew,'" he murmured.

"How old are you?" asked the hussar.

"Some sixty years."

"Pooh! thou art a boy, nephew! I am five years thy senior; forward!— march!"

As the boat put off with the hussars, a *chasseur*, who was observing their motions from the other side, called across the water in German.

"Cannot you see that we are hussars?" was the reply, in Hungarian.

The soldier levelled his musket and fired, and the ball went through the old hussar's csako. He turned impatiently to the recruit, who had moved his head as the ball whistled past his ear.

"Why do you bend your head?—the balls must fall on one side or on the other; and thou, nephew, get from under my horse, and pull away by the rope."

The peasant, who was lying on his face at the bottom of the boat, never felt less inclined to obey in his life, especially as fifty or sixty grenadiers appeared from behind the entrenchments, and began firing on the hussars.

"Dismount and guide the boat," said the old hussar, turning to the recruit.

The *chasseur*, seeing that the balls had no effect, ran down to the rope, which he cut with his sword, as the hussars reached the middle of the stream, and the boat was consequently borne back again by the current. The old hussar, swearing that he was not done with them yet, gloomily reascended the bank with his companion, and galloping back to his troop, which was concealed in a wood at a little distance, he reported himself to the captain.

"What news, Gergo?" asked Gejza—for it was he.

"It would not do, captain, as I said before; they did not like our *numbers*, so they cut the rope when we were half over; they might have allowed me to cross if I had been alone."

"Never mind, Gergo—how did we get over the water before boats were made?"

"Ah, I thought of that, captain dear; but it is my duty to obey, and not to argue."

"Now, lads, whoever likes a bath may follow me!" cried the young soldier, and, spurring his horse, he galloped towards the river followed by his troop.

It was a beautiful sight to see the hundred and fifty hussars go through the water, like a flock of wild birds through the air—only their horses' heads above the foam, and the breeze tossing about the plumes of their red csakos.

The grenadiers having fired one volley with little or no effect, suddenly retired, and were at some distance when the hussars reached the opposite bank.

By this manœuvre the patrol of the Czibakhaza ferry was cut off from Szolnok, while Damjanics was meanwhile rapidly advancing towards the Theiss.

The hussars took prisoners all the couriers and passengers upon the road; and late at night the *avant-garde* crossed at Czibakhaza, and pressed forward on Szolnok, a reconnoitring party sustaining a brisk fire all the way to Kecskemet.

The same night, Damjanics reached the Theiss at Czibakhaza with his whole army, and advanced by forced marches on Szolnok, before the General of the district had been apprised of his approach.

It was a beautiful evening in spring. The sisters sat side by side at the window of their little chamber, silently watching the stars as they twinkled into light. Neither spoke, for each feared to grieve the other by expressing her hopes or fears; but their tears mingled as they sat clinging to one another, each pale face seeking comfort from the other—their hands clasped, and their hearts raised in prayer.

To-morrow, one may return triumphant from the battle to lay his laurels at his bride's feet. And the other—what may be his fate?

Sleep at last brought rest to the weary eyes, and gave back its restrained feelings to each beating heart, and they appeared again in dreams. And one spoke, not of war, nor of his country, but of love alone, eternal and unchangeable; but the other only came to bid farewell, silently and sadly. And then again she saw him; but his dark eyes were closed, and the pale moonbeams bathed his dying brow.

Their mother heard them murmuring in sleep, and stole to their bedsides.

Tears rolled down one pale sleeper's face; while a bright smile was playing on the other's, and illumined its sweet repose.

Damjanics' army halted opposite Szolnok during the night, after two hours' march, and awaited in battle order, and without watch-fires, the signal to resume the march.

The roar of cannon on the opposite side of the Theiss was the expected signal.

The Hungarian General had seen several campaigns. Whenever he came up with the enemy, his quick glance discovered as if by instinct their strongest point, and there he directed all his force, crying, at the head of his troops, "Follow me!"

His system, however, was not generally approved of in the army. Many of the Generals affirmed that it was not enough to gain a battle: attention must be paid to the rules of war, various obligations attended to for which every General is responsible, proclamations issued, harangues made, &c.—with all of which Damjanics dispensed. He was neither a statesman nor a student—he was simply a soldier.

On quitting the Banat, however, he issued the following proclamation to his enemies:—

"Dogs!

"I retire at present, but I will return.

"If in the meantime you dare stir, I will sweep you from off the face of the earth, and then shoot myself through the head as the last Raczien, that no remnant of our race may be left!"[59]

> [59] Damjanics was by birth a Racz or Raczien, who were the
> bitterest enemies of the Hungarians, and committed many
> excesses and cruelties during the rebellion of 1848-9. The
> proclamation is here translated word for word.

The results of this first attempt so much encouraged the General, that he determined, of the many necessary things required of him, to harangue his troops before the next action, and actually made a vow to that effect.

It was the night before the battle of Szolnok.

"Singular!" muttered the General, as he paced up and down his tent; "my spirits were wont to rise before a battle, and now I feel as anxious as if the thought of to-morrow were unwelcome!" And he strove to solve in his own mind the cause of such unusual gloom.

Some time after, an *officier de corps* remarked within the General's hearing, that to-morrow they should have the famous harangue.

"The tartar take it!" exclaimed the General; "it was that made me feel as if I could creep out of my skin. But never fear—they shall have it, and the enemy shall pay for it!"

The General had finished his plans of battle in a quarter of an hour;— the speech was not ready late in the morning.

Having arranged his troops in order, he rode out before them. They all knew that he was to harangue them that day, and they knew that it was as great a sacrifice on his part as if he were to deliver up his battery to a parliamentary tribunal for half a day.

Halting before the standard of the ninth battalion, he lifted his csako, grew very pale, and began:—

"Comrades!"

At that instant, the guns thundered across the Theiss.

The General's countenance suddenly brightened—diction and phraseology were forgotten; and drawing his sword, he cried in a voice of thunder,—"There is the enemy! Follow me!" which was answered by a tremendous cheer, while the whole army dashed after their gallant leader towards the cannon's roar.

Meanwhile, Vecsey's *corps d'armée* stormed the ramparts on the opposite side of the Theiss.

The attack, however, was only apparent: the manœuvre of either party frustrated the other.

The imperial troops endeavoured to entice the enemy within their cross fire by charges of cavalry and feint retreats; while the hussars, seeing the cuirassiers turn in good order, gave the command "right about," and quietly returned to their stations.

And now the Hungarians prepared to storm the entrenchments; and when the battalions were almost within gunshot, they advanced their cannon, and without any impediment poured a vigorous fire on the ramparts—appearing to expend their whole strength before the enemy, while their real aim was totally different.

They were only answered here and there by a gun from the ramparts; but the battery concealed in the wood did not give the slightest intimation of its existence, it being expected that the enemy would make an attack, as the place was apparently feebly defended, and the imperialists engaged on all sides, and, purposely, giving them every advantage.

But the attack was not made. This continued till about noon. The distant spectator could observe nothing but the continual motion of regular masses. One or two troops of heavy cavalry marched quietly up to the field of action, their helmets gleaming in the bright sun of a cloudless day. A division of hussars galloped by with drawn swords: long lines of infantry suddenly formed into squares, and fired on the passing cavalry. At another point, the treacherous gleam of bayonets in the moat betrayed the stealthy approach of troops, upon which the adjacent battery suddenly galloped to a little eminence, from whence they began to fire. But no regular engagement had taken place; the "On, Magyar! on!" and the hussars' "Ha! on!" were not yet heard. The whole was a mere animated play of arms. Trumpets sounded, drums beat, cannon fired; but they were unaccompanied by battle-cries or dying groans—death still greedily awaited the onset.

Suddenly the great guns thundered across the Theiss.

Swift and unexpected, like the descent of lightning from heaven, was Damjanics' appearance at Szolnok, and it was hailed by a tremendous cheer from the besieging party—life announcing death! Again the cannon roared.

The besiegers did not find the imperial army unprepared, although this attack was unexpected; but there were not many troops on that side of the ramparts, which was principally protected by cannon.

The Hungarians advanced in a semicircle, the Szeged battalion in the centre, composed chiefly of recruits armed with scythes, on the right the red-caps, and the hussars on the left.

The enemy's guns opened a deadly fire from every side, and yet they advanced like the tempest-cloud through which the lightning passes, changing its form without impeding its course. The balls made fearful inroads among them—they fell right and left, covering the place with the dead and wounded; and many a dying soldier, raising his head for the last time, gazed long and earnestly after his standard, till it disappeared amidst the fire of the enemy—when, cheering yet again, he sank to rise no more.

The Szeged battalion came up first with the foe, rushing impetuously on—for their arms were useless till face to face with their enemy. They stormed the battery of the terminus, from which the cannon fired incessantly—one ball sweeping off fourteen at a time; but they only hastened the more furiously over the dead bodies of their comrades. One moment more—several guns opened at once, and a hundred mangled bodies and headless trunks rolled in the dust and smoke. The next instant, the troops which guarded the battery were scattered on every side: the artillery stood valiantly by their guns to the last man. As the besiegers advanced, they were assailed by a hot fire from the windows of the houses, and from behind the barricades. The conflict was long and desperate. At last, the tricoloured banner waving from the windows announced that the besiegers were victorious.

This was the first action in which the Szeged battalion had been engaged, and for numbers among them it was the last.

Meanwhile the red-caps marched steadily on to the flying bastions. Unlike the young corps, these troops knew how to give place to the enemy's balls, and never fired in vain; nor did they cover their eyes from the fearful carnage around them, as most of the young troops did, for death was familiar to them in all its forms. This was their seventeenth engagement, and in each they had been foremost in the attack.

The entrenchments were guarded by a body of *chasseurs*, who kept up a constant harassing fire on the advancing troops.

The latter quickly thinned their lines, and forming into chain, rushed on the entrenchments, heedless of the musket fire—their standard-bearer foremost in the attack. A musket ball cut the staff of the standard in two, and the soldier, placing the colours on his sword, rushed on as before—another ball, and the standard-bearer fell mortally wounded, holding up the colours with his last strength, till a comrade received it on the point of his bayonet.

They reached the bulwarks, and, climbing on each other's shoulders, their bayonets soon clashed with those of the enemy. An hour later, they were in possession of the ramparts. The *chasseurs*, repulsed by their desperate attack, retreated to the *tête de pont*, where they rallied, under cover of some troops which had come to their assistance. The red-caps were soon engaged with these fresh troops, and their battle-cry was heard on the opposite side.

Meanwhile Vecsey's troops advanced impetuously to the redoubt, part of the garrison of which had hurried towards Szolnok, where the action had begun; but the most desperate engagement was below the chapel. A regiment of *chasseurs* were drawn up *en carré* on the plain, and were twice charged by the hussars, and twice repulsed; the third time they succeeded in breaking the square, the horses dashing in among the bayonets, and in an instant all was confusion. The *chasseurs* retreated to the chapel bulwarks, where they endeavoured to rally, but were pursued by the artillery, and, cut off from all possible retreat to the town, they fled in disorder, and were pursued to the Zagyva; there, although the most desperate once more made a stand, the rest were driven into the stream, and many an empty csako was borne down the blood-stained water.

Suddenly a cuirassier regiment was seen galloping from the opposite side, towards the scene of action, their helmets and swords gleaming through clouds of dust. The hussars quickly formed to receive the new enemy, and, without waiting for their attack, dashed forward to the encounter.

It was like the meeting of two hurricanes: one a mighty, moving bastion, advancing in such exact order, it seemed as if the thousand men and steeds had but one pulse; the other troops, light and swift as the wind, their spirited little horses neighing and dashing on before, as if each wished to be first in the encounter; the various coloured pelisses and plumes of their riders tossed about in the wind, and their swords flashing over their heads.

"Hurrah! hurrah!—Rajta! rajta!"

The mutual collision broke the order at once. The troops on either side divided into parties, fighting man to man; here a cuirassier was surrounded by the hussars, and there a hussar in the midst of cuirassiers; the attacking party now advancing, now retreating, as the antagonists on either side gained strength.

For some time only the two standards waving high above, and here and there a soldier's face, and the gleam of straight and curved swords, were seen through the smoke and dust; and now the wind blew the dust aside, and exposed the bright helmets, the excited countenances, the maddened horses, many of which galloped about with empty saddles, while their riders lay trodden on the field.

The clash of swords resounded on all sides, mingled with cries of victory and the groans of death.

A tall and powerful cuirassier galloped about like the genius of battle— death seemed in each flash of his sword; he rode his third horse, two having already been shot under him.

Clouds of dust and smoke again veiled the combatants, and nothing could be seen but the two banners—now pressing forward, now retarded, but slowly approaching, and cutting a deadly passage towards each other.

Old Gergo was engaged with two cuirassiers, his ardour unmingled with the impetuosity of youth; and even in the midst of the fray he found time to instruct the young recruit, illustrating his theory by many a prompt example.

A troop of hussars now dashed forward and were met by an equal number of cuirassiers; their leaders, being on the right of their troops, had not yet met face to face, but, foremost to the charge, they showed a good example, while each man fought as if he alone were responsible for the honour of his party. The right flank on either side pressing back the foe's left, they both turned round the centre, like a stiff axle—the hussars occupying the place of the cuirassiers, and the latter that of the hussars.

In the heat of the action, their leaders recognised each other—Laszlo and Gejza! But the discovery produced no wavering—both were determined to conquer or to die.

Meanwhile another troop came up to the assistance of the cuirassiers, and the hussar captain was obliged to cut his way out from between two fires, and thus came face to face with his antagonist.

"Surrender, comrade!" cried Laszlo.

"Never!" cried the hussar, as he galloped to the charge.

The sword of death was raised in either hand, their glances darted fire; for a moment they remained motionless, as if spell-bound, their swords still raised—the next both turned with one accord upon the nearest foes. Laszlo's sword pierced the heart of a hussar, while Gejza dealt such a blow on a cuirassier's helmet that he fell without a groan, and then, without turning, he cut his way through the enemy's ranks—"Hurrah! hurrah!—rajta!" And the battle-cry mingled with the clash of swords and the groans of the dying.

Meanwhile a division of cuirassiers marched rapidly through Szolnok to take the hussars in the rear.

Suddenly, at the turn of a street, two hundred red-caps stood before them. Both parties were taken by surprise at the unexpected encounter. It was but a moment. The next, an engagement took place of which we find few instances in history, namely, infantry attacking cavalry. The two hundred red-caps suddenly fired on the cuirassiers, and then, shouting wildly, rushed upon them with their bayonets; and the veteran troops, who had stood so many fires, whose valour alone had turned the day at Mor, were obliged to retreat before the fearful attack.

This circumstance occurred but twice during the whole campaign.

Görgei was the first who attempted it, with the Inczed battalion, at the time of his first retreat; that same battalion (eleventh) which so gallantly defended the bridge of Piski,60 where more than half their number fell.

[60] In Transylvania.

An old Polish soldier who witnessed the combat, made the following remark:—"I have seen the battles of the *ancienne garde*, and fought with the Polish legion, but I never saw men fight like the red-caps!"

By this attack the cuirassiers were cut off from their head forces, and, pressed by Vecsey on the opposite side, they retreated hastily, without having time to save their cannon or destroy the bridge after them.

The imperial forces, thus pressed between two fires, were obliged to evacuate Szolnok, and retreat among the Zagyva morasses.

After their desperate conflict with the red-caps, the cuirassiers were again routed by a fresh regiment of hussars, and driven into the Zagyva; but few of the weary horses had strength to struggle through the water, and their heavy armour prevented the men from swimming: thus many sank in the stream.

It was evening when the battle was over. Horses without riders were galloping about the plain, while here and there a wounded steed neighed mournfully, as if searching for his master. Powder-waggons and cannon lay overturned on the field, which was strewed with the dead and dying.

The trumpet sounded the retreat, and the hussars assembled from every side, their horses rearing and prancing as if they had come out for the first time that day.

An hour afterwards, the sound of music was heard in every *guinguette*, and the hussars' spurs clinked to the gay cymbal and clarionet. The battle was forgotten; it was now the time for mirth.

Old Gergo treated his comrades. He was rich enough—for he had killed an officer of rank; and though his pupil the recruit could scarcely keep his feet, he continued to treat him in spite of his resistance.

"But if we drink it all now, corporal, we shall have nothing left for to-morrow."

"Don't argue with me, but drink; that's the order now, and to-morrow will take care of itself;" and the soldiers drank on, while their companions danced and shouted to the gay sounds. All was feasting and revelry within the town.

But without, upon the battle-field, what painful sounds hailed the fall of evening?—it was the fearful groans of the dying! What sad thoughts called forth those sighs from the parting spirit! Home, glory, mother, and beloved ones,—never to meet again! The evening breeze bears them away: whither?

An officer of hussars went over the field with a military surgeon, while his soldiers bore the wounded away on their arms.

The young officer turned mournfully from one sad spectacle to another. Here lay a young soldier in the bloom of youth, the point of a sword had pierced through his cuirass and come out behind; and from whose hand had that thrust come? a little farther, lay another, whose face was so cut, and disfigured by the dust, that none could have recognised it! and now his eye rested on a young hussar who lay on his back, his outstretched arm still grasping his sword, over which the fingers were closed so stiffly that it was impossible to release it; near him an old soldier had died, with his arm around the neck of his horse, which had been killed along with him, like two old comrades whom death could not part.

The young officer carefully surveyed the field, and his quick eye passed none over. He had reached a little knoll, where, half concealed among some bushes, a white form seemed to move. It was a young cuirassier officer, who lay with his face buried in the long grass.

The hussar knelt down to raise his head, and called for assistance.

"Thanks, comrade!" said the dying youth faintly, as he turned his face towards him.

The last rays of the setting sun shone on the handsome, pale countenance, the closing eyes, and the deep wound just below the heart.

"Laszlo!" groaned the hussar, "is it thus we meet?"

"Lay me on the grass, brother; I am dying," said the cuirassier faintly. "Alas! my bride will wait in vain!"

The surgeons examined the wound, and pronounced it mortal; he had but a few moments to live.

"Tell my bride," said the young man, in scarcely audible accents, "that my last thought was of her—and bury me where she may come and"—

The young hussar sobbed bitterly beside his dying friend. "Alas! that we must part—that one of us must die!"

"God bless you, brother—be happy!" murmured Laszlo, convulsively grasping Gejza's hand; "poor Aniko!" and his head sank on his comrade's breast.

The sun's last rays had set, and the pale moon rose, shedding her quiet beams on the closed eyes and silent lips!

The long-looked-for day had come and gone; that day so full of hope and fear for the young sisters.

It had brought grief and joy; but the joy was not for the hopeful, nor the tear for the trembling heart, though one stood at the altar, and the other at the lonely grave; and one indeed wore the white and the other the black dress, but neither wore that which she had prepared.

THE BREWER

Nature had endowed Vendel Hornyicsek, the brewer of B— —, in the county of Raab, with five hundred and seventy nine pounds of standard weight; and he was not the man to turn tail before a stuffed lamb and any given quantity of beer.

His head was a complete circle, a worthy rival for any pumpkin produced on the sunniest plain; and Mount Ararat itself might have blushed in the vicinity of his nose. He had only one eye, which you might have suspected he had borrowed *ad usum* from some misanthropic mole—it was small, green, and peculiarly adapted to sleep; but mother Nature was not unjust, and what she curtailed in one feature she amply refunded in another, by bestowing more than ordinary proportions on the mouth, into which capacious aperture the four-quart tankard would certainly have disappeared altogether had it not been held fast by its two handles. Except, however, to receive the contents of the tankard, the good man seldom made use of this feature. It is true that he could speak nothing but the German and Bohemian languages, in which he had been born and bred; for though he had lived thirty years in the county of Raab, he had never been able to make himself understood in the Hungarian language, and certainly he found no living creature, unless it were those travelled gentlemen, the storks, to address him in his native tongue. Moreover, Vendel Hornyicsek gazda61 was not a lover of great commotion; he was by no means ambitious. He would sit quietly in the chimney-corner from morning till night, replenishing his interior with ample potions of the genuine barley-bree, and turning in his mind some philosophy peculiarly his own. He never dined at regular hours, or rather he dined at every hour of the day; it was a continual, unwearied struggle with his appetite—that invincible Antæus, who, as often as he was overcome, rose with redoubled strength to renew the attack; and these struggles did not cease with the day, like the labour of ordinary mortals, but he was accustomed to wake at night and strive to satisfy the cravings of the voracious monster. A pitcher of unusual dimensions was regularly placed by his bedside, just within comfortable reach of his hand; for it was his firm belief that whoever goes hungry to bed dreams of being devoured by Pharaoh's lean kine; it was probable, however, that he would have despatched the whole seven had they come to an actual encounter.

[61] The common name for host or master.

In the village of B— — they still exhibit as a relic his flannel stockings, each of which would have contained at least a Presburg peck of anything you liked to put into it; while a wandering Sclavonian family might have harboured snugly in his sleeve.

There was not a vestige of a beard on the broad expanse of face, which was naked as the moon, and blooming as the Pacha's rose. The corners of his mouth extended upwards, as if they were amusing themselves at the expense of the eye placed over them, and there was not the slightest rumour of anything like brow or lash to crown the eyelid. As an indemnity, however, for such destitution, the chin was doubled and trebled; indeed, it would have been difficult to decide where it began and how it ended; and a few orphan hairs endeavoured to keep their ground on the vast and sterile heath above his ears.

Our worthy host had already disposed of three ribs, or in other words, he had followed to the grave three wives, each of whom had weighed above two hundredweight. But what did he derive, after all, from so many weddings and funerals? To be left alone at last, for the house to go to wreck and ruin, for the beer to get sour, the bread to be half baked, and the meat half cooked, while the hawks carried off his poultry, and the rats his cheese; in short, his whole establishment went to auction, like the Csakys'62 straw, till finally in the height of his distress, Vendel resolved—what else could he do?—he resolved to look out for another wife, and actually set about carrying his project into execution. In former times he had been used to contemplate and weigh duly every consideration connected with this most important step, together with the merits requisite in the object of his choice. She must be plain, that he might have no cause for jealousy; of small speech, but ample dowry; and her knowledge and accomplishments must consist chiefly in the noble art of pampuska63 cookery, with which, namely, the pampuskas, our worthy host's most sublime ideas of mortal happiness were connected. Hitherto he had succeeded to the utmost of his wishes, and three wives adorned with all the requisite virtues had rendered the pampuska morsel sweet to his lips. Moreover, he had lived in uninterrupted peace and tranquillity, without having ever had the slightest cause for uneasiness; on the contrary, the first impulse of every one who looked at either of the three worthy dames had been to turn and run as long as there was a road before him.

[62] This family is said to have had once such abundant crops that, in order to get rid of it, they were obliged to let all who would carry it off.

[63] A sort of fritter—a Bohemian dish.

But let no man call himself happy before his death—he may do so afterwards if he has a mind; as the wise Racien said a fortnight after the inundation. Vendel Hornyicsek having for the fourth time resolved to put on the orban cap, so outwitted his good sense in his advanced age, as to take to himself a mate who was both young and pretty, and whose name was Vicza.

The first had been Nani, the second Lotti, the third Zsuzsi, all good, quiet, pious names. Hey! Vendel, Vendel, why should you have stumbled upon a Vicza! and such a Vicza too, whose eyes might have allured the sun from the skies, and each one of whose saucy motions might have charmed the very curd64 into life; a Vicza who, instead of pampuska cakes, baked such witch pogacsok,65 that he must have been a very Saturn who ventured to partake of them; and it must be observed, that although every muscle of this fair Vicza was replete with vivacity and motion, yet the most flexible part of her whole person was that small member designated by anatomists the tongue; indeed, it required no whalebone palate like that of the monster of the deep to emit such effusions as would clear the whole atmosphere.

[64] In Hungarian, the expression is more *naïve—sleeping milk* being the literal translation.

[65] Bannocks.

Scarcely had Mistress Vicza placed her foot in her husband's house when it became an overturned world. Her appearance had much the same effect as pouring vitriol into water, or putting a leech among the foals. Every servant was obliged to be on his feet at cockcrowing, and wo to that cheek on whose sleep the sun shone, for Mistress Vicza's palm was sure to celebrate it; moreover, she was in the kitchen, storeroom, barn, fold, stall, in short, everywhere at once, to see that all was going on in order, and that the folks were not sleeping or stealing. She saw everything, knew everything, and had a word for everybody, persecuted and pursued from morning till night whatever was capable of motion, followed up every command to the very letter, and was unfailing in her promises, which were invariably threats.

These new arrangements by no means pleased the good Vendel. He could never sleep beyond daybreak, for all the windows and doors were then thrown open to let the morning air pass through the rooms; he had nobody to sit and discourse with to make the time pass, for nobody had a moment to sit down—the whole household seemed to be on galvanic springs from sunrise till sunset. He was kept, besides, to regular meals, and they only dished three times a day for him—for him who had been accustomed to eat every hour of the twenty-four; and, oh unparalleled barbarity! he was obliged to forego altogether his nightly repasts.

If the unhappy man complained of having nothing to do, a basket of beans in their husks was placed before him to be peeled, or some other such employment which he would set to work at with a heavy sigh, thinking mournfully the while of his three dead partners, and the happy days which had fled never to return.

But Vendel was a philosopher, and he knew that it was best to submit with a good grace, for how should he set himself in opposition to the rising hurricane, or look the lightning in the face? Who indeed would not have drawn in his head between his shoulders when the capped Bellona turned with outstretched arm to pour forth the vial of her wrath in hailstones and coals of fire, lightning flashing from her eyes and thunder pealing from her mouth? Vendel was not the man to cope with such elements of war; he would have borne even more for the sake of a quiet life.

Our worthy host kept a large beer-tavern in the village of B— —, which had been hitherto the resort of all the cuirassiers and dragoons in the neighbourhood, who beguiled every leisure hour in the enjoyment of the national beverage, while their kind host showed them a never-failing good example.

A tall stripling of a Moravian youth, meagre as a sign-post, was the beerhouse Ganymede. One might have thought his master had chosen him purposely to form a contrast to himself. His mouth was always wide open, and his eyes, which seemed trying to find their way out of his head, stared vacantly before him: if he looked at anything at all, it was apparently with the point of his nose.

From two arms of immeasurable length dangled a huge pair of uncouth red hands, which looked as though they were not really his own, but merely borrowed for the day's work, and his awkward legs he seemed rather to drag after him than to be indebted to their assistance for the act of propulsion.

To complete the singularity of his appearance, this youth was in the habit of wearing a coat with long and pointed tails, the sleeves of which scarcely reached below the elbows, while the ends of the tails dangled against his ankles; his waistcoat had doubtless boasted of some very brilliant colouring in days long past, though it would have been difficult to distinguish the shades at present, and most of the gilt buttons had only left their ears as a remembrance. Wide csikos66 drawers adorned his legs as far as the ankles, beneath which his bare feet, were thrust into a pair of heelless slippers; a high cravat stood up around his neck like a halter, in which no less than three glittering pins of Bohemian stones constituted the especial glory of his toilet.

[66] The csikos, who keep the horses on the plains, are noted for their wide drawers.

It was late in the evening. The dogs were barking about the streets, and the peacocks crying in the neighbouring farm-yard; otherwise the village was very quiet, the good folks having for the most part retired to rest with the sparrows.

Master Hans, or Hanzli, as he was commonly denominated—we have evaded the question as long as possible, but finally we must acknowledge that the youth's name was Hanzli; it was no fault of his, poor fellow! his god-parents were alone to blame; and doubtless, had he been capable of speech when they so basely betrayed his helpless innocence, he would have protested against it—Hanzli thrust his nose and his arm out of the window, then drew both back, and the window was closed.

The village had been deserted for some weeks by the German soldiery; and from that day forward the beer-room had become pitifully empty, for it was only now and then that some desperately thirsty wretch dropped in by chance, and ventured to slake his thirst with a glass of the barm-smelling wine.

A dim light flickered on the long table, round which leaned despondingly a dozen of empty chairs. Vendel-gazda sat near the cupboard, in a red flannel dressing-gown and a pointed white cap with a blue border; his hands, which were placed on his vast stomach, held a plated snuff-box, and with his legs outstretched beneath the table, he snored away to his heart's content, while the much-esteemed goblet stood before him like an old fat dame with her arms a-kimbo.

Hanzli having closed the shutters, and looked about him to see that all was right, listened hard for a few moments to his master's deep breathing, as he bobbed behind the tankard, and then hastily making up his mind, he shambled over with long strides on tiptoe—hands, eyes, and mouth all moving together, as if he were stepping with each of them, and, pausing before the table, he raised one leg, balanced himself on the other, and peeped into the depths of the tankard. It was still half full. This was enough. Having once more peeped into it to make sure that his imagination was not deceiving him, he seized it by the two ears, and, raising it to his month, began to draw in the unoffered beverage, his knees bending under him, and his eyes starting from his head with the enormous exertion.

As he continued raising the huge tankard till half his head was within it, a tremendous explosion was suddenly heard in the kitchen, as if pots and pans were being thrown at somebody's head, which so startled Hanzli that he emptied the remains of the barley nectar over his head and shoulders; and what was his mortification when, on replacing the empty tankard, he encountered Vendel's green eye staring at him wide open, as if to say, "I see you, my lad; and I wish you good health!" but that was not what he said.

"Hanzli, my lad, go and see what is broken in the kitchen." Could he have uttered a severer reproof?

But Hanzli had too much sense and too much confidence in his master's goodness to believe that he was in earnest; he knew that he would probably return with the answer that it was his nose that was broken; and having recovered from his first embarrassment, he merely drew a long breath terminating in a whistle, and shook his head until the shake resolved itself into a wave.

"Poor Master Vendel!" he seemed to say; "it was another world in Mistress Nani's lifetime; you were not then roused from your sleep in this manner."

Vendel-gazda replied by a pitiful gaze at Hanzli. He would have clasped his hands too, but only the tips of his fingers could reach each other. He looked as if he would have said: "My poor lad, Hanzli, you too have a bad job of it now-a-days; in Mistress Nani's lifetime, the key of the cellar lived in your pocket, and you were not then obliged to empty my tankard."

The two countrymen were used to this silent language. They might have conversed in their own tongue, to be sure. But then, who knows— in short, there are cases—and Vendel and Hanzli were of this opinion—in which least said is soonest mended.

And now Master Vendel's head began to wave very disastrously; his whole appearance was one large, living, fat complaint. It was like that feeling which a man experiences when he knows that there is something the matter with him, something seriously wrong, but cannot exactly tell what it is.

"Hanzli, my lad!" he exclaimed at last, in a very weak voice, after they had exhausted their telegraphic repartee; "Hanzli, tell me what is the matter with you."

Hanzli raised both his shoulders to his ears, extending the palms of his hands outwards, and lifted his eyebrows to the top of his forehead— implying by this gesture that he knew very well what was the matter with him, but was wise enough to keep it to himself.

"Hm!" replied Vendel, and was again silent. He would not force the lad to speak—an excellent policy, if intentional; for when words are not forced, they force themselves. Hanzli by degrees shambled up nearer his master, and after fidgeting about, coughing, and standing on one leg, he suddenly turned round, placed his finger on the side of his nose, and stooping to a level with Vendel's ear, whispered into it:

"Indeed, indeed, master, the misfortune is this, and this alone,—that you have no heir."

"What have I not, Hanzli?"

"That you have no son or daughter."

At these words Vendel's eye opened wide, and he struck the table with a force which sent the four-quart tankard dancing about as if the tartar were in it; then, holding up his enormous face, he began to look out of himself. An entirely new idea seemed to thrill through him, as if he had just been assured that perpetual motion had not yet been discovered, and that he was the man to discover it.

"You are right, Hanzli!" he exclaimed; "I have no son or daughter; and what if I had?"

"Why then, you see, master," said Hanzli, looking behind him at each word, "you see there would be something for the wife to do—somebody to quarrel with, that you might not be always disturbed; and then you could sit all day in the large arm-chair drinking and sleeping, and the children would come and kiss your hand morning and evening, and you could take them on your knee and tell them of the far-famed Rübezahl,67 and if they made a noise you could scold them yourself; and then, in after years, all the excellent mysteries of the noble art of brewing would devolve on them, and you would leave a renowned progeny after you; and how nice all this would be!"

[67] The subject of an old German legend.

Vendel's pride felt all the weight of this argument: his eye glistened, his clenched fists were raised to his mouth, and he smiled as complacently as a Tyrolian cheese, and sighed so deeply, that it might have been a hurricane on Lichtenstein's estate. This poetical turn was still more imposing than the melancholy one, but it did not last long. Vendel's ideas were forced to descend from their airy regions, for the door opened, and a profane figure entered, carrying the pole of a cart as a staff, and advanced with heavy steps to the farthest end of the long table, where he seated himself on a bench, and grumbling out, in a tone which would have put a bear to shame, "Wine here!" he elbowed himself out of his mantle, and pushed the long pole behind him.

The intruder was a middle-aged man, tall and muscular; his skin was of a dark reddish brown, and shone as if it had been rubbed with oil; his black knotty hair was divided in the middle, and fell in matted clusters on either side; and his beard was spiral, and twisted like a gipsy's farewell.68

[68] Gipsy's farewell—a byword, because they generally terminate the last notes of their music by various turns and windings of the air.

He wore a high csalma,69 in the top of which was stuck a red pipe; and a large brass monogram, the initials of the lord of the domain, was fastened on one side.

[69] A kind of toque worn by the peasants in some districts.

Wine was placed before him, which he swallowed in silence, only now and then grumbling something inarticulately to himself. When he had drunk a few glasses, he took the pipe out of his csalma, and lighting it at the candle, leant upon one elbow and began to smoke. He seemed upon no ceremony, and was evidently no stranger in the house. Hanzli stood before him with his mouth open, and his hands behind his back; and Vendel reclined in his arm-chair, giving full scope to the flights of his imagination.

At last the silent guest, tired of leaning on one elbow, exchanged it for the other, and, nodding condescendingly to Hanzli, he emptied his pipe; and again leaning on his arm, and drawing his mouth fearfully to one side with his fist, exclaimed: "Well, Hanzli deak,70 have you heard that the French are coming?"

[70] Scholar, student.

"Ah, indeed!" cried Hanzli, starting; "from Turkey?"

Hanzli had studied about two years, and knew something of geography. He could speak a little Hungarian, too, and Moravian, and German—just enough of each to prevent him being sold in any of them (had there been anybody to buy him), and he jumbled all these languages together so strangely, that it would have been difficult to say which one he meant to speak.

"Indeed, I cannot tell that; I do not know where they come from," replied the guest. "But this much is certain, that they all carry their heads under their arms, have eyes in their shoulders, and when they get hold of a man they snap his head off—kakk it goes!"

Hanzli raised his hands to his neck: he thought they had got him already.

"Just so," continued the guest, wiping his bearded chin with the sleeve of his coat. "Then all their generals eat two pounds of iron, every morning, and wash it down with a pint of vitriol."

"By all the saints!" exclaimed Hanzli, opening his mouth and eyes; "have you seen them yet, Andras-gazda?"

"I was at a place where they were talking about them: my godfather's niece has a bridegroom whose brother is serving with the green csako hussars—they have just quartered a troop in the district, and it was he who related it."

At the word 'hussar,' Vendel's attention began to be excited; it was the only word he understood in Hungarian, and it brought to his recollection so much poultry which had been carried off by the kites, and so many barrels of wine which the great bell71 had paid, and still pays for to the present day.

[71] In Hungary, there is a proverb that unpaid debts will be collected by the great bell.

But it is a bad thing to mention the evil one, for he is sure to be prowling about the garden; and Vendel-gazda had scarcely time to summon to his imagination that human being metamorphosed into the inhuman called a hussar, before the door burst open, as if Sisera's army had arrived, and six moustached figures, each one smarter and more agile than the last, entered with a clash of arms, which would have disturbed the philosophy of any honest peace-loving Bohemian in Christendom; and instead of seating themselves at the table, as any other reasonable Christians would have done, they clinked and rattled about here and there, making jests on the pictures of Cossack feats on the walls, with their pendants of Spring, Summer, and Winter.

One among them was a singularly handsome youth, with raven hair, and eyes which flashed like lightning; his pointed dark moustache was provokingly becoming, and his figure as supple as a young leopard's, but he was certainly the most unreasonable of the party: he gave no rest to man or beast, and was the bane of every honest soul with whom he came in contact. Scarcely had he entered, than he stumbled over Hanzli, who was gaping in solemn wonder at the new-comers, his back bent and his neck stretched forward, as if he were trying to personify the letter S.

"Your servant, nephew!" exclaimed the hussar, thrusting his fingers among the youth's hair, and making it all stand on end; "well, what have you been about since we last met?"

As they had never met in their lives before, this question and the cockatoo *frisure* so embarrassed Hanzli, that he seized the bottle which stood before Andras-gazda and raised it to his lips, with as little ceremony as if that good man had not been sitting behind it.

"Have you lost your senses?" cried Andras-gazda, seizing the tails of Hanzli's coat.

"Make haste, man!" cried a voice deeper than any bass fiddle; "thunder and storms! make haste, man, and bring something to drink, or else" — and then followed a torrent of oaths, which it would be difficult and highly unbecoming to render into any known language.

The voice proceeded from under the huge moustache of the hussar sergeant, who had seated himself on the bench with an imposing dignity that became his rank.

Hanzli disappeared, but in a few minutes he shuffled back, and placed a brilliantly coloured plate before the sergeant.

"Did I ask for anything to eat, you stork, that you have brought me a plate instead of a glass?"

Hanzli again disappeared, and returned with a glass of foaming beer, which he placed before the hussar, handing him a fork at the same time.

"What the tartar do you take me for?" cried the hussar furiously, "that you should suppose I am going to drink such confounded stuff, as never before entered the mouth of any of my kindred!"

Hanzli's confusion increased at every step, till at last he could not find his own hands.

Oh, the worthy German dragoons! they were much more reasonable guests; they knew how to appreciate the good barley-bree! Then each had his own place, and his own tankard, beside which he would sit half the night singing honest German songs, or treating of Kant's philosophy, till some had fallen asleep on their benches, and others under them!

But the Magyar people have no conception of the ecstatic, or of beer-drinking; and it would be morally impossible to cut German or philosophy out of their nature.

Vendel-gazda had so completely lost all presence of mind, that he actually raised the tankard three times to his lips before he perceived that it was empty. From his earliest childhood he had grown up with the idea that every honest soul should keep clear of hussar soldiery; but he was not quite certain as to whether Mistress Vicza had been educated in the same principles.

Beneath the cupboard, with its head resting on Vendel's slippers, lay his favourite curly-haired, tail-clipped poodle, emitting now a half sneeze in its sleep, and now a snarl, as if in sympathy with its master's feelings.

"Good evening to you, Master Host," exclaimed the mischief-loving hussar, at the same time striking him on the shoulder as familiarly as if he had been one of his own recruits.

Vendel opened his eyes—that is, his eye—as wide as possible; while the hussar, seizing his enormous palm, gave it such a hearty slap that the room echoed with the sound, and then shaking it after the Hungarian fashion till the whole of the fat Colossus trembled like jelly, he sat down on the bench beside him, and thrust his finger and thumb into the open snuff-box, which the good man held in the other hand. In trying to find a place for his feet under the table, he trod so hard on the stump of the sleeping poodle's tail that it actually crackled, sending the poor animal howling most lamentably round the room, while his howls were re-echoed by all the six or eight dogs in the court-yard.

"Come, come, don't make such a noise," said the hussar; "what if I had stood on your nose?" And as the dog returned to its accustomed place at its master's feet, he got hold of its head between his knees and filled its nostrils with snuff; while the poor animal, endeavouring to bite, bark, and sneeze at the same time, exhibited the most ludicrous appearance. Everybody in the room was ready to split with laughter; even Hanzli ventured to grin, and thereby incurred the displeasure of his gracious master, who turned his eye upon him severely, as if to say: "I take the joke from the soldiers, because they are hussars; but you are Hanzli, and you have no business to laugh."

Meanwhile, poor Vendel's nose grew longer and longer. "What a terrible race!" thought he to himself; "they respect neither heaven nor earth, never drink beer, take an honest man's snuff to give it to his dog, and then laugh at the whole affair! Heaven preserve us! what may not come next?"

What indeed!

Mankind has a singular propensity for thrusting his nose wherever he hears laughter or noise; and considering this weakness, what should be more natural than that all the inhabitants of the kitchen should press to the door of the beer-room to hear what was going on, and consequently that Mistress Vicza, with her eyes burning like two coals, should immediately follow in the track of the "linen folk?"

But no sooner did the sparkling eyes, the rosy cheeks, and the elastic figure of Mistress Vicza make its appearance, than the hussar started from his post beside Vendel, and bounded towards the door.

"Ah, sweet one! I have not seen you yet," he exclaimed, proceeding *brevi manu* to span the small waist of the pretty hostess.

"For shame, sir!" exclaimed Mistress Vicza, extricating herself from the hussar's grasp; and then, running over to her husband, she began to caress and fondle him—drawing his cap over his head, and trying to make room for herself on the bench beside him—though, at the very moment she was kissing the dear old man, her bright eyes glanced slily at the handsome hussar. (*Pro memoria* to every married man—when his wife kisses up one of his eyes, let him look well after her with the other.)

Our hero, in order to repair his fault, after looking about him and twisting his moustache, turned suddenly towards the group of servants assembled at the door, and seizing the nearest, a plump, rosy-faced little girl, with long plaited hair tied with gay ribbons, he imprinted a hearty kiss on her cheek, on which she screamed so loudly that he started back in alarm, bounding over the tables and chairs in his way.

"I'll settle your wits for you, master, if you can't behave better than that!" cried a deep voice in echo to the scream.

"How now! what is the matter, countryman?" said the hussar, peering into the bold countenance of the hardy peasant.

"'What is the matter?' that girl there is my bride; and I'll soon let you know what the matter is, if you dare to touch her again!"

"Ah! is that the case? who knows but that she would prefer me, after all?" replied the hussar, and, leaping over the table, he once more seized this living organ of sound, who screamed louder than before.

"Storms of Karpath!" shouted Andras, starting up, and kicking the bench from before him; then dashing his cap on the ground, he began tucking up the sleeves of his shirt.

"You want to fight, I suppose?" said the hussar, smiling complacently; "but swords are not made out of scythes, and you had better leave a hussar alone."

"That I shall not, when he touches my bride, were he a dog-faced Tartar! I shall beat him not only out of this, but out of the world too, if he had a thousand souls! I don't care for your sword, Master Hussar;" and loosing the mantle from his neck, the sturdy peasant seized the pole he had brought with him, and held it forth with an arm as knotty as an oak.

"Don't be foolish, now, Andras!" cried the little girl, running over to the pole-gladiator, and endeavouring to pacify him.

"Keep yourself out of the way, Panna," said Andras; "this is no time for trifling; I'll show him who is master here!"

"Why now, Andras, if you are determined to fight, I will get a weapon of your own dimensions," and, laughing gaily, the hussar opened the door and went into the court.

"Bring what you like, the beam of a mill, or an oak-tree, I don't fear you, with six others at your back!" cried the athletic labourer, assuming an offensive and defensive position with his back to the wall.

"Don't be reckoning on us," said the sergeant; "we have nothing to say to you—the lad can stand for himself."

"You will probably part company soon," muttered Andras, waiting with open eyes for the hussar's return.

He appeared at length, with neither a mill-beam nor an oak tree, but a long, slender reed, which he had pulled out of the roof.

"What! do you dare to make a fool of me?" cried Andras furiously.

"Not I," replied the hussar seriously, and stepping up to him, he began shaking the reed before his antagonist's face, who tried in vain to catch it, growing more impatient every instant, as the reed tickled his nose and mouth, and the gay laugh of the hussar rang in his ears, till at last, maddened with fury, he swung violently round and dashed the great cart-pole with such violence before him, that it brought down a shower of lime and mortar from the opposite wall, against which it fell, after causing great havoc on its way—several chairs and tables lay despoiled of arms and legs on the ground, and the two-eared tankard before Vendel-gazda was shivered into a thousand splinters; while Hanzli lay below one of the tables contemplating the scene at full length. What became of the hussar, or how he managed to escape in that critical moment, Heaven only knows; but when Andras looked about him, after this feat of annihilating rage, he found the reed still at his mouth, like a cigar twelve feet long, and the hussar standing opposite to him as before.

A general burst of laughter responded to Andras's gape of astonishment.

"Well, if ever I saw a match for that since I lived at Kiliti!" exclaimed the perplexed peasant, rubbing his eyes.

But what were mine host Vendel's feelings during all this excitement? he who loved peace and quiet, to what had he come at last? Disorder and misrule had taken possession of his house, he heard oaths which made his hair stand on end, his snuff-box was rifled without permission, his poodle's tail trod upon, he himself laughed at, and finally, open war carried on in his presence, and his favourite tankard, which had been esteemed and honoured, and had grown old in his house, was destroyed for ever, never to be used again, even beyond the grave, where he hoped to meet the three wives who had gone before him! It was more than a Bohemian-German brewer, who wore a night-cap, and was married for the fourth time, could be expected to bear.

"Go to your beds, my good folk!" he exclaimed, addressing his household in piteous accents, and rising solemnly from his seat; "let me get away from hence, Viczikam; let my bed be warmed with hot irons, for I am ill, very ill, and perhaps I may die. Alas! I am sick, sick! Vicza, I am dying!"

"For Heaven's sake, what is the matter?" cried his wife in a tone of great alarm, which was echoed by all the servants, who were of course much alarmed also.

"Bring elder-flowers from the attics," cried Mistress Vicza; "get a linseed poultice directly, boil water for the tea, and warm the pans; you, Hanzli, run to the barber's for leeches. Beatrice, lay down the bed immediately, and prepare hot irons—the gazda is sick, very sick; his head burns like an oven, and his hand is as cold as a frozen turnip; make haste—fly! two steps for one!"

The servants dispersed right and left to their various appointments, and some, directed by Mistress Vicza, seized Vendel by the arms and legs, and carried him off, neck and crop, to his bedroom, where they rolled him up in three feather-beds and half-a-dozen pillows, and made him drink a quart of camomile and as much elder-tea; while Mistress Vicza sat beside him with a hand-brush, which she applied unmercifully if he attempted to move hand or foot from under the feather-beds.

This is the village cure for every complaint. The patient is boiled in his own soup, and if he does not suffocate, or die of apoplexy, he is sure to be cured.

Vendel-gazda was at first only shamming ill. He wished to be in peace and quiet, and he wished to be made much of; but Mistress Vicza had fairly outwitted him, and he ended by believing what he had himself invented; he felt that it was either the heat or the cold, but some sort of fever it certainly was. The hot tea which he had drunk, the sack of linseed porridge which had been placed on his stomach, the vesicatorium applied to his soles, the anxious faces about him, the tiptoe tread, the odour of vinegar poured on heated iron to carry off infection, the hands laid on his forehead, the whispered opinions, all gave rise to those peculiar sensations experienced at the beginning of an illness—a sort of congealment in the head, and a swarming sensation throughout the whole system.

"Vicza!" whispered the patient from beneath the feather beds, from which only his nose was seen rising like a main-mast; "Vicza, I am thirsty!"

"The czerjo fu72 will be here directly, my dear old man, and then you can drink it; meanwhile, you may suck your lips a little."

[72] Thousand-sweets, an herb.

Alas! it was not czerjo-fu tea that Vendel wanted to drink, but he did not dare to say so.

"See, here it is, hot and bitter, for my dear old man! wait, I will pour some into the saucer—now, drink it, and you will be quite well; but take care not to burn your mouth."

"Brrrrrphü!" exclaimed the self-made patient, shuddering, as he took the first mouthful; "this must be poison!"

"Poison indeed! it is excellent physic. I will drink some myself; there now—delightful! it will cure you perfectly—drink now, my old man, drink it, quick! come now, drink it when I tell you."

In short, *nolens volens*, Vendel was obliged to open his mouth, and swallow what is erroneously called a thousand sweets, but is, in truth, a hundred thousand bitters.

It is a well-known fact that strong bitters produce a strong appetite, and this was the case thirty years ago, just as at present.

Vendel-gazda contented himself for some time by sighing deeply, and grimacing with his nose, which was the only part of his body in active condition, till at last, no longer able to control his impatience, he beckoned to Mistress Vicza, and whispered something in a beseeching tone, accompanied by a cannibal expression of countenance.

"You insatiable cormorant!" said Mistress Vicza angrily, "what will you want next?" and, drawing the capacious night-cap over his head, she bade him go to sleep, and left the room.

A deep and heavy sigh burst from poor Vendel's lips.

What the mystic word may or may not have been, has remained a secret to historians. Psychologians and philosophers, however, who are initiated in the sacred mysteries of gastronomy, may explain it in the simple expression, "I am hungry."

Mistress Vicza, however, recommended the sufferer to forget his tortures in sleep.

But Vendel could not sleep. Fearful and strange apparitions rose before his hungry imagination. Now a gigantic mast of Augsburg sausage sailed past, followed by an immeasurable side of bacon; now a host of rosy, smiling Bohemian pampuskas, their preserves squeezing out from every corner, came flying and leaping around him; anon a respectable beer-flask floated gravely by, with its venerable crown of white foam, accompanied by a roasted pig of unusual dimensions; then followed in diverse rotation, the whole system of bakes, stews, and roasts, and all sorts of nameable and nameless hashes, minces, and rich soups, emitting their savoury odours and aromatic flavours.

"Oh, hundredfold unhappy man that I am, not to be able to devour all these!" said the hungry brewer to himself, as swallowing his saliva, he turned to the wall, and tried to say his prayers.

But how could he pray under such circumstances? hungry and thirsty, with the water actually running from his mouth; besides which, the loud voices in the next room scolding, laughing, and fighting, were by no means calculated to inspire devotional feeling.

While he was thus suffering and struggling within himself—now whimpering, and now gnawing his coverlet—all at once, he thought he felt the pillow begin to move under his head, while certain mysterious whisperings met his ear; at last, something laid hold of his head.

"What is that!"

"Ja—ha—hai! it is me, master," said a voice, accompanied by a chattering of teeth.

Vendel looked round. Hanzli stood before him, his face of a livid green, his knees knocking together, and his hair standing on end.

Vendel thought he beheld a spectre. He tried to cry out, but his tongue stuck to the roof of his mouth, and he could not articulate a syllable.

"Master!" exclaimed the youth with upturned eyes; and, trembling violently, he fell upon both knees, and seized the collar of Vendel's night-dress so tightly, that the latter thought he was going to choke him, but he did not—no, he did not; on the contrary, Hanzli began to weep bitterly, and to kiss his master's huge hand, while he could only exclaim in a voice choked with sobs, "Master, master!"

"I hear, my lad; but what is the matter with you?"

"Oh, nothing the matter with me; but my master is ruined for ever; they are going to seize him and carry him off, and make a terrible job of him!"

"What are you talking of, Hanzli, my lad?" exclaimed the amazed brewer; "what do you mean?"

"Well, do you know, master, what the enemy, this terrible, vitriol-drinking enemy, has come for?"

"Not I."

"Nor did I know it before, but now I know it all. Oh! to think that it was for *that* they have come across kingdoms and worlds with fire and sword! to think that they have been searching governments and realms for *that*!"

"For what?"

"Why, did I not say it?"

"For my wife, perhaps?" cried the ex-patient, starting up, hunger and thirst alike forgotten.

"That would have been a good idea!" thought Hanzli; "they might have done that, but they did not. It is for you yourself, my beloved master—for you alone that all this war is waging," he whispered, with upraised eyes, pointing with his long ape-like arms to his master, who had fallen on his back; for though he did not understand the circumstances of the affair, he was very much alarmed for all that.

He stared at Hanzli, and Hanzli stared at him; both seemed afraid of renewing the conversation.

"But why—what does the French Emperor want with me?" asked Vendel at last, in a voice faint with suspense and terror.

"Ay," replied Hanzli, "that is the thing! They have a great project about you, master. I saw the green csako hussars whispering together, and shaking their heads. 'That is the man,' I heard them say, 'and no other;' and I came as near as possible to listen who or what it could be, and what should I hear"—

"Well, and what did you hear?"

"They said—whispering as low as possible, that nobody might hear them—that the French Emperor would not cease devastating the land with fire and sword, until they delivered him up as a ransom"—

"Well?"

"Until they gave him, as a ransom, a man weighing five hundredweight"—

"And what do they want with him?" gasped Vendel.

"And therefore they are determined to weigh you to-morrow; and if you strike the weight, they will immediately hand you over to the Emperor of the French! All this they whispered very low; but I heard them, master, for all that."

"But what does he want with me, Hanzli? do you not know what he wants?"

"Oh, it will kill you, master, to hear it! Nothing more nor less than"—

"Than what?"

"Than to preserve you in spirits for his museum!"

"All ye saints!" roared Vendel, leaping up on his bed; "preserve me in spirits of wine like the four-legged hen, or the double-tailed lizard!"

"Just so, master, and alive too!"

"But it shall not be!" roared Vendel. "They shall not preserve me in spirits; I have no desire for such an honour—none at all! Come, help me up. Where are my slippers? Holy prophet Jonas! no wish for it whatever! Reach me my jacket and my cap. St. Florian and Habakkuk! help me to dress. My cloak, my cloak, Hanzli—St. Cecilia! my cloak! Let us run, my lad, run"—

"But whither?"

This was the question.

"Where? out of the window, of course. Take the hatchet and knock out the cross beams—that's it! never mind breaking the glass! Now, raise me up, Hanzli; let us run!"

And the next moment there was a terrible crash outside the window, occasioned by the descent of Vendel, which luckily the noise of the revellers within prevented them from hearing.

"But where shall we go now?"

This was the next question, for Vendel-gazda's legs were not exactly fashioned to run away with him. What was to be done?

At last Hanzli bethought him of a large wheel-barrow, which lay under a shed close by; and bringing it out, he placed his master in it, and wheeled him down a by-road which led behind the village; while the gigantic effort of this superhuman undertaking bent his back into a C, and caused his eyes to start almost out of their sockets.

His master tried to encourage him as well as he could: "Push on, my brave boy! I will serve you another time—only push on!"

At last they reached the end of the village. Poor Hanzli still continued pushing his immense burden before him, panting and snorting, while his back seemed ready to break at every step, and Vendel still continued his words of encouragement. "That's right I push on, my boy!—we will rest anon."

They reached the maize-ground.

Hanzli was nearly exhausted; and just as he was exerting his last strength to roll the sisyphian burden over a little mound—while Vendel urged him forward as usual, crying, "Push on, my lad, push out just a little more!"—plump! the barrow turned to one side, and the whole contents were precipitated into a muddy ditch.

"Oh! alas! I am lost! Mercy, Hanzli; save me!" cried the prostrate Blasius.

Hanzli did his best; and after much labour, succeeded in dragging his master out of the mud.

"But now you must get on, master, as you best can, on your own two legs; for if you expect me to push the barrow any more, I must just leave you here—my spine is split already; I shall never be fit for anything."

"Don't be foolish, my lad; you surely don't mean to forsake me! Help me at least to hide somewhere. You know very well how I always loved you—like my own son, Hanzlikam!"

"Well then, don't be talking about it; but just get up and give me your arm. Iai! if you are going to lean on me in that manner, master, I won't go a step farther. Just try to move your own legs—so, so."

And by dint of threats and encouragement, Hanzli succeeded in dragging his unhappy master through the maize till they reached a small shed, the sides and roof of which were somewhat dilapidated by wind and rain. Bundles of reeds, plaited together with maize stems, formed the shed-walls, through which the flowers of the sweet hazel-nut grew up luxuriantly; within, there was nothing but a legion of gnats.

"Am I to remain here?" asked Vendel in a voice of despair, surveying the shed, which was almost filled when he was inside.

"Don't be afraid, master! nobody will think of looking for you here."

"But where am I to sit down?"

"Why, on the ground, master."

"St. Jeremias! that is a hard seat."

"Never mind, master; it is better than being preserved in spirits of wine."

"But it is very cold; and then I am very hungry, too."

"Well, we can help that, master. I will go home and bring you a whole loaf, and some bacon."

"Nothing else? You surely do not wish me to starve, Hanzli?"

"I do not wish that, master; but indeed you must try and get down a little, at least half a hundredweight, unless you intend to spend your life here in eternal concealment."

Vendel looked round in dismay. "Very well, my son, very well—that is, I mean, very bad, very bad; but it can't be helped. Bring my dog, Hanzli, that I may have something to speak to at least when I am alone, and to take care of me."

"Well, Heaven bless you, master, till I come back again! and don't be afraid."

"Hanzli, don't speak of me to *anybody*,—you know who *that* is, Hanzli—not a syllable!"

"No, no; no, no!"

And Vendel was left alone to his own reflections, which were anything but agreeable. Cold and hungry, turned out of his comfortable home and warm bed, to pass the night in a damp maize-shed—and all for the caprice of a sovereign who wished to preserve him in spirits!

In about an hour's time, every moment of which seemed an eternity to our poor fugitive, Hanzli returned laden with various articles. Vendel descried him at some distance, and rejoiced in seeing him thus bent beneath his burden, believing he had brought the whole contents of the larder on his back.

"What is that on your back, Hanzli?" he called to him as he approached.

"A sheaf of straw, and a cloak."

"Iai! nothing to eat? And what is that in your arms?"

"That is the poodle, which I was obliged to carry, for he would not come with me."

"And the bread, and the other things?" asked Vendel anxiously.

"Here it is, in the bag."

Alas! this bag was a very small concern.

"And have you brought nothing to drink, Hanzli?"

"Yes, master, in this bottle."

"That's right! Reach it here; let me draw the cork. Oh! are you a heathen, Hanzli?—there is nothing here but water!"

"But it is quite fresh."

"Do you wish to kill me, Hanzli?" Large tears stood in poor Vendel's eyes.

"Come now, master, don't be grumbling; there is enough to eat and drink. We will hang up the bag on these cross beams, and I will make your bed. See now, you may sleep soundly there, and I will come back again to-morrow. Good night, master; shut the door after me." ·

And Vendel was again alone. Ay, such is human life! Man can be secure of nothing in this world; even when he lies down in a comfortable bed, there is no saying where he may awake in the morning!

Thus philosophized poor Vendel as he lay on his back on the hard earth. It was now quite dark; one or two inquisitive stars peeped through the cracks of the shed, but all was silent as death.

Vendel was just beginning to feel drowsy, when all at once he heard something or somebody speaking close to him in the German accent—indeed the sounds were quite distinct.

"Quak, quak, frakk!"

"Who the tartar can that be?"

"Quak, quak, frakk!"

"Perhaps it is Sclavonian they are talking," thought Vendel: "Jako sza volas, moje dusa?"73

[73] "What is your name, my dear?"

"Quak, quak, frakk!" The voice came always nearer; until at last Vendel summoned resolution to stretch out his hand in the direction of the sound to feel for its cause.

Something cold moved under his fingers—as cold as a frog. What the tartar could it be? as cold as a frog, speaks German, and moves! Vendel could not guess; but he once more addressed the mysterious creature, and then, seizing his cap from off his head, he laid it over it, that he might not find it staring in his face next morning; after which, he took the loaf out of the bag, and breaking off the crust, placed it under his head as a pillow, and slept soundly till daybreak;—for though he was once or twice disturbed by something pulling his hair or scratching his head, he was too much fatigued to take much notice of it, and only shook his head and fell asleep again. Towards morning, however, he began to be troubled by fearful dreams. A vast museum rose before him, in which were divers stuffed pelicans, ostriches, storks, crocodiles, sea-horses, peacocks, long-tailed monkeys, and dog-faced Tartars, embalmed speckled devils, petrified angels, and suchlike _naturæ curiosa,_ all standing in long rows, among which were one or two critics, hung by the legs.

But what most attracted his attention, were two gigantic glasses placed in the middle of the room, both filled with spirits, and bound round the top with oilskin, in one of which stood a meagre elephant, swinging his long trunk before him, with frizzed hair, glazed boots, a wide frock coat, and high collar, from each side of which protruded his long tusks.

But now for the other glass! There floated Master Vendel himself, swelled to twice his original size, in his yellow flannel coat and coloured slippers, and stamping with all his force to break out of his prison. He tried to cry out, too; but when he opened his mouth, the spirits went down his throat. At last he made a desperate leap to get his head through the oilskin, and kicked out—the side of the reed shed.

"Ahhaouhh!" he cried with a loud yawn, infinitely relieved at finding himself there, instead of in the French Emperor's museum. "It was a good thing I did not submit to *that*; a terrible job they would have made of me, no doubt!"

Vendel then sat up, and began to think of breakfasting. He looked about for the loaf; but no loaf was to be seen—only a few scattered crumbs marked the place it had once occupied as a pillow.

"Well!" sighed Vendel, summoning all his philosophy; "I must eat the bacon alone, though I shall probably be ill after it."

But Providence had taken care that Vendel should not be ill through this means: the ham was nowhere to be found—only the empty bag lay on the ground.

Fearful spectres floated across the waste of Vendel's brain. "Filax!" he cried, but the poodle did not answer: there was a mine scratched out under the reeds, by which he had probably made his escape.

Vendel burst open the door, and the first thing which met his eye was his faithful dog quietly gnawing the bones of the bacon.

"Alas, alas! I am lost!" cried Vendel, falling on his back in utter despair.

Fortunately, some secret misgiving induced the faithful Hanzli to return about noon with a fresh transport of provisions, otherwise the poor brewer, like King Eu— — (the tartar knows what comes next!), might have been tempted to eat himself up.

"Hanzli, my son! take away the dog, and bring a cat instead; the mice have eaten all my bread, and the dog has carried off the bacon. But what of the hussars, Hanzli?"

"Oh! they are already beyond the frontiers; they made a great noise till early in the morning, when they mounted their horses and galloped off. Since then, they have probably been in battle."

"And Mistress Vicza?"

"They have not carried her off," replied Hanzli with a bitter sigh. "She is going on in a terrible way, looking for you everywhere. She thinks you are after no good, and promises that you shall smart for it when you return."

"Utcza! I am between two fires!" thought poor Vendel. "On one side the French Emperor, on the other my wife: one wants to have me under a glass, the other under her thumb!"

"But keep yourself well hid, for the enemy is approaching," continued Hanzli. "All the gentlemen of the town are hiding their effects under the beams and in the cellars, and their wives are cooking and baking all sorts of cakes; the very roads are covered with pastry. They say the enemy fires with red powder, and there is a strong smell of pepper all about. Heaven preserve us when they come! for they are a terrible merciless set, it is said, and spare neither man nor child; and they have such a love for torture, that they will bend two trees together for their diversion, and tie a man's legs to them, then suddenly let them go, and whip! he is split in two!"

"Ale! iui!"

"Then they tie the women together by the hair, and drive them off to the markets in Africa."

"I say, Hanzli, how far is it to Africa?"

"I have not heard that yet, master; but I daresay as far as Szerdahely."[74]

[74] A little town about twenty miles north of Raab.

"I should like to know, in order that, if they carry off Vicza, I could reckon in how many days she might return."

"But what if they carry me off? and then some dog-faced young lady in Africa may fall in love with me! sure enough, and then eat me! They say they fatten a man up with currants and other fruits, and then eat him!"

"Alas! my son, Hanzli! if they carry you off and eat you, there will be nobody to bring me anything to eat! For Heaven's sake, Hanzli, take care of thyself!" And the good man seized Hanzli, and kissed and embraced him till the lad thought a bear had got him in its clutches, and was so blinded in consequence of the squeezing, that he stumbled about afterwards like a shell-fish on shore.

Days passed on. Hanzli continued to bring food to his master morning and evening, and to enliven his solitude with the numerous reports he had heard in the village, and which were not unfrequently the cause of sleepless nights to poor Vendel.

Meanwhile, the maize was growing tall and yellow; the pumpkins were ripening beneath their great shady leaves, and the starlings visited the happy fields. Early in the mornings Vendel went up a neighbouring hillock, from whence he could see the village, and watch the smoke of the chimneys, and hear the dogs barking from a distance, and the bells ringing; then, when the sun rose, he would sigh deeply and go back to his hut, where he lay down till Hanzli returned with food; nor would he venture out again till the sun sank below the horizon, when he would creep forth once more, and watch the shepherds' fires on the meadows, and listen to the herd-bells returning to the village, or the merry creaking of waggon-wheels over the plains; and then the moon rose, like a bright silver twentypence—so rare an appearance in those days (not the moon, but the twentypence), and poor Hornyicsek gazed at St. David and his harp in the bright planet, and bethought him of the happy times when he used to watch it from his marble bench, with his head in a state of brilliant clairvoyance, illuminated by beer. The mild evening breeze sighed softly through the leaves of the maize, and the crickets chirped around him. If Vendel had been a poet, he could not have desired more; but unfortunately, as it was, all this was lost to him, and he would readily have been excused the enjoyment of such romantic scenes.

The good man now discovered that his clothes were growing wider every day, and that he mounted the hillock with much less difficulty than formerly. He began to think that he might now with safety return to the village; but Hanzli dissuaded him, declaring that he was still much too fat, though he put him on stricter diet every day.

Thus several weeks passed by, which were unmarked by any incident of great importance in regard to Vendel. True, the ants sometimes took his residence by storm, causing him considerable inconvenience by day and night; once a fearful hurricane nearly terrified him to death; and a mad buffalo kept beating about the maize-ground one afternoon, bellowing fearfully round the shed, while Vendel did not dare to breathe or stir. But there was one adventure which very much disturbed the good man's equanimity; and as it had, besides, some influence on his future proceedings, we shall relate it more in detail.

We have already mentioned that Vendel was haunted by some *uncanny* spirit, which seemed to converse in German, was cold to the touch, and moved. This visit had been frequently repeated, and Vendel had as often covered the intruder with his cap; but next morning, when he raised it carefully, there was nothing to be seen but a hole in the ground, which was quite dark, and seemed to descend into the depths of the earth.

One evening, as he was musing over the mysteries of this secret passage, he thought he heard steps outside the shed, accompanied by low whisperings. Shortly after, a strange phenomenon took place at the mysterious hole; it seemed as if trying to speak—gurgling, hickupping, and sobbing, exactly like a human throat; he thought he heard it sigh, too. By degrees it grew louder and louder; a gulping sound followed, then a terrible scratching was heard, nearer and nearer, and louder! Vendel trembled like an aspen leaf. At last—hah!—at last, a fearful head appeared,—two eyes, two ears, sharp teeth, a red tongue! higher and higher it came, struggling out of the hole. One struggle more, and a terrible, wild-looking, dirty creature, with sharp nails and shining eyes, rushed forth!

It was a water-rat!

"Saint Bartholomew, help!" cried the brewer; "it will eat me!"

And as the creature issued from the hole, a deluge rose after it, squirting and bubbling; and in an instant the rat, Vendel, and his residence were completely inundated.

The mystery may be thus explained. Some mischievous shepherd boys had come to fill up the hole with water, and having found the entrance on that side of the mound on which the forsaken shed stood, they had brought water from a neighbouring pond in buckets, which they poured down the hole; and, ignorant of its telegraphic theory, they cursed the frogs for drinking all their water, while Vendel's residence was undergoing an inundation at the other outlet of the rat's hole.

Meanwhile, the persecuted monster ran round the small shed, and not finding any mode of exit, climbed up the reeds on all-fours, and had just reached a hole which the wind had broken in the roof, when by some unlucky chance it slipped back and fell—right on Vendel's nose!

Our readers may imagine the cry which burst from the lips of the terrified man at this catastrophe: he kicked open the door with hands and feet, and rolled out, making as great a tumult as if three regiments of Turks had been behind him.

But the shepherd boys by no means took the matter in jest. Every one for himself, they scampered off with terror-stricken countenances, leaving buckets, tubs, and water-rat, and never paused till they reached the village, where they immediately alarmed the inhabitants.

When Vendel had recovered from his panic, he began to reflect on the probable consequences of this imprudent sally: he should now be discovered, betrayed, and put in spirits. And this was the fate that awaited him!

The unfortunate man crept up his hill of observation, and strained his eyes towards the village. In a very short time his worst fears began to be realized: a party of men, armed with pitchforks and scythes, were evidently making for his place of concealment. To have remained there longer would have been tempting Providence; and so the poor man took up his mantle with great resignation, and sighing deeply, wandered out into the fields of buck-wheat, where he lay down and listened anxiously to the distant uproar with which the excited villagers hunted the fearful spectre; and to this day the true legend of the "earth-man" is told in the district.

When all was quiet, Vendel rose and withdrew farther from the dangerous vicinity of his hut. For three whole days he wandered through thorns and bushes, sleeping in the open air, and supporting life with earth-nuts and maize. Three miserable fast days they were, which deprived him of at least twenty pounds of bodily weight, but certainly prolonged his life by three years! On the fourth day he heard a great deal of firing at about a mile's distance, and at intervals the sound of great guns. He even saw some of the balls lazily rebounding from the ground at the end of their flight, and, picking up one, he put it into his pocket in testimony of the battle he had seen, and of all he had gone through during the war.

Towards noon, the firing ceased, and in the evening, as Vendel was preparing to lie down under the shelter of a ridge of potatoes, a form started from the treacherous wood beside him in pelisse and dolmany, with a red csako, short boots, and a musket in his hand. He looked about him—perhaps he was pursued, perhaps pursuing—he seemed evidently in a dilemma of some kind; as he approached, however, Vendel recognised Matyas Kormas, one of the noble proprietors of the district—but in what a plight! He who had gone out with such zeal, torn and covered with mud; his hair and moustache, wont to be so stiffly waxed, hanging dolefully about his face, and his countenance expressive of anxiety and alarm. Vendel was much relieved, however, to see that there were no marks of blood about him; but his ardour seemed considerably abated, and he by no means now looked as if he could devour his enemies.

"Good evening, Vendel!" he exclaimed in a mild tone, on recognising the brewer; "can you tell me in what direction the village lies?"

Vendel immediately offered to conduct him, thinking he might have a better chance of safety by returning with an armed man, the whole country being now unsafe.

"I only wanted to know in order that I might keep away from it," replied Matyas, "for the enemy occupy it at present; but let us get down into the underwood, Vendel; we can hide there together."

"Then are they really such ferocious people?" asked Vendel anxiously.

"Hiai! my friend, you had better ask no questions—you never saw such things! if we had not retreated, there would not have been a man of us left! they have a peculiar way of holding their muskets, and never miss a shot!"

"Why did you not hold yours the same way?" asked Vendel simply.

"Why, you see, Providence was against us; there is no firing against that! Come, let us make a hole somewhere, and hide these arms; for if they find out that I have come from the camp, I shall be taken prisoner, and brought back again."

The two patriots hastened to gain that underground which stretches from Cs—— to the Danube, in which they concealed themselves for a whole day and a half, enduring all the glories and privations of war, and encouraging one another through all their difficulties and dangers. On the evening of the second day, however, our heroes were as hungry as wolves, and had began to turn their thoughts to the procuring food. Slowly and stealthily they left the wood, and, not far from the outskirts, they descried a waggon lying overturned in one of the cross roads.

Matyas, seeing that nobody was near it, broke a willow sapling from the roadside, and, desiring Vendel to lie down on the ground and shut his eyes, he rushed towards the deserted waggon, and attacked it with great fury.

"Defend yourselves!—surrender! Who dares resist?" he cried, beating the waggon with his wand; while Vendel, who lay with his face buried in the grass, firmly believed that his friend had put to flight at least three hundred Frenchmen! "The day is ours!" exclaimed Matyas at last, returning flushed and triumphant from the strife; "let us seize the spoil!"

If Vendel had hitherto any doubts as to the enemy's capacity for digesting iron, they were entirely removed on his trying to bite the bread taken from the waggon. They were obliged to steep it for two days in the Danube; but they ate it for all that, and Vendel thought he had never eaten anything with so good an appetite before.

At last, Heaven delivered our country from its scourge. When Napoleon had seen the Miskolcz bread, the Debreczen honeycakes, the Vasvar csakany,75 the Kecskemet kulacs,76 the Ugocsa horned-owls, and the Comorn figs—without having obtained the chief object of his enterprise in the person of Vendel-gazda—he returned home again with his army; or, in other words, we drove them out of the country—which is sacred truth, although envious historians wish to conceal it.

[75] A wind instrument.

[76] A sort of wooden flask.

When these glad tidings spread through the land, the woods and maize fields began to be depopulated; and every one returned to his ancestral abode, to relate his warlike adventures to his anxious family, who listened with breathless interest as he described how he had defended himself against at least thirty of the enemy, and carried off their ammunition waggons; how a ball had been fired into his breast, while he was only saved by a large silver button, and the letters of nobility which he always carried about him; and finally, how his musket, igniting in the heat of the battle, had burst into a thousand pieces! These, and still more marvellous adventures, our jovial ancestors recited after the war. Heaven bless them! if they had allowed themselves to be shot, where should we have been now? and without us—hm!

Among the rest, Matyas-ur and Vendel-gazda left their place of concealment, and returned to the village; and indeed it was high time, for they were both terribly pulled down, especially the brewer, who was a mere shadow of his former self, and only resembled that respectable personage as a dried pear does a green one. Moreover, such was the tattered and dirty condition to which their wandering life had reduced them, that they might have exhibited themselves with perfect confidence at twentypence per head, *sub titulo*—Finns!

The danger once over, it was an easy matter for Matyas-ur. He had only to go home to be recognised and welcomed at once; but with Vendel the case was otherwise. As he reached his home, the sound of music and dancing struck painfully on his ear. "Hm!" he thought, "they do not seem to be mourning much for me!" He listened again, and heard the noise of gay laughter and loud talking. At last he opened the door. The large guest-room was full of gaily-dressed people, who were crowded in every corner; while the space in the middle was occupied by the dancers. With some difficulty, Vendel squeezed through the crowd, and there, in the midst of all, was his beloved wife, with her cap on one side, dancing with Andras-gazda, whose skin shone twice as much as it was wont. Hanzli's subdued-looking face also appeared among the crowd; but the youth was evidently out of spirits, and sat moody and silent amidst the gay revellers. Meanwhile the beer and wine flowed copiously, and the beneficent odour of all species of eatables tantalized the nose of the hungry wanderer.

"Oh! unhappy man!" cried Vendel, clapping his hands together; that was all he said—but how much was expressed in the words!—for a few moments he gazed round him in silence. "Stop!" he roared at last, stamping on the ground; on which his little dog came out from below the table, and began barking at his sorely-tried master. *His own poodle barked at him!* "Who is this man?" exclaimed several of the guests. "Where do you come from, countryman?" asked Andras-gazda. "Give the poor wretch a glass of wine; he must be some beggar!" said Mistress Vicza, adjusting her cap.

This was more than the exemplary patience of the Bohemian could bear. "Hear, all of you!" he roared; "I am myself, and nobody else!"

One and all shook their heads. The voice was Vendel's, but the face, the figure, none recognised.

"Not even you, Hanzli?" cried Vendel in despair; "not even you remember me?"

Hanzli looked at him gravely, then grinned, then again stared vacantly, without the slightest recognition.

"Ah, this is indeed desperate!" groaned the unfortunate man, as, seizing one of the four-quart bottles of beer which stood on the table, he emptied it at one draught; and this was his redemption. By this means he was recognised at once; and "Vendel-batya!" "Vendel-gazda!" "Nagyuram!" "Kisuram!" "Edes uram!"77 resounded on every side; while they all fell upon him, embraced, kissed him, and led him out to dance. He was very well received indeed, and a little explanation set everything to rights.

[77] Great master, Little master, Dear master; these being titles carefully distinguished from each other by the peasants.

The cause of the feasting and merriment was Andras's wedding with Panna, the little girl for whom he had fought with the hussar; which solemnity was celebrated jointly with the retreat of the French; and now that there was Vendel-gazda's miraculous return to rejoice at besides, the festivities were kept up till late next morning.

Thus ended the trials and adventures of the brewer of B— —; and from this day forward, Heaven showered her blessings upon him; sons and daughters grew up around him, some fair, and some dark, but all fat, and each one finer and prettier than the other.

THE SZEKELY78 MOTHER

[78] Szekely (Szekler in German), the inhabitants of the border districts in Transylvania, said to be one of the most ancient tribes of the Magyar race, who came over still earlier than Attila.

The cannons were silent, the battle was over—the brave had fallen.

The field, which so lately had been the scene of wild and desperate contention, was now silent as the grave; only the thunder of heaven and the moaning of the breeze were to be heard, while the lurid lightning gleamed across the plain, as if the spirits of the dead had begun a new and inexorable strife on high, to guard the gates of heaven, as, an hour before, they had defended the frontiers of their country against their foes.

In the churchyard, before the gates of Kezdi-Vasarhely, the Szekely women anxiously awaited, not the return of the beloved, but the news of the victory.

They sat in groups on the gravestones and green mounds, listening all day to the cannon, and trying to distinguish the distant sounds.

"That is ours—that is Gabor Aron79—and that the enemy—and now the thunder of heaven."

[79] A common rustic, who, at the beginning of the late war, astonished his countrymen by his skill in founding cannons, and in the art of gunnery.

And, when the cannon had ceased, they waited with beating hearts to hear of defeat or victory.

And all—mothers, young girls, brides, wives, breathed the same fervent wish—that if the beloved should return, it might be with glory; but that if the day were lost which was to decide the fate of their country, none might return to tell it!

On the threshold of the chapel, by the crypt-door, sat an old man: he was past eighty—his eyes were dim and lustreless, and his voice faint and trembling: he, too, had come out to the churchyard to wait the issue of the battle, for he could not rest at home; beside him sat a cripple, who had one leg shrunk up, but although the body was weak and sickly, every thought of his heart was in the battle-field, and he frequently exclaimed, in bitterness of spirit, "Why cannot I too be there?"

The cripple knelt beside the old man, and read to him out of the Bible. The passage was in Samuel, about the battles of Israel—the holy war, in which thirty thousand had fallen guarding the ark of God.

"Why cannot I be there?" sighed the unhappy youth, and read:

"'And the ark of God was taken; and the two sons of Eli, Hophni and Phinehas, were slain.

"'And there ran a man of Benjamin out of the army, and came to Shiloh the same day, with his clothes rent, and with earth upon his head.

"'And when he came, lo, Eli sat upon a seat by the wayside watching: for his heart trembled for the ark of God. And when the man came into the city, and told it, all the city cried out.

"'And when Eli heard the noise of the crying, he said, What meaneth the noise of this tumult? And the man came in hastily, and told Eli.

"'Now Eli was ninety and eight years old; and his eyes were dim, that he could not see.'"

The cripple could read no more; he looked at the old man, his heart sickened, and his eyes filled with tears.

"Why do you not continue?" asked the old man.

"It is dark; I cannot see the words."

"That is false; I feel the last rays of the sun on my face; why do you not read on?"

The cripple wiped the tears from his eyes, and again began to read:—

"'And the man said unto Eli, I am he that came out of the army, and I fled to-day out of the army. And he said, What is there done, my son?

"'And the messenger answered and said, Israel is fled before the Philistines, and there hath been also a great slaughter among the people, and thy two sons also, Hophni and Phinehas, are dead, and the ark of God is taken.'"

But here he could no longer contain himself, and, sobbing bitterly, he leant his head on the old man's knee, and hid his face in his hands.

The latter did not insist on his reading any more; but repeated, in a low voice, the well-known verse:

"'And it came to pass, when he made mention of the ark of God, that he fell from off the seat backward by the side of the gate, and his neck brake, and he died.'"

Beneath an acacia tree, at a little distance from the rest, stood two females.

The eldest might have been six-and-thirty; her features, though stern and severe, were still beautiful, and her dark lustrous eyes glowed with the fire of enthusiasm. She was very pale, and the lightning which glimmered around her gave a still more livid hue to her features.

Judith—for so she was called—was a true type of the Szekely women; one of those unfading forms who retain to an advanced age the keen expression of countenance, the brilliancy of the large dark eye, the thrilling and musical tones, and slender but vigorous form; while the mind, instead of decaying, grows stronger with years.

Round her majestic figure, a slight girl of sixteen twined her arms, clinging to her like the gentle convolvulus to the stately pine.

Aranka was a lovely blue-eyed maiden, with bright golden locks, and a form so fragile, that it seemed to bend like the lily to the breeze.

She was betrothed to the son of that proud matron to whom she clung, and the eyes of the mother and the bride sought the beloved, as they gazed eagerly through the dim apace.

"Do you not see a form approaching there?" asked Judith, pointing towards the plain.

Aranka drew still closer, that she might see the object pointed out; her head rested on Judith's shoulder, but she could not discern anything, for the starry beam of the blue eye cannot pierce the distance, like the more fiery ray of the black eye.

In a few minutes the form became more distinct, and the timid blush of love flitted over the young girl's cheek, while a deep flush of anger mantled on the mother's.

"It is he, my beloved!" murmured Aranka, pressing her small hand on her heart, as if to still the little flutterer.

"He has no arms!" cried Judith with horror, as she turned away her head, and covered her eyes with her hand; for, though still indistinct to others, the gentle girl recognised her lover, and the mother had seen her son's disgrace.

With slow and uncertain steps the figure approached; his head hung dejectedly on his breast, and he appeared to move with pain.

On seeing the women assembled in the churchyard, he bent his steps thither.

They all now recognised Judith's son, and surrounded the mother as he approached.

The churchyard moat lay between the mother and her son. Unable to cross it, the young man sank on the ground before it. His clothes were torn and covered with blood, and his hand endeavoured to conceal a wound in his breast.

"Where have you left your arms?" cried his mother in a stern voice, advancing from among the crowd.

He would have replied, that he had left it in his enemy's heart; but he had not strength to speak, and the words died on his mouth.

"Speak! is the battle lost?"

The youth made a sign of the affirmative.

"And why did you not fall with the rest? Why did you leave the field for the sun to rise on your disgrace? Why have you come hither?"

The youth was silent.

"Wherefore should you desire to outlive your country? And, if you have come to be buried here, better far to have sought a grave where it had been glory to have died—on the battle-field. Away! This churchyard has no place for you—you can have no part among our dead—leave us, and deny that you were born here! Live or die, but forget us."

The youth looked in his mother's face with an imploring expression, and then at the women who surrounded her; but he encountered no glance—no trace of sympathy—his eyes sought his bride, his heart's brightest hopes, the blue-eyed maiden; but she had fallen on her knees at his mother's feet, hiding her face in Judith's dress, to conceal her sobs.

The youth still hesitated—still waited to see if any one would bid him stay; and when he saw that none spoke, not even his bride, he raised himself slowly and silently from the earth, still holding his hand across his breast, and, with tottering steps, turned once more to the trackless plain, and wandered into the woods beyond, where he sank never to rise again.

One or two of the Szekely youths returned afterwards from the lost field, but the women refused them admittance.

"Seek another home," they said, "than the one you could not defend!"

And the few who survived wandered into distant countries, for none dared return who had outlived his country's ruin.

Bitter were the sounds of weeping and lamentation in the churchyard of Kezdi-Vasarhely—the cry of the Szekely women rose to heaven.

The old man at the crypt-door asked, in a feeble voice, the cause of the weeping.

"Szekely-land is lost!" they cried; "your son and your grandsons have fallen on the field with their leader, and Gabor Aron; and all their cannon is taken!"

The old man raised his hands and sightless eyes to heaven. "My God!" he exclaimed, and, sinking to the earth, he ceased to be blind; for the light of eternity had risen on his spirit.

The old man was dead.

The Szekely women surrounded the body with deep reverence, and bore it in their arms into the town.

The cripple followed slowly on his crutches, repeating bitterly to himself, "Why could not I have been there too? why could not I have fallen among them?"

In all Kezdi-Vasarhely there was not a man to be seen; the brave had fallen, the deserters had been turned away, and the last man they were now placing in his coffin, and he was an old man past eighty, and blind.

Only women and children now remained—widows and orphans—who wept bitterly round the old man's bier, but not for the dead.

The cripple knelt unheeded at the foot of the coffin; and hid his face in his hands, as he heard them say that the *last* man was dead; they did not consider him as one!

The house was quite full, as well as the court—for the old man's grandchildren and great-grandchildren formed a large congregation; and all those to whom he had done good during his life, whom he had assisted with his counsel or supported in their sorrow—how many there were! and yet the greater part was absent, covering the battle-field!—and among all his sons and grandsons, only that one cripple was present, and he was not considered as a man!

They had all their dead to mourn—all their peculiar sorrows, but none more than the high-minded Judith, and the poor cripple,—and yet they alone wept not. A restless fever burned within them, and, instead of tears, sparks of fire seemed to burst from their eyes.

In the midst of the weeping and lamentation, Judith beckoned the cripple aside.

"David!" she exclaimed, taking the youth's damp, cold hand, "your grandfather lies stretched out before you, and yet you stand beside the coffin without shedding a tear! what are you thinking of? Last night I heard you sighing and tossing on your bed—you never slept—what were you thinking of then, David?"

The cripple hung his head in silence.

"David, if you were a strong, sound man—if you could hold a sword or a lance, instead of those crutches—would you hang your head in silence as you do now?"

The cripple raised his glowing face, and his large, dark eyes met Judith's with such a gleam of enthusiasm, it seemed as if the ardent spirit had forgotten for a moment the weakness of its mortal dwelling.

"And you will never be happy," she continued; "no joys await your lot in this life, and yet who knows how long that life may be. Speak! should death appear before you in its most brilliant form—more glorious than on the battle-field—and bid you cast away your crutches and embrace the weapons of destruction, giving you all you loved on earth as a funeral pile to perish around you, that none should remain to whom your thoughts might return from the other world"—

"I do not understand you."

"You *will* not, perhaps. The world is still fair to you, even amidst ruins, and blasted by dishonour; unfortunate as you are, life is still dear—even your crutches are not to be exchanged for wings!"

"Oh! speak not thus; how often would I have given the life I abhor for the death I envy!" exclaimed the unhappy youth; and added, in a lower tone, "for the death of glory!"

"And what death would be more glorious than yours? on a battle-field in which the elements themselves should join, where you would stand in the midst, high above all, like the angel of death, proclaiming resistance to the last, in a voice which would be heard above the battle-cry; and, when all had fallen, when there remained none to help, you alone would snatch the victory from the enemy's hand, and bear it with you—not to the grave, but to heaven!"

"O that I could!" sighed the cripple; "but what is my voice? it would not be heard in battle; and my arm could snatch the victory from none!"

"Listen to me! The victors will arrive to-day or to-morrow; but neither repose nor enjoyment shall await them here—they shall find every door closed, and our weapons shall be the reply to theirs. If the men of Kezdi-

Vasarhely have fallen in defence of their country, the women shall not be unworthy of them! We shall lose—for the arm of woman is weak, though her heart is strong—we have neither the weapons nor the force to resist, only the will; and therefore our aim is not victory, but an honourable death. You will go up to the tower, and when you see the enemy approaching at a distance, ring the bell; we will then carry out the dead to be buried, and await the hated foe beside his grave; and wo to them if they try to enter by force, we shall defend every house to the last—despair will teach us to fight; and should fear or hesitation overcome our weak hearts for an instant, the voice of your bell will revive our courage, and inspire us with new strength. And you must not cease one moment till the combat is over; then take the wreaths of tarred pine, which you will find in a niche of the tower ready prepared, and when the enemy have taken possession of the town, throw them down on the roofs of the houses! Thus you will regain the town from the enemy, and, amidst smoke and flames—the funeral-pile of all you love on earth—you will bear victory along with you to heaven!"

The cripple listened with increasing agitation to Judith's words; and when she had finished, he dashed away his crutches, and, falling at her feet, embraced her knees, and murmured some unintelligible words; but the enthusiasm which glowed in every feature told how the spirit rejoiced to meet the death she had portrayed in such brilliant colours.

"Will you have courage?" asked Judith.

"Oh! I shall rejoice in it! I shall no longer be a cripple—no longer unhappy; I shall die like a hero! and when the flames are bursting around me, I shall sing with the prophet, 'Cry out, ye gates, cry out, O city, for the terrible day of the Lord is come!'"

And the cripple trembled violently with agitation, and his withered arm was raised to heaven.

Judith gazed at him in silence, as he still knelt, with his hands and eyes upraised, as if inspired.

"Come with me!" she exclaimed, after a few moments' pause, raising him from the ground.

David took up his crutches and followed her, with such joyful alacrity that his feet scarcely seemed to touch the earth; he appeared already to possess wings instead of crutches.

As they passed the chamber of the dead, he approached his grandfather's coffin, and, kissing the cold face and hands, murmured, with an expression of unwonted joy, "We shall meet soon!"

The women looked at him with surprise; they had never seen him smile thus before, and thought that grief had estranged his mind. Judith left the room, telling them she would soon return, and herself conducted the cripple to the tower, while he followed with a vigour he had hitherto never displayed;—the spirit seemed actually bearing up the fragile body.

When they reached the top, Judith kissed the cripple's brow, and pressed his hand in silence.

David locked the door after her, and threw the key out of the window along with his crutches.

"I shall want them no more," he cried, as Judith passed below the tower. "I wish to be certain that I shall not fail in the hour of temptation."

He then placed himself at the window, and looked out towards the mountains.

Judith returned to the house of mourning, and found the women still weeping round the bier.

She motioned to them to dry their tears—her majestic form, calm features, and commanding eye, seemed formed to be obeyed. The women were silent, and Judith addressed them in a clear, steady voice:

"Sisters!—widows and orphans of Kezdi-Vasarhely!—Heaven has visited us with great and severe trials; we have outlived all that was good— all that we loved on earth; there is not a house in which some beloved one was not expected who will never now return! However long we may live, no happiness awaits us in this world! we may grow old and gray in our deserted homes, but the best part of our lives lies beneath the sod; and this is not the heaviest stroke which awaits us. Instead of the beloved, those who have shed their heart's-blood will come—we shall see them take possession of the places which our beloved ones have left; instead of the familiar voices, we shall hear the harsh tones, and meet the unfeeling gaze of strangers—of our bitter enemies! Shall we await that time? Death gives back all that life has taken away—and death can take nothing but life! If I did not know that I am among Szekely women, I would take leave of you, and say, I go alone to die! but I know you all—where I am you will be also; you will act as I do, and be worthy of your dead. Go home to your houses, conceal everything you value; make fires in every stove, and boil water and oil in every vessel. At the first sound of the bell, let every one of you assemble here; we will then carry out the dead to the gate of the town, and dig his grave across the road before it, and with this moat the town shall be closed—none shall pass from within alive! Haste! put your houses in order, and return here at the first sound of the bell!"

The women dispersed—with the calmness of despair they went home, and did as Judith desired, and collected all the weapons they could find, but not another tear was shed.

The bell of the tower had begun to toll; it was the only bell left in Kezdi-Vasarhely; the rest had all been founded into cannon. Clouds of dust were seen to rise far off on the winding mountain-path, above Predialo, and the tolling of the bell announced the approach of the Russian troops. Two companies marched towards the gates of Kezdi-Vasarhely; one from without, the other from within the town. One was formed of hardened soldiers, the other of women and girls. On one side the enlivening sound of military music was heard, and colours floated on the breeze; on the other, the dismal tones of the funeral song arose, and mourning veils fluttered round the bier.

A troop of Circassian horsemen paused before the gates. Their dress, their features, their language—all seemed to recall a strange image of the past, of those ancient times when first the Magyar people sought a home in the unknown world—for even then, persecuted by fate, they wandered forth in millions, driven from their own country; and some found a home among the wild mountains of the Caucasus, others wandered still farther, and the parted brethren never met, or heard of each other more, till, mingled with the surrounding nations, both had changed; and when, a thousand years later, the world's caprice once more brought them together, and they met as foes, both were struck by some strange sympathy, some sad chord which touched each alike, and their hearts felt oppressed, and their arms sank, they knew not wherefore.

The leader of the troop was a young chief, whose oval face, handsome sunburnt features, and dark eyes, bore great resemblance to the Szekely Magyar, and if he had worn a dolmany, none would have distinguished the one from the other; but his dress was not that of the present Magyar, and yet the crimson-bordered toque, the short linen vest, beneath which flowed the long coloured kaftan, the curved sword—even the manner of girding it on—all recalled some well-known object, like a portrait once seen, the name of which we have forgotten, or the impression caused by some dream, or bygone scene of childhood, and we sigh to be unable to speak to them, or understand their language, to ask if they are happier among their mountains than their brothers on the plain, or if they, too, weep like us; and bid them, when they return, and sit in the evenings at the threshold of their mountain homes—those which they so bravely defended, speak of us to their children, and point to where the setting sun gilds the home of the Magyar, and breathe a prayer for their suffering brethren.

The grave was dug, and the women stood before it chanting their mournful dirges, while the measure was now and then interrupted by sobs, and the solemn bell tolled the knell of death—the death of the town.

The leader of the troop alighted from his horse, his comrades followed his example, and taking their csalmas from their heads, they clasped their hands and stood beside the grave in silent prayer. Who would have thought that these were enemies?

After a pause of a few minutes, the leader made a motion to approach the women on the opposite side of the grave, but Judith calmly advanced, and waved him back. "Approach not," she exclaimed—"the grave is the boundary between us; there is nothing to seek in the town—none but women and children inhabit it—the widows and orphans of those you have killed; and here, in this grave, lies the last man of Kezdi-Vasarhely, a holy man, whom God permitted to live eighty-nine years, to be the friend and counsellor of the whole town, and has now called to Himself, because the town has no more need of him: his spirit fled at the first news of the lost battle, for he was blind ten years: had he not been blind, the steel and not the news of the battle would have killed him, as it killed the rest. The women of Kezdi-Vasarhely have buried him here, that none may enter the town. They wish to live in solitude, as becomes widows whose husbands have fallen in battle; and therefore, blessed be the grave which shuts us out from the world, and accursed be he who steps over it, both before and after his death!"

The Circassian drew a white handkerchief from his bosom, and placing it on the end of his spear, spoke to the Szekely women in a language unknown to them, although the tone, and even the accent, seemed familiar. He wished to tell them that he had brought peace to their town; that they had nothing to fear from him; that he only desired admittance. The women understood his intention, but motioned a refusal. "In vain you bring peace!" they exclaimed; "as long as there is a living breath here, there must be war between us and you; only death can bring us peace. Seek quarters for your troops elsewhere; the world is large enough—there is no rest for you here; grief reigns alone in this town, where the ghosts of the grave wander through the streets, women bewailing the dead, and driven by despair to madness—depart from here!"

The action of the women, the unknown yet familiar tones, awakened a strange sad echo in the heart of the young Circassian, as he stood supported on his lance, looking on the mourners before him.

Brought up in the stern exercise of military duty, he was accustomed to fulfil the word of command, without regard to circumstances; but now his strength seemed to fail him, and he hesitated to force his way through a party of weak women.

"Take the white handkerchief from your lance," cried Judith, "and steep it in our heart's blood—then you may enter our town;" and as he leapt into the saddle, several of the women threw themselves before his horse's feet, causing the animal to rear and neigh.

But the Circassian remembered that he had a beloved mother at home whose words so much resembled those of that proud matron—and sisters, and a young bride, beautiful as those young girls who had thrown themselves before his horse's feet—with just such dark glorious eyes, sad features, and light forms; and his heart failed him. He turned quickly aside, that the women might not see the tears which filled his eyes; and then, dashing his spurs into his horse's side, he once more waved his white handkerchief to the kneeling women, and galloped from the gate. His comrades hastened after him; their lances gleamed through clouds of dust, which soon concealed them from view; but neither the Szekely nor the Circassian women saw that young chieftain more.

He was summoned before a military tribunal for transgression of duty, and suffered the stern fate of the soldier.

Troops of a different nature were sent next against the town, whose horses trampled down the grave, and whose bayonets forced open the closed doors.

It was a weary strife, without the glory of war; one by one each house was taken, defended as they were by women and children; the contest was renewed in every street; the infuriated inhabitants pouring boiling water and oil over the heads of their enemies, while the fearful tolling of the bell, heard above the cries and the clang of arms, excited them to still greater desperation.

The combat continued till night, when the song of triumph was heard in the streets—the town was in the hands of the enemy. Suddenly, as if it had descended from heaven, fire burst from the roofs of the houses, and in an instant, the wind coming to the assistance of the flames, carried the fiery embers from one end of the town to the other. Cries of despair arose amidst the howling of the blast, but dense clouds of smoke concealed all but the flames which darted through them, devouring as they passed; and high above, the roof of the tower blazed like a gigantic torch, while the solemn tolling still continued, the voice of battle, of fire, of tempest, and of death: a fearful crash was heard, and all was still—the bell had fallen.

The two elements remained joint masters of the field. The wind and the flames contended over the ruins of Kezdi-Vasarhely.

A BALL

Dearest Ilma, — I am in despair! I am very ill, and in bed! Ah! I shall never dance a quadrille again. I will go into a convent, or marry, or make away with myself in some other way. Conceive what has happened to me! Oh! it is too dreadful, too shocking! you never read such a thing in a romance!

You may have heard that the Hungarian troops marched through here last week, after the battle of Branyisko; there was the greatest panic and confusion at the news of their approach; we expected that they would have set fire to the town, and pillaged, and killed us — indeed, mamma said there was no knowing what horrors they might commit, and she desired me to scratch my face with my nails, and disfigure myself, in case they should wish to carry me off! Did you ever hear such an idea?

Well! ere long the national guards marched in with their bands playing. Papa went to meet them with a deputation. Our servants all ran out to see the soldiers, and I could not find mamma anywhere; the day before, she had never ceased searching for a place to conceal herself in — never answering me when I called and looked for her; and if by chance I found her in a wardrobe, or in the clock, she scolded me severely for discovering her hiding-place.

As I was left quite alone, I thought the best thing I could do was to lay out the table with every sort of eatable and wine I could find; that at least these national guards should not eat me, but find something else prepared for them; and I determined in my own mind to give them quietly every thing they asked for, and let them see I did not fear them in the least; and then I waited with the utmost resignation to hear cries for help through the streets.

At last the sound of spurred footsteps and clinking swords echoed along the corridor, but no noise or swearing; *au contraire*, a very polite double knock at the door. In my terror or flurry, however, I had no power to say, Come in. But do not imagine they broke in the door with their muskets — not at all, they only repeated the knock, and waited till I gave permission, in a trembling voice — expecting at least six dog-faced Tartars to enter, with square heads and skin caps — beards down to their girdles, and dressed in bears' hides, with leather sacks over their shoulders, to thrust their plunder into; and covered all over with pistols and knives, as I have heard mamma describe them; but conceive my surprise, when, instead of all this, two young officers walked in; one fair, and the other dark, but very well dressed, and just like other people.

They wore small fur cloaks across their shoulders, and under this, a tight-fitting attila—no idea of skins or square heads; indeed, the dark one was quite a handsome youth.

Their first action was to beg pardon for any inconvenience they might cause; to which I replied, that I considered it no inconvenience whatever, and was ready to serve them in any way they wanted.

The dark youth, glancing at the table, could scarcely refrain from a smile, which embarrassed me extremely, as I thought he must have supposed I had prepared all this on purpose for him. At last the other relieved my embarrassment, by thanking me politely for all my proffered services, and only begged I would show them an apartment where they could take some rest, as they were very tired, not having slept in a bed for six weeks, or lain down at all for two days.

Poor creatures! I quite pitied them—not to have slept in a bed for six weeks!

"Indeed!" I exclaimed, "it must have been very uncomfortable to have been obliged to sleep on a divan, or even in a camp-bed, for six entire weeks!"

They both laughed. "On the bare ground—on the snow—under the clear sky," they replied.

Oh, heavens! even our servants would have died, had they been obliged to pass one winter's night out of doors.

I begged them to follow me, and showed them our best room, in which there were two beds. As the servants were all out, I was going to make down the bed myself.

"Oh, we cannot allow that!" they both exclaimed, "we can do that ourselves;" and seeing they had need of rest, I bowed, and hastened to leave them alone.

Scarcely had I reached my own room, when I heard a terrible shriek, which seemed to proceed from the apartment I had just left, and cries of "Help! robbers! murder!"

I knew the voice, but in my terror I could not remember who it was, and still the cries continued, "Help! murder!"

If you can imagine my situation, you may suppose that I never moved from the spot on which I stood, till the voice, echoing through the rooms, at last approached my apartment.

It was my dear mamma!—but in what a plight!

Her clothes all crumpled, her cap over her eyes, one of her shoes off, and her whole face as red as if she had come out of an oven. It was a long time before I could make out where she had been, or what had happened to her. Well! only fancy. She had hid in the very room where I had quartered my two guests, and where, do you think?—in one of the beds, under all the feather quilts! Now you may imagine the rest, and the surprise of the national guard officer when he threw himself down half dead with fatigue. Poor mamma had good reason to cry out; but what an idea, to hide there!

After much trouble, I calmed her a little, and endeavoured to persuade her that these national guards had not come to rob or kill us; and, finally, I succeeded so far, that she promised not to hide again, and I undertook to explain to the officers, that mamma had the rheumatism, and was obliged to get under all these feather beds, by way of a vapour bath!

Meanwhile our guests had scarcely time to fall asleep, when an orderly arrived, who desired to speak with them.

"You cannot see them at present," I replied—"they are both asleep; but you may wait, or come again."

"Where are they sleeping?" he asked.

I showed him the room, and without the slightest consideration, as to whether it was proper to awake them, after being two whole days without rest, he walked coolly into the room.

I expected they would have immediately cut the man in pieces for disturbing them, instead of which, in a few minutes, they both appeared, completely dressed, and followed the orderly, without the slightest sign of displeasure. The major had sent for them.

How strange this military life must be, how people can submit without the least resistance! I should be a very bad soldier indeed, for I always like to know beforehand why I am ordered to do a thing.

In about half an hour the officers returned—no ill-humour or sleepiness was visible; they did not even return to their rooms; but asked for mamma and me, and announced to us in very flattering terms, that the officers' corps had *improviséd* a ball for that night, to which we were invited, and then they immediately begged to engage me for a *française*, a csardas, and a polonaise (there was to be no waltzing), and I naturally promised everything.

It was our first ball since the Carnival, and they seemed to enjoy the thoughts of it as much as I did, for they would not hear of sleeping any more.

Mamma, however, never ceased making every objection and difficulty she could think of.

"You have no ball dress."

"My white dress, dear mamma; I only wore it once."

"It is old-fashioned."

"A little bow of national ribbon, and you will have the prettiest of new fashions," interrupted the dark officer.

"But my foot aches," persevered mamma.

"But there is no absolute necessity for your dancing, dear mamma."

The officers did not laugh—out of politeness; and for the same reason, mamma did not scold me till they had gone away.

"You foolish child," she said angrily, "to rush openly in the face of danger, and ruin yourself intentionally!"

I thought mamma was afraid I should take cold, as she always was, when I prepared for a ball; and to calm her fears I reminded her that there was to be no waltzing. This made her still more angry. "You have no sense," she exclaimed. "Do you suppose they are giving this ball that they may dance? not at all! it is all finesse—all a plot of the national guards, to get the young girls of the town together, when they will probably seize them, and carry them off to Turkey."

"Ah, mamma! why, officers are not allowed to marry in time of war," I reminded her, laughing.

On this she scolded me still more, called me a little goose, and told me I should find out to my cost; and with this threat she left me to prepare for the ball.

I was busy enough until evening getting everything ready. According to the officer's advice I wore a broad red-white-green ribbon as a sash, and my *coiffure* was a simple bouquet of white and red roses, to which the green leaves gave the national colour. I never observed before how well these colours blend.

The two officers waited on us *en pleine parade*, and paid us so many compliments, I could not imagine how they learnt them all. I was obliged to laugh, to put off my embarrassment.

"Well, you will see tears will be the end of all this," said mamma; but nevertheless she continued arranging and altering something or other about my dress, that if they did carry me away, they should at least find everything in order.

The officers accompanied us to the ballroom. I was already enjoying the idea of the effect which my national ribbon and our two beaux would produce; and, *entre nous*, I could not give up the hope, that if all the others really had square heads, we should have the only two round ones in the room!

But great was my mistake and surprise.

There was not one of my companions who had not at least twice as much national ribbon on her dress as I had; and as to the officers, our two cavaliers held but the third rank among them.

One was more agreeable, more fascinating, handsomer, livelier than the other; how is it possible that men like these can shed so much blood!

There was one in particular who attracted my attention—not mine alone, but everybody's. He was a young captain—his strikingly handsome face, and tall, graceful figure became the braided attila so well, it seemed to have been moulded on him.

And then his dancing! with what animation he went through the mazur and csardas; one could have rushed through the crowd to embrace him—I do not talk of myself; and, what was more than dancing—more than compliments, a *je ne sais quoi* in the large, dark, dreamy eyes; you cannot imagine *that*, it is not to be described—it bewildered, inspired, overpowered, and enchanted at the same moment. In less than an hour, every girl in the room was in love with him. I do not except myself. If they are as irresistible on the field of battle, I do not know what could withstand them. Imagine my feelings, when all at once he stepped up to me and requested the honour of the next quadrille!

Unfortunately, I was engaged. What would I not have given at that moment, had a courier entered to call away my dancer.

"Perhaps the next one?" said the captain, seating himself beside me.

I do not know what I said, or whether I replied at all; I only know I felt as I do when flying in a dream.

"But you will forget, perhaps, that you promised me?" he continued.

Had I not suddenly recollected myself, I should probably have told him that sooner could I forget my existence; however, I only replied, in a very indifferent tone, that I should not forget.

"But you do not know me!"

A country simpleton would have answered in my place, "Among a hundred—among thousands! at the first glance!"

Not I! As if I were doing the simplest thing in the world, I took a single rosebud from my breast and gave it to him. "I shall know you by this," I said, without betraying the slightest agitation.

The captain silently pressed the rose to his lips; I did not look, but I *knew* it. I would not have encountered his eyes at that moment for all the world.

He then left me and sat down under a mirror opposite; he did not dance, and seemed absorbed in his own reflections.

Meanwhile two csardas and a polonaise were danced, after which our quadrille would come. You may conceive how long the time appeared; these eternal "harom a tanczes" seemed absolutely to have no end. I never saw people dance so furiously; and although it was the third night they had not slept, nothing would tire them out. However, I amused myself pretty well by making the acquaintance of the commander of the battalion, Major Sch——, who is a most diverting person.

His name is German; and though he speaks Hungarian shockingly, he will always speak it, even if he is addressed in German or French. Then he is most dreadfully deaf, and accustomed to such loud-toned conversation, one would think the cannons were conversing together.

They say he is a very gallant soldier; but his appearance is not prepossessing—an uncouth, grotesque figure, with a long thin face, short-cut hair, and a grisly beard, which is not at all becoming. But the most amusing thing was, that what I spoke he did not hear; and what he spoke I did not understand. He brought me over a box of *bonbons*; and I complained of the badness of confectionary in our town. He probably supposed from my grimace that somebody had offended me at the ball, and answered something, from which—by the gestures which accompanied it—I could only infer that he intended cutting the offender in pieces; unless indeed what others would express under such circumstances may be the common gesticulation of men who live in war.

At last, my quadrille came. The band played the symphony, and the dancers hastened to seek their partners.

My heart almost burst from my dress when I saw my dancer approach, and, bowing low, press the little flower to his heart.

I fear my hand trembled as he took it in his; but I only smiled, and made some observation about the music.

"Ah, you are carrying off my neighbour!" cried the major, laughing, with one of his "annihilating" gesticulations.

As we joined the columns, somebody whispered behind us, "What a well-matched couple!"

Ah, Ilma! how happy I was! I felt, as we stood there, hand in hand, as if his blood were flowing into mine, and mine into his! We waited for the music; but before it could begin, the noise of horses' feet were heard galloping up the street, and, at the same time, several cannons were fired at a distance, which made all the windows rattle. Suddenly an officer entered the ballroom, with his csako on his head, and covered with mud, and announced that the enemy had attacked the outposts.

The major had heard the cannon, and read from the courier's face what he could not understand from his words.

"Ah, that's right!" he exclaimed, clapping his hands, and again those fearful gestures by which people express killing. "We were only waiting for them, *messieurs*; we must ask our ladies for a few moments' leave—just a few moments, *mes dames*; we shall return immediately, and meanwhile you can rest."

And he hastened to put on his sword; all the other officers ran to get theirs—and I saw the gay, courtly, flattering expressions suddenly change to angry, fierce, threatening countenances; but one and all seemed eager to start, as if they had expected it all along.

My dancer, too, forsook me to look for his sword and csako. His step was the firmest, his eye the keenest of all; if I had hitherto felt happiness—more than happiness—in looking at him, admiration, enthusiasm now filled my breast.

As he buckled on his sword, a strange fever seemed to burn in all my veins; I could have wished to be in the battle with him, to ride beside him, and dash with him into the midst of the enemy!

He still held my rose in his hand, and, as he took up his csako, he placed it beside the cockade; and then he turned back, as if he sought something through the crowd—our eyes met!—he hastened away, and the ballroom was empty!

Meanwhile we remained alone, as if nothing had happened; the major had given orders that none should leave the rooms before his return. It was the longest hour I ever spent.

Many of us stood at the windows listening to the cannon, and trying to guess the result, as they sounded now nearer, now more distant. None judged it advisable to go home, as the combat might have ended in the streets, and they thought it better to await the decision where we were.

Ere long, the sounds began to recede further and further, till at last they ceased entirely. The civilians concluded by this that the national guards had gained the victory. They were right. In less than a quarter of an hour we heard them return with great noise and clatter. And the officers entered the room gaily, as if nothing had happened; many of them wiped something from their dross—perhaps mud or blood—and each hastened to find and cheer his partner.

"Where did we leave off?" cried one.

"At the quadrille," replied several at once, and began arranging the columns as if they had just come out of the supper-room. My dancer and the major were alone absent!

In vain my eyes were fixed on the door—every instant some one entered, but not the one I sought.

At last the major appeared. He looked round, and when he saw me, immediately approached, and, making a grotesque bow, without waiting for me to speak, "Fair lady!" he said, "your dancer entreats your pardon for this breach of politeness; but he is unable with the best will to enjoy the happiness of dancing the *française* with you, having been shot through the leg, which is obliged to be amputated above the knee."

Oh, Ilma! I shall never dance a quadrille again.

I am very ill! I am overwhelmed by despair!

CONSTABLE'S MISCELLANY OF FOREIGN LITERATURE

For our supply of the comforts and luxuries of life, we lay the world under contribution: fresh from every quarter of the globe we draw a portion of its yearly produce. The field of literature is well-nigh as broad as that of commerce; as rich and varied in its annual fruits; and, if gleaned carefully, might furnish to our higher tastes as large an annual ministry of enjoyment. Believing that a sufficient demand exists to warrant the enterprise, Thomas Constable & Co. propose to present to the British public a Series of the most popular accessions which the literature of the globe is constantly receiving. Europe alone,—its more northern and eastern lands especially,—offers to the hand of the selector most inviting and abundant fruits; Asia may supply a few rarer exotics; whilst in America the fields are whitening to a harvest into which many a hasty sickle has been already thrust, and from which many a rich sheaf may be hereafter gathered.

Fully aware of the extent and difficulty of such an effort, the Publishers will spare no pains to make the execution of their undertaking commensurate with its high aim. They have already opened channels of communication with various countries, and secured the aid of those who are minutely acquainted with their current literature; and they take this opportunity of stating, that even where no legal copyright in this country can be claimed by the author or publisher of a work of which they may avail themselves, an equitable share of any profit which may arise from its sale will be set aside for his advantage.

The Series will be made as varied as possible, that there may be something in it to suit the tastes of all who seek instruction or healthful recreation for the mind,—and its range will therefore be as extensive as the field of Literature itself: while, at the same time, it shall be the endeavour of its editors to select, for the most part, works of general or universal interest.

The Publishers are unable to state the exact periods at which their Miscellany of Foreign Literature will appear, but they believe that the number of volumes issued during the first year will not exceed six; so that taking the average price per volume as *Three Shillings and Sixpence*, the cost to Subscribers would not exceed *One Guinea*; while, by the addition of a *special* title-page for each work issued, those persons who may wish to select an occasional publication will be saved the awkwardness of placing in their library a volume or volumes evidently detached from a continuous Series.